On the night that Walter Brownley had arrived to take up his position at a remote mission, set among the hills of the Eastern Cape, he had written in his journal, 'January 27th 1898: At St Matthias there is an odd sense of predestination. It is strange how strongly I feel it . . . what it is I do not know but I shall leave before it takes me in . . .' And yet – despite himself – he had not left: he'd waited for the catastrophic game to end, as he knew it must . . .

Marguerite Poland's spellbinding novel of love and dispossession is a rich and haunting work in which individual destinies are played out against the backdrop of the country's wider conflicts at the turn of the century, particularly the turbulence and discord wrought by the inevitable clash of different cultures.

> *Shades* is a wonderful read, not only in the so-called British 'great tradition' that includes Charlotte Brontë, EM Forster and DH Lawrence but also in the distinguished South African tradition of writers such as Pauline Smith, Olive Schreiner and Nadine Gordimer.
> – Barrie Hough in *Insig*

Marguerite Poland, who lives in Kloof near Durban, is South Africa's most distinguished writer for children. *Shades* is her second adult novel, following the highly acclaimed *Train to Doringbult* which was published in 1987.

Shades

Marguerite Poland

PENGUIN BOOKS

PENGUIN BOOKS

Published by the Penguin Group
Penguin Books Ltd, 27 Wrights Lane, London W8 5TZ, England
Penguin Putnam Inc., 375 Hudson Street, New York, New York 10014, USA
Penguin Books Australia Ltd, Ringwood, Victoria, Australia
Penguin Books Canada Ltd, 10 Alcorn Avenue, Toronto, Ontario, Canada M4V 3B2
Penguin Books (NZ) Ltd, Private Bag 102902, NSMC, Auckland, New Zealand
Penguin Books (South Africa) (Pty) Ltd, 5 Watkins Street, Denver Ext. 4, South Africa

Penguin Books Ltd, Registered Offices: Harmondsworth, Middlesex, England

First published by Viking 1993
Published in Penguin Books 1994
5 7 9 10 8 6

Cover illustration by Leigh Voigt. Back cover from a painting by Thomas Baines,
'Lyndoch, Baviansriver, the farm of Mr Dodds Pringle'

Typesetting and reproduction by National Book Printers, Cape Town
Printed in England by Clays Ltd, St Ives plc

For my husband Martin,
for my mother Hope Brereton Poland,
and for my friend Susan Imrie Ross
who made those three transcendent journeys with me:
pilgrim souls – no companions could have shared them more
completely.

Acknowledgements

There were three events that led to the writing of this book:

The acquisition from the generous members of the Brereton family of the journal of Daisy Taberer Brereton, various papers and photograph albums, and especially Marie McCrae's wonderful gift of our great-grandfather's Bible.

The discovery, with the tireless help of Sandy Rowoldt, of the letter-books of the Reverend Cyril Wyche in the Cory Library, Rhodes University, Grahamstown.

Three incomparable visits to St Matthew's Mission, Keiskammahoek.

During the writing of this book I have had the unstinting support of my own beloved family – Martin, Susie and Verlie Oosthuizen – and my sister Nicki Hamilton; of loved and admired artist Leigh Voigt; of greatly valued editors Alison Lowry and Pam Thornley and proof-readers Susan Clarence, Georgina Hamilton and Cathy Kinnear; of Brenda Richardson and other very dear and caring friends, relatives, research assistants especially at Killie Campbell Africana Library and many other helpers. To all – the deepest debt of gratitude and love.

The rest is between me and my 'shades', especially those of my great-grandfather William Brereton, story-teller and priest; of Charlie Fraser, restored from a long, long exile, and of my great-great-grandfather Charles Taberer, the 'Old Man', who held the light for me. I hope they will forgive me for any liberties I might have taken with their privacy or with the events of their lives but I know they will acknowledge, because I am the inheritor of their history, that I have loved them greatly and respect the memory of each.

Marguerite Poland
1993

Prologue

October 1900

It was already dark by the time they brought the body of Crispin Farborough home. Standing on the veranda of the mission house, Walter Brownley saw the procession of lanterns moving slowly down the hill, accompanying the Cape cart. It rolled like a tumbrel, its wheels hooping the ironstone. He could only see the lights and hear the rumble of the wagon. No voices came to him.

The night wind was hot – the restless, wild hotness of a wind that had blown in from Xhosaland. It came in fierce, sudden gusts across the beaten yard, like spirits disembodied. Walter tugged at his clergyman's collar, easing it. His neck was damp. He could feel the sweat between his shoulder blades and on his face. He might have prayed but he felt only anger at himself for having waited long enough to witness all this madness and a weariness so old, so invasive, that he waited motionless, standing in the shadow of the porch.

The lights moved on, disappearing one by one as the procession dipped towards the drift out of sight below the ridge. There was a stillness then for he could no longer hear the horses' hooves, and only the leaves of the oak before the porch turned restlessly against each other. Beyond, where the bush reached down to the edges of the kitchen garden, the twigs of thorn trees tapped rhythmically: a small, secret tattoo in the dark.

The front door opened. A flat wedge of light widened on the flagging of the floor. Walter turned. Helmina Smythe came out, her steps tentative. She looked at him fearfully, head inclined, listening. 'The cart?' Her voice broke.

He wished he could have comforted her in a way that she deserved. To have lived, dependent, in a household for eleven years assumed a place within the family. Yet he knew she would withdraw in deference to the Farboroughs' loss, recalling her status as a paid employee of the mission, and

1

deny herself the right to mourn. But mourn she would, in solitude.

He touched her arm reassuringly and said, 'I must tell them where the coffin is. The carpenter said he'd put it in the porch of the church when he had finished it. Perhaps you should prepare something. Mrs Farborough will need reviving.'

She nodded and slipped away, closing the door behind her.

Walter took the path to the yard as, one by one, the lights reappeared and the cart came into view. He could hear the voices. Benedict's. Then Victor's. He hurried on to meet them as they took the stretcher down. It lay on the ground, dark figures gathered round it, lantern beams catching the angle of a face, the hollow of an eye. The mission people waited silently in the lee of the church. Then Walter heard their voices, the soft beginnings of lament. A hymn, counter-harmony to wind surging in the trees, echoed up and out into the night.

He could see Father Charles Farborough climbing down from the trap, the white of his helmet in the gloom, and Emily, his wife, so small and upright at his side, reaching for his arm. They seemed to cling together, just a moment, two bewildered old people, and then they turned and came towards him, walking slowly, and Walter went to meet them. 'Father Charles?'

Charles Farborough raised his head, his white beard jutting. 'Brownley?'

Arms reached out for Walter and he felt his own armour quake. Steadying the old man, his hand on his shoulder, Walter said, 'I went for the doctor. He'll be here in the morning. The coffin is ready. It's in the church porch.'

Emily Farborough looked up at him. She paused as if gathering her words. 'I want Crispin home first,' she said, bridling the tremor in her voice. 'Tell Victor to bring the coffin to the house.' As Walter turned from them to speak to Victor, Emily put out her hand and rested it on his sleeve. She said – oh, brief and fierce it was – 'Thank you for coming so far. We never doubted that you would.'

Walter returned alone to the yard. Victor Drake, Benedict Matiwane and Mzantsi the catechist were standing by the

2

stretcher, a troop of watchers in their wake. Even in the cold of the night air, the smell of death was close about them. Walter said to Victor, 'The coffin is ready. Your aunt would like you to bring Crispin to the house in it.'

Victor nodded and Walter could see that he breathed shallowly, assailed by nausea. His face was pale and sweat crept along the edges of his hair. Together they carried the stretcher, Benedict and Mzantsi easing the load. They turned towards the church, bearing Crispin Farborough between them in silence. They laid him in the coffin and drew the lid up across his face. They stood a moment to recover themselves, to breathe again, and then they bent to the coffin and lifted it among them and took it down across the yard and along the avenue of trees and brought it to the table in the house where Helmina Smythe had placed a linen cloth and lighted candles and a lamp.

Benedict and Mzantsi withdrew. Emily Farborough turned towards the table and she said, 'I wish to see him.'

No one moved.

'Victor' – and steady – 'just his face.'

Victor Drake obeyed, stood sentinel a moment at Crispin's head. Strange to see him so. Strange to see him, eyes cast down, face bent to face, almost tender. Only the tendons in Victor's neck betrayed him. He stood back for Charles and Emily Farborough and moved to the window and waited, his hands behind his back, staring out beyond the panes.

The shadows of the watchers loomed and fell away across the whiteness of the walls, loomed and fell away beneath the gaze of portraits looking down at Crispin Farborough, the bloodied mess of his chest concealed from their gaze. His eyes were closed, his once unruly hair lay pale and limp. Walter turned his eyes away, striving to recall the living face, the voice, the schoolboy laugh, great with exultation: Crispin enticing eels from the water-furrows, mimicking the neddickies and bulbuls, luring them to him with secret words, dragging a brace of birds behind him in triumph for the pot. But he could not find that face, only fleetingly evoke those watchful eyes as they'd looked back at him the night they'd sat in vigil together at Mbokothwe and Walter had read the passage from

Isaiah: 'Behold, I have refined thee not with silver; I have chosen thee in the furnace of affliction . . .'

Emily and Charles Farborough stood and looked down at their son. Emily put out her hand and touched his cheek: nor did she recoil but let her fingers linger a moment at the contour of his brow. Then she straightened and she said to Father Charles, 'You may close the coffin,' and she turned and looked about the room, appraising each of them. 'Helmina, where is Benedict?'

'He went outside, Mrs Farborough,' whispered Helmina. 'Victor?'

'Aunt Emily?'

'Call him in. He must be here with the family.'

But Victor, his back to them, seemed to hesitate and Walter said, 'I will go.'

He left the room. His steps, in the stillness of that house, were loud and measured as he walked across the hall and onto the flagging of the veranda. The catechist, Mzantsi, waited still at the edge of the porch, a group of the faithful behind him. Tears hung webbed in his greying beard. He clasped Walter's hand as he came to him. Walter scanned the gathering for Benedict but he was not there. He said, 'Go in while I find Benedict. Take the people with you. We will say a prayer together.'

Benedict Matiwane was not in his room in Mzantsi's cottage. He was not in the teacher's house. Walter turned away and went towards the church. He entered the porch and hesitated – as he had on his arrival that morning – hand on the door, unwilling to go further. He turned the knob tentatively: it was a sacrificial moment.

The door still stuck as it always had for there was a roughness in the boards that only another generation would wear down. He pulled it closed behind him, waiting. He gazed about at the deeply shadowed arches, the small dim light of the sanctuary lamp way up beyond the chancel steps. Once he had served as assistant in this church, faith and humour still intact: matins and evensong and three services on Sunday; choirs, confirmations, baptisms and burials. It had all been so familiar. Now he stood, a stranger at its door.

4

'Benedict?' he said and his voice hung in the stillness, echoing among the arches of the nave. 'Benedict?' There was no reply.

Walter trod softly up the aisle, running his hand along the polished edges of a pew. The scents were still the same, of wax and dusty kneelers. And there – sudden and fugitive about him – the smell of lavender and lemon balm and laundered vestments: once Frances Farborough had walked along this aisle with the starched white linen folded on her arm and he had startled her and caught the sudden fragrance of her as she had bent her head from him and laughed.

He moved on, quickening his pace: that a scent can shake the heart – oh, to its roots.

'Benedict? Are you there?' He reached the altar-rail. 'Benedict?' The vestry door stood ajar. A soft grey light trembled on the floor beyond, glimmering and fading with the moonlight and the breath of trees stirring outside the windows. He did not approach. He could not go there now. He had returned to it in dream and thought so many times since he'd been gone that it had seemed the sanctuary of all remembrance. Later, perhaps. Later – just before he saddled his horse to ride away. He retreated, leaving the church and closing the great porch door behind him.

He hurried then, his step brisk on the path to the workshop, to the smithy, to the stables. The night wind surged in the branches of the trees. Above the spur of the Kaboosie the moon had risen, heavy and misshapen. Walter turned from it and took the track that led along the avenue towards the printing-room. Benedict would be there. Yes. Sitting with his papers and his press. Walter scrutinised the window, saw the furtive flame behind the panes.

He was right. Benedict was hunched at the table, his hat laid aside, his hands quiet before him. How many times had Walter seen him sitting so, late at night, surrounded by print, asleep or dreaming, reams of paper strewn around: poems, articles, hymns and invoice sheets?

He opened the door softly and went inside. Benedict turned. The planes of his face flared and dimmed in the tongue of light. 'Benedict?'

5

Benedict looked back.

Tentatively, Walter said, 'Mrs Farborough is asking for you at the house. She wants you there with the family.'

Benedict was silent. He glanced at the papers on the desk and he said, his voice flat. 'With the family . . .'

'She sent me to find you.'

'I am always told that I am a member of the family.' He did not parody the words or mimic but spoke them quietly. His eyes held Walter's. 'But that is one of the great delusions. One is given a hat and a pair of breeches, a name and a present at Christmas and a sponsor to pay the fees and one is suddenly a member of the family. Where is that family? Where were they in all those other times? Who cared?'

'Crispin did.'

'Crispin did. Yes.' Benedict took up his hat. 'And now he is dead.'

Walter hesitated. 'I wish I understood the reason for it all.'

'You must look for the reasons with Victor Drake,' said Benedict, and a distance washing in. 'You will see it in his face. And yet he will never understand what part he had to play. He will protest that he was in the army fighting for his country. And so he was.' He paused. 'It goes back long before that. Long, long before. Perhaps it was something decided by our shades when we were born.'

Walter said, 'Will you stay away then?'

'I will come,' said Benedict. 'For Crispin.' He took up his hat and blew out the candle and followed Walter from the room. Wordlessly, he walked a pace or two behind and Walter could hear the small, defiant cracking of his knuckles in the dark. They reached the house and made their way among the mission workers gathered in the hall.

The family was standing round the table: Father Charles and Emily; Victor at the window; Helmina in a corner of the room; Mzantsi hovering at the door. Nowasha, the housemaid, hid her eyes with her apron, face to the wall.

Father Charles said, without looking up, 'Now that we are all here, Mr Brownley, will you lead the prayers?'

Walter hesitated, deferential, but Father Charles took up the prayer-book from the sideboard and gave it to him.

6

'Please,' he said and his eyes were weary beneath the drooping brows.

'I am the Resurrection and the Life, saith the Lord: He that believeth in me, though he were dead, yet shall he live, and whosoever liveth and believeth in me shall never die.' Walter looked up from the prayer-book in his hand.

Father Charles, Emily and Helmina had knelt at the table's edge. Mzantsi knelt too, beyond the circle of the lamplight. Victor Drake had turned from the window. He stood behind his aunt. Walter felt the presence of him, felt the weight, the height, the shadow shouldering the walls, the military coat, the shining boots astride the floor.

Benedict, alone, waited in the doorway. Walter turned to beckon him inside but he did not move. His hands were not clasped before him. His head was not bent. He remained – he with his fob-watch and his hat and his fledgling cleric's suit – seemingly unmoved, and Walter's words faltered as he spoke, to see the blackness in his eyes.

It was after midnight when Walter returned to the retreat house. Father Charles walked with him to the gate, carrying a lantern. He raised it up and lighted Walter's face. He said, his hand on Walter's arm, 'I have not even asked you how you've been.'

'Do not speak about Mbokothwe now,' said Walter.

'That bad?'

'Most times.'

'I need you here. You can see what an old man I've become.'

'No doubt they will send you a zealous young priest when one is available.'

'I had one once and he left me for Mbokothwe.'

'There was little choice.'

Father Charles nodded. The hand holding the lantern shook. The broad shoulders were stooped, the alpaca coat that he had always filled so vigorously hung about his limbs, the great lion-like head, the straight, grey brush of hair, the clipped beard, were still the same but the eyes were old and their outward droop which had given his expression its uni-

7

que humour, made his face look frail and weary. 'I wish I knew,' he said, 'what had happened to our son. I wish I knew what he'd been thinking.' Walter waited. 'I wonder, if I'd known, if I could have counselled such despair.' He turned from Walter and he said, 'God bless, old friend. How glad I am to have you home tonight.'

Home. Walter might have smiled – with something close to bitterness – to hear the word. He watched the old man walk away and then he took his tobacco pouch from his pocket and he went, not to the retreat house where a bed had been prepared for him, but to the long veranda of the curate's lodge. He trod the length of it, passing the doors of the small, plain rooms. One. Two. Three. Four. Five. The last had once been his. He sat on the step outside it and lit his pipe. He looked up at the sky. How many times he'd done it in the past. How unfamiliar it once had been: how well he knew the Southern Constellations now.

The stars were large and clear, the incandescent green of planets, dimmed by neither dust nor light. He could feel the silence of the Amatolas pressing in around him: aloof, distant, covered with black-green bush. There was no poetry in any of his books to describe such a landscape – no poetry, no words. He had decided, long ago, that his God – his most dependable, predictable Creator – had retreated in defeat before the God who had invented this. One day those same dark-sapped bushes would march in and reclaim the mission and its cultivated lands. He was sure of it. There was nothing like the ruins of settlements to underscore the impotence of man against a place like this. The great church, buttressed in stone, would one day be the haunt of owls.

He knew it now and he had known it then for he had written in his journal on his first night at the mission – listening to the secret dark beyond his window: 'January 27th, 1898: At St Matthias Mission there is an odd sense of predestination. It is strange how strongly I feel it . . . what it is I do not know but I shall leave before it takes me in. I shall leave before I am its victim.'

And yet, despite the clarity of his perceptions, despite some instinct shouting in his head, he had not left. He had written those words and then he had put them away. For two and a half years they had lain in his journal unrecalled. And now he was leaving – fighting a rising desolation: not a victim eager for escape, but an exile sent from home.

The catastrophic game had ended as he knew it must. It had claimed them all. Tom, Reuben and Sonwabo gone. Crispin gone – dragging himself out into some remote and hostile darkness. And if Benedict Matiwane was still there, he had ensured a distance more divisive and complete than death. Tomorrow, when the funeral was over, when Crispin had been buried beneath the oak at the east side of the church, then he himself would go, a passenger in Klaus Otto's transport wagon. No inducements and no remembrances would keep him back.

No inducements.

No remembrances.

He stood and walked towards the corner of the curate's lodge. He looked across the drive and yard towards the mission house. The last time he had stood like this, he had watched the moon's reflection in the panes of Frances Farborough's window, the night she'd gone away. Then, he'd felt a primal cry, rising like a flame in his throat. Now he stood in quietness, hearing only the breathing of the trees, the shadows grey and still across the shutters of her empty room.

Chapter One

Ad anum extremum mundi. Arse end of the world. That is what Walter had said – oh, so drily and dismissively – when Klaus Otto, the transport rider, gesturing at the surrounding countryside with his driver's whip, turned to him and asked, 'What do you think of it?'

He should have kept his trite replies to himself, asked Klaus Otto to leave him at Debe Nek to wait for a cart going back to town, heeded the mounting apprehension that he'd felt ever since he'd loaded his trunk onto Klaus Otto's transport wagon at the station in King William's Town. Instead of passing by cultivated farmlands, hamlets and orchards as he'd expected, they'd turned east and journeyed on towards a low, dark ridge of bush-clad hills. He should have taken warning when Klaus Otto told him that along those distant valleys the Frontier Wars had once been fought and that the bones of warriors remained unclaimed in the more isolated reaches of the countryside. Scanning the silent slopes ahead, it seemed to Walter as though the land had been abandoned, not from choice but from compulsion, and that something of the brooding of a battlefield remained: a frontier such as this – so much dark monotony – seemed to be a place for soldiers, not for priests.

Nor should he have been lulled into complacence by the sudden and unexpected sight of the abundant mission gardens, the large grey church, the houses of the catechist and carpenter and the Reverend Charles Farborough's bungalow with its fragrant garden – a small enclave of order and repose – when the wagon breasted the last hill and started the dusty descent towards the little settlement of St Matthias. He should have fled the wide, hot madness of those plains.

Klaus Otto set Walter down at the gate of the mission and lifted his trunk to the ground. Walter scanned the avenue of trees leading into the yard. Way off, where pasture was lush around a water-furrow, three young men and a girl were fishing. They did not turn to watch him. Perhaps they had not heard his approach. One of the young men was black, dressed in a suit and waistcoat, his hat tilted at an angle and decorated with a long, grey crane's feather and Walter could distinguish, in the still midday hush – even from that distance – that they spoke now in English, now Xhosa, shifting from one to the other as if it were one language.

Walter turned his gaze from them, shook Klaus Otto's hand and stood beside his trunk, feeling an immense and unexpected loneliness as the wagon lumbered away. He wanted to call Klaus Otto back, climb up beside him again, hear the ponderous German voice. He had travelled with him for enough hours to feel some tenuous kinship – even that of being two men alone in an empty landscape. He stood abandoned in the avenue, his isolation heightened by the sight of the foursome bending to each other, parting, mingling back and forth in some languid communion. Leaving the trunk concealed beneath a bush, carrying his carpet-bag and coat, Walter walked down the avenue of trees towards the mission yard. The small, furtive rustlings in the undergrowth along the driveway where the shade was flat and dusty, made him feel that there were watchers at his back. The very thorn trees held him in their gaze, retreating once he'd passed, into the deep malaise that oppressed them in the stillness of noon. He paused at the big stone church and, shading his eyes, looked up at the abandoned swallows' nests colonising the eaves, scanned the wagon workshops where the great doors stood closed in the heat of a Saturday afternoon. At a distance, a grizzled man – a carpenter or a blacksmith – sat smoking a pipe at a cottage door and a buxom, tow-haired girl greeted him incuriously. He raised his hat to them and hurried on.

He walked between a collection of sheds and outbuildings, unsure of his direction. In the shade of a wall, a tall Xhosa holding a broom glanced up as he passed. His head was like a skull across which the skin was tightly stretched, moulding the hollows of his jaw, his sunken lids. Near him, a small gathering of old black men, dressed in uniform drabness and indistinguishable from each other in their age and emaciation, sat side by side, like a row of ragged rock-martins: a bond of brotherhood or blood or dispossession must be theirs – Walter

11

could not tell. They turned their heads to watch him walking down towards the missionary's house and as he went, the man with the broom began to sing. That there was a connection between the words of the song and his arrival seemed evident enough and as he reached the porch and tapped at the door, the singing stopped, the secret drift of words that instant stilled. Walter hesitated, suspended a moment between the watchers in the yard and the gloom of the hall beyond the door, held open by a servant. He took his hat from his head and all but plunged inside.

In retrospect, it seemed strange to Walter that he had set out from Grahamstown for St Matthias with so much anticipation. Missionary work had never been his intention but the Bishop had spoken so engagingly of the missionary, the Reverend Charles Farborough, and his urgent need for an assistant, that he had wavered. St Matthias, the Bishop had added, was one of the oldest and most prosperous missions in the Colony with a flourishing wagon-making concern and a tin-smithy. He had mentioned – slyly, Walter decided – that St Matthias had a printing-press in embryo, knowing that this information would intrigue him, for books were Walter's love and scholarship his talent and the idea of a hand in publications, no matter how rudimentary, was inducement enough. He had not mentioned that the embryonic printing-press was an ancient 1835 double-crown Albion and that it lay encased in rust and cobwebs in a wagon shed at a distant mission called Mbokothwe, unused for years and awaiting recovery. Walter soon discovered that almost every expectation he had had was oddly inappropriate and he had almost smiled at his naivety.

Charles and Emily Farborough were waiting for him in the living-room of the mission house. If he had felt an aloneness in the avenue when Klaus Otto had left him, it was momentarily forgotten. The old man came to him, holding out both his hands in greeting and taking his in a grip that steadied him against the wish to retreat.

Charles Farborough was not tall, but broad-shouldered and sturdy: a man who had been a workman all his life. His grey hair was cut close, his beard clipped short. His eyes – a quiet, pale blue beneath deeply drooping brows – searched Walter's. He smiled, the leonine head inclined. 'It is a long journey. No doubt you thought you'd left civilisation for ever?'

As if offering consolation – with a small touch of triumph – he turned and drew his wife forward, keeping her hand in his a moment before he said, 'My dear, you will be as glad as I am to welcome Mr Brownley to our home.'

'How do you do.' Emily Farborough's voice was clear and light. Her voice, her eyes, the brisk but delicate movement of her hands; clear and light indeed. And her little living-room, clear and light as well, restrained in its furnishing, each piece set to the best advantage to show line and craftsmanship: china, prints, a wooden screen, a pianoforte bearing silver frames. Uncluttered but complete. This small house in a wilderness of thorn bush and plain was testimony to something else – another place, another time – and Emily Farborough was its custodian, standing there before him with her small handsome face, her upright carriage, a hint of the austere about her mouth.

'Let me show you to your room,' she said. 'There are bees in the curate's lodge at present so you shall stay in the house until we have smoked them out.'

'Besides,' said Charles Farborough, 'company for a day or two will be more settling, I'm sure. The bees are not as unwelcome as my wife would have you think.'

When Walter had unpacked his suitcase, he came out onto the veranda where tea was served. Emily Farborough presided over the teapot while Miss Smythe, the governess, hovered about offering plates of scones and bread and butter. She reminded Walter of a mouse he had once startled in a vestry cupboard, small and brown, twittering almost in deference and fright. She peered at him from across the table, with brief, sideways glances as though snatching scraps of information, too diffident to meet his eye, her thin fingers tight about her cup.

Seventeen year old Crispin was the first to return from the water-furrows where Walter had seen him fishing. He sidled through the front door and held out a sturdy hand. His hair had been wetted and hastily combed flat. As the wetness of his head dried in the warm afternoon air, his pale hair escaped and stood up here and there as if with a life of its own. He had an engaging face. It was boyish and brown-skinned and there was humour in his mouth. Walter noticed that Helmina Smythe, so achingly shy, had an ease with Crispin, endearing in its brief display. Crispin did not speak, but sat on the bench close beside her and ate a prodigious helping of bread and butter with an unselfconscious appetite. Food was good and to be enjoyed. Helmina Smythe kept his plate full, eating nothing herself, slipping him her share.

They had not been gathered round the table long when the garden gate opened and a tall young man came up the path between the daisy bushes at a trot. He took the veranda step in a bound, suddenly among them, his eyes sweeping them, resting a moment on Walter before he turned enquiringly to Emily Farborough. She put up her hand and touched his arm and she inclined her head to Walter, saying, 'Mr Brownley, this is our nephew, Victor Drake. He's visiting us from Grahamstown, as he does each holiday.' She looked up at Victor as though she were reproaching him and said, 'But now that he's left school and works for the Native Affairs Department he'll be far too busy for us and I don't know what we'll do without him.'

Victor Drake patted her shoulder absently and greeted Walter, exchanging a word or two about his journey. He stood with his hand resting at his hip – a detached elegance – surveying the tea-table. His sleeves were half rolled up his arms and he leaned across and helped himself to a cup and plate with a slow, humorous bit of repartee to his Aunt Emily.

He had the air of someone teasing, knowing to which point of familiarity he might stray which would flatter and not offend. He paid no attention to Miss Smythe beyond a perfunctory greeting. As he drew up a chair, he glanced expectantly at the door. Walter followed his gaze. There was the sound of footsteps in the hall. A young girl stepped out onto the porch. Victor turned back to his tea. He did not rise as she approached and it was Walter who stood, both to greet her and to offer her a chair.

'Ah, here is Frances,' Charles Farborough said. 'Mr Brownley, may I present our only daughter, Frances. Come here, my lass, you shall have a seat next to Mr Brownley and look him over and tell me if he'll do.'

'Really, dear,' his wife interrupted. 'You will embarrass Mr Brownley.'

'Not at all!' Father Charles smiled over at Walter with a slow, half-wink. 'Mr Brownley was assisting at a parish among coalminers near Nottingham. Do you think a bit of a girl could embarrass him?'

Frances Farborough's greeting was soft and gruff. A girl of about eighteen, she was small and tousle-haired, brisk in her movements like her mother, vivid in her smile, but – in contrast – with her father's deep-set, quiet eyes. She raised those eyes to Walter's briefly and then she sat in her chair, contained within it, her plate before her. Despite the fact that she seemed to be listening to the conversation of the others, Walter was aware of her appraisal for she looked at him now and then with some candour, her expression one of unselfconscious absorption. He smiled at her, amused by her ingenuousness: no doubt she thought him middle-aged although he had only just passed thirty. Too short, perhaps, too slight, too dark when compared with the broad athletic blondness of her cousin or her brother.

As they talked and drank their tea, a young black man appeared suddenly at the edge of the porch. By the hat that he wore – punctuated by an elegant crane feather bouncing in its brim – Walter recognised him as the last of the foursome that he had seen fishing at the water-furrow.

'Ah, Benedict.' Father Charles looked up and beckoned to him. The young man approached, carrying a pair of fishing rods across his shoulder. From his hand dangled an eel. 'Come and meet Mr Brownley, our new assistant.' He turned to Walter. 'Mr Brownley, this is Benedict Matiwane, one of our students.'

Benedict Matiwane carefully leaned the rods against the veranda railing and stood waiting at the step.

Realising that he would approach no further, Walter went to him and shook his hand. 'How do you do?' he said and

Benedict Matiwane returned the greeting briefly with averted eyes.

'Benedict will be an invaluable help to you, Mr Brownley,' said Father Charles. 'With lessons, with translations, with anything you need to know about St Matthias. He has lived here all his life.'

Benedict smiled momentarily. A fine face, light-boned and smooth; a quickness in his glance and in the fleeting expressions round about his mouth.

'I shall be consulting you often, I think,' said Walter.

'I shall be glad to be of service,' said the young man courteously and then he looked across at Father Charles and said, 'I have brought Mr Victor's rod and the eel that I caught, if you would like it.'

'Put the rod in the shed,' said Victor, his mouth full of cake and leaning across to appraise Benedict's catch. 'Clean the eel and leave it in the kitchen. Do you wish to cook it, Aunt Emily?' turning to her and wiping his fingers against each other, brisk in dispensing with both eel and cake.

'Thank you, Victor, that would be very nice.'

Victor nodded at Benedict and held out his cup to Helmina Smythe to refill.

Benedict, raising his hat to Walter, picked up the fishing rods to leave. As Walter returned to his seat he saw Crispin Farborough slip a pair of griddle-scones into his pockets. He rose unobtrusively and followed Benedict Matiwane down the path. He whistled as he went, his straight, short, spiky hair bouncing with his easy step.

When tea was over, Helmina Smythe helped the maid to clear the tray and Father Charles excused himself, saying, 'It's Sunday tomorrow and I have a sermon to write.'

Victor Drake stretched and suppressed a yawn as he said, 'I'm going riding. Hector needs some exercise.' He went inside and returned with a riding-crop and was starting away when Emily Farborough called him back, saying, 'Do take Mr Brownley with you, Victor, and show him the places of interest while I see to dinner.' She turned to Walter. 'Do you ride, Mr Brownley?'

'I do, Mrs Farborough,' Walter said.

'It might be more pleasant to go on the horses. You will see the country to greater advantage that way.'

Walter sensed Victor's impatience, saw the fleeting exasperation cross his face, and he said, 'Any time will do.'

'It's a lovely afternoon.' Emily Farborough was insistent. 'Victor will be delighted to go with you, I'm sure.'

'Come along then,' said Victor.

As Walter stood to follow him, he caught the glance that passed across the tea-table between Victor Drake and Frances Farborough. Infinitesimally, Frances shook her head and frowned.

Victor led the way to the stables, flicking his riding-crop against his boot, preoccupied and silent. He unlatched the stable yard gate and held it open for Walter. Loitering near the trough was the tow-haired girl Walter had seen earlier, trailing her hand in the water, idling with the tap. Waiting.

Walter greeted her, raised his hat, but Victor only glanced in her direction, wiped the back of his wrist across his lip and sauntered on, saying conversationally, 'You may take Hector, the grey. He's our best horse.' He paused. 'I must tell you, he's a little stubborn.'

Walter made no objection and so the tall Xhosa, the keeper of the broom, was summoned with a whistle. 'This is Kobus,' said Victor as the man led the horses from the stables. 'If you ever want a mount, just call him.'

The groom nodded and cast a shrewd glance at Walter but he neither spoke nor smiled. He stood impassively and picked at his stump-teeth with a twig. The big grey horse moved restlessly, his ears laid back, jerking at the rein. The girl had withdrawn a little way. She stood at a distance, watching.

'Who's the lass?' Walter said to Victor.

'Where?' Careless. 'Oh, her?' Victor barely turned his head. 'Uncle Charles is always taking in some unfortunate family or other. They come and go all the time, mostly on their way to the coast or Kimberley or wherever they think there's work. Her father's a wheelwright. He's helping out at the moment but he drinks himself stiff each night and knocks his wife around. They'll be moving on before long, I should think.'

Victor cupped his hands and gave Walter a leg up. Then he mounted the bay mare and swung her out of the yard. Walter had barely time to collect himself before Hector plunged after her.

Walter knew nothing of the place where Hector balked and ran for home, nor that he was never ridden by anyone but Charles Farborough or Victor Drake, but he was a competent horseman and he followed Victor out on the road towards the drift, looking about him with some interest. He raised his hat to Frances and Crispin as he passed them standing in the orchard. They were peeling quince laths and they glanced up at him, and something in the expressions on their faces should have warned him.

Victor led the way along the road, curving east towards the hills, going ahead at a brisk trot. They crossed the drift and were almost cantering down the slope towards a wide bend in the road when Hector, without warning, suddenly shied. Walter almost fell but he righted himself, pulling himself steady on the pommel. Shaking his head, tramping with his hooves, snorting in alarm, Hector wheeled around, impervious to instruction, and then launched out for home. Walter gave him his head while he regained his composure and adjusted his seat. Hector jumped the stream running down towards the mission furrows and surged up the far bank without mishap, Walter anticipating the path that he would take.

Hector swung into the stable yard and stopped abruptly. Walter leaned forward and soothed his neck, talking gently to him. He'd remained quite calm, as steadfast as a gnome upon a unicorn. Only his hat had fallen off.

Looking up, he saw Frances and Crispin Farborough peering at him through the quince hedge. Victor cantered into the yard, somewhat sheepish, and offered his own mount.

But Walter declined and suggested an alternative route for their tour. Crestfallen, Victor led the way past the cattle kraal towards the pasture.

Later, when Walter came up from the stables alone and stopped to extract his pipe from his pocket, he saw Frances Farborough standing in the orchard with Victor and Crispin and he heard her say – clearly, and a triumph in her voice –

'What a show-off you are, Victor! I bet he's the first parson you've lured out who hasn't fallen off at the sight of the ancestral shades waiting for Hector in the road!'

'Still,' retorted Victor, 'you should have seen his face! Clinging like a monkey with his coat tails on end.'

'He looks much more of a sport than the other priests we've had,' Crispin said. 'And anyway, he rides well. Even you might have fallen off.'

'What bosh!' said Victor, giving him a playful shove. 'Doesn't he remind you of that little Jewish fellow who runs the haberdasher's in Town? Big nose. Black eyes. Just the same. If he hadn't arrived wearing a dog-collar I'd have thought him a wandering smous.'

'Don't be mean, Vic!' said Frances. 'Anyway, whatever you think, he's got the nicest voice I've ever heard, so there!'

'He has to have something to recommend him!' said Victor flippantly.

'He'll do very well as a hero for Miss Smythe,' said Frances, with a small chuckle.

'And what constitutes a hero for you, Miss Farborough?' Walter said, coming up behind them on the path.

Frances spun around, the flush hot on her face. He looked at her steadily and without rancour, startling her into a blunt admission. 'Soldiers, Mr Brownley,' she said.

Walter laughed. 'It's fortunate that I'm to teach you Latin,' he said. 'There are enough soldiers in the Roman texts to keep you happy for months.'

And as he walked away from them, he realised that he'd won a small measure of approval from the two young Farboroughs. That he should have sought it was an unexpected but spontaneous response and he felt annoyed at himself for his reaction.

Walter had never lacked acceptance – not from his fellow students, not from the coalminers, not from his colleagues in the church, nor from the large and boisterous family of his sister Daisy who had clamoured for his attention – pestering him for stories, hiding his hat so he would stay, climbing all over him in search of sweets – whenever he had visited them. But here, he suspected, there were preconceptions. He was an interloper, another of the Bishop's offerings to be discarded. The world was ordered not by what it was but by what Victor Drake ordained it ought to be.

And as the days passed, Walter's first impression of Victor seemed confirmed: his manners were just beyond reproach but his assurance was matched with a condescension inappropriate at twenty-one. Despite his vigour, his broad shoulders, his extraordinary height, the clipped, amusing manner of his speech, there was something indulged about Victor Drake, an edge of arrogance. And something secretive as well. On that first night as he sat at dinner at the Farboroughs' table, Walter was alert to something undisclosed, some odd dissimulation with Victor at its core: when Father Charles left the table to speak to the catechist Mzantsi, waiting on the porch, and Emily Farborough said, 'Why should Mzantsi come at this time of night?' he saw a small, silencing signal of command pass from Victor Drake to Crispin Farborough. No one answered. Frances toyed with her fork and when Helmina Smythe looked pointedly at Victor, he returned her gaze with a brief, sardonic glance, momentarily insolent. Emily Farborough, apparently not wishing to let her exasperation show in the presence of a newcomer, enquired about Walter's impressions of Grahamstown, but when her husband reappeared, she said, almost sharply, 'What did Mzantsi want so late?'

'Nothing of importance, my dear,' he replied.

'Indeed, it must have been to bring him out at dinner time.'

'It was in connection with Benedict,' Father Charles conceded reluctantly.

'What has he done?'

'Nothing to concern us here.'

'What Benedict does is always my concern,' Emily persisted.

'Mzantsi was looking for him, that's all. It appears that he has been going out at night.' Charles Farborough turned to Walter and smiled. 'Young fellows of his age are inclined to be restless.' He raised his glass to his wife. 'I shall deal with it tomorrow, my dear.'

'It's against the rules of the boarding-house! What would

his sponsor say?' Emily Farborough retorted. 'I am in the middle of a letter to her and she has such high hopes for him!'

She turned to Walter and said, 'Benedict Matiwane was abandoned here when he was an infant. A vagrant woman had been seen about the district, poor godless wretch, and the baby must have been hers. We baptised him and put him in the care of one of the families of our servants. I'm sure that when you met him today, you could see what a promising young man he seems. He was always a clever child and has spent much of his time with Victor, which has been of the greatest benefit to him. They're of an age, you know, and we consider him a member of the family. There's a Miss Prudieaux-Brune in England who is sponsoring his education and now he's almost ready to sit the final teacher's examinations, we're hoping he'll follow in Mzantsi's footsteps and become a catechist. God willing, he might even take Holy Orders one day.'

She looked across at her husband then and said, with a touch of asperity, 'Still, despite our best efforts and our most fervent prayers, we are always having to contend with the influence of the old men and their heathen nonsense. Perhaps Mr Dwane and his Episcopalians are more shrewd than we, for they trade on the old traditions of the natives and the heathen flock to hear them. Still, I do not like to have unconverted people like Kobus about the place for it sets a bad example.'

'How are we to convert if we do not have the unconverted to begin with?' Charles Farborough said. 'There is nothing to fear from Kobus and the old men. Kobus is our sweeper and our groom, Mr Brownley. No doubt you have seen him, armed with a broom and always followed by a collection of old men. We seem to be a haven for the displaced. I could tell you a number of extraordinary stories about the origins of some.'

'I do not like Kobus's influence,' Emily Farborough exclaimed. 'And we are all far too soft with Benedict! Behaviour like this upsets the other boys and undermines Mr Mzantsi's authority. Perhaps we should put Benedict in the care of Mr Brownley.' She inclined her head. 'You could teach him Latin, Mr Brownley. It would be of the greatest advantage to him.'

'I'd prefer to be the pupil to start with, Mrs Farborough,' Walter said. 'I would like to learn Xhosa. I won't be of much use if I cannot speak the language of the people. In return, I shall be glad to instruct in anything you choose, Latin included.'

And, as he spoke, he was aware of Frances Farborough's sudden attention. Fleetingly, despite the grave appraisal, he saw her smile. A small salute, locked hastily away, as if she dared not show it.

Rebuffed, Emily remarked a little archly, 'It was Benedict of whom *I* was thinking, Mr Brownley. Mzantsi is always there to act as interpreter, should the need arise. Besides, it is a rule in our senior boarding-school that only English may be spoken. Pupils are required to use it among themselves. How are they to get on if they continue to speak in Kaffir?'

The night of his arrival was not the time to engage in debate with his senior's wife and Walter, despite long-considered opinions, let the matter rest, but when he went to his unfamiliar room, he could not dismiss the small but insistent desolation that he felt. He sat on the chair and looked bleakly at his jacket hanging in the cupboard, at his hat upon its peg, at his books arranged on the table. He observed the starkness of the room with its narrow bed, its washstand and strong oak cupboard, unadorned by carpet, chest of drawers or easy chair. He felt monklike sitting in his shirt-sleeves with his parson's collar hung on a hook behind the door, abandoned, like a man set down in an unfamiliar plain, with neither map nor path to show the way. He could smell, he could breathe, he could taste, he could hear and yet he felt suspended as though he was waiting for something to make sense of the uncertainties.

Beneath the seeming calm of the mission and Father Charles's unassailable tranquillity, Emily Farborough's cultivated conversation with the echoes of another, fuller world, beyond the mission house with its old and fragrant garden, there was another order, another truth.

He walked restlessly about the room, filling his pipe. He stopped and listened. Above the tossing of the wind in the trees outside, he heard singing, now clear, now faint. He would not have heard it if he had followed Helmina Smythe's advice and closed himself away with the sound of his own voice saying his prayers. Out in the dark, gathered within some firelit circle, were the people of the mission. Their song, phrased in harmonies he did not understand, drifted back and forth in minor keys, like the calls of unknown night birds.

Listening still, he sat on the bed, wearily undoing his shirt buttons, and he glanced up at the text which hung above it on the wall. The words were embroidered in a careless riot of colourful silks in a childish hand, signed by Frances Farborough and dated 1893. Reading them, he wondered that a girl so young had chosen such an unforgiving verse:

> Blessings are upon the head of the just: but
> violence covereth the head of the wicked,
> The memory of the just is blessed: but the name of
> the wicked shall rot.
> The wise in heart shall receive commandments:
> but the prating fool shall fall.

He read the words again, holding his candle close to the frame, to light them. Then he went to the table, opened his bottle of ink, turned to a clean page in his journal, dipped his pen and wrote:

'January 27th 1898: At St Matthias Mission there is an odd sense of predestination . . .' He looked up and gazed a moment at the text on the wall, returned to the page and added, 'It is strange how strongly I feel it. What it is I do not know, but I shall leave before it takes me in. I shall leave before I am its victim.'

He paused, alert, disturbed by a furtive scraping and the squeaking of a sash. He went to the open window and looked out into the night. From the next room Victor Drake emerged. He clambered into the garden below, straightened and glanced around. It seemed to Walter, watching him, that by the way he moved, his swift retreat, he was quite familiar with the path in the dark.

Unhesitating, disturbing nothing as he went, he walked away. He disappeared at last and Walter drew back and lit his pipe. What tryst would Victor have so late at night? Watching still, Walter half expected the next window to snap open and Crispin or Frances Farborough to fly out in pursuit. But it remained closed against the night.

Walter had his own ideas about the purpose of the nocturnal wanderings and within a fortnight he had witnessed a scene which seemed to confirm his suspicions. He was walking across the yard with Father Charles on their way to the church to take a confirmation class when they were startled by a commotion at the door of the wagon shed.

'Hello, what's going on?' Father Charles said, changing direction.

The wheelwright, surrounded by workers attempting to restrain him, had Benedict Matiwane by the jacket and was lifting him off the ground, shaking him like a terrier. Close by, one of the apprentices, Sonwabo Pumani, was sitting on the ground, holding a bloody rag to his head.

'I'll have no words from you, you insolent kaffir,' the man shouted and Walter, approaching, smelt the scent of him. Unwashed clothes and liquor.

'Put him down, Truter.' Father Charles's voice was calm. The workers parted as he walked among them. The wheelwright let Benedict go, half throwing him back so that he staggered into the watchers, almost falling to the ground.

'What is the trouble?' Father Charles addressed Benedict first.

This seemed to offend the wheelwright and he pushed his way forward, fist clenched. 'See here,' he said. 'I'll not work if you take a kaffir's word above mine.'

'I will take each on his merits,' Father Charles responded evenly. 'What is your complaint?'

'That idle, lazy boy,' elbowing the watchers aside, he pointed to Sonwabo, 'was insolent to me. I did my duty and chastised him, only to be set upon by this . . .' he almost spat in Benedict Matiwane's direction, searching for a word. 'I won't abide insolent kaffirs.'

'What have you to say, Benedict?' Father Charles turned to him.

'He struck Sonwabo with a mallet for no reason but that Sonwabo laughed.'

'I'll have no horseplay in my class. I'll have no impudence,' Truter interrupted, glaring about at the workers.

Father Charles bent to Sonwabo and examined his head. The wound was deep and bled copiously. He straightened and said to Walter, 'Take the lad down to Mrs Farborough, will you, Brownley? I shouldn't wonder if we have to call on Dr Fraser for stitches.' He turned back to the wheelwright, 'Perhaps, Mr Truter, you should come down to the office and we'll have a word in private.'

'In private, you say?' and Truter's eyes blazed red. 'What's there to say in private? There's a lot of "private" going on here indeed,' and he laughed, the gin strong in the air about him. 'This fellow,' indicating Benedict, 'has his own "private" at night, don't you, Master-High-And-Mighty? Scratch the surface of a popinjay nigger like him and you'll find a heathen underneath, running about in the dark, singing songs with red-blanket kaffirs.' He insinuated himself closer and said, breathing heavily, 'And what's more' – and a cunning in the way he looked up and sideways at Father Charles – 'if we're discussing "private" now, you'll not blame me if I take the quince stick to my own daughter. It's a father's right, wouldn't you say? For I will, you see, if I get another whiff of "private" with regard to her and a certain gentleman and neither will live to tell the tale.'

Father Charles regarded him a moment and then he said, 'Will you come with me, Mr Truter? I'll discuss nothing with you here.' He looked around at the apprentices. 'Back to work, lads. Tom Pumani, take charge till recess.'

As Walter helped Sonwabo Pumani away, he heard Father Charles say to Benedict, 'I'll speak to you after evensong, Benedict. Go to the church now and read with the class. We were busy with St Paul. Corinthians, chapter one, if you will.'

Emily Farborough dispatched Victor to The Hoek in the trap to take Sonwabo to Dr Fraser. They returned at dusk and Walter saw Sonwabo at evensong, a great white bandage wrapped about his head, the centre of attention with the students from the girls' school, craning from their side of the aisle to see him sitting proudly in his pew.

Father Charles, accompanied by Benedict, went down to his office after service. He came in late for dinner and Victor looked up apprehensively from his plate.

'I'm sorry to have kept you waiting, my dear,' Father Charles said to his wife. 'I'm glad you began without me,' and he sat in his chair and said his grace silently to himself and ate his meal with some preoccupation.

Emily said, 'Will we have some music after dinner? I believe you're a musician of note, Mr Brownley.' She smiled. 'Oh, don't protest! The Dean told me everything and we're looking forward to hearing something new.'

'By all means let us have a song,' Father Charles said, 'but you'll not be offended if I excuse myself tonight? And Victor too?' He leaned towards Victor and said quietly, 'You'll come and help me in the office after dinner, will you?'

'Can't Vic stay and sing?' exclaimed Frances. 'I want to teach him a duet.'

'Not tonight. I've matters on my mind.'

By the calmness of Father Charles's tone, none might have suspected his purpose in taking Victor with him. But Walter knew, and he observed the darkening in Victor's face, the apprehension with which he left the room.

Nothing was said. Whatever passed between Victor and his uncle went unremarked by the rest of the family and Father Charles returned with him after an hour, enjoyed the tea Helmina made for him and read a calm and reassuring passage from the Bible, before bidding them all good-night.

The next day, as Walter went to his duties in the schoolroom, he saw an old Scotch cart drawn up outside the wheelwright's cottage. A shabby pair of mules stood drooping in the traces. A meagre load of household goods was piled in the back.

By midday, when he passed that way again, the cottage stood empty, the door padlocked at the bolt.

There was no more word of nightly ramblings.

Chapter Two

Victor's attention returned to Frances. If it had been briefly vagrant, she was not aware of its cause, only puzzled by the change in him and irritated by the sudden swings from capricious baiting to studied indifference. She did not understand the restlessness in him, the sudden disconcerting scrutiny.

'What is the matter with you, Victor? One minute you're sunshine, the next you're sour and horrid,' she said crossly, but he did not reply.

In the days that followed, Victor's bouts of indolence preceded spurts of high activity when he and Crispin swam and hunted, accompanied by the carpentry apprentices, Tom and Reuben and Sonwabo Pumani or Benedict. Resentful at being ignored, Frances took out her ill humour on Helmina Smythe or loitered about the garden.

She had always been part of every game, she had dared things which would have brought the severest censure had she been caught. As a child she had escaped from her room at rest times to go hunting with him and Crispin, forced herself to gut the eels she caught so she might be accepted, cooked birds over fires in the bush, running wild with them and never being excluded. But this game of Victor's – this intrusive attention or studied indifference – was a new and vexing pastime.

And she was angry with him. Some time before, he had taken to slipping out at night and when she had confronted him, he had said – and quite severely – 'I've been going to listen to Kobus prepare the boys for initiation. And you know I can't tell you more because of Xhosa custom, so don't even ask. You'd better keep a look out for me too because I'll be skinned alive if Aunt Emily catches me.'

Accepting the truth of this, she had willingly become a conspirator. She had been aware of his nightly exits through the window and listened for any steps in the passage so she could divert attention from him or shield his absence from discovery. She was relieved when, without warning, these excursions had stopped.

27

It was only a chance remark of Crispin's that alerted her. She said to him, 'What do you learn at initiation, Crispin?'

'How do you know I've been going to initiation?' And he flushed and glanced round to see if there were eavesdroppers.

'Silly!' she said. 'As if I'd tell! I asked Victor.'

'What would he know?' said Crispin crossly and then he looked confused and pulled at his ear and said, 'We only learn songs and Kobus talks about manhood and things. Benedict wanted me to go with him. He hasn't any other way of understanding about being a Xhosa and neither have I.'

Frances laughed and rubbed her hand across his hair, making it stand up. 'A Xhosa indeed! You're such an old heathen, I wonder where you came from?' And she went away, knowing Victor had lied to her.

She challenged him as he came back alone from hunting, his rifle slung across his shoulder and a brace of birds dangling from his belt. He was leading Hector down the path towards the stables and she saw him and marched up to him and said, 'Why did you tell me you were going to initiation with Benedict when you weren't?'

He glanced down at her and away and she could see that familiar expression of his, mustering the supercilious. But he waited for her to speak, a lead – oh, she knew it – so he could make up an excuse from whatever she offered. She looked at him with her arms folded resolutely, waiting.

He laughed then, moved a little closer to her, half leaning against Hector's neck, surveying her. 'You're a girl. You wouldn't understand.'

'Don't be an idiot,' said Frances. 'What wouldn't I understand?'

He only smiled.

'What wouldn't I understand?' she said again and ready for battle. 'Here, I have been covering for you when you go out and now you won't tell me why.'

'I felt restless,' said Victor. 'That's all. Penned in. I've been at the river. And off into the Pirie Bush.'

He turned to Hector and unsaddled him and led him to the stable. Frances followed. Victor said, the old conspiratorial tone, half a whisper, half a laugh, 'I'll take you with me, if you like.'

28

'Don't be an ass!' she retorted, still stung by his subterfuge. 'Anyway, can you imagine the fuss if someone saw? I've got you out of trouble often enough in the last three weeks as it is. And anyway, what for?'

'For fun,' he said. 'But seeing you're scared . . .'

'No, I'm not!'

'Yes, you are! You weren't afraid that time when we cooked the meercat and stayed out half the night. A real little heathen daubed with sacrificial blood and baying for more.'

'Don't be disgusting!'

'Still, you revelled in it.'

'I was only thirteen and you should have known better,' she said. 'Besides, it was a game.'

There was a silence.

'So is this,' he said lightly. But his voice belied him.

Frances was about to reply when she was aware of a movement in the adjoining stable. She took a step backwards and glanced in through the half-open door. Walter Brownley was rubbing down the mare. He turned when he saw her. 'Good afternoon, Miss Farborough,' he said quite evenly.

'Mr Brownley.' She knew the colour in her face was high. She said, to cover her discomposure, 'Why don't you let Kobus groom her? That's what he's here for.'

'I saw him busy over at the workshop with your father. And anyway, when a horse has carried me for as many hours as this poor old girl has done, I think she deserves a bit of consideration. She is very hot and dusty!' And he went about his work again, with a low whistle, under his breath, rubbing vigorously with the brush.

Victor came from the stable, took up his rifle and the birds that he had shot and walked away, beckoning to her with his head. 'Do you think he heard?' he said.

'Not everything. Only the last bit. So what?'

'Damn him,' said Victor so vehemently that Frances glanced at him in surprise.

It was another of Victor's games. Victor's great parade of games, astonishing in their inventiveness. Games like the ones that he had played when he first came to the mission, or the

29

later ones when he was sixteen and Frances and Crispin had obeyed his every bidding, awed by his height and his age and his *savoir-faire*. Childhood games where Victor exercised his power and ascendancy over all of them. They surrendered willingly. They had never questioned that they should.

The night before each holiday was always the same: Crispin – no more than twelve – sitting on her bed, legs drawn up, encircled by his arms, chin on his knee, unable to sleep because Victor would be home. Terrifying, wonderful Victor, coming from town in the wagon with his cricket bat and his rugby ball and his wild imaginative entertainments. Frances had to stay with Crispin and tell him stories in an attempt to make him sleep.

There were rugby matches in the yard, goals constructed from wattle poles, dares to go far up the Ndwandwe stream and never breathe a word of fright at the rustlings in the bush or at the sight of a snake in the undergrowth. Another sacrifice perhaps: cooking a meercat in the moonlight with its skin stripped back and only its nose still moist and black and glistening.

Or the War Game. Played down at the river, out of sight of the mission house and a whole range of scouts to give the warning should an adult come near, a whistle echoing from place to place and the fishing rods hastily retrieved and cast in seeming innocence into the stream.

Oh, the War Game! Hector saddled and bridled and brought by Kobus at Victor's request! He was part of the ritual, for none but Father Charles or Victor could ride him, and the fact that Hector always shied at the same bend in the road confirmed Kobus's view that he was disturbed by some restless shade that kept about that place: a warrior perhaps, whose people had never found his body and had failed to lead his spirit home. Hector's divinatory powers made him an object of awe and Victor's ability to ride him added to his already considerable prestige.

The War Game, devised to re-enact Victor's father's finest hour. A tribute to a hero. A means of creating another in the eyes of all of them – his own included!

Victor's father, Claude Drake, had been a major in the

Frontier Light Horse and Victor had concocted a uniform to resemble a cavalryman's. He possessed a tunic and a belt which he had found among the things that had been sent home on his father's death. He had a bugle which had the name 'A. O'Flaherty' roughly engraved on it.

When he first showed it to Frances and Crispin, bringing it covertly from his bag and secreting it inside his shirt until they were alone, Frances said with suitable reverence as she fingered it, 'Who is A. O'Flaherty?'

'Trooper O'Flaherty died defending my father at Ulundi in the Zulu War,' Victor replied. 'There was an ambush on the riverbank and O'Flaherty lost his mount. The Zulus were closing in and my father tried to save him by lifting him onto his own horse, but he couldn't. He tried and tried but O'Flaherty was a giant. At last O'Flaherty cried, "Leave me, sir, for God's sake and save yourself." The Zulus rose out of the bush with a yell and flung themselves on him. There was nothing more my father could do, so he fired his revolver right and left, right and left until it was empty and then he rode away with the spears raining round him. When they went back later to find O'Flaherty's body, they counted a hundred stab wounds and they had to chase the crows away and bring a sack to gather up the pieces. They buried him where he fell. This bugle was all that was left to remember him by and they played the last post on it and made a wooden cross.'

Frances stared at him, hearing some distant grandeur in the words. Surely Major Drake must have ridden such a horse as Hector! Muscle and sheen and red-rimmed eye! Surely he must have looked like Victor, but with a military moustache and whiskers and a jacket in gold-braided scarlet.

'My father was decorated highly for his action,' Victor said, eyeing them to ensure they were conscious of the privilege of sharing such information. 'It's a famous story. My mother has pieces from the newspapers and pictures of the regiment. One day I will show them all to you.' And a look on his face to make Frances reach her hand gently to his sleeve. But he shook it off impatiently and said – a transforming enthusiasm – 'Let's play the War Game!'

The sound of those words, Crispin creeping closer! Let's

play the War Game! An apprehension and yet, it was what she and Crispin had both been waiting to hear.

The battle scene down at the river.

Victor as Major Drake.

Crispin as O'Flaherty.

Frances his widow, black-draped and loitering in the bushes, waiting for the end.

Tom and Reuben and Sonwabo were instructed to bring the other boys from the school to play the Zulu *impi*. The forces were ranged at either side of the Mtwaku river, hidden from view by the thorn bush growing thickly on its banks.

'The object,' Victor said – and Crispin translating into Xhosa – 'is for O'Flaherty to try and reach camp.' Victor pointed with his riding-crop. 'It is down there, near the water pump.' A long way off, at a bend in the stream. 'O'Flaherty is the scout. You are the *impi*. It is your purpose to stop O'Flaherty from reaching camp. If you catch him, you are to drag him back to your kraal near that tree.' The imperious indicator swung in the opposite direction. 'There' – choosing a large thorn among the brush – 'I will give you five minutes to find him and try and capture him. Then I will blow the bugle and you will know that the Frontier Light Horse has started out to rescue him! Frances' – looking round for her among the crowd of anxious faces – 'you will be the widow at home.' He gestured behind him. 'Stay there and wait. Benedict. You will be a trooper with me until you are the military chaplain.' And he turned Hector and trotted off down the mission lands to the pump at the bend, obediently followed by Benedict on foot.

The greatest apprehension was Crispin's, the prize dragged from side to side. Frances knew it by the small nervous movements of his tongue along his bottom lip as he crept along the riverbank, listening for the bugle.

She stood in the heat in the black drapery, tearing it on the thorny bushes and peering through the leaves to see how well concealed Crispin was in his progress towards the imaginary camp. She could see Tom and Reuben Pumani and the rest of the *impi* gaining on him from behind and she wanted to cry out to warn him but it wasn't part of Victor's game. She turned her back and tried to imagine herself as Trooper O'Flaherty's wife, complacent in her parlour, awaiting news of war.

The drumming of hooves and the sound of the bugle. The flat, lone toot in the midday hush. A pause. An eternal pause because Victor took delight in suspense, knowing the terror that the sound of his approach occasioned the mission boys.

There was Victor, charging down through the bush, red dust flying, goading Hector towards the stream to rescue the beleaguered O'Flaherty: a display of horsemanship at sixteen which none of them could ever hope to match.

Mostly the mission boys just ran away as Hector reached them and Crispin hid his head in his arms as if to ward off the flying feet, half springing up himself – despite having been instructed to play dead – to avoid being trampled.

Victor's irritation at the cowardice of the *impi* always spoiled it at the end. In reality, O'Flaherty had been killed and if Crispin did not have a similar fate, Victor could not ride to Frances and bring her on the horse to the site of the carnage. He could not stand with her while she prostrated herself on the riverbank awaiting Benedict's approach: 'Reverend Parmiter, pray accompany us to the grave', and Frances trying not to laugh because she knew that Reverend Parmiter was Victor's school chaplain and the joke of Grahamstown. But Benedict didn't know and he opened the old prayer-book and took the service somewhat peremptorily because he did not approve of the game and had no way of avoiding it.

The mourners left, the corpse stood up and departed, the Reverend Parmiter turned his shirt around, dispensing with the prayer-book, and Victor lifted Frances onto the horse and mounted up behind her and rode her home, pretended he was departing again for some desperate front, gallantly promising to return for her. A lingering look, a chaste kiss, an outstretched hand as she dismounted. Then he flung himself into the saddle and rode away, blowing the bugle loud enough to send Hector into a frenzy and make the mission boys scatter once again: across the grazing camp, flying over the quince hedge, urging Hector at it at a gallop. How he survived without breaking his neck was a miracle!

Victor's game had ended abruptly. Not because he'd fallen from Hector nor because he'd trampled a child but because, in jest, he'd padlocked Sonwabo Pumani in the vestry cupboard and Sonwabo had had hysterics.

Benedict had started it all by refusing to be the Reverend Parmiter. He had heard Victor mimicking the chaplain to Crispin and was humiliated to discover who it was that he'd been playing so unwittingly.

'You will not make fun of me,' he said angrily, omitting to call Victor 'Master Victor' as he was supposed to do.

'Oh, come on, Benedict. Don't be a prig!' said Victor.

Benedict glowered, unable to retort but small Sonwabo did, drawing himself up and delivering an oath in Xhosa which would have made them laugh if Victor had not turned on him and ridden after him.

Sonwabo fled to the porch of the church, the other children racing after him. Victor dismounted, throwing Hector's reins over the hitching-post, and caught Sonwabo with a deft hand. He picked him up, put him over his shoulder, said – half in annoyance, half in jest – 'I'll teach you, you insolent little beggar,' and marched him kicking down the aisle of the church and into the vestry. Victor opened the cupboard, deposited Sonwabo inside and clicked the padlock closed. 'I'll make your mother pay a tickey for your release,' he shouted. 'And if she hasn't got one you'll have to stay there for ever.'

He had forgotten to check for a key.

Crispin and Frances, Benedict and Sonwabo's brothers ran into the church after them. 'Let him out, Victor,' said Crispin breathlessly, pushing back the vestry door.

'Not for a bit!' Victor laughed. 'No one swears at me like that without a hiding.'

'Let him out!' And Crispin was angry. 'Don't you know he's frightened of closed places?'

'I'd prefer him to be frightened of me!' said Victor.

There was a muffled banging and a shouting, as if the cupboard might fly for the tumult inside it.

'Give me the key!' shouted Crispin, his face flushed. 'You're cruel, Victor. Give it to me.'

34

Victor looked around, patted his pockets. 'I don't know where it is,' he said.

Frances went to the cupboard, tapping gently at it. 'Hush, Sonwabo, hush. We'll get you out.'

But the frenzy continued. Frances and Crispin and even Victor – somewhat alarmed – searched the vestry for the key to the padlock but they could not find it.

'Dad will have it,' said Crispin. 'He keeps it with the others on his belt.'

'I'm going for a hammer to smash the door,' said Benedict defiantly, starting away.

'Don't be a fool!' said Victor. 'I'll fetch the key.'

Crispin and Frances crouched with Tom and Reuben outside the cupboard door and tried to calm Sonwabo but he did not seem to hear: the fear was too great and the racking sobs did not abate.

Benedict reappeared with a hammer and smashed it into the lock but it did not yield. Sonwabo started to scream with renewed vigour.

They heard Father Charles coming up the aisle. Benedict put the hammer aside. Father Charles thrust open the door and everyone shrank from his sweeping gaze. Victor, following, stood hesitantly at the threshold.

Sonwabo was pried from the cupboard. He had soiled himself, his eyes started in his head and he looked back at them as if he recognised no one. So small for his age – no more than eleven – he took great gulps of air, shuddering in Father Charles's arms, oblivious of the tears and mucus that bathed his face. When he was quiet at last, Father Charles said, 'Tom and Reuben, take your brother to the kitchen for some food. The rest of you, go about your business quietly now. Victor,' and with a voice to burn, 'to my study, if you please.'

Frances and Crispin, walking silently down towards the house, heard the sound of the cane. One stroke. Two strokes. Three strokes. Four.

A shocking sound it was. They went away for they were more afraid to witness Victor's shame than the wrath of a father in whom they had never seen anger before. Profoundly disturbed, they went together to the loft and stayed there in the hot dustiness among the boxes and trunks until evening came. When they descended they found only their mother and Helmina Smythe in the house. Victor was gone all afternoon. He returned at dusk and went to his room without a word. Their father did not come out of his study until after dinner and ate alone in the parlour. When he had finished, he took a tray to Victor himself. He stayed for almost an hour and then Frances and Crispin heard him close the door quietly and walk down the passage and go out onto the porch. Their mother read the Bible to them that night. Just a short verse before she sent them off to bed.

Victor emerged next day, temporarily subdued. Nothing more was said. But Hector was out of bounds for the rest of the holidays and the games by the river were at an end.

But that was long ago. Long, long ago. And yet it seemed that Victor had the need for games again. Despite young adulthood, despite having left school and taken a position and learned to smoke cigarettes with elegant ease, and to talk of politics and business and send cables to important men, Victor was inventing games, as he had always done. And he wanted Frances to go to the river with him at night 'for fun'. A truly risky entertainment! She had laughed at him. And yet he'd been annoyed! Besides, how could he be so rash when they knew that Walter Brownley must have heard what they had said? Her father's colleague and a priest! She didn't dare. Not even she. The holidays had passed and Victor, restless to the end, had somehow seemed relieved when it was time to go.

Victor and Crispin had been gone a week. And Frances had been thoroughly unsettled and preoccupied. Walter found it difficult to engage her attention at the few lessons he was obliged to give her and felt some exasperation at the waste of time.

He was tutoring her Latin one Tuesday afternoon in the stuffy schoolroom when she wearily pushed her books aside and rose to open the window. Hearing the familiar squeal of the sash, recalling suddenly his first night at the mission when he'd seen Victor climbing out, aware of how he'd listened for it since the conversation that he'd overheard in the stable, Walter said – on an impulse – 'Tell me about Victor.'

'Why?' Her tone was wary.

'He seems to be the most important person here.'

'Is he?'

'Do you listen to him from admiration or fear?'

'Fear?'

'Yes,' Walter said. 'Fear.'

'I'm not afraid of Victor!' she retorted, the flush hot at her ears.

'Aren't you?'

She turned away, said defensively, 'Victor doesn't ever mean any harm. It's only his manner.' And she glanced at him searchingly with a small expression of unease that betrayed the lightness of her tone. 'Most things he does are a kind of game or a tease or a dare,' she said. 'You shouldn't mind him, you know.' She fumbled. 'I don't.' She paused. Walter waited. 'You don't like Victor, do you?'

'Did I say that?'

She did not answer and Walter took his pipe from the drawer and filled it slowly. He lit it and said, 'Well, tell me about him. Entertain me with his exploits.'

She turned to the window again and looked out. 'I first saw him when I was very small,' she said. 'He must have been about seven when he came with my uncle to visit. I don't remember it well because I was only four, but I do remember that I had been given a sweet and Vic said he would marry me one day if I let him have it.'

She flushed and Walter picked the threads of old tobacco from the edge of his pipe bowl.

'My uncle was his stepfather,' she said, 'and although he adopted Victor, I don't suppose Victor's really related, if you think about it. His own father was a hero in the Zulu War. He won a medal for trying to save a trooper in an ambush. Victor's mother still keeps it on a silky cushion in her parlour. Later he was killed. Shot. Victor was only a few months old. We used to play a game about it all. About the trooper he tried to save and about the *impi* capturing him on the riverbank.

Crispin was the trooper and the school children were the *impi* and Victor was Major Drake. He used to charge Hector down the bank and across the stream at them. Mostly, they just ran away.'

'I'm hardly surprised,' said Walter drily.

'They weren't supposed to. Vic used to get furious with them.'

'I see.' Walter scrutinised her, tracing her finger round the edge of the window-panes. 'Wasn't this game of yours a bit macabre?'

'It was our favourite.'

'Whose favourite?'

'Victor's.'

'And the others?'

'Crispin does anything Victor asks.'

Walter noticed that she failed to mention her own devotion. 'Go on,' he said.

She hesitated, looking for a way to proceed. Then she said, 'Victor's mother married my uncle when Victor was only two. He was my father's elder brother. A barrister, nearly a judge. Perhaps you've heard of him? Mr Melville Farborough?'

Walter had not heard of him and Frances continued. 'Victor's mother never comes here. She doesn't like to leave Grahamstown. She's a grand lady from England, so my mother is marvellously impressed by her.' She pulled a small face. 'When Victor was fourteen my uncle died and after that, Victor asked to be called Drake again instead of Farborough. I was sad because people used to think he was our brother and now they don't any more.' She fiddled with her cuffs, pushing them up her wrists and pulling them back. 'Anyway,' she continued, 'he's been here each holiday since. He's always had his own room in the house, with his own things in it. My mother wants him to be ordained so that the mission will be his one day. "At all costs, my dear" – a perfect imitation of her mother's tone – "we must keep St Matthias in the family. If Crispin cannot take Holy Orders, Victor shall."' Frances rolled her eyes. 'Poor Crispin! He can hardly be blamed for being a little slow at school. He hates being cooped up there! He was much better when Miss Smythe taught him. She took endless trouble with him. Really, she did. He ought to be allowed to leave and be a hunter or a transport rider. Those are the things that'd suit him, don't you think? Besides,' she inclined her head and said half-jokingly, 'he's a heathen, so it wouldn't do trying to make him a priest.' She paused. 'I don't think Victor would be a very good one either.'

'And you fervently hope he won't try,' remarked Walter, watching her face, 'because soldiers are your heroes and not priests.'

She reddened and glanced over at him. 'I'm sorry, Mr Brownley. I didn't mean it like that!'

But he only laughed and said, 'What a rush to the priest-hood there'd be if clergymen were the objects of adulation! I'd have to take to soldiering to escape the eager hordes!'

'When he first arrived,' Frances said, hurrying on, for she could tell that he was amused with her and the blush was still hot at her throat, 'Victor brought a cricket bat and wickets and a proper fishing rod and a rugby ball.' She smiled. 'Crispin loved that rugby ball. He'd been asking for one end-lessly and started praying for it aloud at bedtime. My mother caned him once for kicking gourds off their vines and aiming them over the hedge. Sometimes Victor let him play with the ball, but when he didn't feel generous, he locked it up in the cupboard for days. Crispin would do almost anything for him, hoping he'd take it out again.'

It was evident to Walter from the way she spoke, that from the moment she and Crispin had hidden behind the quince hedge and watched Victor Drake come up the path towards the house for the first time, they had been enslaved.

'Even I was allowed to kick a bit,' she said, 'when my mother and Miss Smythe were out of sight!' She laughed. 'Benedict and Sonwabo Pumani and his brothers used to come and join in. They'd be one team and Vic and Crispin the other. Victor used to coach them, but he always won the matches. He could kick much higher and further than any-one. He could run faster. After that they always went about together, Vic leading them. I sometimes followed, when I managed to escape Miss Smythe.'

'Through the window at rest times?' Walter said.

'How do you know that?'

'Ah, I have my sources!'

'I don't do that any more,' she said primly. 'Only when I was very young.'

'Is that so?' Walter cocked an eyebrow and chuckled.

She turned from him, suddenly flustered, saying hastily, 'Before Crispin was sent to school it was very dull for us when Victor wasn't here.'

'What did you do when he was gone?'

'Oh,' she said, 'we played Benedict's games again, like we used to. The bird game. Naming them, calling them up. Silly really' – she tossed it aside: perfidious Frances. But then – unexpectedly – she sang a little incantation, the gruffness of her voice changing, catching an echo of something else, distant from him and strangely sad:

> Oh you, *unongub'endala*, are a little ragged one,
> And you, *ikhwebula*, the one who waits to call
> the cattle home,
> And you *unomaswana* are the drop of calabash
> milk, so white and fat.

Averting his gaze from her face – despite the starched whiteness of her petticoats and pinafore – Walter could not have distinguished her voice from those of the Xhosa girls he came across at homesteads in the hills, heathen girls half naked and working in the fields.

Frances came back to her seat and picked up her Latin book and opened it. 'I suppose I had better finish my lesson.'

Walter put his pipe away and set an exercise for her and waited as she worked. His mind, in the sultry heat of the afternoon, drifted back to the story she had just told him. It was evident from her words that – by their games – she, Victor and Crispin had created a truth that was more powerful than the real events from which it had originated. The distinction between past and present, imagination and reality, were blurred and as he watched her, Walter knew that he, too, was capable of creating myth where none

40

existed, of devising games that might yet grow to overwhelm.

He did. Reluctantly at first. Then knowingly. He might as well have put a noose around his own neck and pulled it taut. Such a game indeed: he came to watch for her, despite himself. Green-eyed, she was. Small and vivid in her movements. How interchangeable the sweet and the sardonic in her smile. At times she was reflective and then, in sudden counterpoint, impetuous and boyish. She was also vexing. She learned with a puzzling blend of competence and indifference. Quirky, warm, capricious, all in turn, she often made him laugh, loud enough to bring a glance of censure from her mother, if she happened to be passing by.

She was also insatiably curious.

Walter was sitting at his desk one day, writing, when she appeared at his door. Without knocking, she came in and looked enquiringly at the sheets before him and said, 'Miss Smythe is a mean thing! I'm far too old for the schoolroom but she has given me a history essay to "entertain me", so I hope you are not planning any unseen Latin.'

'No, I am not,' he said, drawing the papers towards himself and looking up at her pointedly for she was staring at the words he had written, quite unabashed. 'I am writing a letter,' he said.

'Who to?'

'To whom, Miss Farborough. To whom.' It was out of his mouth before he could stop himself.

'Oh bother that,' she said, and she pulled out a chair and sat and looked at him, waiting.

'If you must know, I am writing to my niece in England. Her name is Miranda. She is often ill and my sister Daisy used to like me to amuse her with stories. Now I am here, I have to write them instead of telling them.'

'Can't someone else entertain her?'

'No one else knows the characters that she especially likes,' said Walter.

'What characters?'

'They are not in a book,' he replied patiently. He smoothed the papers and took them up and tapped their

41

edges on the table-top and then slid them into a drawer out of sight.

Her eyes followed his hands. 'Are they your own inventions?'

Walter saw the fleeting suspicion and intrigue on her face. 'Yes, I make them up.'

'What are they about?'

'Is this an inquisition or a conversation?' he asked. And then he smiled and said, 'Nothing of consequence. Just a character we had between us, that's all. A rather eccentric fellow.'

'What's his name?'

Walter hesitated, guarding something from derision, then he said cautiously, 'My niece, Miranda, is only nine, you understand? She is confined indoors because of her health and her brothers are away at school. She is sometimes lonely.'

'What's his name?' Frances persisted. 'The man in the story.'

'His name?' said Walter, touching the drawer as if in apology to its occupant. 'His name is Plotz.'

'Plotz?'

'Mr Plotz is a story-teller and he gets his stories confused. Rather like Mrs Malaprop and her words. Red Riding Hood meets the Billy Goats Gruff . . . It is all rather foolish but it amuses Miranda.' He took up a pencil and tapped it in the palm of his hand. 'She is very dear to me and I miss her.'

Frances stared at him. Walter looked back. Perhaps the idea of his having a family or a past beyond the moment when the wagon had delivered him in the yard, had not occurred to her: a clergyman's correspondence could not go further than a letter from the Dean or an information sheet on the progress of the Mission in India or Tibet or Nigeria. Letters from a child named Miranda, eagerly requesting the next instalment in the adventures of a Mr Plotz, were doubtless unimaginable.

'And what does Mr Plotz do?' she asked.

'All sorts of things. This episode is called, "Mr Plotz goes to Africa. The Green Lion and other stories".'

'The green lion?'

'Well, yes. Mr Plotz has not seen a lion yet so he is unsure of what colour it ought to be.'

42

'Oh.' Frances gazed at him.

Walter expected her to follow this with something arch – as she would have done, he knew, if Victor had been near – but instead she traced her finger down the spindle of the chair and said, without meeting his gaze, 'No one ever told me stories like that.'

'Surely,' he said, detecting the wistfulness.

She drew herself up a little, but still she did not look at him. 'Only Bible stories. Except when our father told us about when he was young. And sometimes Nowasha the cook, when we were small and ate in the kitchen.' She glanced up then. 'She had wonderful stories,' she said. 'Xhosa stories, and she taught us all the rhymes and songs until my mother stopped her. She said they were heathen and full of black magic.'

'Oh, a bit of magic never did any harm,' said Walter. 'White or black. The Bible's full of magic formulae – burning bushes and talking doves and staffs turning into serpents.'

Frances looked aghast.

'A great dollop of folklore, Frances. Stirring stuff. Nearly as good as the Greek myths.'

'If my mother knew you'd said that . . .'

'Your mother will not know unless you choose to tell her.'

Frances did not reply, nor did she look at him. She resumed picking at the splinters on the chairback. 'Would you like me to tell you the story of the girl who went to get clay and the *zimuzimu* cannibal caught her?' she said hesitantly. 'Perhaps Miranda might like to hear it. It is a Xhosa tale that Benedict once told me before he was confirmed and became all holy.'

'Yes, indeed,' said Walter.

She seemed suddenly embarrassed and said a little gruffly, 'Really, it is a very silly story.' She stood. 'There is tea on the veranda, if you want.'

'Mr Plotz is intrigued by the green lion,' Walter ventured. 'I am sure that the story about – what did you call it? – would be delightful.'

'*Zimuzimu.*'

'Will you tell it?'

43

'Oh,' she said, idling with the buckle of her belt, 'I think I've probably forgotten.'

'Perhaps you'd rather not tell *me*,' said Walter. 'However, Plotz is most discreet and there is nothing that he considers nonsense if it is entertaining.'

She gazed back at him from the doorway, half perplexed, humouring him lest he was humouring her and she said, 'I shall tell Mr Plotz when I meet him.'

Walter laughed and watched her go. '*Zimuzimu*,' he said to himself. 'Well, Plotz, that should please you.'

Had he listened he might have heard Plotz laughing at his back, relishing his folly. Instead, paying no attention to the voice, he extracted the pages from his drawer and continued with his tale.

Walter sat alone that afternoon – as he often did – to write a letter to his sister Daisy, and to Miranda, to retreat in his mind to the old house in Alton with its busyness and its odd, dusty corners and its ash tree in the garden. He closed his eyes a moment and felt himself transported back and he remembered when little Miranda and his sister Daisy had put their arms around him and Daisy had said, 'You can't go to Africa, Walter. We love you so and we'll be quite lost without you.' Then she had peeped at him teasingly and said, 'Why don't you marry one of the Misses Parsons? They're mad for you and rich as can be. You'd be happy as a lark and right next door!'

The prospect of marriage with one of the Misses Parsons might have tempted him to accept a post in China, despite the fact that they were Daisy's neighbours. But now, writing here in the silence of the mission house – a strange, transplanted monument to England, an imposter in the wild stretch of veld – even the idea of the Misses Parsons, all three in a row and smelling of chlorodyne and mildew as they took the front pew in church, filled him with longing.

He rested his forehead against his hand, trying to recapture the vision of Daisy's face and Miranda's eager eyes: 'And what happened to the green lion then, Mr Plotz?' she might say.

'Never mind the green lion, Miranda. I have lost my Wor-

44

cester Sauce' – Plotz always deferred the end of his story by going in search of his elusive Worcester Sauce – 'but I shall tell you exactly what happened . . . tomorrow.'

There was no Worcester Sauce at St Matthias. Only the green lion of which he had been writing to Miranda – oh, with such deft humour, he had laughed out loud to read the conversation between the trusting Plotz and the beast! He did not know that the green lion might be waiting at his back, no buffoon this, despite what he had said, but some malignant presence. That day, sitting in the schoolroom with the afternoon resting softly at the window, how could he have known?

In the months that followed, Walter came each afternoon, when his other duties were done, to teach Frances Latin or English grammar or mathematics and Plotz and his stories crept into their conversation, their way of speaking to each other. His presence allowed a kind of intimacy that would otherwise have been impossible. A solitary Latin lesson was not so tedious when shared – just now and then – with Plotz, the green lion and Miranda. Plotz had no need to observe the formality of calling Frances 'Miss Farborough' and, in consequence, a new character – Mrs Brodowski – was added to the cast.

Walter invented her the day that Charles Farborough left for a Synod meeting in Grahamstown and he saw Frances standing mournfully at the gate watching the trap drive away. She stood quite still in the sunlight and gazed down the road long after it was empty. He walked up towards her and said, 'What can we think up to make you look less miserable?'

'Nothing in Latin!' she retorted brusquely.

He did not take offence. He laughed. 'I won't inflict that on you at present. By the way,' he said as he walked beside her, 'yesterday, when Mr Mzantsi brought the post, I got a letter from my sister Daisy. There was a note in it from Miranda. She wants to hear more about you. I believe she thinks you are some sort of African sprite accompanying Plotz on his adventures. I don't suppose you'd care to write to her and tell her something of yourself? She'd love that.' He glanced at her. 'After all, you'd be able to describe green lion country far better than I. Mr Plotz is too preoccupied with England to do it justice.'

45

'Why?' she said. 'Are you going back?'

'I don't know. It's too early to decide. Should I stay or go?'

'I don't care what you do,' she remarked rather petulantly, glancing back up the road where the trap had disappeared.

'If you're lonely I can understand why,' said Walter. 'You're very isolated from people your age.'

'Daddy promised that when he next went to Grahamstown, I could go with him. I so wanted to see Crispin and Victor again. Mother spoilt it all and said I'd be a hindrance.'

He could see that she struggled with herself to keep from tears and he said, 'I have Miranda's letter in my room. Will you wait while I fetch it? Perhaps you could sketch the school and the church and other things to give her an idea of how it looks here. Miss Smythe has shown me your drawings and I know how good they are.' He walked on slowly, despite the resistance which he sensed in her. 'I knew a lady once who was an artist. Her name was Mrs Brodowski and she wore a gypsy shawl and drank tea from a Russian samovar and she had an astonishing dogcart for her children, all decorated with plumes.' Frances made no comment but she did not move off. 'Mrs Brodowski,' Walter continued, 'did bizarre paintings of Gothic creatures and she was interested in metaphysics. She could interpret dreams. Most extraordinary . . .'

He fell silent. Frances said, 'And?'

'And? Oh . . . Mrs Brodowski? Yes. I suppose I shall tell you some time. She wore a monocle. It seemed to magnify her eye enormously.'

'I am sure you are inventing this,' Frances said and she looked at him shrewdly.

'Invent Mrs Brodowski?' He pretended great offence. 'How could I? She lived at number seventy-one Garrick Street. How could I invent that?'

'Next you'll tell me she was a friend of Mr Plotz and then I'll *know* it's all a story.'

'In a sense I suppose she was. But only in a sense.'

'Did Miranda ever meet her?'

'Heavens no! Mrs Brodowski was rather too exotic for Miranda's acquaintance. Daisy would not have approved of that!'

46

As he had suspected she would, Frances followed him to the steps of the curate's lodge while he fetched the letter. She took it without comment. She did not even glance at the stamp while he was there. Nor did she look back. He watched her go, the letter in her hand, holding it carelessly, as if it had no interest for her. He went indoors amused, knowing well enough that she would read it eagerly once she was alone.

He was not surprised when he saw her, a few hours later, deep in work, sitting with her back against the wall of the church, painting a view of the school with the hills beyond, her hair tied up in a twist of scarf which gave her a Bohemian air. He went away before she saw him, knowing that – at that moment – Grahamstown had slipped for a while from her thoughts.

Over the next week or two Frances painted more and more scenes for Walter to send in his next letter home. She sketched Nowasha the cook, shelling peas, sitting on an upturned tub on the porch. There was a drawing of Benedict with his high white collar, his little hat worn on the back of his head, and another of Crispin – sketched from memory – fishing from the riverbank. She even did one of herself with a faintly gypsy air, just a hint of a Mrs Brodowski about it.

'There,' he said as he scanned it, 'I see a close resemblance here to Mrs Brodowski herself. You must be a changeling. Plotz' – as if summoning an unseen presence – 'may I present Mrs Brodowski. Mrs B – Plotz.'

'Do you think Miranda will be pleased?' Frances said, spreading the drawings out on the table.

Walter bent over them. There was the schoolroom, the gable of the church, leaning a little, as if straining to a stiff wind, the curate's lodge. She had pencilled 'Plotz here' in small, faint writing. 'I have written a letter too.' She held it out. 'Read it, if you like.'

She had watched him unfold it. Clearly, despite her carefully composed expression, she was eager that he should see it. It began tentatively, describing the mission and her family. It became easier as the paragraphs grew. He turned the page. He read, 'Mr Plotz is quite well although I think you would find that his nose has grown. The dust seems to aggravate his hay fever. I have heard him sneeze fifteen times without stopping.'

Following all this girlish nonsense there was a sketch of himself and, despite the exaggerated nose, remarkably like. She ended the letter by saying, 'I know you miss him and I am sure that he will come back to England as soon as he has discovered the green lion and is quite satisfied that he may return.'

Walter looked over at Frances and smiled. 'This will make Miranda very happy.'

He gathered up the paintings and stacked them neatly by his books. 'Miranda thought me quite the handsomest of her uncles!' he said. 'After seeing your sketch I fear she might change her mind. Sit! It is time for your lesson. I have a meaty piece for you to translate from Livy.'

And so the apprehension and strangeness of those first days were put aside by Walter. The words that he had written in his journal on the first night at St Matthias had been forgotten and for six months he allowed himself to be lured into a contented complacence and routine. He should have marvelled at his own insanity at inventing Plotz against every rational instinct of self-preservation! Ah, Plotz – how many times he learned to bless or curse him for intruding! It was Plotz – and not himself – in whom Frances came to confide, to whom she fled in times of need, fugitive from loneliness and isolation. Plotz could be ugly, droll and foolish and still be liked because he was invented. Had he acquired this privilege because he demanded nothing in return and could be disregarded when his usefulness had ended? Walter felt like a puppeteer shadowing a little sawdust man to whom he had given life. Having made him, would Plotz turn on him at last and extract something as his due? Half his heart, perhaps?

Chapter Three

And in the game that Walter had invented, it was not only he and Frances who were players. Helmina Smythe hovered at the edges, aware that Walter Brownley and Frances seemed to have some joke between them from which she felt excluded. No amount of rationalisation could convince her otherwise, despite Walter Brownley's unaffected ease with everyone in the household, despite the small attentions that he paid her, despite their frequent walks and games of chess when he would challenge her with a quizzical, cajoling humour and make her laugh – oh, such a small, restrained little laugh, kept inside, fragile as a bubble.

Helmina Smythe knew that Walter Brownley was the final hope against the fading of her youth. And now, Frances had intruded in some indefinable way, despite all the prayers and supplications. In Frances, there was a spontaneity which had been extinguished in herself, long before it had ever learned to flame and which – Helmina knew – had found response in him.

At Frances's age, Helmina had nursed her widowed mother and kept her vigil at the sickbed through days and nights, constantly moving in and out of that twilight world. Her mother's chief delight had been to have Helmina sit at the window, peering through heavy lace curtains – for no window in her room might be opened – and describe to her the street outside and who walked by with whom. Helmina had often wanted to run down, burst from the house, fly to the gate and call in greeting to the passersby, 'Here I am! Helmina! Do you know me?' But she never stirred. Never stirred. Only waited.

Once a young man had smiled at her as she stood in the garden and another time the same young man had stopped at the gate and raised his hat and said, 'Good-day' while she had been emptying the slops and she had been so alarmed to be found there with the bucket in her hands that after greeting him – oh, barely civil – she had fled inside for fear of appearing improper or menial with her sleeves rolled up. She had wondered if he thought her a servant girl with whom he could banter, unaware of her standing in the house.

But despite these reservations, she, in her lighter moments, had often imagined conversations with him: 'Ah, Mr Fox, how good of you to call. Shall we walk about the orchard?' And the stand of scrofulous fig trees would be transformed, in an instant, into a grove drifting with pear blossom, bright as butterflies, and the old brown patches of grass which a neighbourhood dog visited so abundantly, would be starry with little flowers.

After that first approach she had hurried indoors and sat behind the dusty curtains in her mother's room for days, waiting for him to go by again. He did quite often, but he never saw her watching and she, afraid, had never shown herself again. After some time, it seemed, he chose another route.

When her mother died, her uncle and his family had moved into the house. She was asked to stay, but she felt unwelcome with so few rooms and so many mouths to feed and when her uncle had told her that a Reverend Farborough wanted a governess for his children, she knew she must go. Her removal to the mission was accomplished before she had adjusted to the idea of leaving the house in which she had lived for nineteen years.

She had shared the Farboroughs' home since then. For eleven years her salary had been paid discreetly in a way that made her feel not a dependant, but as if she were an elder daughter receiving an allowance. And yet, despite this, the sense of belonging evaded her. Once Frances and Crispin were grown, would she have a role or would she be sent away? It was something that was never mentioned, but as Frances and Crispin grew she felt the time approaching when Father Charles might say, 'Helmina, my dear, what are your plans?'

But Providence had intervened. Providence had sent Walter Brownley. A reward for her steadfastness and patience. And yet, Helmina feared – she had read enough romances to suspect the truth – Providence also championed the beautiful and passionate and young. Once, she had been young, but beauty was denied her. As for passion, Helmina would not put a name to it nor dare explain it to herself or of herself: but she knew that in every man there lurked something primal and urgent which could only be expunged by self-sacrifice and denial. She had read of it. She had seen it. It was there in young men like Victor – just behind the eyes: a questing, a certain restlessness which could not be concealed. Once she had seen Victor passing the washing line, pause and nonchalantly glance over her underwear hanging there. She had recoiled with shame and yet – deny it as she might – this unsolicited invasion held for her a curious triumph. Did she – even she – possess that slow-burning secret which sent men to fury or to hell, that had caused wars and duels and the downfall of the Righteous?

Whatever it was that urged Victor to do a thing like that, could not such impulses interest Walter Brownley too – more honourably, more acceptably? Could he not step in to arrest her youth at the moment of its setting?

And so she watched him and she was solicitous about his study, keeping the desk dusted and neat, renewing the water in the jug twice daily, opening the drawers discreetly to slip away a stray pencil or ruler. And there, one morning, she saw the pictures that Frances had drawn for Miranda and her eye fell on the painting of the curate's lodge with the words, 'Plotz here', written faintly beside the fifth door.

Frances was working in the sewing-room when Helmina Smythe came in. Helmina closed the door carefully behind her and she said, 'What is "Plotz"?'

'Plotz?' Frances drew back.

'Yes!' Helmina's tone was conspiratorial, faintly wheedling.

'I have no idea,' replied Frances coolly.

'"Plotz" was written on one of those drawings you did for Mr Brownley.'

'Did he show them to you?'

Helmina looked away, flustered. 'They are very nice paintings . . .' Frances saw the flush at Helmina's throat. 'It looked like your writing. I was just wondering . . .'

'I wrote nothing, Miss Smythe. I simply drew.' Frances held Helmina's eye.

'Do not be tedious, Frances,' said Helmina in irritation. 'I know you did and I was hoping you meant no disrespect to Mr Brownley by doing so . . .'

Frances did not retort as she might have done. She said, 'No, Miss Smythe,' and continued with her sewing.

Helmina went away and Frances pushed her sewing aside. She went to the living-room and opened the piano. She sat at it and she played her scales. Fast. Faster. Up and down. Up and down. Careless of mistakes. And when Walter Brownley came in in search of her father, she closed the lid with a snap and said, before she could stop herself, 'Why did you tell Miss Smythe about Plotz?'

He was taken aback. 'Whatever makes you think I would introduce Plotz to Miss Smythe?'

'She asked me who he was.'

Walter raised an eyebrow. 'Is that so?'

'And you showed her the pictures and you told her.'

'I did?'

There! That infuriatingly ironic tone of his! She was not fooled by it!

'My dear Miss Farborough,' he said, 'Plotz would be invisible to certain people no matter how hard they tried to believe in him. It would be futile to show himself. Besides, you should not talk about him so loudly, you would make him uncomfortable. Someone might hear.' And he cast her a conspiring glance as if the room was full of eavesdroppers, took his hat and went away.

It was soon after this that Walter acquired Boggis. Boggis the gelding. Reliable, droll, participant in the invented kingdom. Boggis and Plotz. One presupposed the other. He acquired him the day Victor and Crispin returned to St Matthias – Crispin on holiday from school, Victor sent for a stint in the divisional office in The Hoek for which he had volunteered for a month. Walter, anticipating the need for a discreet retreat from the family circle, taking a protesting Plotz with him, was relieved at the prospect of having his own horse. He could escape the mission and spend the month travelling daily to the outstations which fell under the mission's control.

The need for another horse had become urgent. He could not travel to the outstations without one and with two men constantly in the saddle, visiting the far-flung chapels and schools, the mission horses were overworked and frequently went lame. He and Father Charles had been riding out on alternate days, one remaining at the station to attend to affairs, the other taking a saddle-bag packed to hold a dawn service, medicines for the sick, equipment for teachers and a box of sandwiches and a bottle of cold tea.

In England, Walter had had a bicycle for parish visiting and had never had to travel more than five miles. Now, between them, he and Father Charles covered three hundred square miles every month over countryside uncharted but for one rough wagon road that ran from Debe Nek to Stutterheim.

The purchase of a horse would take a large portion of his annual stipend and buying extra fodder would erode it more, but they could not work without another mount and Father Charles suggested he accompany the family to King William's Town and attend the monthly stockfair when they went to meet Crispin and Victor's train from Grahamstown.

Emily, anxious to buy supplies for the girls of the St Agnes Guild, had promised to take Helmina Smythe to assist her, and Frances was festive in her anticipation of the home-coming. She had not been to Town in six months and on the morning of their departure Walter saw her picking sprays of banksia roses and tying them onto the trap's hood and climbing up and down arranging travelling rugs and a parcel of food for the journey, singing to herself. Kobus harnessed the horses and Walter led Hector from the stable. Victor would ride him back and Walter, once he had bought a horse, would return to the mission on his own.

'You're very jolly this morning, Mrs B,' he said as he tethered Hector to the hitching-post outside the front porch.

'And you look very grand in your travelling coat, Mr Plotz. Are you going courting?' returned Frances.

'I am sure the young ladies of King William's Town are gathered in their ardent dozens to welcome me,' he said drily.

'Well then, you must have a buttonhole,' and she reached

53

up and stuck a rosebud in his lapel and then clambered into the trap and settled herself with the air of a maiden aunt. 'I shall have to keep my eye on you, I am sure.'

The sun was already high by the time the family were ready to leave and the last instructions had been given. Kobus had been spoken to and Mzantsi had gone over his notes for the confirmation class with Father Charles.

Nowasha stood in the garden laying the laundry out on the bushes, her small grandchild in a pinafore hovering at her side. They waved hands in farewell as the trap drove off along the track past the church and the catechist's cottage. The carpenter looked out of the wagon shop and called, 'Take care at the drift, the water's up,' and Tom and Reuben and Sonwabo, sitting outside drinking their sour porridge, stood to attention and saluted as they turned west along the road. Then Tom threw his hat in the air and caught it and flourished it and Frances called '*Sobonana*' gaily and Emily turned and admonished her but she subsided into the seat, unconcerned. She turned and surreptitiously waved at the apprentices again and dangled her hat over the side of the trap by the ribbons so that it dipped and rose like a kite.

Walter rode ahead to open the gate and Father Charles urged the horses on. Beside Frances, Helmina Smythe sat straight and expectant as if the end of the journey was in sight. 'I haven't been to Town in over a year,' she said breathlessly.

The wind was brisk and it blew from behind. They made good progress and within an hour or two the horses were taking the long hill towards Rabula where the road wound up above the river. The shadow of the trap's wheels slid across the bushes at the side of the track. Doves resting in the warm dust were set to flight. Walter watched them veer away with a wickering of wings. The folds of the hills were deep with bush and forest trees. Euphorbias grew in serried ranks on the drier slopes and here and there *msenges* shook their grey-blue plumes.

They passed ochre-blanketed herders and young girls carrying firewood who called, '*Mfundisi, Mfundisi!*' They paused to greet the catechist from Gwili Gwili, riding on his horse towards the village. A gracious old man in an alpaca jacket, he took his hat from his head and held it in one hand against his chest, bowing to Emily, bowing to Father Charles.

All day they travelled and the wind, which had subsided at midday, came up again, flurrying the dust and sending a spiral pirouetting out behind the wheels of the trap. Father Charles took out his pipe and lit it. Frances slept, her head resting against a strut of the canopy. Emily remained alert, speaking now and then to Father Charles when she suspected the pipe might drop from his mouth as he dozed. Walter kept a steady pace, watching the country dropping down towards the plains and Hector, wearying, pulled less at the bridle, balked less often at movements in the grass, and as the sun retreated a deep blue dusk filled the bowl of the valley. The highest ridges, a spur of krantz, a hilltop in the distance, caught the last shafts of light. The first star emerged in a pale sky.

The trap clattered down towards the ford in a river. Small drifts of mist wisped the water's surface. It was unusually full for June for the rains had been late, and Father Charles drew the horses to a halt and waited for Walter to come up beside him. 'It's rather high,' he said and indicated a pole planted at the edge.

'I'll ride in and see,' said Walter, coaxing the reluctant Hector into the cold stream.

He went carefully, picking his way. The flow was strong but not too deep. 'We'll do well enough,' called Walter, beckoning with his arm.

Crossing just ahead and to the side, Walter rode beside the pair as Father Charles guided them into the water. The sound of turning wheels on the flat stones of the ford was muffled by the surge of the water. Frances leaned out to watch the river curling brown and swift beneath the floor.

Halfway across the trap stuck, its wheel caught against a rock. The horses strained forward but Father Charles reined them in. 'Whoa, Barton! Whoa, Sultan! Brownley,' he called to Walter, above the sound of the water, 'if we could lighten up, we may be able to loosen it.' He turned to Emily. 'My dear, you shall stay with me, but I think that if Mr Brownley could take Helmina and Frances to the other side we shall relieve some of the weight. Bring your horse up close. Step across Helmina, my dear. Put your foot on his boot – here, take her arm, will you? Steady now.'

The trap swayed as the horses strained forward and Helmina placed her foot gingerly on the toe of Walter Brownley's boot. Taking his hand, held out firmly, braced against a fall, she crossed between the side of the vehicle and the pommel of his saddle.

Walter felt Helmina's foot on his. He felt the tentative pressure of her hand as she gripped his fingers. For one precarious moment he thought that she might fall but he encircled her waist with his arm, easing her down into the saddle. She sat in the small space between him and the pommel, drawing herself up, containing her body as if she did not wish it to intrude on his and offend him. He leaned away from the awkwardness of her hat brim probing at his with the movements of the horse. And when they reached the other side and he dismounted, Helmina thrust her fingers under the pommel, gripping it, seemingly afraid that Hector might shy.

Walter returned to the trap. As Frances prepared to spring up behind him, a group of young men, herding cattle, appeared over the crest of the hill. Two or three started towards the river to free the wheel but Frances, determined to lose nothing of the adventure, would not resume her seat. The trap dipped and bounced as she stretched towards the horse and Emily said sharply, 'If you must ride, go in front, Frances. Young ladies do not sit astride horses!'

Frances pulled a face but she obeyed, placing her foot lightly on Walter's boot. She reached for his hand and sprang, wriggling back against him. Hector, shaking his head, made his way towards the bank where the herders were discarding their blankets and sticks.

'Look at the buttermilk star,' said Frances, pointing up above the ridge of hills.

'Why is it buttermilk?' asked Walter.

'Because it is really a gourd of buttermilk, not a star at all,' she explained, her head tilted so she could see his face. 'It is a lamp which is lit when the dark comes and then in the morning the wind blows it out when the sun rises. That's what Nowasha used to tell me.'

He looked at the sky, at its translucent, brief green before the twilight faded and then he looked down at Frances watching the star, unconscious of his gaze.

A buttermilk star! Small, warming lanterns strung across the dark. Frances leaned unselfconsciously against him, while his hands held the reins just above her lap. He could sense, rather than feel, the bony curve of her back. Her hair, as she turned her head aside to watch the water, brushed his neck. Hector stumbled slightly and she caught the pommel to steady herself and jostled in his arms. They reached the other bank and Walter sat, just an instant, and looked at the buttermilk star before he dismounted and lifted her down. She placed her hands on his shoulders and laughed as he swung her.

He watched her as she bent to smooth her frock and to retrieve her shawl which had fallen to the ground. Quite still he stood. Quite still before her. Then he turned from her and busied himself with Hector's saddle blanket, not looking at her. 'No,' he said – the word half-spoken. 'No!' And he tugged at the bridle quite sharply and Hector jerked his head in surprise.

The herders were splashing through the shallows towards the trap, laughing and shouting to each other at the coldness of the water. They reached it and tried to push it clear, straining together. A voice sang out a word. Another. It was caught up into a phrase. The phrase gathered to a chant as they lifted the wheel free and the horses pulled away, eager to reach the side.

As the trap crept towards the bank, Emily Farborough leaned over to her husband and said quietly, her hand on his sleeve, 'Charles, I have this idea that Walter Brownley might court Helmina.'

Father Charles placed his fingers over hers and said, 'You're a romantic after all, my dear. Whoever would have thought it?'

'It would be very appropriate,' she returned briskly, as though he had contradicted her. Father Charles smiled down at her and squeezed her hand but he said nothing: he had seen Walter Brownley's face as he had lifted Frances from the horse. He had seen it as he'd turned away.

57

That evening they stayed with the Rector of St Mildred's, Thomas Blacklock. He was an old friend of the Farboroughs and had half a dozen married daughters and quantities of grandchildren running about the house. His conversation was distracted, he left sentences hovering in the air, as though he anticipated interruption. His pleasure at seeing Father Charles and Walter was marked. He all but hustled them into his study for a pipe while the ladies unpacked. 'Well, old man . . .' he said at intervals, absently patting Father Charles's sleeve.

Walter had been looking forward to meeting Thomas Blacklock, to inspecting someone else's library of books and journals, to seeing vehicles passing down a street and rows of houses and shops, goods displayed in their windows, no matter how small or provincial they might seem. He had anticipated talking to a colleague of matters beyond the interests of St Matthias. But he sat in Blacklock's study, silent and preoccupied, taking little notice of his surroundings. He hardly spoke, despite the enthusiastic welcome. All that evening, he watched Frances, unconscious of his absorption.

When the tea-tray was drawn up in front of the fire, Walter sat in his large chair, almost submerged, oblivious of the conversation going back and forth around him. He did not even hear Mrs Blacklock say to Emily Farborough, not a yard from him, 'Your Mr Brownley is a rather solemn man,' or Emily's rejoinder, 'He is a talented musician,' as if that were reason enough for a lugubrious nature.

'Half a sugar and a touch of milk, am I right, Mr Brownley?' said Helmina, standing before him with a cup of tea. Almost startled by her voice, he stood abruptly and took it from her. He turned from her and, despite himself, his eyes went restlessly to Frances.

She was bent over a book with one of the Blacklocks' daughters, admiring it as it lay open on a table, lit only by a tall candle. Light edged her dark profile, the wing of hair that had slid across her cheek. Walter looked away and caught, momentarily, the sight of Helmina's pale face turned to his. He drank his tea and then went to place his cup on the table near which she stood alone. He did not meet her eye nor brazen out a conversation to hide his discomposure. It would

58

have been deceitful and he had no wish for that. He fought, with some alarm, the sudden, small tumult that assailed him for the second time that day. Despite himself, despite his dry self-abrogation, he could not deny the uninvited, unexpected sting in his arms, his throat, as he had guided Frances down into his saddle or now, as he glanced across at her, inclined to the light of the candle's flame as she read. Such feelings were not only inappropriate, they were inconceivable. He would have to deny them. Extinguish them. Laugh at them. Scorn them to death.

He linked his hands behind his back and looked at his boots, trying to follow the conversation of Emily and Father Charles and their hosts, but he was aware only of Frances who sat – oblivious of him – across the room. He forgot Helmina Smythe standing a pace away, the corner of the table interposed between them, his teacup empty on the cloth beside which her hand – taut and brittle as a small bird's claw – grasped its edge.

And that night, when he was shown by Mrs Blacklock to his spartan back room in the rectory and had closed the door, he took his writing materials from his bag and he wrote a letter to his sister Daisy. He began with general news of the mission, a description of the Blacklock family, an account of the dusty town. And then he said, his pen chasing across the pages, 'A madness has overwhelmed Plotz! Plotz is the unhappy victim of a strange and (though he doesn't realise it), most inconvenient sorcery. Picture, my dear, the previously practical Plotz, as a youthful and ardent lover! He has quite forgotten the shape of his nose. He has ignored his raisin eyes. He is unaware of his large ears. He has overlooked the prodigious size of his extremities. In short, he is delighted with the notion of his own attractions! No Bottom in an ass's head could be more deluded! There are more dangerous things in green-lion country than the beast itself, but Plotz – braggadocio in person – has decided that *he* is the lion. The best we can do is humour the poor fellow, and leave him to his fate!'

Walter put down his pen in irritation and looked up at the ceiling. How the gelatinous geckos ran – little clockwork parts visible against the light of a pane, eyes lustrous with the chase for moths. Once, he had closed one between the window and the frame. He had seen the small foot protruding, the supplicating fingers. He had unlatched the hasp, appalled, and taken the little body in his hand. The delicate white throat had pulsed in death as it had in the quick expectation of life. Blood had squeezed from the minute threads of veins. He'd felt a regret, quite disproportionate to the act.

Walter walked about the room, sending the geckos scuttling behind the curtains and the dresser. Discontent seemed burrowed in his limbs, like the strange friction of unfamiliar cloth. He moved the books which he had borrowed from Thomas Blacklock's library from left to right, from right to left, adjusted the chair, pulled back the cover of the bed to expose the starched, rust-spotted whiteness of the sheets.

He lay on the bed, his hands behind his head and tried to think of Daisy's drawing-room, the warm, worn chintz of the chairs, the placing of the china upon her dresser, to recall it, to keep alive his place in it all, ensuring somehow that he'd have a right to it when he returned.

But he could not find the images. He lay alert to the sound of the curtain moving in the slight breeze which came through the window, the small lift and rustle of the pages on which he had been writing. He swung his legs over the side of the bed and sat with his elbows on his knees, his hands hanging loose, fighting off inadmissible thoughts that usually lay submerged, surfacing sometimes when he slept to wake him with some after-taste of loneliness and shame. And now, here, they arose, unwanted, precipitating a headlong need – the desire to cry unrestrained at some long-gone grief, to be sunk entirely in the warmth of some other being: to hold, to touch, to be held within a complete and affirming embrace. To love.

Walter stood and fetched his pipe and went to the window. He lit it and fingered his clergyman's collar – some futile insurance against temptation. He sat at the table and drew one of the books towards him but he laid it aside soon enough. What could Brightman's Liturgies tell him with the night pressing up against the window-panes, with a little wind lisping at the door, with the sky scattered wide with a pale gold frosting of buttermilk stars?

Victor and Crispin arrived early the next morning. From the dining-room where the household was gathered round the breakfast table, Walter heard the tap at the front door, knowing by its tone, its brisk assurance, who it was that knocked. A servant went to attend to the guests and he heard the quick step in the hall and, from the porch, Crispin's laugh and the clatter as he dragged a trunk across the threshold. Walter did not turn his head to look at Frances as Victor appeared in the doorway, filling it. Broad. Immensely tall. Victor in his travelling coat and boots. Victor astride the world: confident of their pleasure at seeing him. Victor's eyes, scanning the room briefly, before he went to greet his hosts, sought Frances. And Victor smiled.

The Blacklocks and the Farboroughs were too preoccupied with the arrival of Victor and Crispin to say more than a brief goodbye to Walter before he went in search of a horse and to Dyer's General Dealers, armed with a list from Father Charles. Only Helmina followed him to the hall and said, 'I hope you will find a good horse, Mr Brownley.'

'Thank you, Miss Smythe,' he said. 'Enjoy your shopping and a safe trip back to St Matthias. I shall see you on Friday.' And he raised his hat and went away and stood on the porch a moment and heard a shout of laughter from Victor as Crispin told – in jest – of some incident on the train. And there was Frances! Ah, that small, gruff, boyish laugh! They were closed in there, in some exclusive, family communion from which the rest had been excluded. He stepped into the street and walked away.

Walter returned to St Matthias at the end of the week with a brown gelding. The horse was half-lame by the time it reached the mission gate and he led it the last mile, the reins slack across his arm. He looked down at the little settlement below: at the grey church and the white-walled mission house, the sheer slant of the roof of the curate's lodge, the garden and the ploughed land. He saw Father Charles coming out of the church in his cassock and he saw Frances at his side. Friday at four: he had been taking confirmation class. Walter went down towards them, covered in dust and trudging before his horse.

'Ho, Brownley!' called Father Charles. 'What a thorough-bred you have there!'

'Best I could do,' said Walter, wiping his forehead with his sleeve and raising his hat in greeting. 'It must be the slowest in the Colony. And the worst schooled.'

Father Charles laughed and inspected the gelding's feet. It contemplated him balefully, refusing to lift a hoof. 'I doubt he'll carry you beyond the nearest garden,' he said. 'Where on earth did you get him?'

'There's not a horse to be had,' said Walter, appraising his acquisition ruefully. 'Still, he has a look in his eye that appeals to me.'

'How was the ride?' asked Father Charles.

'Rather slower than the outward trip!' Walter laughed. 'At least Hector won't feel he has a competitor!' Walter glanced at Frances but she was rubbing the horse's nose and talking softly to it. 'I have the newspapers in the saddle-bag and the post. A great heap of it. Everything will be along with Klaus Otto tomorrow. The rose plants Mrs Farborough bought on Tuesday were waiting with the other supplies. I hope they'll survive the journey. I asked Dyer to douse them well. The price of paraffin is up. Any excuse to wring the last penny out of us. Dyer says the shortages are going to be worse and we should think of bringing in our own wagon for a full consign-ment of meal next month.'

Frances said, 'Are you sure it's a horse and not a mule, Mr Brownley?'

'At the price, it should be the source of bloodstock for the Colony!' He led it to the trough.

'Come down to the house for tea, Brownley,' said Father Charles. 'You must be parched yourself. I'm glad to see you back, I must say. If I'd known what sort of beast you'd pur-chased, I shouldn't have been too confident of your return!'

He went off down the avenue, the Punch, the Church Quarterly Review and a package of letters tucked under his arm. Walter took his pipe from his pocket and turned to Frances. She sat on the edge of the trough, dragging her fingers in the water.

'What will you call him?' she said.

'Boggis.'

'Boggis?'

'Yes. Boggis.' Walter contemplated the horse as it drank, blowing and sucking in turns. 'He's a rather unfortunate-looking beast. Just like his namesake.'

'Who was Boggis? Is he another of your inventions like Plotz and Mrs Brodowski?'

'Mr Archibald Boggis was my tutor at Canterbury,' said Walter. 'He had just such a look as his namesake. If he hadn't been a priest I'd have suspected him of being a rogue. But in the end, I was rather fond of him. I think Boggis and I shall do very well together. After all, the rides to the outstations are rather tedious and I have no one to talk to.'

And so Boggis was taken to the stables and billeted with Hector, and inspected with some disparagement by Victor and Crispin. And Boggis went out on alternate days with Walter, in heat and rain and wind, when he rode to Gwili Gwili or Sidenge or Rabula. And Boggis, in his awkward, shuffle-footed way, became the repository of all confidences. He knew the doings of each day, especially those of Friday afternoons and Saturdays when Victor returned from the Native Affairs Department's offices in The Hoek and he and Crispin and Frances were off to the river with their fishing rods, or up on the hillsides, or picnicking with Emily and Miss Smythe by the Ndwandwe stream, or practising for the Choral Union Glee Evening with those left at school for the holidays, or playing tennis on the rough court or croquet on the dry brown lawn beneath the bare oak trees. Walter pointed them out to Boggis when he caught sight of them down by the river or on the path along its bank, or reading or playing bagatelle on the veranda.

Ah, Boggis knew. He knew about the day Walter had walked down to the river in search of him: it was the only time Walter had been angry with Boggis and ready to give him a good kick for straying, for in searching for him, he had blundered into the open above the fishing spot and there, below him, on the sandbank, were Victor and Frances, alone in the shade of an overhanging tree. He'd felt naked, exposed, standing there above the stream in his cleric's collar and his jacket, red-faced from the heat, and they, turning to look up at him, startled and defensive. He had blundered in, intruding in the intimacy of words, the closeness of their shoulders, almost touching, almost brushing together as they sat, the fishing pole idle on the bank. They had moved apart imperceptibly and stared back, silent, and he had raised his hat. How fatuous the gesture! How trite! How his greeting stuck in his throat and how foolish his voice had sounded in his ears when he had said, 'Seen Boggis?'

Seen Boggis, indeed! They would not have seen a cavalcade of thoroughbreds had it passed by. Victor had shaken his head and stood and stretched and picked up his fishing rod and waded off down the stream without glancing at Frances. He had said, over his shoulder, 'I'll chase him up if I find him.'

Frances had remained mute, her eyes on the water as Walter had turned away and walked hastily back along the path. He had stopped, his breath unruly in his chest.

There they had been, sitting on the sandbank – she with her bare toes in the water. Ah, he knew those feet, for he had seen her once run bootless. Humour they had, and spunk, if character can be told from feet: high-arched and broad and the toes short and even, like a child's. She had sat with her arms linked about her skirted knees, Victor lounging beside her with his hair wet from bathing. It had clung to his head, short, darkened by the water. His skin was brown. The fine contour of his face caught light at the cheekbones and brows. He had been speaking, the crook of his elbow resting on his knee and his forearm bare, gesturing with his hand and she laughing. A small laugh, untutored by other girls to coyness or affectation.

How Boggis had looked at him when he'd come up towards the garden and found him, standing under a tree, head mulish, tail twitching at flies and muttered, 'Get on with you, you absurd donkey', and chased him unceremoniously into the pasture and closed the gate with a clang and walked off without a glance. If he had not felt so absurd himself he might have laughed at the affronted cast of Boggis's eye, the droop of his lip!

But Boggis did not hold grudges, and uncomplainingly – without going lame all week – he'd carried Walter from outstation to outstation beyond the usual round of duty on Walter's insistence. They often left before sunrise when there was frost on the grass and ice in the water trough. Walter held early service before the people went to their fields or took their cattle out to graze. Mounted on Boggis, he would ride quietly past the sleeping house, its curtains drawn and only the light in Father Charles's study showing that he was already at his work. Boggis would even shamble on, finding his own path, his gait erratic, while Walter practised sermons, tested his embryonic Xhosa, or sang. He would continue walking, head down, when Walter abandoned the reins and brought out his pipe and filled and lit it without attending to where he was going.

It was Boggis, in his unchanging, lazy, clod-footed way, who kept at bay the fear of empty places, of forest paths or deserted hillsides or bushed ravines where even the birds were silent. There was something so predictable, so sure in Boggis's progress from mission to outstation and back, that Walter felt a strange security with him. Boggis did not shy at rustlings in the grass, he was disdainful of all passersby, he held cattle and goats in contempt. Nothing seemed to intrude in his own ruminations. The five, six, even seven hours Walter spent in the saddle, were hours spent with Boggis.

And Boggis had been there – dependable Boggis – when Walter had come upon Helmina Smythe standing by the quince hedge and, startled by their appearance, had exclaimed in astonishment, touched with triumph, 'Victor is impudence itself!' her hand fluttering to her mouth. 'He has just kissed Frances under my very nose and no scruples.' Boggis had rescued Walter from framing a rejoinder by lifting his tail and relieving himself, suddenly and noisily. Helmina Smythe had fled.

Boggis became Walter's daily companion, the confidant that could snort – oh, almost on cue – at signs of preoccupation with Victor and Frances. He became, too, the sharer of Walter's greatest triumph when he pulled the cart all the way from Mbokothwe, dragging the old diocesan printing-press that Walter had been given permission to resurrect by the

Bishop. On that occasion Boggis had been as spirited as Walter. He had all but trotted the last mile to the mission as if anticipating a hero's welcome!

Small were their preoccupations, small their secrets at that time. Looking back, Walter had wondered at himself. He had thrown himself into the publication of tracts and texts with a redirected passion. Every minute not spent attending to his duties was engaged in the printing-room with the Albion, inadequate though it was, the door closed against intrusion. He had hoped unashamedly for rain on the days he was supposed to visit the outstations so that he could clean up the type and tinker with the machine, closeted from the sight of Victor and Frances. He avoided meals, asking Nowasha to prepare a plate of sandwiches instead. Sometimes he worked into the early hours of the morning.

But, in the end, what did the printing-press and the Choral Union and the excursions on a horse, armed with prayer-book, cross and chalice in some dry and isolated valley, matter? What game, Walter wondered, had God been plotting while they were toiling with their small affairs? Which God – as great, indifferent Imperialist-in-the-Sky – had taken the tribesmen's lands, extracted the poll tax and sent them – oh, they passed daily up the road – to entrain for the goldfields? While they fretted at the mission with the Rules for the Boarding-School and Miss Prudieaux-Brune's letters of request for a picture of Benedict for her to display at the Ladies' Institute Mission Morning, and the fitness of the fifteen current candidates to be confirmed, He dealt each card, with deliberate precision.

But Walter did not know it then. Instead he harnessed Boggis in the Cape cart, enlisted Helmina's help in preparing a meal for the journey and set off for the mission at Mbokothwe with a letter authorising him to remove the printing-press from a shed. The missionary in charge was the Reverend Hubert Brompton. Walter had not met him. He had never been to Mbokothwe. He left St Matthias one Monday morning. No one saw him off. He went before anyone was awake.

He would not think of Frances. He would not think of Victor. He turned the cart eastwards. He did not look back.

Chapter Four

Walter left St Matthias for Mbokothwe with relief, glad to be gone, glad to be working, impatient with the carnival atmosphere in the Farborough house since Victor and Crispin had come home. At weekends, his duties were punctuated by the explosion of guns as the two of them hunted in the surrounding hills. There were always game birds, thonged by the feet, hanging on the back veranda, heads lolling obscenely.

Frances was a stranger to him and he had not eaten at the Farboroughs' table for over a week. Only Helmina haunted the vestry and the yard or came to the room he was preparing for the press, to ask if he needed help. His exile was decreed as surely as if he'd been forcibly confined to the curate's lodge. He was glad to go. Glad to leave them. And if Boggis overturned him in a river, so be it.

He had driven the dusty miles alone, camping the first night at a stream, the next in open plain beyond the town of Stutterheim, and passed into new country, taking roads and tracks he had never seen before. As the afternoon of the third day wore on, the light had lain long upon the hills and he had begun to sing, chorusing every glee and hymn and ditty he could think of. When he had exhausted his extensive repertoire and the mission station was in sight at the top of a long, winding track, he had ended by singing 'God Save the Queen' and Boggis had pricked his ears, aware somehow that he was soon to be released from the harness.

The church and the missionary's house stood darkly in silhouette at the crest of the slope. Beyond, the sky lifted in a great blue and pewter-coloured arc of clouds above a pale horizon. A bell on a pole stood at an angle and the privy leaned in towards it, a little windy edifice, the earth around quite bare and leached. St Matthias was a hub of development, society and industry in comparison with this.

The mission grounds were uncultivated. No other habitation was in sight. No homestead, no cattle, just the hillside and the wind and the spare, high calls of grass birds.

As they drew into the yard, Boggis snorted and shook himself. Walter pulled up the collar of his coat and climbed down. He thrust his hands in his pockets, for as the sun dipped below the hills, the cold seemed to seep up from the ground through his boots. Wind fretted in the thatch of the church. There was no one to greet him.

He began to unharness Boggis when a movement caught his eye. Someone was watching him furtively from the lee of a thorn-fenced cattle kraal. 'Good afternoon,' Walter called, aware of the apprehension in his voice. An old Xhosa shambled out. He was dressed in castoffs from a mission-box, in a jacket so ancient in design, with a high-standing collar and tails, it must have been all of fifty years old. His hair was knotted in dusty nodules, his skin was so dark it seemed that within its hollows it was shaded with blue. He wore a luxuriant moustache, upswept and greying and waxed at its ends.

Walter greeted him and he grunted in reply, shuffling forward, scrutinising him with a wayward eye. When Walter enquired about the Reverend Brompton's whereabouts, he pointed down towards the small square cottage that abutted the church without taking his eye from Walter's face. He took Boggis's reins and Walter, raising his hat in acknowledgement, walked down towards the mission house. The wind sent up spirals of dust. Gravel pattered at the walls.

Walter knocked at the door. It was opened abruptly as though the occupant of the room had been watching through a keyhole, or standing ear to the wall, to hear the sound of his approach. Hubert Brompton stood before him in his black clergyman's suit, his collar blue-white and stiff against the yellow pallor of his skin.

'Brownley? How do you do?' There was no indication of surprise: Walter might have been a regular caller at his door. 'The Dean sent a letter,' was all he said.

The Reverend Hubert Brompton was young, more slightly built, though taller than Walter. His voice was silvery, edging along the tenor. He wore pince-nez. Trailing a thin gold chain, they were attached to the bridge of his nose, an adjunct to its narrow refinement. They caught the light as he moved his head and shuttered out his pale stare. And yet the stare was there, behind the small, blind deception of those lenses. 'Come in,' he said and stepped aside.

Walter entered a room lit by one small window. Off it led a narrow white apartment, chaste as a nun's cell, in which stood a bed. The living-room was furnished with a table, a pair of chairs and a shelf of books. On the walls, black-framed, were etchings of Hubert Brompton's College at Oxford, his school, a country church in England and among them, the rest clustered about it, a mezzotint of the Queen. On the table was an ornate oil lamp and a fringed burgundy-coloured cloth. Beside it, a prayer-stool with a tapestry top in rose and grey and pearl. On the bookshelf stood a stuffed lark, surrounded by stiff paste leaves, confined under a glass dome. A large mahogany musical-box, inlaid with rosewood and ivory, was displayed beside it. It was a shrine, here on this windy, isolated hill, full of icons of another age.

The door opened and the servant came in, his ancient jacket pulled straight, a dirty white stock at his throat. He wore knee breeches but his feet were bare. Such wild feet, dusty and broad, and he thrust the tray that he carried on the table, set with a cloth and fine bone china cups and a pewter teapot. The Reverend Brompton said, ceremoniously, 'Thank you, Pusey. You will attend to Mr Brownley's horses, will you? That will be all until dinner time.'

The servant made a small bow and retreated, casting again a curious look at Walter sitting in his coat with his hat on his knee. The Reverend Brompton turned to the table and the tray and poured the tea.

The liquid was pale, so often were the leaves wrung out and reused, and the milk was sour with the taste of milkweed from the pasture in the valley. Hubert Brompton sipped from his cup with a detached air. He did not speak until he'd laid his cup aside and then he regarded Walter and said, 'Are you an Oxford or a St Augustine's man, Brownley?'

Walter wished he could have escaped that room and the Reverend Brompton watching him, eyes as still as a basilisk's, and before he could answer the question he'd been asked, Hubert Brompton said abruptly, 'The printing-press is in the shed. I wonder if it will ever work again. I have retrieved a boxful of type from oblivion. I was told that when it was moved some years ago the cart overturned in a stream and the print was muddled. I fancy it will still need some cleaning if you are determined to resurrect it. Of course,' he looked across at Walter, 'you know that Reverend Albert who was here before me, lost his mind in the end?' He was silent a moment, contemplating Walter. 'He used to print hymns in Kaffir. He was compiling a hymnal when he died. Pusey says he was bewitched.' The Reverend Brompton's voice was high and light and quavering. 'If one lets the standards drop, one becomes prey to such things.' There he sat, in his upright chair with the little shrine of lamp and prayer-stool and table behind him and the Queen – ah, so solemn, despite the garland of roses wound about her name – to shield him from contagion. 'Pusey will not go near the printing-press. Really, he is too trying sometimes. You will have to commandeer half a dozen red boys and ask them to put it in the cart.' He was silent a minute and then he said, 'This is a place full of spirits. So wrote my predecessor. It had been recommended that Reverend Albert be relieved of the post long before he died. But no one listened.' He stood, his hands linked behind his back, and went to the pictures on the wall and contemplated them. 'What did you say, Brownley? Are you an Oxford or a St Augustine's man?'

'St Augustine's,' said Walter.

'Ah, I might have guessed,' said the Reverend Brompton, a touch of condescension in his voice.

Night came and Hubert Brompton closed the shutter at the window and lit the lamp. Walter took a candle and, shielding it with his hand, he went to the privy across the yard. The flame was blown out in a gust. He fumbled his way to the door and closed it behind him. He lit the stub of candle and set it on the small shelf beside the seat and leaned against the wall. He could feel the whole small building shaking, its odd, sudden moaning as the wind lifted under the roof. The shadows of spiderwebs fluttered up against the corners.

He was weary from the long journey, a deep tiredness in bones and heart. What was he doing in this remote, desolate place, escaping to a privy to keep his thoughts about him?

70

The mission seemed all but derelict – no mention had been made of evensong, no worshippers had presented themselves at sunset. The bell whimpered every now and then as a gust shook it. Walter bolted the door – a cotton-reel on a string, wound about a nail – and sat on the lavatory seat, his elbows on his knees, and listened to that wind. Voices, cries, laments. He could have imagined any of them in that place.

The predestination he had sensed at St Matthias on his arrival was stronger here. Perhaps it was the night. The wind, the blackness of the hills against the sky. Or the strange wild face of Pusey – surely Brompton had chosen such a name in jest. *Pusey*, in a tail coat and breeches – here at Mbokothwe! Where was God, in this strange, small outstation at the edge of the world: a bell, a church, a house and a grave – that of Father Albert – unweeded in the lee of the hill? He and his Xhosa hymnal. He and his printing-press. Walter wondered if – like Father Albert – he might end in a grave on some abandoned slope? His only memorial a piece of machinery that squatted like a beast in the dusty shadows of a shed?

Walter waited, reluctant to leave, as if he'd found a subterranean shelter, burrowed here with a point of light, tunnelled deep where none might find him. God had always been so clear to Walter. In the hardest times, in indecision and in fear, there had always been God. Dependable, predictable. Decidedly English.

But here he felt alone. Abandoned. God could not live here. Despite Hubert Brompton and his picture of the Queen. Despite his charming teacups and his etchings and his little English lark, silenced in a bell-jar. God had turned His back on this insidious madness while Brompton drowned in it, unheeded. Perhaps Mbokothwe was the Bishop's penance for those who had erred or the mortification for those who wished to test a steely resolve. 'Please God, not Mbokothwe!' Walter said aloud. 'Not Mbokothwe, God.'

He paid his respects to the privy, lest he be forced there again in the night, and then left it, walking in the wind, its coldness sharp as a blade.

Pusey brought the dinner. It was served in silence, spooned from fine serving dishes with a silver ladle and fork, although it was nothing more than a piece of boiled sheep, wild spinach and steamed maize bread. There was no accompaniment of gravy or sauce. There was no wine. Another pot of tea was brewed when the plates had been cleared and a damp, chilly fire flickered in the grate.

Brompton rose and moved the chairs closer to the hearth. He said, 'You may smoke if you wish, Brownley,' and sat with his hands peaked together, forming a little arch before him. Walter took out his pipe and pouch and looked at Brompton while he filled it. His face was thin, hollow just above the contour of his jaw. Two lines – not deeply etched but the mark of battles fought too young – ran down beside the corners of his mouth. His straight black hair, close-cropped, grew upon his head like the beginnings of down. He appeared to breathe shallowly as if only a little breath, drawn swiftly, would suffice. And always, his eyes were either closed away by a trick of light reflecting on those small oval lenses, or magnified and large and black and still, watching him.

Walter cleared his throat and said, 'I have been through barren country today. It seems as if no crops were planted last season.'

'Nor were they,' said Brompton. 'There was a plague of locusts and everything was ruined. I have heard that the government is constructing a fence on the borders of the colony in an attempt to contain the cattle plague.'

'Surely that is an impossible task.'

'So it is. I have read that the herds have been decimated right through Africa. Locusts and rinderpest and drought all at once,' said Hubert Brompton. 'I have my theories on this, Brownley.' He pressed his fingers together in their slim arch and he cleared his throat and said, '"And this shall be the plague wherewith the Lord will smite all the people that have fought against Jerusalem; Their flesh shall consume away while they stand upon their feet, and their eyes shall consume away in their holes, and their tongue shall consume away in their mouths. And so shall be the plague of the horse, of the mule, of the camel and of the ass and of all the beasts . . ."' He broke off and the silence in the room was disturbed only by the shifting of the logs in the grate. He continued, '"And if the

72

family of Egypt go not up and come not, they shall have no rain; there shall be the plague wherewith the Lord will smite the heathen that come not up to keep the feast of the tabernacles. This shall be the punishment of Egypt and of all nations.' ' He turned and he looked at Walter. 'It is prophetic, is it not? It will not be an unmixed evil if this rinderpest comes. It will humble all. The Kaffirs here are too independent. They shun labour on the farms and will not go to the mines. They rarely come to this church and grow fat on their depravity. I have great hopes of Mr Rhodes and his Glen Grey proposals. Effectively, only the eldest will inherit now and the rest will be forced to find work. This life of sloth to which they are accustomed encourages the evil of their beliefs.'

Walter said, 'Good cattle husbandry and farming methods hardly constitute a life of sloth. And statutes such as those you mention, admire Mr Rhodes as you might, are clearly the first step towards dispossessing them altogether.'

'Ah, I might have expected such a reaction,' said Brompton, as if Walter's being a St Augustine's man instead of a graduate was the reason for his lapse in understanding. 'You have been here too short a time, Brownley. No doubt you are filled with idealism. The cruelty, barbarity and thanklessness of the old-time heathens brought about their fall as a nation. Look at the cattle killing . . .'

'I think we would serve them better if we understood their customs and respected their age-old rights,' said Walter. 'It is a great arrogance simply to impose ourselves on them.'

'Customs!' Brompton snorted. 'My dear fellow, you have clearly not witnessed the circumcision dances! The rites last days while they gorge themselves. I have sat up here on this hill and observed the whole procedure taking place below. You cannot begin to understand the depth of sensuality and grossness to which barbarian natives can sink, or grasp the extraordinary power the lust of the flesh has over the mind. Custom, you say! They are fraught with wickedness and vice. The people appear to believe that in the carrying out of these very customs they are performing the requirements of religious belief!'

Brompton would allow no interruption. He took a turn

73

about the room, pacing. 'But,' he regarded Walter, 'there is a worse peril, Brownley, and you at St Matthias had better be aware of it, for it is something far more insidious and dangerous than men in red blankets who are so easily identified with the work of Satan. You have heard of Dwane and his Episcopal Methodists? He has been to America where he has met with Negro preachers and other trouble-makers. No doubt it is ambition, power-seeking and a distaste for control that motivates him. These are the characteristics of the generality of natives, you will agree?'

Walter was given no opportunity to agree or disagree, for the Reverend Brompton paced about the room again and continued, 'Dwane went away to fraternise with his coloured brethren. He joined a Negro sect and was promptly made a bishop! The mischief of it all is that his movement has a distinct political side and his preachers do not hesitate to stir up race prejudice. A colleague of ours, misguided in his wish to unite all Christians, invited one of these preachers into his church. He might as well have opened the door to the Serpent of Eden! They are even ridiculing the idea of praying for the Queen! I have heard,' he stood then before the picture of the Monarch, drew his breath as if he struggled with some keen emotion, 'I have heard it said that these Episcopalians believe she is the enemy of the black man! Dwane and his cohorts are responsible for this.'

'It is interesting to hear you speak like this,' said Walter, knocking out his pipe on the hearth and sucking it noisily. 'I have a young assistant, Benedict Matiwane, with whom I wish to start a newspaper. He was very keen to ask the Reverend Dwane to make a contribution to it.'

'Fatal!' cried Brompton, turning on him. 'Fatal, Brownley! I cannot allow you to speak like this, unchallenged! It is our duty to ensure that a true standard of Christianity is set. One cannot put a lower idea before the heathen by way of making the path easier! I am appalled! Are you telling me that Canon Farborough would agree to such a thing?'

'He didn't seem to object.'

'There! Isn't it just as I said to the Dean! Leave people more than five years among the heathen and the heathen sloth overtakes their sensibilities.'

'Steady on, old man,' said Walter evenly. 'Father Charles is the sanest and the finest churchman I have encountered here or anywhere and the Methodists would have you before a court for speaking of Bishop Dwane like that!'

'Canon Farborough is a farmer!' retorted Brompton. 'He labours with his hands, not his head.' He raised his finger impatiently, 'Pray, do not interrupt. I am well aware of the success of your trade school. There have been objections from the tinsmiths of East London at the mission's prosperity – I am privileged to have been privy to the correspondence of the Dean. I am aware of the success of St Matthias's wagonworks and carpentry shop. I know you plan to publish books and papers in the vernacular. Very noble, my dear Brownley, but entirely misguided. English is the language of the church, not heathen grunting! St Matthias is a commercial success indeed. But it is not commerce in which the church should be engaged.'

'And there were over a thousand people at worship last Sunday,' said Walter quietly, 'and in excess of two hundred at evensong each day. The regard in which the people hold Father Charles is remarkable to witness.'

Brompton was silent. Walter saw him wipe away a drop of sweat at the edge of his hair. Another slid down the plane of his cheek. There was a pinched blueness at the corners of his mouth. He touched, a moment, the struts of bone at the outer edges of his eyes as if, in pressing them, he found relief. He stood, looking up at the pictures on his wall.

A large moth, bullet-bodied, droned against the glass funnel of the lamp, fell, grounded on the tablecloth. It clung there, furred and sticky with the strange exudings of some twilight sap. It flew up heavily, leaving a dark down trace on the glass, bent on some self-destruction of its own.

Brompton took up the small candlestick. He let himself out and Walter heard him walk away towards the privy. The door of the house banged in a gust and the moth danced cumbersome parabolas across the dark blue space beyond the reaches of the light.

When he returned, Hubert Brompton showed Walter to his room. It was a small hut detached from the house and below

75

the slope. It was inhabited by spiders and a coarse horsehair mattress and blanket were his only comforts. It was so cold inside, lit only by a small oil lamp, that Walter was obliged to spend much of the night pacing about. He was startled by the faint scutterings of insect wings and the dry, light patter of wary feet as a mouse or rat skirted the wall.

He went outside and looked up at the sky. It was black as a crow's wing and banked with cloud. He took his lamp, the flame turned low, and walked up the slope towards the kraal, to check on Boggis and the mare. They stood apart from the goats, backs to the wind. He went to them and eased his way between them, sheltered by their warm sides. 'There, old man,' he said to Boggis, patting his neck. Boggis turned his head and looked at him, sniffing with wide nostrils. 'What a God-forsaken place I've brought you to.' He lit his pipe and held the bowl in his frozen fingers and leaned his head against his horse. 'Not Mbokothwe, Boggis. That I promise you, now. That poor man is disintegrating, going mad. He'll never last another month. Anywhere, Boggis. Anywhere, but not Mbokothwe.' And as he stood there, he heard a sound. Small, jerky. The tune was faint but instantly familiar on the night air. The musical-box in Brompton's room was playing 'Abide with me, fast falls the eventide'. Over and over and over it played. Over and over.

Walter stood and listened. Sometimes there was silence as if the trinket had been taken up and rewound and then the hymn would begin again, smoother, faster. Three or four times the phrases would repeat and then the notes would lengthen and falter and silence would follow. And as he listened, Walter saw a shadow detach itself from the back wall of Brompton's house, where the shuttered window gleamed. It was Pusey. He stood, a blanket wound about him, head inclined. There was an alertness, an intentness in his stance, quite at odds with the dull, shambling clown that had waited on them at dinner. When, at last, the faint, stumbling notes had died, he turned and walked away, sure-footed and swift, and disappeared over the lip of the slope.

76

And while he had been gone, all through the long journey and the long night of waiting, Walter had kept St Matthias from his mind. Perhaps exile to a place like Mbokothwe would expunge Frances from his consciousness. The business of surviving in such isolation would consume all his energy, all his imagination. The night had been endless on his small, hard, vermin-infested bed.

In the morning Pusey appeared with a tray of tea and a basin of hot water. He had returned to the state of shuffling simpleton. By the time Walter had shaved, four young heathen men, dressed in ochred blankets and armed with hunting sticks, were brought to him by Pusey and together they had heaved the press onto the back of the wagon and loaded the boxes while Pusey harnessed the horses. Walter had paid his helpers and then gone in search of Brompton.

Brompton was in his church. He looked up restlessly as Walter came in. His face was drawn and yellow. Walter said, 'Come back to St Matthias with me. I'd be delighted for the company and I'm sure you could do with a break.'

'I could not possibly leave the mission,' said Hubert Brompton, distractedly. 'There is far too much to do. Too much. I cannot take time off without an assistant. Good heavens, what would the Dean say? And here the heathen are, preparing for initiation. It would be quite overtaken if I should leave. There would be bonfires in the church . . .' His voice trailed away. 'No, I shall write to the Dean when I have time.' He hovered impatiently, then he picked up his pith helmet which had been lying on a pew and ushered Walter out.

'I am sure the Dean would be sympathetic, Brompton. A week or two would do no harm.'

'Absolutely not!' said Brompton and a pulse beat in his throat. 'Absolutely not! There may be priests and catechists and nuns and lay preachers all about the place at St Matthias but I am alone and I will not desert my post! No, Brownley, one has to be made of sterner stuff at Mbokothwe.'

Walter inclined his head. 'Very well, Brompton,' he said. 'However, if you should change your mind, we shall be very glad to see you at St Matthias.' He shook Brompton's hand.

There was nothing more to say. The little church was desolate, the altar cloth, set for a celebration that had not taken place in days, was laden with dust, fine as pollen.

He had shaken the reins and guided the horses down the hill. As soon as he was back at St Matthias, he would write to the Dean himself. He would speak to Father Charles. Someone would have to be sent to relieve Hubert Brompton. He could not be left as he was. Walter turned Boggis and the mare along the track. He did not look back until he knew that the mission would be out of sight. But all that day, and the next, during the long drive home, he could not rid himself of the refrain that repeated itself over and over in his mind: 'Abide with me, fast falls the eventide, The darkness deepens, Lord with me abide, When other helpers fail, and comforts flee, Help of the helpless, O abide with me . . .' and he said a prayer of thanks that somewhere at his back, no matter how distant, was a thread of kinship and support, linking him to others, making such implacable aloneness impossible.

Chapter Five

Victor had devised a new and intriguing game. With some nuance of intent. Months before, Frances had laughed at him when he had suggested a nocturnal jaunt. She would have dared if she could have been sure that Walter Brownley had not overheard their conversation and if Victor had not spoiled it all by a display of unexpected temper when she had suggested that Crispin come too. Crispin had never been excluded before and Victor had no right to sulk because she had mentioned it. Now, since he had been posted to the divisional office in The Hoek for a month, he kept a certain distance from her, was less familiar but oddly intent. He came back to the house at dusk, took to smoking cigarettes in the garden after dinner, and often went off on Friday evenings to have a drink or play cards at the inn with his old school friend Charlie Fraser and another clerk, even leaving Crispin behind.

He was different and Frances, in her turn, watched him. The bantering had ceased. It had been replaced by a more studied wit. He listened to the things she said as if he were looking for something among her words, and the irritation that she had felt with him six months before was tempered with something else: her own restlessness. Victor wished to speak and for the first time, seemed unable to say it. She felt poised to hear it. Her ease with him had gone – just as if he kept a secret from her, excluding her from an old intimacy, with the promise of a greater one.

The greater one was claimed on the day Walter Brownley was due to return from Mbokothwe.

Hot winds blew that Saturday and the clouds of dust hung above the plains stretching out to Xhosaland. The thorns on the acacias were drying out, the longitudinal slits of their shards held by honed points. Frances, coming out onto the veranda after lunch on her way to the orchard to pick lemons for her mother, watched the sky a moment and then bent her head to the wind, closing her eyes against the driving dust. Sheltering in the lee of the quince hedge, she noticed a bright congregation of young men dressed in heathen red sauntering down the slope below the Nolovini ridge towards the river. They were followed by a concourse of girls. They disappeared into a culvert beside the river but their voices reached her clearly.

After a time the disparate sounds of a gathering took on a form. The voices developed a rhythm, from which, at lessening intervals, some phrase flew off, pitched differently. Above the sound of voices was the hollow clash of sticks. The thud of feet was matched – with thrust and parry – to the metre of the words.

Hurriedly, Frances took half a dozen lemons into the kitchen where her mother and Helmina were making cordial, and then escaped back to the garden. She slipped down the steps and through the orchard and climbed the fence at the bottom where an oak supported the strands of wire, and then ran off across the pasture, through the thorn bushes, towards the culvert. Watching any heathen activity was strictly forbidden and speaking Xhosa within hearing of her mother a punishable offence, but she knew the reason for the gathering, the meaning behind the singing and she could not miss it. An *umngeni* was in progress, an event which happened sometimes before boys went for initiation, a stick fight to display their prowess, an exciting and often dangerous event for which young men and girls dressed in all their heathen finery. It was a sight to see!

Frances turned briefly and scanned the house and then she hurried along the bank, keeping behind the bushes, not wanting to intrude upon the notice of the players. She climbed a tree with low, spreading branches, balancing against the trunk and watched the gathering below.

It was divided into two groups. Opponents faced each other, one to one, in traditional pose. Each carried a pair of sticks and around the left hand was wrapped a cloth to protect the knuckles. How the dust flew up from their stamping feet and how their shouts echoed on the slope! Among the mêlée of spectators, glimpsed sporadically in the crowd, was Crispin, head and shoulders taller than the rest, half savage himself and accompanied by Tom and Reuben and Sonwabo

Pumani, come down from the carpentry shop with him. There were not many combatants and the spectators far outnumbered them. The few boys left at the mission for the holidays stood on the bank and watched.

The heathen boys jousting in the hollow were ranged against each other, unhampered by shoes or jackets or tight, rough trousers. All trailed the tails of genets and other wild adornments. One wore a bright square of cashmere round his head and strutted up and down provokingly, proud-plumed as a rooster, while all along the edges of the bank, girls clapped and called. Bare-breasted, they swayed collectively, linked by gesture as if a little wind had touched them and sent their hands fluttering in unison here and there.

Sonwabo, brimming with impertinence and high spirits, discarded his shirt and cap and leapt down the slope. He called for a pair of sticks and with much swagger and bravado he challenged Crispin to fight with him. Crispin fell on him with a howl, dancing in and out, hot and laughing.

On the far bank, Frances recognised Kobus the groom's daughter, younger child of his junior wife and sister of Sonwabo. Beautiful, she was. Beautiful and fine in her little ochred shawl and strings of beads. Sometimes she came to the mission from the homestead in the hills near Nolovini, bright as a bush bird, and walked in her heathen beauty into the yard and asked for her father or her brother or Tom and Reuben, sons of the great wife, and then went away again when she had said what she had come to say, careless of the mission boys hanging from the windows of the boarding-house to see her pass.

She sat among the girls who had come to watch the *umngeni* battle, holding a Xhosa harp, the bow leant against her shoulder, the calabash resonator resting at the curve of her naked breast. She used a twig as a plectrum. The string vibrated plaintively, an accompaniment to the song that the girls chanted in between the ribaldries, encouraging the boys to meet in battle. The taunts, though delivered stridently, were followed by laughter and good-humoured posturing.

Only Benedict stood at a distance, detached from the rest, his hat thrust to the back of his head, his hands in his pockets.

81

It was as Frances was watching from her perch that Victor, rifle in hand, came down from the slopes above the school. She did not see him until he stopped beneath the tree in which she was perched and rested his rifle against the trunk. Half prone along the branch, she peered down at him, her boot an inch or two from his head. He stood, his back against the bole, watching, seemingly oblivious of her. Then suddenly, he put up his hand and clamped it over her boot in a vice-grip. She gave a small, startled cry. He tugged and she slithered down beside him, almost tumbling the last few feet.

'Caught!' he said, standing with his arms up against the trunk at either side of her.

'Beast,' she replied.

'Shall I just step over to the house and tell Miss Smythe where I found you?'

'Why not?' she retorted, trying to muster the old familiarity and pertness. But it sounded false. He stood across her, so close she could smell the heat of him. 'It's the *umngeni*,' she said, indicating slightly with her head. 'Do you remember it? It's just as well that Daddy's gone to an outstation or he'd have stopped it! Listen to the girls!'

'What are they saying?' He did not turn or allow her to escape. He was examining her face, unabashed.

'Taunting them and calling them cowards to egg them on.'

Beyond, some of the audience had risen and were swaying back and forth, clapping and calling derisively.

'I suppose those reds are going for initiation,' said Victor, 'and won't see a girl for months. So,' he looked at her again, 'their blood must be up.'

She pressed her back to the trunk, feeling the damp tendrils of hair at her temples clinging to her skin. She could see the little pulse beating in the hollow of his throat.

He stood away suddenly and rested his hands on his hips and he said, 'Are Tom and Reuben and Sonwabo going for initiation too?'

'I expect so, although Mother is trying to stop them. I don't know why she bothers. You're not a man until you've been and that's a disgrace.' She rubbed her wrist across her upper lip and shook back her hair. 'Just look at Crispin,' she said. 'He's such a barbarian! If he was caught, he'd be whipped!'

Victor stooped, gazing between the branches of the thorn bushes. The heathen boys strutted insinuatingly. The girls laughed. 'Watch,' said Victor and he began to unbutton his shirt, to shrug it off. He stood a moment before her, conscious of her gaze. 'Here,' he gave the shirt to her, dropping it into her hands and then he sauntered down the bank into the culvert. For a moment – just a moment – the momentum of the fighting was arrested, and the ranks of boys fell back as he shouldered in among them. He appropriated a pair of sticks from a heathen boy and, brandishing them, he cried, 'Who will fight?'

Unexpectedly large and naked-looking among the others, his trousers buckled up about his waist, he punched at the air with his weapons but no one came to challenge him. Victor gave a shout of exasperation. He stood, berating the players.

Now the girls were calling for a challenger for Victor. He walked up and down before them, urging them to name an opponent. They responded to his swagger, staring candidly at him and he at them in their near-nakedness.

'Benedict!' cried Victor, seeing Benedict at a distance. 'Come, Benedict.'

Frances crept forward and scanned the watchers, searching for Benedict. Victor sprang up the bank towards him. 'Come on, Benedict,' he said. He turned, swooped at a combatant, arrested his weapons and thrust them into Benedict's hands. Benedict half laughed, held the sticks out, returning them. The girls whispered among themselves.

Then Sonwabo's sister called out clearly, mockingly, and Benedict turned and regarded her a moment. She looked across at him with her harp crooked elegantly in her arm, her provocative head tilted in challenge.

Slowly he took off his jacket and laid it down. He undid his tie, watching her all the time. Piece by piece he removed his clothing until he stood in his trousers. Last of all, he took from his head his little hat with the crane feather and the curled brim and he laid it on top of the neatly folded pile.

The sticks were handed back to him. The boys from the

mission moved in around him but he stepped aside from them and walked along the row of girls sitting at the edge of the culvert. He stopped before Sonwabo's sister with her harp. She did not look at him, she went on tapping at the string. Then slowly she put down her instrument and drew from her shoulders the ochred shawl. With a languid gesture she dropped it over his arm. He took it and wrapped it round his left hand in which he held the pointed parrying stick.

Everyone watched silently. Then, swiftly, suddenly, he confronted Victor, shaking his weapons in the air. Victor leapt at him. Back and forth they went and the other boys fell on each other with renewed vigour.

Concealed by the bush, Frances held Victor's shirt against her, hugging herself in rapt attention as he sparred with Benedict, blow for blow. Benedict, smaller though he was, countered each attack with a dexterity that kept the broader Victor from advancing. The ranks of the heathen boys closed around them. Reuben, Crispin and Sonwabo cheered and Tom threw his hat in the air.

It was then that Frances saw Mzantsi approaching. He half ran, half walked, propelling himself at speed. His shadow jiggered across the ground before him. Its bulk seemed to revolve on the small spindles of his legs, his feet to paddle at the air. He was caught in a sudden momentum beyond his capabilities, and his helmet, clutched in his hand, rotated wildly on its leather strap. He plunged into the culvert.

'*Yimani*! Stop!' he cried dramatically, his arms raised. Laughing and panting, Crispin and Sonwabo, Tom and Reuben turned to see who the intruder was. They stepped back, jostling at each other good-naturedly. The heathen boys continued to fight, unconcerned, but Mzantsi went among them, crying out in a loud voice. The fighters broke up nonchalantly – here the thrust of a stick, there a wrap flicked across a shoulder – and only Victor and Benedict continued, the bravado and strutting and swagger gone. It seemed that the game had ended. 'Fight, man!' cried Victor as Benedict continued, merely defensive. Victor rebuked him: in English, in Xhosa, the words giving impetus to his efforts. Benedict countered enough to keep himself from being injured.

84

Back and forth they went and Mzantsi wrung his hands, begging them to halt. His words were drowned by the shouting of the watchers.

Round and round. Round and round.

At that moment, Frances saw Benedict step back and to the side as Victor lunged. The girl with the harp, silent until then, sent up a shout and Benedict, as if pierced by the words, wheeled and pounced. He caught Victor a blow on the hand which made him stumble and fall to his knees. Victor rolled over, his arm clutched to his stomach. He pushed himself up, stood hunched, shielding his fingers. Frances could see that he fought the pain.

Benedict stood a moment in victory, then he put down his sticks and came towards him. Victor straightened suddenly and with his good hand swung out. Delivered with temper more than anger, his fist caught Benedict on the side of the head and knocked him off his feet. He lay in the dust. There was a hush.

'*Bafana, bafana!*' cried Mzantsi, 'End this violence . . .'

He bent to Benedict, to help him to his feet, but Benedict pushed him away and rose unsteadily. He turned on his heel. He pulled the girl's cloth from his hand, stood before her and held it out. She took it, eyes cast down. He walked away, past the *umngeni* lads, past Mzantsi. He walked away from the silence of the watchers and disappeared beyond the drift.

Mzantsi spoke. His voice quavered in admonition and the apprentices, gathering up their discarded belongings, trailed back towards the yard. The maidens clung together and retreated, the heathen boys swung off behind them, with neither haste nor concern. Kobus's daughter stopped where Benedict's clothes lay on the grass. She picked them up. Holding them before her, precisely folded, she bore them off. The crane feather in the brim of his hat fluttered in the wind.

Mzantsi watched them all retreat and then he turned to Crispin and Victor and said, almost apologetically, 'Mr Victor, there are children that are killed in this way. Indeed, it is strictly forbidden to fight the *umngeni* here. Mr Victor, I am sure you remember the rules? It is these heathen boys. Whenever it is time for initiation, these things happen. It is against

God's law.' He fumbled. 'The influence is very bad. I do not know what to say to *Mfundisi* Charles when he returns.'

'There is no need to accompany me in order to inform my uncle, Mr Mzantsi. I shall tell him myself,' returned Victor curtly. He went up the bank.

Mzantsi watched him go and then he hurried after Tom and Reuben and Sonwabo, twittering abjectly.

Frances followed Victor at some distance as he entered the house with Crispin. She waited until they had gone before she walked up the garden and along the edge of the veranda. She carried the rifle and still held Victor's shirt in her hand for she had stayed out of sight as Mzantsi climbed the bank, herding the mission boys before him. As she reached the steps she could hear her mother's voice from the living-room. 'What did you mean by this, Crispin?' she was saying. 'And Victor, I will not have you going about the mission like that. Where is your shirt? What have you done to your hand? Who did that to you?' Frances paused. Her mother continued, her voice rising as she said, 'Was it a heathen boy? They are most unhygienic, Victor. I've no doubt Doctor Fraser will have to look at it.'

Helmina came through the front door before Frances could slip away unseen. 'Frances?' Helmina appraised her untidy hair and hot face swiftly. 'Come in at once.' She gestured with her head. Frances mounted the steps, holding Victor's shirt surreptitiously at her side. She did not meet her mother's quick glance as she passed the living-room door. She placed the rifle on the gunrack in the hall and went on down the passage.

Helmina followed her closely. She said, 'What is that?' catching at the shirt sleeve.

'Victor's shirt,' said Frances, tugging it from her fingers.

'What are you doing with Victor's shirt?'

Frances did not reply. Helmina said, 'Have you been watching the fighting?'

Frances looked back at her. Helmina snatched the shirt from her grasp. She bore it off to the washing basket, holding it as though it were something shameful. She pressed it down among the soiled linen and let the lid fall.

She said, wiping her fingers delicately against each other, 'I wish you'd realise that they only get you into mischief.'

'Who?' Frances was mulish.

'Boys,' said Helmina. There was an odd jerk in her voice. 'Men.'

'What mischief?' Frances folded her arms. Her voice was half disdainful, half quizzical: a passing imitation of Victor.

Flustered, Helmina said, 'Do not bait me, Frances.'

What did Miss Smythe know of boys that she did not know herself? What could she know, cloistered as she was? Had she ever watched Victor bowl a ball, rubbing it against his groin before he turned and ran and hurled it over-arm? What did she know of the smell and feel of a shirt hastily discarded, cool and damp to the touch, or the scent of it, of a body well exercised and unashamed? She knew only the musty, ecclesiastical odour of vestments, clerics battened in by collars and studs and unassailable cuffs.

'I suppose you will tell my mother I was there,' said Frances.

'It's clear from your appearance that you were, I don't have to tell her anything.' Helmina looked at her reprovingly. 'Why are you so wild, Frances? Young men are alarmed by reckless girls.'

Frances laughed scornfully.

'Do not be unpleasant, Frances,' said Helmina. 'I am only trying to help you. You are far too free. We sometimes despair of you . . .'

'Who despairs of me?' retorted Frances.

'Come along now,' Helmina said, not intending to be led.

'My father doesn't despair of me,' persisted Frances.

'He is very fond,' began Helmina.

'Who then? Crispin and Victor certainly don't. They'd box my ears if I was namby-pamby.'

'Crispin is not a good judge in a matter like this.' Helmina did not mention Victor. She did not dare. Great, vigorous Victor. The tension in him was explosive.

'Who then?'

'Well, your mother is a great lady herself, I am sure she would like to be emulated.'

Again Frances laughed. 'You and my mother!'

'And Mr Brownley,' said Helmina suddenly, roused by her insolence. 'His experience, his family connections, must make your behaviour appear most unrestrained by comparison. I believe he finds you very tiresome at times.'

'Did he say that?' The words flew out involuntarily.

Helmina turned away to hide her deceit. 'Indeed, he has. Often.'

'I do not give a fig for what your Mr Brownley thinks,' said Frances hotly and she turned on her heel. She could feel the heat creeping up her neck. Treacherous, tell-tale blush! She had no means of suppressing it. Tiresome, was she? She marched down the passage, assailed by a stinging sense of betrayal. She went through the hall past the parlour door. Her mother was alone in the room, standing at her bureau with a muslin cloth in her hand, dusting a small rose-patterned teacup. The wall cupboard in which it was displayed with others of the set, stood open. Frances hurried by but Emily, without looking up from her task, said, 'Not so fast, Frances.'

Frances stopped in mid-stride, turned, clenching her teeth.

Emily said, 'I have no doubt you were watching when this unfortunate incident took place, so do not annoy me by denying it. You know the rules.' She replaced the cup in the cupboard, removed another and looked round. She said, 'I have a meeting of the ladies of the St Agnes Guild in The Hoek at four this afternoon. I was going to take you with me but I do not feel inclined to allow you an outing under the circumstances. When your father returns from the outstations he will be speaking to all of you. Until then, you are to stay in your room and think over what you have sanctioned by your presence. Victor is beyond my control but Crispin has had his rifle confiscated for the rest of the holidays. Like you, Crispin would be confined to his room if I did not need him to drive the trap. I expect it will be penance enough for him to sit outside Mrs Nettleton's house without tea or company for a few hours. Miss Smythe will be vigilant, so do not defy my instructions. You may come out to make your father his tea when he returns.' She resumed her dusting. Frances said impetuously, 'That's unfair, I didn't take part . . .'

'You may go.' Her mother was distant.

Frances went, not to her room, but to the privy. No one could follow her there or deny her access. She was too angry to cry. Her punishment was quite unjust. She raged at it, pushing aside Miss Smythe's remark. It was inadmissible anyway. Would Plotz have said those things?

. . . He finds you very tiresome at times.

The words would be expunged, obliterated by anger at her mother. In passing, if Walter Brownley never returned from Mbokothwe, she would be glad. Indeed she would. She closed the privy door resoundingly. Perhaps he'd be bitten by a cobra or drown in a river or fall down a cliff. She envisaged his death throes with satisfaction. Having dispatched him, she sat on the seat, in the confines of the small, hot little room and watched ants trailing back and forth. From her vantage, through a small chink in the door, she could see a wedge of her mother's rose garden.

The blooms bobbed in and out of view. She said aloud, in imitation of her mother, repeating words she had so often heard expressed to visitors: 'In England' – she intoned with exaggerated reverence – 'when I was a girl, my father had a rose garden. Oh, the varieties and fragrances! I have set mine out just as he did his . . .'

England had become synonymous with any discord with her mother, synonymous with the heat-plagued flowerbeds full of irises and roses wilting and pest-infested against the vigorous backdrop of thorn and aloe; synonymous with the porcelain tea-set and figurines and glassware in the wall cupboard that could not be touched, synonymous with the ban on speaking Xhosa anywhere within the confines of the garden and the house – even to Nowasha, at whose knee Frances had learned it – should echoes of some insidious barbarity penetrate the sanctuary. Frances knew, as soon as she had seen her mother standing with the muslin cloth and the cup in her hand that she had 'gone home' – she with her bride-of-the-morning and her little posset cups. She took them out and dusted them whenever she was angry. No punishment, no words of reproof could be more divisive than this action. By it, her mother distanced herself beyond their reach. They had neither rights, nor privileges within this secret world. Their exclusion – and the rejection it implied – was absolute. She would stand aloof and take out her cloth and shake it and lift down the china, turn the pieces over and inspect the names – as though each held a vision that was sacrosanct from children and from housemaids.

It was stifling in the privy and Frances returned to her room and lay on her bed. She heard her mother's quick steps as she went down the passage, the rustle of the skirts of her afternoon frock, the click of her sunshade as she opened it. She heard the trap's wheels as it drew away from the yard and the dogs barking excitedly as they ran alongside as far as the gate. When it had gone, she listened to the wind in the tree outside the porch. A hot wind, gusty and dry. Doves called softly, fat murmurings from their hidden perches.

She closed her eyes.

. . . He finds you very tiresome at times.

. . . Has he said that?

. . . Indeed, he has.

She was roused by Helmina's step as she hesitated outside the door. She seemed to pause, listening. Frances put out her hand and picked up a book on her side table. She dropped it noisily and deliberately on the floor. Satisfied, Helmina crept on. Frances heard her door close and after some minutes the creak of her bedsprings as she lay down.

Frances sat up and paged through the book. It held no interest for her and she put it aside. She looked out of the window and saw the sun glistened on the thatch of the curate's lodge and a flock of goats browsing among the thorn bushes close by. The fowls that frequented the backyard had gone to rest under the hedge. The late light of afternoon sank in quietly about the mission grounds.

. . . Very tiresome at times. Traitorous Plotz.

She thrust the book away and forced her mind to Victor. She wondered where he was. His room had been empty when she had come to her own. He had not helped Crispin harness the horses and his rifle was still on the gunrack in the hall. She lay down again and summoned one of her many daydreams about Victor: heroic, romantic and improbable and then she thought about the sudden nearness of him that morning, the

90

clean, damp smell of him as he'd leaned towards her. The pulse in his throat, the sinews of his neck. He'd dropped his shirt into her hands. It had been as if she'd touched his flesh.

Frances went quietly to her door and locked it. She put the key in the pocket of her skirt. The roof contracted sharply. Startled, she stood, listening. She took off her shoes and placed them next to the bed. She drew the curtain closed, gently easing the rings across the rod. How they seemed to squeal! She waited, her breath shallow. Then she slipped behind them and pulled herself across the sill and slid down to the back porch. Helmina's sash was closed. Frances lowered her own gently behind her.

Barefooted, she ran swiftly across the backyard. She scrambled through the fence and down the slope beyond. Here was sanctuary. Safe from view, she stopped and breathed again. The bush that stretched down to the banks of the Mtwaku river drooped in the heat. She would wade upstream to the place where the boys bathed in summer and lie in the shade of the yellowwood that arched above the bank. She would return long before Miss Smythe discovered she was gone. She admitted to herself no idea of meeting Victor somewhere here. No idea that she'd come out to find him. She'd acknowledge neither motives of defiance nor of quest. And yet, she moved with a sort of reckless alertness, listening every now and then for footsteps in the undergrowth.

Bush willows were decked with new, light leaves. The pale sand was streaked with leaf-mould. It was cool and dry beneath her feet as she picked her way down the bank. Here, above the spreading bush, the yellowwoods thrust up into the sky. Their concentric crowns traced against the cloud, bearded with parasitic growth, ancient as the Amatolas themselves.

A great dun-coloured bull loomed suddenly among the bushes. Frances caught the startled flash of his eye. So large and yet so cryptic among the afternoon shadows. He lumbered on, a truant like herself. She tucked up her skirts as best she could and waded into the stream, choosing her path with care. She came out into the sunlight where a narrow sandbank curved beside a wide, shallow pool. There, stretched out and motionless, lay Victor. He appeared to be asleep, his injured hand trailing in the shallows. He was sprawled on his stomach, his left arm crooked under his head. His shirt lay on the bank beside him. Frances stood transfixed. She gazed at the long back, the smooth thickness of his neck, his damp head, those sculptured boy's arms.

Victor looked up with a start. He stared back at her. She did not look away. She felt the sweat on her lip. She wiped her sleeve across her mouth.

Then Victor laughed, comprehending. He laughed, easily. 'So,' he said, 'you escaped?'

She nodded.

He turned over, sat, his elbows on his knees, his forearms hanging loosely.

She came towards him then, wading tentatively. The heat seemed unbearable. She could feel the sweat again. She could feel it crawling down her spine. She pushed up her sleeves and wet her arms and she splashed her face and mopped it on the hem of her skirt and took in a sandy, warm draught of water. And then she climbed up the bank behind him and sat on the tangle of grass in the shade. Victor stood and stretched. He followed and reclined beside her. She did not look at him. A drop of river water fell from her hair and slid down her temple. Victor pulled a grass from its sheath and dismembered it, extracting the soft, naked end and dissecting it with his thumb-nail. He traced the plume down her sleeve to her wrist, down her skirt from knee to ankle. He pulled it lightly across her toes. 'You came to find me,' he said.

'Yes,' she said. 'You were unfair to Benedict and I'm angry with you.'

'I know.' He put the end of the grass in his mouth. 'I lost my temper. I really didn't mean to.'

'Well, it wasn't sporting of you.'

'Have you come to give me a lecture? Is that why you're here?'

'Just to tell you,' she said and not looking at him.

'I'll make it up to him sometime. I'll take him fishing. Show him there are no ill feelings. Will that satisfy you?'

'No,' she said and he looked up at her, scanning her face.

'Anyway,' he said, 'I did him a favour, making him fight.

The girl with the harp went off with his clothes. He'll have to find her to get them back. If that doesn't please him, nothing will.' He laughed. 'Maybe she'll come looking for him, like you.'

Frances made to stand but Victor reached for her arm and pulled her down, holding the wrist easily between finger and thumb. She struggled, saying crossly, 'Leave me, will you?'

But he laughed again and held her prisoner so effortlessly that she began to laugh as well. 'Quiet now!' he said. 'Quiet!' And he smoothed her fingers to his palm and she could not tell if he were mocking her or not. She looked down at those hands, her fingers caught between them. Brown hands. Prominent sinews, a small white scar curved at a knuckle.

She felt as if she had been allowed the intimacy of a stare, to explore, uncensured, light on forearms, their springy down, the veined smoothness of his inner wrists. She could smell him again – him with his bare chest – bending in beside her, briny and warm with river water.

Victor linked his fingers into hers. She glanced at him: he would grin and release her. But his fingers tightened. His face was close then. She could hear, somewhere on the riverbank, a frog chirruping secretly from the undergrowth. She waited, poised. Now. As she had imagined it. Not just in jest. Not just to tease her, to show off to Miss Smythe. He would kiss her. Yes. And look into her eyes and say something that she would hold sacred, like a talisman.

'You wouldn't come with me before,' he said. 'Why have you changed your mind?'

Frances did not reply.

'Is this a game, Frances?'

She looked up to laugh at him, to push him away, as she could have done once. She might have brushed at her skirt and run off carelessly.

She did not move.

Her first tentative breath at the touch of his lips was swept aside. Her most fatuous imaginings of bashful embraces and lingering looks with the river running by, were routed. No words, no tendernesses. No boyish kisses and foolish laughter. No complicity on a stolen afternoon. Victor bent across her and she could feel the sudden weight of him, fierce to draw her closer.

Frightened by his urgency, her heart surging, it seemed to her as if he were in anguish or in pain, locked against her inviolable petticoats, engaged in some heedless struggle of his own. She turned her face away but he would not let her go until she gasped for breath. Then he drew back suddenly, alert and listening, and glanced across his shoulder at the riverbank below. Far off, from beyond the church, she could hear the goatherds calling to each other. Victor said, 'I think you'd better go back to the house.'

Frances lay as if she had been winded. Above her, a beetle hung suspended, affronted on a leaf. She brushed it aside, pushed herself up and watched Victor mutely. She put her hand out to reach for him, let it fall, for he had turned from her, as if shielding himself from her gaze, and said impatiently, 'Go on, will you, before someone comes.'

She pulled her clothes straight and fled up the bank towards the path. She hesitated, looked down at him. She said, as if she had injured him, 'I'm sorry.'

She had walked out in defiance. She ran back in fear, listening to the sound of her own footsteps, announcing her. She went the long way round, past the beehives and through the pasture and under the oak where she and Crispin had played as small children, making houses among the roots. There was the curate's lodge and Mzantsi's goats had got into the vegetable garden. They stood, stupidly chewing, staring at her. Accusing. Ah, they knew. They knew. They could sense her. They could smell her. They could smell the strange secret dampness of her. They knew.

The shade of the veranda that ran along the curate's lodge was deep and mauve in the afternoon light. All the doors were closed. Walter Brownley had not returned. She looked up at his window. Perhaps, after all, he was inside the room. Perhaps he would open the door as she passed and pull her in and stare at her and say, 'Confess!'

She came to the corner of the veranda, surveyed the house across the yard. Miss Smythe's curtains were drawn back. Perhaps she had gone to her room and tried the door? Frances ran over the open ground and round the side of the house. She dared not open her window in case someone heard. She took her key from her pocket and, glancing into the living-room to see if it was empty, stepped quickly through the open window. She tiptoed down the passage and fitted the key in her lock. She turned it, opened the door, slipped inside and leaned against it. She let out her breath slowly and looked up. Helmina Smythe was sitting in the chair in the corner. Frances gasped.

'Your Father came back early,' said Helmina evenly. 'When you did not answer my call, I fetched the spare key.'

The breath ached in Frances's chest. She said, 'Are you going to tell on me?'

'Why do you make it so difficult for yourself and for me, Frances?' Helmina herself seemed distressed, afraid of what she had discovered. She hardly looked at Frances, averted her eyes. Frances felt suffocated by fear and by the close dankness of her clothes.

'Where have you been?'

'I was at the river. It was hot here.'

'Were you alone?' The question was so tentative, it seemed as though she were begging for some answer that she knew Frances could not give.

'I went alone but I saw Victor there.'

Helmina nodded then, as if confirming something to herself. She said, 'I was asked to be vigilant of you and I neglected my duty. I will say nothing to your parents, Frances, and I'll confess it is because I am too afraid of the consequences. I shall have to think of a way to salve my conscience.' She went to the door and she said, 'Your father was asking for you. He was waiting for his tea. I have taken it to him. I said you were asleep. You had better go to him, he wished to see you.'

She was gone. Frances sat on the edge of her bed. She felt a close, clinging heat and unwashedness sitting there in her dishevelled clothes. She wanted to be cleansed with warm, soapy water. And yet, within that need to cleanse, she was alert to something else: some embryonic yearning in some quiet dark. She walked down the passage to her father's study. Would he see the mark of it in her eyes? Would he see the stain of Victor's urgent tongue on her neck and in her mouth?

She knocked at the door and she opened it and her father looked up from his desk. 'Have you had a good sleep, darling?' he said and he held out his hand for her to take, to encircle her, pull her head down to his, to give her cheek a faint, cajoling caress. She all but cried as she felt his beard against her forehead. 'Shall I make you another pot of tea, Daddy?'

'Do. And bring a cup and share it with me.'

She went to the kitchen and searched for a cup. Disquiet burrowed in her flesh and the salt was strong in her throat as she swallowed back the tears. As she went from the room she looked through the pantry window and saw Victor sauntering past the curate's lodge. He was whistling, his hands in his pockets. His trousers were damp as though he'd swum in them, his shirt clung to his chest. He walked like a raja, lightly, expansively. He greeted a herdboy chasing a flock of goats, made some ribald remark, laughed, sauntered on. Victor – triumphant – vaulted the orchard gate in a stride.

And it was then that Boggis and the mare shambled into the mission yard drawing the Cape cart. Walter Brownley saw Victor swinging along through the orchard whistling and he raised his hand. Victor returned the greeting and came across and took Boggis's rein and said, 'Good afternoon, Mr Brownley, had a good trip?' with an air so affable, Walter glanced at him in surprise.

'Thanks,' said Walter, getting down stiffly. 'Far too long for comfort.' He untethered the horses and helped Victor with the traces. 'How many brace of partridge and guineafowl have you and Crispin massacred since I've been gone?'

Victor laughed. 'None! Crispin went to The Hoek with Aunt Emily.' Then he said. 'Did a spot of fishing at the river this afternoon.'

Walter led the mare to the trough. 'Successful?'

'Highly successful,' said Victor impudently.

'Good,' said Walter. 'I should try my luck sometime.'

'I wonder if you'd have the knack,' said Victor with a small sardonic smile.

Chapter Six

Helmina told him. It was she. Walter could not look at her or escape her gaze as she spoke. The words – banal and pedestrian – orchestrated images far beyond what she could possibly intend: 'Mr Brownley, I am most disturbed. I do not know how to tell you, but really I must ask your counsel. I have let Mrs Farborough down – I hope not gravely – and I simply don't have the courage to tell her . . . Miss Farborough has not taken me into her confidence . . . I don't know what to think . . . perhaps you will have a more considered view.' The words, in her high, light monotone beat at his head. She floundered from innuendo to denial, from conviction to doubt. Frances had been out at the river – secretly – with Victor. She had locked her door and climbed from the window. Was that all? 'She looked so wild.' He had turned away. What, in God's name, had Frances done? What had Victor done? Helmina Smythe seemed unable to say.

'I am worried. I can't think why. They are both so reckless.'

'They have been in each other's company most of their lives,' Walter said flatly. 'I am sure it is perfectly innocent . . .'

He remembered Victor's insouciance, his air of self-congratulation as he took Boggis to the stable. 'Did a spot of fishing . . .' God Almighty! What was there to fish for in that drought-raddled river? He would obliterate Victor! Saddle Boggis, Plotz, arm yourself and run him through! Walter looked at Helmina hollowly, patted her arm and went away.

He did not see Helmina watch him as he walked away nor know the sudden fear she felt for what she'd done. She might rationalise her motive in speaking to Walter: she had assured Emily Farborough that she would be vigilant and she had failed. She needed a confessor. And yet, she knew that she could hardly be blamed if Frances took it into her head to climb out of windows and run about barefoot. She was eighteen, after all.

It was something Helmina needed Walter Brownley to know.

She needed him to know that Frances had left her room and run down to the river and met Victor alone and come back in a high state of agitation and dishevelment. And when she had said what she'd felt compelled to say, she went to the church and dusted the vestry and put all the sacred vessels neatly in the cupboard in rows, and knelt on the floor by the table and said a prayer, wishing some penance could be devised to absolve the shame she felt at her small triumph. Oh, she knew Walter Brownley. She'd watched his face at meals, when on Sundays he was invited to share the family dinner. He betrayed nothing – nothing, but to those with a jealous heart. It was at these times that she'd seen him – a jealous heart he had himself – watching Victor. She had seen him snatch at glances that might pass from Victor to Frances, snatch at any word between them and never give a sign that he was watching. Just as she did. Deny it as she might – fighting with her finer instincts – Helmina wished that Walter Brownley might be vanquished by Victor. And then she would be there.

Through all the years at the mission, Helmina's days had been filled with sameness. Then Walter Brownley had come and they had changed. There followed an autumn of lightness. An autumn in which the falling of the leaves from the oak was a joyous, airy dance. She gathered them and pressed their moist gold into her Bible, forgetting they would turn dark and brittle.

At the start, when Walter Brownley had accompanied her on her walks, they had discussed Frances's curriculum and plans for a school and points of theology. They neither sauntered nor went briskly on these outings. Walter Brownley always set a steady pace, his hands clasped loosely behind his back, looking ahead as he talked, speaking with a quiet ease as if she were the most entertaining companion when she knew that all her words followed stolidly, one behind the other like donkeys or mules plodding in a train: plod, plod, plod. Why did they not skip from her tongue as Frances could make them, in small, gruff cadences, punctuated by that low easy chuckle? She had heard her confidences shuffle out, one here, one there. She had hastily inspected each to see if it were fatuous or trite. It took some courage to speak at all and yet Walter Brownley listened without the slightest indication that he might find her tedious.

And on these walks she might gather something small – a feather, a stone, a flower – and put it into the plain wooden box on her dresser for remembrance. And sometimes, when despair raised itself, she would look at these things as if they had a radiance, adjuncts to what she held inside her heart. Helmina stored these treasures, in hope. With the quiet desperation of a pilgrim, she journeyed towards the shrine.

And then, one day, Helmina had come across a set of paintings that Frances had done for Walter Brownley. Sketches of the mission and environs, portraits of the mission people. They were pleasing enough. But there was something in them. There was something in them that she could not explain, something of a secret, of a joke. 'Plotz here' had been faintly pencilled in beside the picture of the curate's lodge. 'What is Plotz?' she had asked. Ever since she'd said that, Frances had accompanied their walks. And after that, there was no earthly way Helmina could have restrained herself from saying, 'Frances was down at the river with Victor this afternoon . . .'

Walter Brownley's face had said it all. She had caught him at the brink.

When Crispin returned from The Hoek he went in search of Benedict. He went to the boarding-house and the carpentry shop but only old Mr Groenewald was there planing planks and the apprentices had already gone to work in the mission fields.

Crispin had sat all afternoon in the trap outside the Nettletons' house. He had been forbidden to stir from it except to water the horse at the trough in the backyard. His mother had not spoken to him either on their journey there or on their return. Her silence enforced her disapproval. Crispin would have preferred to be caned than to endure her silence. She seemed preoccupied and grieved and when she had turned at the Nettletons' gate and told him to water the horse, her voice had been reproachful.

All his life he had tried to please his mother. She seemed impatient of him. His scholastic efforts would never earn praise, the gloomy letters from his form master brought on bouts of irritation at the start of every holiday. His father was too weighed down with work, too seldom there, too often gone to outstations in the early mornings, returning only at dusk, to give him time.

Crispin was only a boy, his concerns a boy's concerns. He could shoot, bring down a bird with a hunting stick, lure fish from the river. These were his preoccupations. And to match Victor. He followed him unswervingly. If he suffered any rebuff from Victor, there was Benedict. Like Benedict, Crispin had stood many times before Victor, either dispatched by his wit or diminished by his patronage. And yet, Victor held them still, within his magic circle, enthralled.

Crispin went to the boarding-house but Benedict had not returned. He would forfeit his food if he did not come back by supper time. If he missed Mr Brownley calling the register before the lights were turned out he would be punished. Like a shadow, Benedict's sponsorship went with him at all times: what would Miss Prudieaux-Brune say? Crispin blamed himself in some obscure way for what had happened that morning. It was he who had called the mission boys down to see the red boys fighting the *umngeni* in the culvert. It was he who had broken the rules by leading them outside the mission fence. It was he who, in jest, had challenged Sonwabo. Sonwabo, always eager to bring himself to the notice of the heathen girls, had leapt down beside him.

But then, Victor had intruded and humiliated Benedict. For the first time, Crispin felt some vague, some uneasy sense that Benedict had been betrayed. Not just by Victor, but by himself. He had allowed him to walk away.

Benedict had turned his back on all of them. Without a word. There was nothing he could say and nothing could expiate the small, bitter sense of betrayal. That he knew. He had gone, just in his trousers, barefooted. He had walked with care. His feet, accustomed always to boots, were unfamiliar with grass and stones and the heat of the sand between the thorn bushes.

Victor had taunted him and though it had been in jest, the words had stung, said, as they were, in front of the heathen and the apprentices. Said for the daughter of Kobus Pumani to hear. He knew that Victor would forget the incident within the hour or recall it with laughter at some other time – as he had when Mzantsi had reported Benedict to Father Charles for going out at night. Victor had asked him the following day what he'd been up to, disbelieving him when he'd denied that girls were part of the excursion, insisting that he'd simply accompanied Crispin to listen to Kobus preparing Tom and Reuben and Sonwabo for initiation. Victor had been passingly sympathetic when Benedict had been gated for a fortnight from all entertainment or sport but seemed to have forgotten him until he re-emerged from his detention.

Benedict could find no evidence that Victor had been punished for his own excursions in the dark. The departure of the wheelwright and his daughter had brought the incident to a discreet close. There had been no public explanations, no penances exacted for the satisfaction of a Miss Prudieaux-Brune. Clearly, interest in traditional practice, the need to know the customs of his people – the need to be kin with his companions – amounted to depravity. Lust did not.

Benedict walked and walked, tracing a great circle about the hills that ringed the mission. It lay below him, small, diminished by distance. Around it, the homesteads of the people were spare on the hills, the fields stretching down to the edges of the mission gardens.

He had lived here all his life but he had no claims to this. *Iranuga*: stranger, wanderer. That was the word to describe him. Here were no ancestral lands of his. No relatives, no shades. He had no name but that which Emily Farborough had chosen for him. Benedict. A blessing.

On the day of his confirmation he had felt so proud, sitting in his suit in the front pew of the church. A certain aloofness from those around him. He was the chosen one, the protégé. After the service, he alone had been allowed to eat his supper in the Farboroughs' kitchen instead of in the boarding-house with the others. He had sat with his hat placed neatly before him and no one to talk to but Nowasha, the cook. Mrs Farborough had sent for a kitchen plate and set out a heap of dainties for him. Benedict had sat very upright on the wooden chair.

There are some corners of the heart that cannot be probed too closely, some hidden griefs that cannot be expunged: Benedict did not think often of who his parents might have been, for then the magnitude of his aloneness would assail him. He had been raised in an institution. There was security in its rules and routines. Like Mzantsi, like Miss Smythe, like the nuns and the orphans and the children who had nowhere to go in the holidays, like the old men who followed Kobus about the yard: they remained in a strange state of bondage and dependence, born not of love but of need. Like long-serving prisoners who had grown old in captivity, they were afraid of freedom. Each guarded his place jealously, was greedy of possessions itinerantly earned.

Where had he been born? In what ditch? What hovel? Perhaps he had arrived under the aloof and dispassionate eye of one of the nuns, his mother turned out before she could hold him to her breast. A child of God. Which God? Whose God? God was a White Man. That he knew.

A child is conceived in conjunction with the shades. This he had learned from Kobus when he and Crispin and the apprentices had sat with him at night. The shades worked in the blood of the parents, shaping the spirit. These were the child's people. It was they who were vigilant at its conception. It was they who guided it. But if he had been cut off from them, denied knowledge and access, how could they care? They, surely, had withdrawn, taking with them their gift of continuity and weight. Perhaps, at the moment Father Charles had touched his infant forehead with baptismal water, the shades of his forebears had abandoned him and he had emerged, empty of a past. 'We bring this child into the light.' That is what was said. Stripped of its provenance.

Benedict walked down towards the mission buildings as the bell rang for evensong and the girls from the boarding-house filed, white-pinafored, towards the church. He reached the fence and there, waiting at the stile, was Crispin. He held a fishing rod and a spare jacket. He said, gruffly and without looking at Benedict, 'Thought we might fish until you have to go in for supper.' It was a peace offering, Benedict knew.

He took the rod from Crispin and turned along the path towards the river. They sat in silence on the bank, the water unfolding between the shallow sand-bars. They stayed until a new moon emerged, pale as a young bull's horn, hanging distant and translucent in the sky.

Mbokothwe had shaken Walter. He had wished to escape as soon as he had seen Brompton, alert to his approach, crouching at his door. St Matthias, after that desolation, nestling in its valley, was a haven. He had swept his eyes across the lawn, probed the veranda railings. Perhaps Frances was somewhere about the church or the garden or painting a picture underneath the trees, or accompanying the schoolgirls in their singing: the quick, vivid sight of her; a step on the stone flagging of his porch to quicken the heart. 'My mother says, do come over to the house for tea, Mr Brownley.' And then – glancing back to see if she was overheard – 'Did you discover the green lion, Mr Plotz . . .?'

But she had not been there and none of these things had been said. He had only met Victor and Victor had been fishing . . .

And then Miss Smythe, lurking among the banksias at the edge of the curate's garden, twisting her hands into a penance of a shape, had come to confess her breach of vigilance. He did not wish to hear it. He did not wish to know. Why choose him as confidant?

Walter went in search of Father Charles. He found him in his study with Mzantsi. 'Ah, Brownley! Come in and make yourself comfortable.' Father Charles gestured to a chair. Mzantsi was standing at the window. He hardly greeted Walter but faltered on, as if in apology, with a small, unrehearsed sermon, delivered unhappily, about moral decay, the deep sin of superstition and ignorance. Father Charles gave him full attention. Walter half listened, his mind on other things. He caught the drift as he filled his pipe and lit it. There had been a fight. Some heathen ritual in which the mission boys had joined. Crispin, Victor, Benedict and the apprentices.

Father Charles said gently, 'My dear Mzantsi, what happened this morning is not your fault. I have already had an explanation from Victor and Crispin. Both are entirely to blame, but in the end, thanks be to God, no harm has been done. Boys are high-spirited. That is all.'

'But the gospel says, *Mfundisi* . . .'

'The gospel says many things, but it acknowledges that boys are often tempted. You have not failed.'

Mzantsi turned and turned his hat as if struggling with himself and then he said in a low voice, 'It is not necessarily the *umngeni* itself, *Mfundisi*. It is what it may lead to. It leads to much immorality. I have spoken to Kobus about this many times. It is he who encourages these things. These heathen boys are going for initiation soon. He is the *Khankatha* for these initiation rites. You do not know this word, Mr Brownley,' he turned to Walter, 'but it is the *Khankatha* who instructs the boys in all the filthy doings that arise from initiation. What do you think these girls are doing here at this time? It is they who lead the boys to indulging in *umetsho*.'

He stopped abruptly and said in a low voice, 'I should not speak of these things here in front of a man who is unmarried. I apologise . . .'

Walter watched him, the small, cowed movements. He stood before them, a displaced old man, a man from whom the spirit had been extracted and replaced with trappings: an alpaca coat, a watch chain and a helmet. And this is what they hoped for Benedict Matiwane. This is what they wished for Tom and Reuben and Sonwabo Pumani. Young they were and free, as they swung along between the buildings, carrying planks and singing and watching – with exaggerated nonchalance – the girls that drifted by: ochre-clad heathens or the mission girls in pinafores and stiff long sleeves and collars buttoned to their chins.

Mzantsi drew his handkerchief from his pocket and wiped his face. He reminded Walter of an old tortoise that Frances had shown him, his head thrust up from the protective shell of his collar, leading his bulk, his legs at the corners, pushing him along.

'I shall go to the boarding-house and take the register myself tonight,' said Father Charles. 'I shall speak to the boys about the *umngeni*. These things take time. It will be years before such practices disappear.'

When Mzantsi had gone, Father Charles stood and went to a corner cupboard. He took two small glasses from it and a bottle of sherry. He filled each and handed one to Walter. 'A long drive begs a drink at its end,' he said. He eased himself into his chair and contemplated the bowl of his pipe. He said, 'Mzantsi is a man of the finest intentions. He is an Mfengu and he was born and raised on a mission near Grahamstown. There is no one more willing than Mzantsi, none more dedicated to the service of the Church, and no one whom the spectres of the past more haunt. He seems to race from a darkness that none but he himself perceives. I hope he gets his rest one day for he could not deserve it more.'

'Why should a fight distress him so?'

'The *umngeni* is forbidden and Victor and Crispin know the rules. Tempers flare and I have seen a boy killed from a blow on the head. But it's the attendant customs, the general atmosphere that disturbs Mzantsi. There is a practice – and I must add, one not sanctioned by tribal law – among unmarried boys and girls, which is rather distasteful to discuss. Here,' he pushed his tobacco pouch towards Walter to share. 'No doubt it has its function within the society as it is very common, although I believe that the elders frown on it. I'm not an advocate of the belief held among my colleagues that the natives are steeped in sensuality and vice. That is naive nonsense. All societies are prey. However, this activity is indulged in by most young people – not just heathens. It is a sort of mock-intercourse by which the girl's virginity is left intact but which requires an enormous amount of self-discipline and restraint. Of course, this is not easy to sustain – hence the waifs we take in from time to time. The atmosphere before initiation seems a little more charged than usual. Nature puts temptation before us daily, so who are we to judge?'

Who, indeed. Walter inspected the toes of his boots.

'So,' Father Charles smiled. 'You have come back to a contretemps and my wife is in a rage with Victor and Crispin and has confiscated Crispin's gun. I fear she will regret it for we shall have no end of trouble with them loitering about the house and looking for new mischief. Tell me, what did you find at Mbokothwe? Did you get your printing-press?'

'What did I find at Mbokothwe?' Walter stood, his hands behind his back, and went to the window. Dusk was falling fast. 'I got my printing-press and I found a man on the brink of despair.'

Father Charles rubbed his hand across his eyes. His white, drooping eyebrows drew together. 'Another casualty. They didn't tell us at St Augustine's – such far-off, carefree days, despite ourselves – about the loneliness, the need.'

No, they did not tell us. They did not tell us about the loneliness and need. And the loneliness and need did not lessen nor become something to which one grew accustomed.

When Walter had reported on Brompton's condition and gone away to his room, he seemed to take with him – as if it were baggage – all the events of the day. Assailed by an immense weariness, he was glad to find a hipbath placed on the mat and several ewers of warm water standing by it.

He fetched his Church Review, filled his pipe, undressed and dropped his clothes in the corner. When he had washed he leaned against the backrest and lit his pipe and picked up his paper and read and smoked until the water was quite cold.

Loneliness and need. Exacerbated by Frances's presence. She was within his reach but leagues away. Loneliness and need would have to be expunged. He would pay her no more attention. He had been content before he knew her. Content with himself and with God and sure in his vocation. Victor and she could do as they pleased. If they behaved like heathens preparing for initiation – as Helmina Smythe would have him believe – then let them.

And so, the next day, he went to the printing-room and he called for Benedict and he set about cleaning the Mbokothwe printing-press as if it were one of the Herculean tasks. He paid no attention to the distant preoccupations of Benedict. He sent him scurrying from trough to table with brushes and turpentine.

Walter took off his jacket and rolled his sleeves up above his elbows and he took off his collar in the heat and knotted his handkerchief and put it on his head. A workman. And so he was when Frances came into the printing-room with a basket of tea things sent from the house and a plate of bread and butter. He did not glance up from what he was doing but he said, 'Put it on the table, thank you, Miss Farborough' and continued with the work, rubbing the rust from the parts. He could feel her at his back, waiting. She could languish there as long as she liked, he would not turn around. He levered a chisel against a rusty plate. Still she stood. He looked up peremptorily and said, 'Yes?'

Such a look she had. Tremulous. Wistful. She recoiled at the sharpness of his tone.

'The tea will be cold,' she faltered, 'if you do not drink it now.'

Knives and goads. He would dismember Victor on a rack.

'Thank you.' Distant, he bent to his work. He would not look up again. He'd betray himself so entirely she would retreat, laughing, tell Victor, triumphant. Oh, he could just hear her: a peal of girl's laughter, clear and thoughtless. He'd go to the devil before he'd give her the satisfaction of that.

He ignored her, hearing only the clink of the tool against the ancient metal of the press. He began to whistle softly, to block out any sound that she might make. 'Abide with me, fast falls the eventide . . .' When at last he did glance up, she was gone and the tea was cold in the bottle and Benedict was loitering at the trough, talking to Kobus's daughter, standing there in all her heathen splendour, as if it were a Saturday afternoon.

Kobus Pumani's daughter moved from the homestead on the hill to her father's hut at St Matthias Mission and exchanged her traditional beads and skirt for a print pinafore and headscarf. Walter was surprised by the sight of her as he entered the church one morning and found her, wrapped in her father's dishevelled coat, sweeping the porch with his broom.

'Where is your father?' he enquired in Xhosa, surveying her changed appearance with some regret.

'He is gone,' was all she said and she continued to sweep, placidly moving the broom about the flagging as if it were a task that she'd known all her life.

Walter opened the door and went down the aisle. Benedict was putting out prayer-books and counting the hymnals. Emily Farborough was in the vestry.

'Good morning, Mr Brownley,' called Emily. 'I see we are low on candles. Why did no one tell me? Victor left for work not ten minutes ago and I could have asked him to bring them back this evening.'

'Good morning, Mrs Farborough,' said Walter, going through to her. 'I'm sorry if I've overlooked the candles. I have been too preoccupied with the press.'

'Have you printed the programme for the Choral Evening?'

'Yes, and I would like you to see how good it looks on the paper we had sent up from Town.' He watched her as she hung freshly laundered vestments in the cupboard.

'I heard you practising with the choir the other night and it sounded very creditable to me.' She looked at him, sideways and up – a particular mannerism of cocking her head when offering praise – and he smiled.

'I hope we can persuade you to sing, Mrs Farborough. Father Charles has promised an item and there's a space on the programme that needs to be filled.'

'Goodness, Mr Brownley.' She laughed. 'I haven't performed since I was a girl! I shan't ruin any reputation I might have by standing up in company!'

Walter carried the vases through to the church for her and put them on the altar. He turned to Benedict. Benedict looked up at him and then away. 'What is it, Benedict?' Walter asked.

'They are going for initiation today.'

'Who is going?'

'Tom and Reuben and Sonwabo. Kobus Pumani is taking them.'

'Do you wish you were with them?'

'It is a heathen thing,' said Benedict woodenly and he glanced at the vestry door. 'How can you think I would go?'

Walter appraised him shrewdly but he did not reply for Emily Farborough came out with the polished candlesticks and Benedict put the prayer-books carefully on the front pew and left the church. As he opened the door, Walter saw that the girl was idling with the broom and as Benedict reached her, she laid it aside and went with him, unobtrusively, following where he walked.

What a day to leave for initiation, with the bushes along the river parched and scudding in the wind! Despite the gale there was a carnival atmosphere when Walter returned to the yard. Tom and Reuben and Sonwabo Pumani, surrounded by the younger apprentices, Sonwabo's sister, Benedict and Crispin, were gathered near the workshops.

The mission people came from the fields. The old men from their sweeping, the grooms and the farm-hands and the women from the washhouse, old Groenewald from the carpentry shop. Father Charles walked up from the office.

It was only Emily Farborough who did not emerge from the church. Walter could hear her playing the piano, a small, thin sound washed out now and then by the wind.

The chanting, boisterous cavalcade was led by Crispin. It accompanied Tom, Reuben and Sonwabo to the drift. The three stopped at the ford and unlaced their boots. They slung them round their necks. Under the thorn bushes on the other bank, a group of young men from the homesteads around, lounged in the grass. They rose and gazed across at the gathering. A little way off, still and vigilant in the deep shade of a tree, stood another, half turned away. The configuration of plants against which he stood seemed rearranged into a new pattern of shadow and light from which a form emerged. Clad in a kaross the colour of bark, was Kobus Pumani. No longer in his ragged coat, no longer with an old felt hat, almost brimless from use, moulded to his head, he waited, leaning on his stick, his kaross folded round him, his snuff spoon – a magician's little talisman – stuck into his hair.

The apprentices stepped into the stream, bent to roll up the legs of their trousers. On both banks the watchers waited and there was no sound but the water running between the stones.

As the brothers reached the other side the young men converged on them.

'Three weeks,' called Father Charles, in a last bid to hold them.

The apprentices raised their hands.

It was three months before Tom and Reuben and Sonwabo Pumani reappeared.

Chapter Seven

So small an act, so unwittingly performed: had he known, Walter would have stayed in the church after matins and written a sermon instead of walking down to the house to tell Father Charles he was leaving on a circuit of school inspections for the day. But Father Charles was not in his study and no one came when he knocked.

He was writing a note to leave on the desk when he heard the sound of the piano. Impatient, inaccurate notes chasing across the keys. Frances was practising the piece he had selected for her weeks before to play at the Choral Union Evening. He was going away unobtrusively, unwilling to speak to her, determined to maintain his distance, but she called out as he passed the living-room door.

'It's a dreadful tune,' she said, without looking up. 'The notes run away with me. Won't you show me this part?' And she pointed to the music.

'I'm supposed to be saddled up and gone,' he said stiffly. 'Where's your father?'

'At the boarding-house with Mother, speaking to the matron.' She tapped the score with her finger. 'Just the very fast bit, please. I can manage the rest.' Still she did not look at him and she spoke as if she wished to make amends for something and could not find the words.

He went into the room and took his seat on the piano-stool. She stood at his shoulder and watched. 'It's the bass,' she said. 'My fingers won't move fast enough.'

Walter played the offending passage.

'I don't know how you do it,' she said. 'You never seem to practise.'

He could feel her standing close behind him. He relented a little and he said, 'Try the left hand while I play the right. Concentrate on the fingering.'

She sat tentatively beside him on the long stool.

'One, two, begin,' he said.

She played slowly.

'Good! One, two, three, four. Again.'

'May we start from the very beginning?' said Frances. 'I like it as a duet. It's so thin when I play it alone.'

'I'm late,' he said, ready to walk away.

'Just once.'

He subsided: the cracks were opening before his feet. 'Once,' he said.

Frances followed him, gaining confidence, then hastening too far and losing her way. He held the chord, waiting for her to find her place. He played it again. She fumbled.

He pointed at the score. 'Come along,' he said and his fingers ran through a small improvisation back to the original bar.

'Why can't my fingers do that?' She banged them down on the notes.

'Come now! We are abusing this instrument! The Choral Union Evening is a serious occasion,' he said drily.

'If you run across the keyboard like that,' retorted Frances, 'how on earth will I run after you?'

'It would be most brazen of you if you did,' replied Walter, despite himself, and Frances laughed.

'Let's do it for the concert just like this. Please,' she said. 'It's much more fun,' and she looked up at him – hesitant, as though she were afraid he might rebuff her – and again, the trace of wistfulness in her voice and he could see the little dappled freckles on her skin and sense the buttery scent of warmed starch as she moved. Warnings shouted in his head and he looked away.

'Start again,' he said, not quite master of his voice. 'One, two, begin.'

They did not hear the back door latch nor Victor's quick, lithe step in the passage. They were not aware of him standing in the doorway watching them. They increased the tempo as they went, intent on the music, eyes on the score. When they had reached the end they sat a moment, in silence, sleeve to sleeve, side by side. Walter was about to speak, the beginnings of a word, but something made him turn, some instinct nudging at his back, and he saw Victor leaning against the jamb, his arms folded. A glance at his face, watching them, and he knew he was exposed. He stood, said evenly, 'Well, Miss Farborough, I think you have mastered it. We can try again another time.'

Frances inspected the music. 'I'll tell my father you've gone to the schools, if you like,' she said.

'Thank you.' Walter picked up his hat from the top of the piano, glanced at Victor. 'Good morning,' he said in a voice that was foreign in his own ears. And he went without another word but he paused in the passage and he heard Victor say, 'Poor old Brownley,' and Frances's terse rejoinder, 'Why "poor old Brownley"?' and he could hear her tapping the pages of the music together.

'I never suspected what purgatory it must be for him to sit next to you.' Victor laughed. 'I should think that Latin conjugations are not the only kind he'd like to teach you.'

'Whatever are you talking about?' Frances replied. 'If you're going to be tiresome, go away.'

'*Amo, amas, amat.* Is that the favourite among his conjugations? I must say, looking at him, it's very bold of him.'

'Don't be annoying!' Frances said hotly. 'I asked him to help with my piece, that's all.'

'I'm sure he was very willing.' Supercilious Victor.

'Don't be horrid, Victor.'

'Mr Brownley's quite a hero, if one considers him! Manly? Well! Athletic? Sadly, we must decline to comment. Charming? In the eyes of the ladies of this house, quite devastating!'

Frances must have picked up her music and thrown it at him for Walter heard a thud and then the sound of paper scattering across the floorboards.

'He'd have the devil of a job taming it!' Victor again, and laughing aloud.

There was a scuffle and then Victor spoke, teasingly, softly, 'And now?' as if he held her captive.

Having dared to eavesdrop, Walter could not walk away. There were small sounds then: the sigh of Frances's skirt, the heel of Victor's boot, a half chuckle in his throat. 'That's better.' Just a breath – and still he heard it. 'Come down to the river.'

'No.'

'You don't need to be afraid this time. I promise.' A pause. 'I'll be gone in a fortnight, Frances. Maybe for ever.'

A silence then. Walter walked away, not caring if his steps announced him.

If Victor had wanted to appropriate the riverbank, he was thwarted. It seemed that Benedict had chosen the site for his own trysts with Kobus's daughter for she was often seen in the early evenings, gathering kindling, loitering at the bank expectantly. Then, when Saturday came, Emily Farborough had sent Victor with another of her interminable orders to Nettletons in The Hoek and accepted an invitation on his behalf for an afternoon of tennis at their house. On Sunday, Walter had heard Father Charles ask Victor to accompany him to one of the farthest outstations so that, while they rode, they could discuss the letter that had arrived from the Native Affairs Commissioner in Grahamstown, proposing the possibility of a promotion to the Cape Colony's Representative's Office in Johannesburg. A reply must be drafted and a telegram sent. With relief, Walter saw Victor ride out on Hector, leading the way for Crispin and his uncle, but he turned from Frances when he saw her watching from the sewing-room window and went briskly into the church.

He had not been there long when she came through the door from the side porch with freshly laundered altar linen across her arm. She was humming to herself. A small, detached, repeating phrase. She raised her hand to her hair, adjusting the ribbon at her nape and, briefly, he saw the hidden outline of her arm within the blouse.

She had not seen him and she hurried down the aisle leading to the vestry door. Not realising it was locked – Walter had absent-mindedly turned the key and put it in his pocket – she leaned her weight against it and pushed. When it did not yield, she rattled the handle impatiently and kicked it with her boot.

Walter came up behind her and she turned with a startled exclamation of surprise. He took the key from his pocket and said, 'Let me rescue you – not to mention the toes of your boots which will not last long if so violently treated.'

He followed her into the vestry. 'Do you know,' she said,

'Miss Smythe is in one of her awful, gloomy humours and is singing hymns about sin and death and all those things.' She glanced back at him. 'It's enough to put one off living at all. And she seems to think it's good for my soul to run up and down to the church. It's the fifth time she's sent me on an errand here today.'

'A hundred journeys won't cure your soul if you're not inclined to have it mended,' he said. 'But' – with mock severity – 'kicking down the vestry door demands strict repentance.'

'I could kick more than the vestry door!' she said darkly.

She put the cloths in the drawer of the dresser. Bend, tuck, smooth. Bend, tuck, smooth. The small movements of her hands were neat and sure. He smiled to see so maternal a gesture and the straightness of her back and the mutiny of her hair escaping from its ribbon. It revealed the nape of her neck – so sudden, so unexpectedly tender. He gazed and then he turned away and went back to his abandoned notes. Nor did he glance up as she walked away and opened the church door. She did not go out. She stopped and turned and she called, her voice echoing in the nave, 'We have visitors. Mr Otto is here.'

Beyond the porch, drawn up in the yard, Walter could see Klaus Otto's transport wagon. He came down from the chancel and joined Frances, standing in the porch.

'Good morning, Mr Brownley,' said Klaus Otto, raising his hat.

Walter shook hands. 'Good morning, Mr Otto. Good morning, Ma'am.' He bowed to the young woman sitting on the seat beside the transport rider.

Walter could hear the pride in Klaus Otto's voice when he said, 'This is my wife, sir. We have come from Stutterheim. We are going to see the farm I have just bought and my wife will decide where we shall build our new house.'

Walter smiled up at the young woman. She was a girl, no older than Frances. She waited at his side, quiet in the shade of her white cloth bonnet, her hands resting in her lap. Walter could see, by the folds of her dress, that a child would soon be born.

Klaus Otto spoke then of the lands he had bought, the sheep he had raised, the timber he would cut for the roof and the floors. Great Klaus Otto, tall as a windmill, who had driven his wagon for years from King William's Town to Stutterheim, who could carry a calf in his arms, guide a team of sixteen, fell a yellowwood alone, was so solicitous, so tender to his wife, it seemed as if he were fearful she might slip away if he took his eyes from her and he glanced at her closely every now and then as if his words were for her and not for them.

'Will you come down to the house, Mr Otto?' Frances said. 'Would Mrs Otto care for tea? I am sure my mother would be glad to welcome you.'

Klaus Otto thanked her, but declined. He said, 'We have a long way to go before outspan.' He turned to Walter. 'I was asked to deliver this letter to Reverend Farborough,' he said. 'It was given to me by the trader up the Donsa. He said he'd been waiting for someone to pass and bring it down.' He handed an envelope to Walter.

Walter glanced at it and put it in his pocket. 'Mr Farborough is away today but I'll see he gets it,' he said.

Klaus Otto raised his whip in farewell. His wife inclined her head to Frances. Walter stood with his hat in his hands in the blue-green shade of the gum trees and watched the wagon as it started away: a word from Klaus Otto, a crack of the lash, the wail and creak of the wheels.

'How can such a lovely girl have wished to marry old Klaus Otto?' said Frances suddenly. 'I'm sure when I get married I shall choose a man who is handsome and witty and young and we shall live in a big stone house full of elegant things and go riding in a spider. I shan't trek about in a wagon looking for a place to build a mud bungalow with a reed ceiling and a grass roof.'

'Building a house is a good thing to do,' said Walter.

'Klaus Otto is really very ox-like,' observed Frances.

'Klaus Otto is newly married. He is a happy man.'

'I should never allow a suitor of mine to look at me so foolishly!'

'He may not be able to help himself,' said Walter and he settled his hat on his head with great care to avoid her eyes

116

and ensure that no hint of foolishness should be detected in his own face.

Frances walked away briskly, back to the sewing-room. Walter watched her go. Mr Plotz might well have smiled but Walter Brownley didn't. He went down to the lodge to write his sermon. He pulled his chair up to his table and looked about at the small white room. A dresser, a cupboard, a bed. There was something defeated about that bed. So narrow, so impressed with the loneliness of the curates that had gone before. A solitary place, a room like this. No one ever ventured near besides Nowasha to dust and clean and go away again. There was no companionship here but for the creatures that whispered between the loose plaster and the clay-brick walls. Living here, he might as well be one of the bagworms that Frances had once shown him, cocooned and unassailable within the armour of twiglets. Did bagworms ever turn to moths, he wondered, and fly free?

Until he had come to St Matthias, Walter had always valued his aloneness. He had always needed time, between his duties and his studies, his choir and companions, to smoke his pipe and read and think. These things had been his happiness. He had loved the quiet of his rooms at Canterbury. Now it seemed so distant, like a lost chime, like a summer scent he was unable to recapture.

He wished he could retreat, feel pavements beneath his feet, hear the sound of wheels on cobblestones. He must return to England. If he were generous, he would take Helmina Smythe with him and save her from herself. She would not prescribe – so haughtily – that a husband should be witty, handsome and young. She would not insist on an elegant stone house.

Walter leaned across the sill and stared out at the trackless veld beyond the mission grounds. One day this wasteland would triumph. Inexorably it would march in and reclaim this place. Listening, he could hear the students in the smithy tapping with their mallets, fashioning new basins and dishes and mugs. Beyond, in the forests that edged the river, he could hear a tinker barbet calling as it had for centuries, hidden in a deeper, darker shade. When the hammers of St

117

Matthias ceased to ring, it would be there still, striking at the sun.

When he had completed his work, Walter walked across to the house to deliver the trader's letter to Emily Farborough. He saw her prop it against a small vase of daisies on the mantelpiece. There it stood for the rest of the day. Innocent, unobtrusive, framed by the soft, yellow-centred blooms, its news secret under its seal.

Walter forgot about it. He went away and attended to a dozen different duties about the home-station. He took an extra catechism with the confirmation candidates, repaired a water-furrow that was leaking despite its being Sunday, chased a pig from the vegetable garden and wrote to the Colonial Under-Secretary, explaining – for the third time – the reason for the signatures on marriage certificates sometimes not tallying with the names in the register: Xhosa custom was an intricate thing. The Colonial Under-Secretary could be obtuse! A month at the mission station in charge of the register would do him the world of good!

At six o'clock he dragged on his cassock and hurried down to the church to take evensong. He was late – but vigilant Helmina had lighted the candles and laid his prayer-books open on the choir pew and was leading the students in a hymn in readiness.

And so the letter stood there and it was only when Father Charles had returned from the outstation and had had his dinner that it was inspected. Walter heard his slow tread on the path outside the curate's lodge and saw the lantern's beam strike up against the thatch of the long veranda. He opened the door and stood aside. 'Come in, sir,' he said.

Father Charles stepped into the room and took the offered seat. 'Ah, well, Brownley,' he said. 'You were right about Brompton. We should not have waited to hear from the Dean.'

Walter looked at him enquiringly.

'The letter brought by Mr Otto this morning.' He sighed. 'It was from the trader up the Donsa to say that he has heard reports from the natives that one of our ministers is acting strangely. The trader says – to cover himself, I expect – that it is rumour. His words, "the natives believe the priest has been bewitched. *Thakatha*'d." Apparently the station is deserted in the day. We shall have to help.'

'I'll go,' said Walter.

The old man said, 'Five, ten years ago, I wouldn't have heard of being left behind.'

'I know,' said Walter, 'but it is a very arduous journey. I had better take someone with me. Benedict and one of the mission workers.'

'Choose whoever you like.'

'I'll use the cart again. Can you spare the horses?'

'Victor will need Hector,' said Father Charles. 'It's unfortunate you cannot take him with you but he has to finish up in The Hoek this week before he leaves for Grahamstown Tuesday next and I know he's going into King William's Town with the magistrate tomorrow.'

Walter did not answer. He would rather have a missionful of Bromptons baying for his blood, than take Victor with him to Mbokothwe.

'I will deal with the school inspector for you, Brownley. I believe he'll be here on Thursday,' said Father Charles, rising. 'I think you should go at first light. Mrs Farborough will see to food and bedding.'

It was Crispin who asked if he could accompany Walter. Walter found him waiting on the veranda of the lodge half an hour later and Crispin said, 'I heard Dad tell Mother you were going to Mbokothwe.'

'Yes, Crispin,' said Walter. 'Early tomorrow.'

'May I come?'

Walter looked at him. 'Why, Crispin? It's a long journey and Mr Brompton may be ill. We might have to stay longer than expected.'

'Please, Mr Brownley,' said Crispin. 'I've always wanted to go beyond the Donsa . . .' He inclined his head and nudged at the step with the toe of his boot. 'It's wild country.' He spoke, half wistfully. 'I could shoot for the pot. Guinea-fowl or duck. You won't have much to eat without me.'

Walter considered, watching the eager face. 'If your father has no objections and your mother will reconsider the confiscation of your gun, I'd welcome a provider,' he said.

'Will you speak to my father?' said Crispin. 'If you asked, I think he'd let me.'

So Walter followed him back to the house and asked Father Charles. He said, putting his hand on Crispin's shoulder, 'He will be a good companion and he's undertaken to supply meat for the pot.'

Father Charles looked uncertain and then he said, 'Very well, lad. You shall take the mare.'

At first light they were gone. Walter drove the cart, Benedict beside him, Boggis in the traces. Crispin mounted the mare and tethered a mission horse to a leading-rein. As they started away, Walter saw Frances watching from the veranda. She waved and blew a kiss to Crispin and when they reached the drift and he looked back, he could see her still, sitting in the shadow of the old wistaria creeper that grew along the railings. He nudged the horses forward. The sky over Kaboosie mountain was turning pale – arum-white and gold.

Victor went to King William's Town soon after the cart left for Mbokothwe. He saddled Hector and trotted down to the house to say goodbye. Frances was out in the yard feeding the chickens. He reined in at the gate and watched her. She threw the grain, summoning the hens, and would not look up.

He called, 'What do you want from Town?'

'Why should I need anything?' She was dismissive.

He said – an afterthought – 'I might be sent straight on to Grahamstown. Perhaps I'll just ask Klaus Otto to bring Hector back and stay on and catch the first train out. There's no reason to wait.'

Her eyes flicked swiftly up to his. Then she looked away and said, 'Suit yourself,' with perfect composure.

'You can send on my clothes sometime.'

She shrugged. 'I'll tell Miss Smythe.'

Victor scanned her. This time the game was hers. She was playing with him, pretending not to care. But he knew her. He knew she was afraid he'd go and leave her there at St Matthias. Not come back. There was an escape for him. But not for her. Not without him. 'Tell Uncle Charles not to expect me before tomorrow afternoon, if at all. I'll send a message.'

She continued to feed the chickens, ignoring him.

'Goodbye then,' he said carelessly as he swung Hector round and sat back in the saddle as the horse sprang forward.

She would watch him go, fighting not to call him back: an equal challenge. He would not turn, goaded though he felt to see if she still stood there. That would vex her!

Or would it?

He could not be sure any more. Suddenly, the certainties evaded him. He had achieved, with ease, all that was expected of him, and yet some obscure disquiet remained. Success had always been assumed for him by others; his ability to impress far beyond his triumphs on cricket pitch and rugby field, far beyond his elegant essays and competent mathematics and the open admiration of the young ladies of Grahamstown, the hero-worship of new boys, competing to fag for him, to carry his boots, fold his rugger jersey, make his tea in the prefects' study. And on leaving school, the universal predictions of his 'brilliant future' hung like a sword above his head as did his mother's vanity and her fond incomprehension of his needs, as did Aunt Emily's aspirations, thrust on him because Crispin was unable to fulfil her hopes.

In compensation for usurping Crispin's place he had protected him, both at school and at home. In consequence, Crispin would die for him – a word, a gesture would suffice. It was another burden, heaped on all the other fulsome presumptions.

Only Frances knew the truth. She understood his fears too well – Victor, the hero, had cracks in his armour – and if, subconsciously, he had relied on her to shield him from discovery, such knowledge still remained a powerful weapon in her hand. It hadn't mattered until now. She was his. Devoted since he had first come to the mission. And yet, despite this, he had always known that Frances could match him, could lead as well as follow. And could also go. But the possibility of a usurper had not occurred to him before and the unlikeliness of his competitor left him suddenly exposed. The game must end. Swiftly. Before she changed her mind and slipped beyond his reach. He would not relinquish her – she was the constant, the only insurance against his own vulnerability: the memory of a cold nursery, empty of real affection, of the imaginary ghost of his father, blood-stained, bearing the body of O'Flaherty up the stairs at night, shouldering his way into his childhood room, listening for his hidden cry in the dead ear of his pillow. The spectre of that father followed him – deified by his mother – virtues entombed: ribbons, medals, ornamental swords.

It was imperative that he should be a hero too.

Only Frances knew that he might fail.

He dared not fail. He dared not lose her now.

He had told her that he might not return next day, knowing she'd scarcely believe him but if he stayed away until long after nightfall, her anxiety might be real. He had seen it before: an odd fear of separation, fed by a vigorous imagination, quite at odds with an otherwise rational nature. She would be repentant for having kept her distance, fiercely glad to have him back. The advantage would be his and he would take it.

The manner in which he would have liked to secure her – and he indulged himself with improbable imaginings – occupied his mind on the long ride to King William's Town. A restless need he understood well enough obsessed him. Nor was his desire stirred by some half-known, adolescent yearning: Victor's initiation into manhood had been swift and his recall of it spurred his need unbearably.

The wheelwright's daughter had been priestess in the rite. Sloe-eyed, small-hipped, a world-weariness in the way she gazed, an odd innocence in her unashamed sensuality, Victor had noticed her at once on his return to St Matthias during the last Christmas holidays. And she had noticed him. A bargain had been struck without words. She had waylaid him one day when he'd been hunting up beyond the mission.

A trysting-place was easy to arrange. Victor had left his room by the window each night and met her in the wagon shed. The meetings had been brief, closed away in the dark where he could not see her face for shadows nor look into her eyes. Within a fortnight of their meeting, her small demands had become a little strident and her father had begun to suspect them. Victor had not known how to retreat and he'd had cause to thank Sonwabo Pumani for securing his escape: when the wheelwright had struck Sonwabo on the head with a mallet for insolence, his Uncle Charles had told him to pack his mule-cart, take his family and go.

Relieved, Victor had bought her a trinket as a token at Nettleton's when he'd taken Sonwabo to the doctor to have his head stitched. She had held it in both hands and strung it slowly about her neck and tucked it into the bosom of her dress and looked at him from the corners of her eyes, sideways and down, and a small, rueful twist about her mouth as if she had something to say but did not know the words. That was all, and he had turned away and gone off with his rod to fish with Crispin and Benedict. When he'd returned from the river, she'd been gone. He could forget her, put her away before she might demand anything beyond their brief transaction. It was not long before he had forgotten her name.

But he recalled the moments with her often. And that recall preyed on him relentlessly. The power of it. The ascendancy. Yet that ascendancy – that fierce, brief ascendancy – was far from all that he wished of Frances. The bond that they had forged in innocence throughout their childhood must be forged again. Made indissoluble.

Chapter Eight

Crispin was the only one not filled with foreboding on the road to Mbokothwe. He looked around him with the greatest interest, rode off here and there to explore. Once he flushed a francolin from the grass, later a guinea-fowl. He shot them both and brought them to Walter and Benedict in the cart. 'Good eating,' he said with satisfaction.

Sun-shadow raced across the plains and the forests were dredged with blue against the shoulders of the Amatolas. The rivers were low, stony at the fords. Walter measured in his mind each step to Mbokothwe, wishing he were in retreat.

Perhaps his own preoccupation had communicated itself to Benedict, for he too sat silent, watching the sky. 'How far?' he said as the third afternoon drew to a close.

'We'll be there before dark.'

And indeed they began the long climb towards the mission as the last of the afternoon light was laid down across the hills. Walter pointed to the little church rising from the slope with the bell beside it. And suddenly the sun dipped, and as they pulled into the yard the shade was deep and blue about them.

They sat a moment and looked around. Walter said nothing of the strange watchfulness he had experienced when he had first come to Mbokothwe but both Benedict and Crispin seemed apprehensive. Boggis stamped his feet and turned his head as if reproaching Walter for bringing him back to the cold hillside without the comfort of a stable.

Walter climbed down from the cart and crossed the yard to the church. Benedict and Crispin followed, walking close together. The door stood open and dust and leaves were shored up against the peeling planks. A pig foraged in the aisle. It turned to them, furtive and wary, not with the curiosity of a farm animal diverted from the absorption of feeding, but with the cunning of the feral. They gazed at it distrustfully. The wind tapped the loose lead strips of a window against a pane. The chinks of glass had fallen in. They lay in confusion on the floor. The pig raised its snout, probing at the air.

The deterioration in so short a time alarmed Walter. Where was Brompton? What had happened? Crispin went towards the pig to drive it away but it bunched and stood its ground and he retreated. 'Leave it,' said Walter and led them out. They returned to the horses and unharnessed them. Walter took Boggis to the trough and looked up at the bare facade of the church. It stood bleak and still on that wind-swept hill, its drunken bell suspended between two posts like a felon on a gibbet.

Leaving Benedict to attend to the horses, Walter went down to the house. Crispin followed behind him, keeping close. They came to the door – the same behind which Brompton had seemed to crouch, listening – and Walter knocked. There was no reply. He turned the handle. The door swung open. The room was empty.

And yet, it had none of the neglect of the church, none of the desolation. The floor had been swept, the bed was made, the grate had been cleaned and the cloth on the table was not unlaundered. With its icons, it remained a little shrine, stead-fast before the forces ranged against it. Crispin glanced at Walter, moved nearer to him. 'It's like my mother's writing room,' he said, almost whispering, as if he might be heard.

'No one here.' Walter was brisk. 'I think we should feed the horses and put them in the kraal behind the church. The sack of fodder is in the back of the cart.' He took out his pipe and filled it. 'There is a small guest hut just below the edge of the hill. We'll try and make ourselves comfortable there, al-though you might have to chase out the rats. Perhaps you and Benedict could collect some firewood – we should cook that guinea-fowl you shot. I'll be with you in a moment.'

Crispin went with relief, trotting up towards Benedict standing with the horses. Walter found his matches, struck one against the iron grate and lit his pipe. The furniture about the little room seemed to stare back at him, the empty chair to hold a presence he could not dismiss. The musical-box stood on the shelf. Beside it, the small stuffed lark. Walter stepped up to the jar under which it perched, poised for per-petual song.

He left the house and went further down the path and

around the back. Where was Pusey? He called. There was no reply. He knocked at the door of a hut. The thatch sagged in over the lintel. The walls were stained, moulded up out of the earth. There was no response to his knocking but he could not bring himself to try the door.

He retreated to the guest hut on the slope below the yard. Benedict was laying the fire on the earth outside, making it with care from tinder and bits of thorn brush gathered from the nearby bushes. Crispin was cleaning the bird. He secured it on a skewer of wood and balanced it over the flame. Walter unpacked the tea things and a kettle and dragged a log near to the hearth to use as a seat. They gathered round the flame, moving closer as dusk deepened into dark. They went together to see that the horses were secure for the night and Walter told them stories about Canterbury as they drank their tea, but his words trailed off every now and then as if he were listening and the place and time seemed too distant to recall. They sat together, alert to the sounds of the night beyond the circle of light cast by their fire.

'I do not like it here,' said Benedict, taking a twig and stirring up the embers. 'There are unhappy shades. Omens.' He drew his jacket closer.

'A good Christian lad like you?' Walter's tone was light, without conviction.

'There are things that none of us can explain,' said Benedict. 'Not even Father Charles.'

A small chill wind sent them in to their hut long before they felt the need to sleep. Walter suggested an evening prayer but the words hung about them, intruding on their separate preoccupations. It was a long time before they slept.

Much later, Walter awoke, sweating. He pushed his coat back and listened. Something had roused him. Wind was plucking at the roof, plaintive and distant. He lay in darkness so deep he could not distinguish any feature in the room. He sat up and listened.

He knew the hollowness of nights where imaginings ride the blood. Taps and knocks and little rustlings invade the mind until it is understood that this is all inside the head and that the outer silence is deep as an abyss. Walter felt for his

126

boots. He pulled them on and moved cautiously towards the door. He opened it and the night came in, soft with moonlight, bleeding pale shafts across the ridges and the valleys.

The sound again. Walter heard it clearly. He knew then what it was. The musical-box. The tune playing over and over . . . 'Abide with me, fast falls the eventide. The darkness deepens, Lord with me abide.'

That sound. On and on. That sound, faltering and stumbling. He could feel the sweat standing on his forehead, the cold lance of fear at the nape of his neck. He went out and walked towards Brompton's house. He could hear the faint shuffle of the gravel under his feet.

The door stood ajar and the light inside was faint. The notes floated out into the night. Walter hesitated and then he stepped firmly towards the door and pushed it so that it swung open and the light fell out across the threshold. The room was empty but the lid of the musical-box was raised to reveal the velvet plush inside.

'Brompton?' Walter heard the tremor in his voice. It hung in the air, discordant, fading like the mechanical notes. He turned swiftly, defensively, for there was a soft tread on the path behind him. But it was Crispin. His face was pale, taut in the moonlight.

'I heard music. What is playing?' Crispin looked towards the house. 'Is he there?'

'No. No one is there.'

The notes were failing. The box needed winding. Fading, fading. It was silent. Walter and Crispin stood waiting. Someone would come. They would come to start it again. Someone would come.

Walter glanced at Crispin. He put his hand on Crispin's arm in reassurance for Crispin's lip was sweating, his eyes intent. His tongue flicked across the edge of his teeth and he breathed shallowly.

'Can you hear anything?' Walter said softly.

Imperceptibly Crispin shook his head.

Many minutes they stood, many minutes at that silent doorway and then Walter took the lamp and went outside and the shaft wavered round like the beacon of a lighthouse, running over the grass and the bush at the edge of the clearing, but the beam caught no flash of vigilant eyes. 'Come, Crispin,' he said and he closed the door and used the lamp to light them back to the guest hut.

Benedict sat up as they came in, startled by the beam.

'Sleep, boys,' said Walter. 'I will read a little.' And he took his pocket-Bible from his jacket and opened it.

It was Crispin who said, 'Read to us, Mr Brownley.'

So Walter read, and once or twice he looked up at the faces – at Benedict half crouched with his arms linked about his knees and at Crispin, the light on his hair.

> Behold I have refined thee but not with silver;
> I have chosen thee in the furnace of affliction . . .

Walter did not know why he had chosen that passage from Isaiah. He had read randomly: '. . .the furnace of affliction.' Words forged in that small, vermin-infested room at Mbokothwe. And Crispin, head resting on his arm, had watched him: the still, grave attention of his shadowed face.

As Walter lowered the lamp and extinguished the flame he heard the musical-box again, far off and swift, newly wound, the notes racing with each other, steadying, then marching, softly in the night air.

Frances resisted going up to the gate before tea and gazing along the road, looking for Victor. She went about her duties at the mission, helping her father with numerous tasks, staying close to him as if he were some insurance against events. By four o'clock she had crossed the road three times going from school to church to boarding-house, but she had not glanced off towards The Hoek, straining for the sound of hooves.

Her vague impatience for Victor's return became anxiety when her mother said, 'I wonder why Victor isn't back yet? Put aside a plate of sandwiches for him, Frances. I hope Hector hasn't gone lame. He has been ridden so much of late.' And the afternoon passed and the shadows were long where the gum trees laid them down on the open ground behind the church, and still he hadn't come.

Dusk was falling and her parents walked across for evensong. Helmina called for her to hurry and she followed, dragging on her cape and dropping her prayer-book in the dust. She glanced restlessly towards the stables but the stalls were empty. She sat in the church near Helmina and she felt a small, cold wind creeping between the pews. She hardly sang the opening hymn for she was listening for the gate, for Hector's snort, for a greeting from someone in the yard. The voices of the students filled the church and closed her in:

> And some are pressed with worldly care
> And some are tried with sinful doubt
> And some such grievous passions bear
> That only Thou canst tear them out.

God could see her. He could see what she was hiding in her heart. Why had that hymn been chosen for this evening's benediction if He didn't know? He knew her. He knew her well. He knew, too, that it was her fault that Victor had gone so suddenly. She had been gruff with him, avoided him, made excuses not to meet him, annoyed him. Led him on and then retreated from him. She had sinned by going to the river, knowing he was there, defiant at Helmina Smythe's instructions, stung by her words of reproof.

The sin of pride: that was hers. And some restlessness inside her that wished to bait him, to cause in him – and in herself – that strange and powerful affliction that she'd witnessed.

Miss Smythe had once said, inadvertently blurting out the words, 'The passions of men are easily provoked and can cause them the greatest distress and harm, Frances. Ensure that you are never a cause of their sudden arousal, for that is your sin rather than theirs and any consequences would be your fault entirely,' and her face had been so flushed when she had spoken that Frances had wanted to laugh. But she had not understood. Not until the moment at the river.

Had she angered him? Had she harmed him? Had she really distressed him? Perhaps he had gone and Klaus Otto would come in the morning with a letter. 'Dear Frances, I have decided to go after all. Cheerio and good luck . . .' And then what? She would be abandoned here in this place with no hope of escape. She had never imagined a prolonged separation from Victor. Its impossibility was implicit in both their lives. And yet, perhaps his pride would not permit him to retrieve her after this. She would become like Helmina, a little bird, empty of blood, with a heart beating so faintly but so inexorably, without expectation, without life. A punishment, indeed.

She pushed the small, cold fear aside, recalled hastily her private repertoire of day-dreams about Victor. Victor the hero, Frances the heroine. Foolish fantasy beyond possibility, adaptations from the few romances she had read covertly in Helmina's room when no one had been around. She had thought sometimes – half dreaming, half conscious – of what it would be like to marry Victor. She ventured no further than the wedding ceremony: Victor in a kind of ancient, red-coated, military splendour, medalled – like the picture of his father – and Walter Brownley taking the service. But somehow the dream stuck at the chancel steps, for no matter how she insisted, Walter Brownley would not conduct the marriage as she wished and when she saw him standing there in his vestments, the church empty, the guests gone, the look on his face was designed to make her tear off her veil in shame.

The choir was singing again and Frances fumbled for her hymn book, waiting out five verses silently, ignoring Helmina's frown and sidelong glances. The notes faded and her father turned from the altar and gave the benediction. He spoke in Xhosa and his voice rose up around the church. Frances said, 'Please, dear God, bring Victor now.' And she promised all kinds of penances in payment for his safe return, all kinds of small mortifications. Anything to expiate the possibility of retribution. But there was still no sound of hooves and all she could hear was the shuffle of the congregation.

Evensong was over and he did not come. Supper was served and still he did not come. Frances read Strickland's Queens to her mother and Helmina after tea, alert to the slightest sound from beyond the curtained windows.

Father Charles opened the Bible at nine and read. He, too,

was listening. 'I am sure that something has kept Victor in Town and there is a perfectly sound explanation,' he said, looking over at his wife.

'I do prefer it when we're all at home,' said Emily bleakly. 'Thank the Lord the weather is fine. Put a light in the window, Frances, although I expect he will be here in the morning. He may have stayed over at Crewe's in Debe Nek. Perhaps Hector has dropped a shoe.'

And so they went to bed.

Frances lay under the covers, her eyes open. There was a full moon and the light drifted in across the floorboards. The wind was high. The gum tree in the backyard by the fence tossed and raced. She woke and slept and woke again. Imaginings at night: the slow march of minutes. All the mythologies of her childhood arose. *Thikoloshe* the mannikin, *Chanti* the water snake, haunter of pools, denizen of bushed ravines. The shades of warriors walked again, silent companies on deserted paths where once they lay in ambush. Jackals. Leopards.

Frances rose from her bed and went softly from her room. She tiptoed past Helmina's door and crept to the kitchen. She took a mug of water from the pitcher on the table, held the familiar object, wishing it to banish the spectres, to still the slow, strong beat of her heart. She opened the back door and stood on the porch. The loft ladder leaning against the wall sent a crucifix of shadow lancing across the whitewash. Pewter-grey and blue, the night. The stars were locked away behind cloud but the moon rode pale in a pool of sky.

She walked barefoot along the veranda that ran around the side of the house. The light still glowed unextinguished on the window-sill of the living-room, the flame steady in the glass. She went down the steps and along the path towards the privy, treading carefully for night adders sometimes lay in the warm gravel. She bent and took a sprig of mint from the place by the water-furrow where it grew in abundance and ate a small, spiky leaf. She left the door open and looked out across the grass and the low droop of banksias that spread over a fallen tree. Far away a kraal-dog barked, a lone cry, a howl to the moon.

So deep a silence, so still the clear, long sweep of Kaboosie mountain, set against the eastern clouds. She went out and stood by the gate, gazing towards the church and stables, too hunched in gloom to distinguish in the trees.

He must be somewhere there, out in the dark. Hurt, perhaps. Thrown from the horse, head dashed against a stone. Calling and no one to hear him. A long time she waited, the wind in her face, warm here in hollows, cool there. It lifted her cape, wound her nightdress about her bare legs.

She went back to the house and she opened the door to Victor's room. The curtains were undrawn, letting in the moon's light. A ghostly grey, without colour, each object distinct. His tennis racket stood in a corner, his second pair of riding boots by the wardrobe, a packet of cigarette papers lay on the table. Frances went to the cupboard. Had he taken anything? Had he really gone? She opened it soundlessly. His shirts and jackets hung there still. She put her face close to them, breathed them, touching the empty arms a moment, listening all the time. But there was only the wind scattering dust across the yard, jerking at the shutters fastened back against the walls. Please, God, send him now . . . send him now. She stood at the window. Waiting. Waiting, her head resting against the frame, staring out into the dark.

Quietly he came. No hoofbeats, no sound of his approach to rouse her from her vigil. She did not hear him fasten the kitchen latch, remove his boots in the scullery nor walk softly down the passage to his room. It was only as he closed his door that she was startled into wakefulness.

Fear and imaginings had taken Frances's restraint. The denizens dissolved, the painful knot of fright. No spectre, this. No restless shade. She went to him and he reached for her. His hands were cold, roughened by the wind, his shirt glimmered pale. 'Where were you?' she faltered.

His face sought the warmth of her neck. He buried it in her hair. 'I thought I saw my father in a donga at Rabula.' His breath touched her ear, lingered there. 'Full of blood, ghastly white,' he said. 'I rode so hard, Hector went lame. I had to lead him. Oh God' – the last resistance in abeyance – 'hold me, Frances.'

And so the secrets of the heart are forged in prosaic places. Small echoes, under-harmonies, dyadic notes, haunt like dust motes the most familiar rooms, lie undiscovered in the shadow of a wall.

The lamp still burned to light a traveller home. The trees still breathed outside the cottered panes of Victor's room and far away a dog still barked, lonely in its homage to the moon.

Such a day, such a bergwind blowing, hurling itself around the yard at Mbokothwe! A wind with the breath of inland plains, of mountainsides and desolate ravines. It brought no sound from distant homesteads, no cry of goats, no voice of cattle in fallow lands. It blew steadily from the hinterland.

Walter heard it and battened the door of the hut against it as he went out, leaving Benedict and Crispin asleep. He walked up the path towards Brompton's house. His examination of it the evening before had been cursory. Perhaps there was some sign, some clue that he had overlooked, something to be gleaned. He reached the door of the house, put out his hand tentatively. He paused at the threshold, looking about. The musical-box stood in its customary place. It was closed. He could detect the mark of fingerprints, dulling the smooth, polished patina of its lid.

He stepped into the bedroom alcove and went to the cupboard. There, in ordered, serried rows, were Hubert Brompton's shirts, his well-starched cleric's collars, jacket, overcoat and sun helmet. Walter could have done an inventory at a glance. And then he stopped. An empty ammunition box lay at the back of the cupboard. An odd, discarded bullet had rolled into a corner. He picked them up and looked at them. There was no gun in the house. Brompton must have taken it with him. He bent and searched beneath the bed. Dust lay in small wreaths against the corner. He ran his eye along the edge where the thatch and the top of the wall met, forming an uneven shelf no more than six inches wide. It appeared to be empty but, intuitively, he brought a chair from the living-room and stood on it, examining the ledge.

There, above the cupboard and thrown into gloom by the shadow of the door, was a small disturbance of the thatch: a lumpiness as if a rat had burrowed in between the grass stems. He took the chair closer and reached up, searching hesitantly with his fingers. Wedged in and cunningly flattened between the layers of grass, was a piece of cloth. Carefully Walter tugged at it, easing it out. The hidden cloth was wrapped around a number of objects. He could feel them through the weave. He pulled at the parcel but it stuck and he took his knife from his pocket and pried at the thatch.

When he had freed it, Walter lifted down his discovery and examined it. It was a flour bag, knotted with string. Walter cut the fastening and emptied the contents onto the floor. A collection of strong-smelling items tumbled out. Walter drew back, startled. There was a small cap made of animal fur, a double string of white beads, a flat container of pale ointment that looked like river clay, a snake skin, a collection of leaves, and a lump of bulb or root or animal fat which had begun to decompose, covering the bag with its sticky oozings.

He stood, repelled, his breath quick in his chest. Then he bent and looked at the strange objects again, impatient with himself. It was ludicrous to be standing there with these primitive amulets crouching at the toe of his boot while the Queen, garlanded with roses, watched balefully from the wall. She seemed to catch his eye and he laughed.

He eased his cleric's collar – his own insurance against magic – and looked distrustfully about the room. Why would Brompton have secreted such twilight objects in his roof? What was the purpose of them? The smell of the bag was pungent and he took out his handkerchief and blew his nose. Gingerly, he shuffled the amulets into the bag. No, he would not retreat into parlour-games with Lucifer. Such notions had long been dismissed from his theology. He would not be daunted by potions and spells, just as his own creation, Plotz, would not be defeated by the green lion. Logic. Reason. Rationality. These were still at his command.

He pushed the ammunition box back into the cupboard and latched the door. Its long mirror reflected here and there the angles of the room. Secret watchers leaning in. And far beyond the window, a hill – a dark, bushed slope, ablaze with aloes in the morning light. Crispin and Benedict appeared in the doorway.

'What is it?' said Crispin, looking at Walter's face. 'Is something wrong?'

Walter picked up the flour bag and held it out. 'Some accoutrements,' he said. 'Ritual or magical or necromantic. I found them hidden in the thatch.'

'Who put them there?' asked Crispin, bending and then withdrawing from the odour clinging to the cloth.

Walter shook his head. 'One of them. Brompton or Pusey. I'm damned if I know what game they've been playing.'

He turned away and walked down the front steps into the yard. He laid the bag in the shade of a bush growing by the wall of the house. 'Saddle up,' he said. 'It's time to look for both of them.'

He hurried towards the kraal where the horses stood together. Seeing him, Boggis came towards him, thrusting his head over the rough poles that blocked the entrance. Such a reassurance in the feel of Boggis's nose, the soft blowing of his nostrils as he searched Walter's jacket.

He fetched the tack from the shed and when he had saddled Boggis, he mounted him and waited by the gate for Benedict and Crispin to follow. He looked about the yard, searching with his eyes, examining the buildings and the edges of the bush pushing up to the lip of the slope. And he felt, suddenly, as if his own scrutiny was met with scrutiny in turn. 'Brompton?' he said involuntarily. 'Pusey?' Nothing stirred but the rope of the bell tapping against the struts of its frame.

'Come along, lads,' he called, leading briskly through the gate and out into the mission lands. Alert to every movement, every shifting shadow, they searched the garden, the silent, stony hillside below the church where boulders shrugged off layered skins of rock. And as they searched, it seemed to Walter – despite himself – as if they were being stalked by some intelligence, tuned to touch their instincts in a way they could not grasp: they rode together, closely and in silence, listening.

The buildings, the gardens, revealed nothing. They went on, out onto the hillsides that stretched up towards a bushed ravine. Well beyond the mission fence they encountered a group of herders with their cattle. Young heathen men, they glanced up warily at their approach. Walter reined in and Benedict spoke to them. A small silence trailed the formal greetings.

Benedict asked if they knew the whereabouts of the *mfundisi* from the mission. The twitch of a shoulder cloth, the probing of the tip of a herding stick at the sand. Perhaps. The remark was given reluctantly. One of the herders spoke then. They were not mission people, he said. They were red. The speaker glanced at Benedict directly. A faint disdain. Did they go to the mission? Rhetorical. He paused for effect. No, they did not! The mission was not of interest to them. He looked at Benedict and Crispin, as if challenging them to contradict him. Indeed, he conceded, he had seen the white *mfundisi*. Fleetingly, Walter envisaged an exchange between this young man and Brompton. The futility for both. The great, unfathomable divide.

The white man, the herder said, the one with four eyes, stayed up on the hill in his church. That is where he stayed, night and day. What the *mfundisi* did was his affair. They had their own business to take care of.

Walter asked about Pusey. Benedict translated.

Pusey? The name hovered there. The absurdity of it. Yes, they knew about the servant. He was not their concern. He came from another place. Every man knows that it is not wise to talk to strangers. In speaking you might give them something with which to trap you. The hearts of men are full of thoughts of witchcraft. That place where the mission was built was full of omens. Were there not the signs for all to see?

Walter sighed. He said, 'We, too, can feel the omens. Indeed, we have heard strange noises in the night and we are anxious to return home as soon as we are able. But we may not leave without the *mfundisi*. We are afraid that something has happened to him for he has taken nothing. A man does not make a journey without his clothes. We have come to fetch him. We wish to pay his servant off, to close the house and go.'

Walter glanced at Benedict as he translated, sitting rigid on the horse, rapping out the words without inflection.

136

Then Crispin spoke in quiet, faultless Xhosa and Walter caught the quick glance of appraisal that passed between the herders. He said, 'If you were looking for a man in these parts, one who has gone away because of the burden in his heart, where would you look?'

'This is an empty place' – the reply was cautious – 'but if it was my concern, I should look where a man can shelter.' The herder's gaze encompassed the grazing-lands, the sparse hillsides, drifted up towards the bushed ravine. 'It is said that there are caves.'

That was the answer. Given obliquely. The herder drew his snuff container from his belt and took a pinch. He sneezed. It was a dismissal.

Walter thanked him and touched the brim of his hat. Countering the small contempt for Benedict that he had witnessed earlier, he said, 'Lead on, Benedict.' Benedict swung his horse, raised his hand solemnly to the herders and rode ahead.

'*Imihlola*,' Crispin said. 'Omens.'

Chapter Nine

The paths winding up through the ravine among the undergrowth of bracken, ferns and fallen logs were ill-frequented,
used more by animals than men. Still, the evidence of men
was there: at the margins were places where brushwood had
been collected or where a woodcutter's axe had struck the
limbs from trees.

Walter, Benedict and Crispin stopped and surveyed the bush
rising before them. In this forest, beyond the boundaries of the
sunlight, beyond where the more garrulous birds plied back and
forth, there was a brooding that was more than just the absence
of light, more than the sudden, startled flick of retreating wings,
the cryptic flight of moths from trunk to trunk.

They tethered the horses at the forest's edge and Walter
said to Crispin, 'You and Benedict had better lead. If there
are tracks you'll find them more easily than I.' Crispin hesitated, then he pushed his way in among the undergrowth.
Walter paused, shrinking momentarily from the darkness of
that bush. He had heard of forests such as this – of voices, of
strange uprootings, of unknown spoor, of caves haunted by
bats and of places where pythons – heralded by the sour,
ancestral smell of curdled milk – lay among the rocks. Here,
indeed, would be the shades of warriors, the last retreating
armies of the Ngcayecibi War, hunted down, killed, spears
defiant, daring still to parry. Spear to gun: no match for the
distant death of bullets.

The path that led into the undergrowth was only visible
when the wind touched the thickly shingled leaves, showing
briefly where secret feet might have passed. Crispin chose this
path, going ahead, leading them up a steep incline strewn
with tall, lichen-covered boulders. The great, soaring trunks
of ancient trees leant in above them, the distant crowns spiralled out against the morning blue of the sky.

Crispin led them further and further, Benedict at his heel.
Walter could feel the sweat, born of apprehension, crawling
across his chest and down his arms. Nothing stirred. Nothing

but small, unobtrusive things. Here, even the most familiar seemed furtive and wary, as if offering warning against intrusion. Gnats danced in the empty spaces between the leaves, copulating flies clung to bark, a long-horned beetle droned clumsily through the undergrowth.

Suddenly the path widened and there before them was a hole – not a game-trap – but a depression in the ground, overlaid with moss. Near it stood a small cairn of stones. Walter turned to Crispin and Benedict. 'What is it?'

'An *isivivane* cairn and a confessional,' said Crispin softly. He pointed to the hollow in the earth. 'This is where people come to tell their secrets to the shades.'

Walter looked across at him, Benedict beside him, staring down into the mossy bowl, linked in some private meditation. It was a sanctuary, there in the green cathedral gloom, a place where men might go and so confess the burdens of their hearts, relieve the leanings of the spirits on their shoulders which made them bent and which disturbed their dreams. He felt a fleeting moment of reprieve, as real as any he had known in any church. He gazed at the place, smelt the rich, soft scent of leaf-mould and then he turned away to lead the others further into the trees but neither Benedict nor Crispin followed. He stopped to beckon them on but they stood beside the cairn and each had taken up a stone. He heard them speak – a soft incantation – as they laid their offerings on the mound.

Then Benedict came towards him and scanned the forest, searching for the hidden paths. 'This way,' he said.

As Walter started after him, he glanced back and saw Crispin still standing by the cairn. Then, head bent, Crispin turned away from it and trotted up to join them.

Benedict pushed his way through the sheltering leaves, Walter and Crispin walking a pace or two behind. He led them across slopes and through hollows and down the length of shadowy ravines. They seemed to walk for hours, picking their way where the ground was damp and boggy or where stones lay loose and treacherous. The silence deepened and the light was locked away by crowding branches. Shadows hung suspended in among the trees. A parapet of krantzes rose ahead of them. Water oozed from the rockface, streaking it with jade and orange slime. They paused to catch their breath and there – closer than Walter had ever heard its note – the tinker barbet called, a secret harbinger among the boughs. He followed Crispin's gaze as he sought the bird in the canopy above. Then there was a sudden stillness, a breathlessness. Benedict shifted uneasily.

Walter said – remembering the empty box of ammunition on the cupboard floor – and his undertone seemed loud among them, 'I will lead now. Follow at least thirty paces behind.' Crispin began to object but Walter touched his arm reassuringly and put a finger to his lips. If Brompton was here – and Walter could sense it – he must be close for the forest pressed up against a krantz and high above, two hundred feet or more, was the empty, windy brow of the ridge.

Walter went on, walking with difficulty over a fretwork of branches which had long fallen to the ground. Cautiously he trod, alert to the sound of Crispin and Benedict's steps some way behind him. Ten minutes, fifteen. Half an hour and still the silence pressed in about him. He skirted a granite boulder thrusting up through the vegetation, loosed from its moorings on the cliff high above. A shot exploded into the leaves beyond him.

Walter threw himself to the ground.

The report echoed and echoed, reverberating back and forth among the rocks, ringing in his ears. He raised his head slightly and he called. 'Brompton!'

Brompton . . . Brompton . . . Brompton: a sardonic echo mocking in the trees.

Another shot, fired wildly, up into the air. Walter heard the quick tear of leaves far above his head. Silence was a long time coming. A leaf spiralled down, turning gently.

Listening intently, Walter heard muted sounds some way off, saw the shadow of a shelter in the cliff-face.

'Brompton?' Tentatively. Still the silence.

Walter sat up, waited a moment. 'Brompton. This is Walter Brownley from St Matthias. I have come to talk to you.' He listened. There – the sound again – like the scratch of metal on stone. Brompton was ready with his gun.

'The Dean has sent me,' Walter called out.

The Dean . . .The Dean . . .The Dean. Softer still, a whisper among bracken.

'We will go to Grahamstown.' Another sound, like a grunt. Walter spoke again, louder. 'Sunday Service at St Michael and St George.'

The reloading of the weapon. He could hear it. Click, click, click.

Walter leaned against the boulder, peering back along the path. He could see Crispin and Benedict, crouched near a log. He indicated that they should remain where they were. The sweat clung to him like oil. He wiped his sleeve across his brow and looked up at the dense, tangled web of branches above him. So far the sky, so far, so distant beyond the net of leaves. Dear God, what do I do now?

Walter knew he was taking a chance. He knew he might unleash a volley of angry shots. He had no choice but to try. He drew himself into the lee of the rock and he began to sing.

Softly he sang, tentatively at first. 'Abide with me, fast falls the eventide; The darkness deepens, Lord, with me abide.'

Silence. No shot, no sound.

More confidently he continued, 'When other helpers fail and comforts flee, Help of the helpless, O abide with me . . .' He had never really heeded the words of the hymn before. He'd sung it first as a choirboy at St Paul's School when he was twelve. Since then the tune had always conjured up the great shadowy magnificence of the Cathedral's dome, incense at Benediction; or Daisy's parish church, the Misses Parsons, the ruddy-cheeked lads in the choir, the smell of damp shoes and musty umbrellas in the porch and the rain – the interminable rain – soft-drenching on gardens and the may hedge beside Daisy's gate, silvered and bent with drops. He could not have imagined that he might use it as the lure for a madman nor sing it in this wild ravine, among these strange primeval rocks, closed into a green-cavern gloom, making supplication – on his own account – with every word. What was he doing here? What recklessness had brought him to this place? What absurd and futile vocation?

There was neither shot nor movement. He continued to sing through two verses, three, four. How strangely his voice faltered. How strangely the notes leant against each other:

141

I fear no foe with Thee at hand to bless,
Ills have no weight and tears no bitterness:
Where is death's sting? Where, grave, thy victory?
I triumph still if Thou abide with me.

Soundlessly Benedict and Crispin eased their way forward,
sinking down beside him as they reached the rock. Together
they sang the hymn again. Once, twice, standing side by side:
such solemn words and Crispin's face drained and still.

As the last harmony faded, they heard a sound: a sob
wrenched out and suppressed, a cry choked into silence.
Walter stood then and walked firmly towards the cleft in the
rock.

There are things to shake Faith at its core, that turn it to
anger or to fear, that make it flame or die in the heart of a
man. There are things that precipitate a glimpse of the void:
implacably dark and still. And so it was when Walter stood
and gazed at Hubert Brompton, crouched on the earth as if
rapacious insects had lapped his blood, the gun discarded at
his side. The eyes looked up, stared a moment into his. It was
as if some small, furtive creature was captive in the skull,
detached from the thing that sheltered it.

Walter recoiled, steadied himself. 'Brompton? It's Walter
Brownley. I have come to take you home.' Slowly he squatted
before him – looking all the while into the terrible face – and
slid the gun away out of reach. Then he said, hardly raising
his voice, 'Benedict? Crispin? You can come now.'

They came, hastening, their feet slipping on the fallen
branches and the ooze among the leaf-mould. The light was
shut away briefly as they stood across the mouth of the shelter
and Walter said, without turning his head, 'Take the
weapon.' Crispin picked it up. Walter extended his hand to
Brompton, 'Do you know me?'

Brompton did not move. The still, uncomprehending face
was turned to him, the skin seemed scaled like a reptile's,
crepuscular and pale as parchment.

'Come.' Walter touched the shoulder.

Brompton's mouth moved. It opened and it closed. It was
as if his tongue too had been eaten away by the thing that

142

sheltered in his skull. No words came. No sound but a hollow hissing of air. Walter reached for his hand, gripped it. As Brompton swayed towards him, the smell of putrescence assailed him. He could feel the emaciation, the brittleness of the fingers in his palm as if, in life, Brompton had begun to decompose. Nausea flooded him but he fought it down. Benedict crouched beside him and together they lifted Brompton out of the shelter. Walter looked over at Crispin, indicating that he should take the gun and lead the way. Crispin's face was ashen. His jaw, clenched though it was, shook perceptibly: a tremor at the curve below the ear. 'Take us out, lad,' said Walter quietly. 'Easy now, we will have to carry him.'

Supported on either side by Walter and Benedict, propped in their strong grip, Brompton's legs seemed to propel him in a strange, disjointed momentum of their own, quite at odds with the rest of him. He was an exhausting burden. Through hours, until the sun stood way past its zenith, they bore him from the forest, their feet tearing at the undergrowth, their breath scouring their gullets. The denizens must have crouched to hear them pass.

When at last they reached the horses, Walter mounted Boggis while Benedict and Crispin lifted Brompton up and over the pommel. Walter encircled him with his arm, stoical, despite the stench that clung like a hide.

Their progress towards the mission was slow. Even when they reached the yard, Brompton seemed unaware of his surroundings. He allowed himself to be dragged from the saddle and propped against the wall of the house while Walter handed the reins to Benedict. Benedict led Boggis and the other horses away to the kraal.

'Help me lift him indoors,' said Walter to Crispin. 'Then come back and light a fire. There's wood in the shed around the back. Bring whatever food we have. Is there any bread left?'

Crispin nodded.

'Just a little then. I doubt he's eaten in days. After I've cleaned him I'll make a broth to soak it in. He must take it slowly.'

Crispin leaned the gun against the mantelpiece and helped

Walter carry Hubert Brompton into the house. They laid him on the bed. Then Crispin turned and hurried outside. Walter could hear him retching painfully. Over and over. Wringing himself out. He stepped into the living-room. 'Crispin?' He listened. 'Are you all right?' But Crispin was half running towards the guest hut. Walter turned back to the bedroom alcove. He stopped, swept his eye along the bookshelf. Something in its configuration was different. A gap. A space. An empty place between the lark and brass candlesticks and photographs. The musical-box that had stood there that morning, with the finger marks upon the lid, was gone.

It was tedious heating the water. Benedict and Crispin tended the fire, feeding it dry twigs and logs, sitting beside it, a little bread and tough cold guinea-fowl between them. When they spoke it was in Xhosa in soft, subdued voices. Alone in the house, Walter trickled liquid into Brompton's mouth from a cup. Brompton spluttered and gagged. Walter put the cup aside, laid him back against the pillow and began to strip off his clothing.

Shoes, stockings, trousers. Piece by piece Walter dropped them into a bucket. Brompton had soiled himself. Walter hardly breathed for fear of unleashing a wave of nausea. He clenched his teeth, felt the sharp metallic rush of spit at the back of his tongue. He turned his head away, panted rhythmically, returned to his task.

There were cuts on Brompton's hands and knees, gashes below his eye and in the stubble of his beard. The blood had dried and bruises stained the skin. Walter took the bucket outside. He handed it to Crispin. 'Bury these, please. There is no point in trying to save them.' The cleric's collar, the underclothing, the shirt and jacket lay limp and damp as if Brompton's life had oozed into them. 'You should also bury the bag of things I found this morning in the roof, Crispin. Put them all together.' He went to the bush where he had hidden the bag, stooping to retrieve it. Then he stepped back, startled. It had gone.

Pushing the problem of the bag aside, Walter hurried back to the room, looked down at the man on the bed. He lay inert, disarrayed, his eyes closed. Walter had never seen such a hopeless, desolate nakedness.

A man who has hidden his body all his life, grows to fear and despise it. He closes it away, crouches over it lest it be discovered. Hair grows on it like secret moss, strange and repellent. It is familiar to no one, loved by none, decaying slowly in seclusion.

Walter felt shamed at seeing Brompton naked, as if he had been lewd in glancing at the mushroom-pale skin, the thin, slack flesh, the prominent blue veins that crept across the naked groin. He turned to the cupboard and took a gown from a peg and laid it over him. Here was a man who had never celebrated life, never felt the surge of it within him. The great exhilaration. The power. Walter turned from him in fear. Might he, too, in age or sickness, be tended by a stranger, with pity, not with love? Would no one ever reach for him, caress him, wish to touch him, with warmth and familiarity? Would he wither in some twilight world, repel as Brompton did, arouse the same restraint and distance? He went to the door and called for Benedict and Crispin. 'Bring the bath, please. He's ready.'

Crispin and Benedict heaved the tin tub into the room and placed it on the floor. The luke-warm water tilted back and forward to the rim. Together they lifted Brompton into in. He snorted and shook, paddled with his hands in a bid to escape. Head, face, trunk, genitals, feet. The water was grey and scummed with dirt and hair.

'That'll have to do. Another rinsing would be a strain on him,' said Walter and he laid a towel on the bed inside an old sheet. Streaming water, Brompton was wrapped in them. He shook as if he had a fever, stared about, grunting in his chest. Walter reached for the mug by the bed but Brompton turned his head away. 'I wish we had brought some brandy,' said Walter. He sat back on his haunches. 'Benedict, please go to the church and see if there is any communion wine in the vestry.'

Benedict looked aghast.

'It won't be consecrated. It's only wine till then.'

Benedict went. Walter dipped a corner of the sheet in the

bath and mopped Brompton's face, speaking soothingly. 'What happened, old man?' he said, but Brompton did not understand his words.

They heard Benedict running. He burst in, breathless, his eyes starting. 'There's a horse tethered at the church and a man drinking wine, sitting on the altar.'

Walter strode outside, followed by Crispin and Benedict. As they reached the yard, a horse hurtled down towards them. It was Brompton's bay. Mounted on it was Pusey. In one hand he carried a bottle of communion wine. The musical-box was clenched against his side. The beads that Walter had found in the flour sack in the thatch were strung diagonally about his chest, the roots and fat pendulous at his waist. His face was daubed with clay, his military moustache was whitened. He wore his frock-coat, its tails lifting like the wings of some great black bird behind him. Around his head was wrapped Brompton's surplice, twisted turban-like, a sleeve trailing. Bouncing like a thin-tipped feather, it achieved a wild, pagan elegance as he advanced.

He glanced at Walter as he circled past him and he laughed. Light flashed across his stare, refracted from the spectacles he wore: Brompton's pince-nez precarious on the bridge of his nose. Flecks of spittle flew from his mouth as he uttered a great declamatory monologue. A defiant exultation. The walls of the buildings round the yard rang with the sound of his words. Uncomprehending, Walter turned to Crispin and Benedict. They stood mesmerised.

Pusey reined in a pace or two away and flung back his head and emptied the contents of the bottle in a gulp. He shuddered and turned his attention to the musical-box. He opened it, cocking his head. The tune jangled out.

Walter commanded him to dismount, reaching for the bridle. Jerking the horse's head from his grasp, Pusey wheeled about the yard, coming to a halt some way away. He saluted with the bottle by twirling it once around his head and hurling it against the wall of the house. Then he opened the musical-box again. The notes scratched out, stuck. He shook the box and the notes limped on as if afraid to withhold their magic.

146

It was then that a furtive movement in the doorway of the house made Walter turn. Behind them Brompton wavered on the step. The sheet had fallen from him. Naked, he stumbled towards the horse, an animal howl rising in his throat, lips drawn back across his teeth. 'Give it. Give it . . .' he moaned. 'Give it . . .'

Pusey looked over at Brompton. A moment of stillness. Then, almost slowly, almost gently, he took the box and he tossed it. It cartwheeled up and over, arching through the sunlight. The lid opened as it fell and, as it hit the ground, the notes twanged deep inside it, chips of iron falling, falling.

Pusey swung about. The horse sprang forward at his command. Resplendent in his frock-coat and vestments, the diviner's accoutrements and pince-nez, he rode along the lip of the hill. They could hear the hoof-beats long after he had disappeared.

Walter turned to Brompton. He grovelled on the ground. Mucus streaming from his nose was smeared across his face. He was reaching for the musical-box. The top had come loose from one of its hinges, the innards chinked together, broken somewhere in the heart. Shielding it, he held it in against his chest, rocked it, rocked it. Crispin went to him and lifted him with tender hands.

Walter did not think often of the vigil of that night in the little house, nor of the journey from Mbokothwe to Stutterheim. Both were long and distressing. Brompton had fallen into a delirium from which he sometimes woke and into which he sank again, on and off, throughout the hours of darkness and then throughout the miles between the mission and the town. Only occasionally did he have moments of near-lucidity. Like the mechanism in the musical-box, it seemed that Brompton's reason had broken up inside him, leaving only fragments of coherence.

An unseasonable rain overtook them an hour or two from Stutterheim and Benedict rode ahead to prepare the Rector of St Barnabas for their arrival. Walter drove the cart and Crispin sat in the back, shielding Hubert Brompton from the squalls, hunched close to him under a canvas sail, raising him sometimes to give him water from a flask. The musical-box was stored at his feet, wrapped protectively in his shirt. Walter saw Crispin bend and speak softly – too softly for him to catch his words – and take Brompton's hand in reassurance: a compassion such as Walter had not seen before. He turned away, humbled.

They spent the night at the rectory at St Barnabas, glad of good food and dry clothes, while a doctor attended to Brompton. A cable was sent to the Dean. It was arranged that two orderlies from the hospital in Queenstown should accompany the sick man on the train to Grahamstown once his strength had been sufficiently restored. In the mean time he was sedated and put to bed in a darkened room. Walter sat awhile by his side, sunk in exhaustion himself.

The stories of casualties in the mission field were legion. Walter had heard them all, long before he had embarked for South Africa. His tutor had spoken of them and they had had talks from visiting missionaries and priests: work-worn from India, from the West Indies, from China or Malaya, each with a tale to tell. This was not a calling for those who might falter. With regard to South Africa, they were told of those members of the Society for the Propagation of the Gospel who had been murdered, those whose houses had been burned, whose stock was pillaged and those – the lecturer was either faintly apologetic or brisk – dismissed for immorality, victims of the isolation of remote country districts.

News filtered through of students from previous years who had gone out crusading and succumbed: Seedley in a hospital in Calcutta; Rogers missing in Nigeria; Clarke sent home under a cloud – something about his wife; Rodbard's suicide on St Vincent. The news of Bishop Twells's flight from Bloemfontein in 1869, accused of sodomy, was an old story circulated continuously – morbidly – among the students twenty years on. Disgrace, sin, aberration. All these were spectral in that tale. It was as if the Bishop had taken the honour of the clergy like a thief – dishonour to one is dishonour to all – and made off with it, so that each of them, by association, stood exposed to censure and to scorn. One man's pain – whatever pain, whatever moral collapse – was inadmissible, could

148

make every recruit look into his heart and fear the thing he saw. There must be no such gazing, no such introspection. Among themselves, like a pack of hungry dogs, they dissected his fall, goaded by fear of their own susceptibility. In time, like the Bishop and the wasted priests, Brompton would be the subject of a similar analysis:

- Do you remember Hubert Brompton? An Oxford man. He wouldn't let you forget it. In imitation – Are you an Oxford or a St Augustine's man, sir?
- Did you know he named his servant Pusey! I fear he meant offence in giving it.
- Poor old Brompton. Anyone been to see him?
- Doesn't remember a soul, poor beggar.
- They say he sits all day and listens to a musical-box that no longer plays.
  Laughter.
- If you ask me, they should take it away. It's obsessive with him. He has an extraordinary attachment to it. Seen him myself. He looks off into space for all the world as if a choir of angels is singing.
- I doubt it's angels. More likely some denizens of the Inferno!

Oh, Walter could hear them. That was how it would be in the chapter house and cathedral stalls and the dinners at the Dean's. None of them, in the safety of the cures of Grahamstown, had known the silences of this place nor sensed the presence of another God. None had fought so great a battle. There were few of them who ever would.

It was only when they had left Stutterheim early the next morning, when they had started down the Donsa Pass with the sun coming up behind and the long blue shadows of the horses darting across the track, that Walter said to Benedict and Crispin, 'What did Pusey say?'

'Have you heard of *mshologu*, *Mfundisi*?' said Benedict.

'*Mshologu*?' Walter shook his head.

'That is the thing that was troubling the man on the horse.'

'Explain.'

'He said that the *mfundisi* at Mbokothwe took his things away. Medicines and gifts. He would not let him make a

149

sacrifice with a white goat. It seems that this man had *thwasa*'d.'

'What is *thwasa*'d?'

'It was his vocation to be a diviner. By the power of a snake. That is what he said.'

'A snake?'

'A person is called to be a diviner. There is nothing he can do if he is called. He can only listen. The shades speak to him in dreams and in these dreams he will see an animal. A leopard or a wild cat or a snake. It is one of these that stands beside his heart when he learns. If this person is not allowed to become a diviner, if he does not complete his preparations for his calling, this animal becomes an *mshologu* sent by the shades, an evil to trouble his heart and cause sickness and even death.'

'So, the shades, being angry, send the *mshologu*?' said Walter cautiously.

'The *mfundisi* did not believe in the *mshologu*,' said Benedict. 'He took the divining things of the man and told him God would punish him with death if he did not give them up. So, he took the *mfundisi*'s things in turn, the things belonging to the *mfundisi*'s shades – the music-box and the wine and the vestments too, because he was angry and afraid.'

Walter did not scoff. He sensed that Crispin was watching him. 'Do you believe that?' he said to Benedict.

'No,' said Benedict. His voice was flat. He half laughed. 'Why must I believe it? I'm a Christian. I'm only telling you what the man said. It is his belief, not mine.' He did not look at them but continued to stare out over the valley where the smoke from homesteads was rising now, lifting up into the morning sky.

'I do,' said Crispin softly.

'Why?' asked Walter. His tone was not challenging.

'We all have an *mshologu* we're afraid of. We just give it different names. Satan. Fear. Death. Lots of different things. Mr Brompton had one. I think that he couldn't get away from his past. That's why this has happened.' Crispin bent down and brought out a bundle from beneath the seat of the cart. He unwrapped it in his lap. It was the musical-box. He said, 'This was Mr Brompton's magic thing. The servant must have had one too. I suppose it depended which was stronger.' He was silent a moment, then he said, 'I didn't want to leave this with the orderlies. I'm going to repair it and when I go back to school I'll take it to him, wherever they send him. I expect they'll put him in the mental hospital in Grahamstown.' He ran his finger across the lid. He polished it carefully with a corner of his shirt as if cleansing it from defilement. Benedict rode ahead a little and Crispin worked at the musical-box. Then he said suddenly to Walter, 'Why did you become a priest, Mr Brownley?'

Caught unawares, Walter glanced at him in surprise. Crispin's face was flushed as if the question had taken some courage to broach. 'I sometimes wonder, Crispin. There weren't many opportunities put in my way. My father died young and my grandfather, who was a parson, had his expectations. Besides, I loved him, I admired him. To follow him seemed the happy thing to do.' He laughed. 'In my defence, I was intrigued by the philosophical aspects. The debate. I don't expect that constitutes a vocation. I don't think I ever asked if God might want me. Seriously,' Walter drew on his pipe, 'I can't remember considering anything else – except teaching, perhaps, or doctoring, like my father.'

They drove on a little way and then Crispin said, 'If I were a priest at St Matthias . . .' He paused and added carefully. 'If I were ever clever enough to be one . . .' He faltered again, searched for words, 'I'd remember the shades. They'd be the most important thing in my belief.'

Walter smiled. 'The conventional church would call that dabbling in idolatry.'

'Would you?' Crispin glanced across and down, expecting a rebuff.

'Once I might have thought so. But not now. How could I comment when I know so little about it?'

'It's the key,' said Crispin simply. 'It's the key to understanding everything here.'

'Have you ever thought of being a priest?' said Walter.

Crispin's hesitance was palpable. 'I'm a dunce,' he said. Walter was about to speak but Crispin pointed suddenly, searching awkwardly for a diversion, 'Look at the quails,' he said. A small group, wings purring, fled across the grass some way away. 'There's a belief that quails turn into frogs when the rains come and back into birds in the winter time. That's why frogs disappear in dry weather without a trace.' He half stood. 'See, there they go again.'

He would not be drawn further on the subject of priests and he turned to Benedict and said, 'Tell Mr Brownley about the quails and all the other birds, Benedict.'

Benedict drew alongside, matching his horse's pace with that of the cart. He whistled a soft, beckoning call. Crispin whistled back, imitating, echoing the note. They repeated the duet: this is a pipit and this a lark and this is the boubou shrike talking to its mate and this is when it imitates another and this is a bokmakierie and this the river-warbler, comforter of birds by the stream. Walter was enchanted.

'Who taught you?' he said.

'Benedict taught me,' said Crispin.

'And Tom and Reuben and Sonwabo taught me,' said Benedict. 'And Kobus Pumani, their father, taught them.' He laughed. 'And so it goes.'

'And now we're not allowed to play the game,' said Crispin, 'because it's supposed to be heathen!' He licked his lips – some faint defiance – and whistled at a different pitch. 'Here is the mourning dove,' he said. 'My mother is dead, my father is dead, all my children are dead.' And Benedict, taking up the beckoning note, 'My heart is falling over. Dudududududududu.'

And so they rode together with the lament of the little dove between them, flitting back and forth from throat to throat, a soft duet exchanged.

Frances heard Boggis's whinny as he reached the gate of the mission yard, putting his head up in a proprietary manner and announcing himself. She got up from her seat in the sewing-room and said to Helmina, 'They're back,' and went out without excusing herself, leaving the door swinging behind her. She took the path to the church. There was Benedict. There was Crispin.

And there – thank God – was Walter Brownley.

She saw him stoop to light a match and settle his pipe between his teeth in that predictable and consoling way. There was a little catch in her breath as she hurried on. But as she reached the yard, not far from where the cart was parked, she saw Victor come around the side of the church, his gun across his shoulder, swinging a francolin from the other hand and she stopped. She would have retreated if Crispin had not already seen her and waved. Walking sedately, she reached them as Victor did. She turned to Crispin and put her arms about him and kissed him and said, 'I missed you. Did you have an adventure?'

And then, under the eye of Victor, standing nonchalantly, with the gun poised at his shoulder, she turned to Walter Brownley. 'Good afternoon, Mr Brownley.' Oh, so small and stiff! She dared not raise her eyes to his.

'Good afternoon, Miss Farborough.'

'Can I help? Is there anything to carry in?'

'We can manage, thank you,' he replied evenly. He paid more attention to the pipe than to her.

'If you want something to do you can take this bird to the kitchen,' said Victor, holding it out to her. 'I'll help with the horses.'

'It's all bloody.'

'I haven't noticed that worry you in the past,' he returned, half mockingly.

Frances flushed, put out her hand and took it.

Crispin was reaching into the cart. Carefully he brought out the musical-box, still wrapped up in his dirty shirt.

Victor said, 'What's that?'

'Reverend Brompton's musical-box,' said Crispin. 'I'm going to try and fix it for him.' He tucked it under his arm and he took it to the church. Victor led the horses to the trough. Frances glanced up at Walter Brownley then, but he was piling the bedding rolls on the grass. She hesitated, almost spoke.

Plotz. She needed Plotz – to hear him say 'Mrs B' in a secret voice full of laughter, to be able to meet his gnome-man's dark eyes and see herself reflected steadily: to restore the thing that

153

was gone, to reassure and comfort her, to explain away her sin. She had held the tears until now, but, seeing him, she could feel them gathering.

Victor was coming from the trough. He looked over at her. Lingered at her eyes. How new his expression was. How it shouted his possession of her. She turned and walked towards the house, the bird dangling at her side.

Victor might have watched her go, but Walter heard her: the soft tread of her soles on the fine sand of the driveway, the rustle of the bird's feathers brushing her skirt. Her shadow slid momentarily past him, reaching for his feet. He felt it as if she had touched him with her breath.

He looked up at Victor watching her. And as he scanned that face, a sudden certainty assailed him. He felt the blood beating in his ears.

Chapter Ten

The certainty was compounded the next day when the Native Affairs Inspector and the Magistrate and a gathering of friends from The Hoek and Debe Nek came for a Sunday lunch. That such conviction should confront one in a crowd of people, amidst the hubbub and the talk and the passing of plates and the pouring of tea! Walter would have retreated to the printing-room with Benedict if Emily had not insisted that he participate in all the sports that she'd arranged. He cried off but she would not hear of it. A party was so rare, his presence was compulsory.

Unable to escape, he offered his help to Helmina and watched as she arranged the tea-table on the lawn. He carried chairs for her and brought benches from the hall. He talked to her as she set the cushions and cut some roses for a vase which she placed as a centre-piece. He admired her handiwork, bringing a quick flush to her face and a ready smile that he had not seen in a long time. He felt wretched for misleading her.

The Nettletons and the Dohnes and the teacher came from The Hoek, the trader from Rabula and Reverend Butler from Debe Nek. The Dohnes had a trio of daughters and a son and Reverend Butler's boy had brought a cricket bat and wickets.

The Magistrate's wife sat with Emily Farborough on the bench under the oak near the tennis court, watching Frances play with Victor and Crispin and the Nettletons' eldest girl. Helmina ran back and forth with Nowasha and a pair of housemaids brought from the school, bearing trays of tea and cordial and bringing more and more to eat. Emily Farborough's hospitality would not be forgotten.

Father Charles had retired to his study with Harold Stanbridge, the Native Affairs Inspector and Mr Erskine, the Magistrate. Victor was called in to them. He tossed Walter his racket and asked him to partner Frances in his place.

'I shan't do all the running, Mrs B,' Walter said to her with a smile, 'so you'd better be nimble.'

155

Frances glanced up at him. Then she frowned and inspected her racket strings and pushed back her hair. Disquiet and defensiveness side by side. He could not decide which was in the ascendant. He turned from her and looked off beyond the fence, feeling the soft, dry wind through his shirt. Half hidden in the grass, a small group of mission children watched the game, small, dark heads ducking down below the bank of grass should anyone stare in their direction.

Way beyond, outside the boarding-house, Walter saw the schoolgirls in their starched white Sunday pinafores, sitting in the sun along the walls and further on, two or three walking slowly with a nun, drifting like flowers in the wind. The boys, forbidden to approach, were playing rugby on the field by the water-furrow, Benedict among them. They would meet for service – boys on the left of the aisle, girls on the right. Only the sacristans at the altar-rail might kneel side by side, sleeves touching.

Walter turned back to his game. Frances was waiting desultorily. Usually she had to be admonished by her mother for her lack of restraint on the court – her dashes for the ball, wielding her racket like a machete, tearing her dress, allowing her hair to escape its ribbons and combs. Today she played woodenly, and when the set was over she sat fanning herself with her hat. Far away and a darkness in her face, he knew she was not listening to the chatter of the young women gathered round her and, when addressed, her eyes seldom met the speaker's. Walter bent to her and said – unobtrusively as he passed – 'Are you all right?'

She replied, 'Yes.' But her bottom lip trembled – oh so slightly – and despite a small grimace of impatience, he sensed that if he had put out his hand she would have grasped it. She turned her head away and spoke to Miss Nettleton and asked her when she had last been to King William's Town.

Ignoring the dismissal, Walter sat down on the grass beside her. Her white skirt pooled about her, her hat floating in her lap. The toes of her boots, turned in towards each other, pushed out beneath the hem of her petticoat. They were just within his gaze, stub-toed, buttoned tightly. He wished he could have put out a finger and touched them in reassurance.

Miss Nettleton was speaking. Frances listened politely but suddenly she looked beyond her, distracted. Following her gaze, Walter saw Victor emerge from the house and walk across the lawn towards them. He was rolling up his sleeves as he came: brisk, confident, long-legged in white twill trousers, he reached the table and said, smiling engagingly, 'Can I pour anyone a glass? Miss Nettleton?' He handed round the cordial and then he helped himself. He drank a moment, glanced at Frances.

What is there in a look that momentarily strips a man? What – by the minute dilation of an eye, the fleeting light and dark, the flicker of a muscle in the jaw – that renders him so naked? In Victor's quick appraisal of Frances, there was some secret knowing, some hesitation, some anxiety. His eyes swept her briefly, gathering her in with his gaze. She must have looked across at him for Walter saw his eyes dart up, suddenly intent. Discomposure, nakedness indeed. He could not hide it.

Walter turned from him, unable to deny what he had seen: one could challenge or deride infatuation, lust, greed, mawkish sentiment but one stood back in deference – or defeat – from love.

They sat in the shade of the oaks and the flocks of redwinged starlings twittered mournfully from the grove at the bottom of the garden, disparate sounds from the liveliness of the conversation round the table. A melancholy interchange in the quiet of the midday.

Harold Stanbridge, the Native Affairs Inspector – an expansive patron – proposed a toast, raising his glass to congratulate Victor on the imminent appointment to the department's office in Johannesburg, using his remarks as a vehicle – self-enhancing – to describe his own work and achievement. Victor was suitably gracious and self-deprecatory in his thanks.

The ritual complete, the conversation became general but Walter, at Helmina's side, listened as Harold Stanbridge turned to Charles Farborough and Victor and said, 'There is a deal of money to be made in recruiting, I hear.'

'Recruiting?' said Father Charles.

'For the gold mines,' said Harold Stanbridge. 'I was in Johannesburg not long ago and was most interested in the work of the Witwatersrand Native Labour Association. Do you know of it?'

'No,' said Father Charles. 'The gold mines do not really affect us here.'

'They will,' said Harold Stanbridge. 'A sleeping giant that must be fed with men. If I were younger I'd be interested in the prospect of recruiting myself. I'd take my chances and I'd certainly be a richer man.'

Charles Farborough took out his pipe and filled it. He did not comment and Harold Stanbridge continued, 'The amount of labour needed is inexhaustible but the natives here are not keen to go to the mines and we have to find a way to induce them. The recruiters elsewhere earn a capitation fee so there is brisk competition between them and they are naturally very persuasive in inducing the natives to sign up. What we need is to get headmen on our side for they have the power to order the people to work. Oil the palm and you'll have no trouble at all. Set up a chain of traders to act as agents, with a system of loyal runners among the natives. Pay the price where need be – to the headmen and chiefs, with a bit of flattery and a bottle or two – and you're away. If one could get the monopoly of the market, there'd be a river of black gold running north and straight through your pocket.'

Father Charles said, 'I believe, sir, that the people wouldn't benefit in general from leaving their families and their lands. They'd need to return all the time for ploughing or to attend to ceremonies or to care for the cattle. I do not see how it would suit the situation.'

'Well, it depends very much on your vision for the future of the Colony,' said Stanbridge with a touch of condescension. 'If we don't fill the mines in the Transvaal with units of labour, the gold simply won't come out and that will affect us all. There are wider interests at stake here and an honest day's work never did the native any harm. On the contrary it would benefit him and bring revenue into the Colony. What a resource waiting to be harnessed! Cattle advances and credit are the weapons of the clever trader-recruiter who plays on the susceptibilities of the people in hard times. A fortune can be made.'

'Such practices are open to abuse by the unscrupulous,' said Father Charles. 'I should not encourage such ideas.'

Harold Stanbridge retreated then, mollifying the missionary. He said smoothly, 'The Native Affairs Department would be very thorough indeed in ensuring that things proceed in an orderly way.' He turned to Thomas Nettleton. 'Have you ever considered becoming a recruiting agent, sir?'

'I've thought of it,' returned the old man. 'The store is situated very favourably for the area. However, I would be wary of cattle advances and credit. Times are hard and with the rinderpest already in the Colony I would feel uneasy about calling in the debts.'

'You are conscientious, sir,' and Stanbridge bowed a little in Thomas Nettleton's direction. 'There are fellows I know in the Transvaal who have men, desperate for cattle, who have pledged their children for the future in return for an advance in cash or oxen. Three or four years hence, you understand. Oh, I can hear your objections,' he raised his hand as if to sweep them aside, 'but if a native wishes to pledge his child to a recruiter, that is his choice. There are lads on the mines of fifteen or sixteen – passing for eighteen – who are perfectly content with their lot. The doctors up at the Chamber turn a blind eye to it. Besides, these fellows who've been out herding cattle since they were five or six are as strong as titans. Earn a good wage. The fixing is thirty shillings a month. If I were looking to the future I'd go into recruiting. All a fellow needs to start out is to have some connections in an area, to be able to speak the native tongue in order to earn trust and then to keep it by fair dealing and making sure the headmen are happy. Put them in your pay, give them advances, outlay a bit to corner the market. Then a fellow's in a position to tap the heart of it.'

Under the trees, with the white cloth lifting at the corner in a little breeze and the ladies retired inside to refresh themselves for lunch, Walter listened to the desultory conversation. Men, on a Sunday afternoon, dallying with ideas and the sound of the cricket bat tapping at the ball where the children played and the laughter of girls from the house and the wind in the trees high, high above. And Victor, lounging in his chair, with his arm crooked across the back of it and his legs crossed and the half intentness, half languor as he listened to Harold Stanbridge.

The conversation turned to other things – to the approach of the rinderpest and to the idiosyncrasies of colonial officials who had not done a round of duty in a frontier town and to the newest difficulties with a headman at Lady Frere who was inciting people not to pay their taxes. And Victor sat. Was it then that the idea first struck him? Or did the words drift into his consciousness and out again unheeded? Or settle, dormant for the time? Destinies are fixed against the passing of a moment, dynasties conceived which are the nidus of their own destruction.

And yet, Walter's remembrance of that day was not of Harold Stanbridge's words or of Victor's close attention to them as they sat under the trees, of empires in recruiting or of mines or rinderpest, but that it marked the occasion of their first public confrontation. And though the act that precipitated it aroused legitimate indignation, he knew that his anger arose from another, deeper impulse. It was a front for the desolation and the impotence that had overwhelmed him when he'd seen Victor look across at Frances as she'd sat on the grass with her hat in her lap. Such an end to the entertainments on that sultry afternoon!

Victor was central among the young people, leading the croquet and the tennis and the cricket and the banter round the lunch and tea-tables. Crispin sat at his side, his jester or his fool, the brunt of some of the repartee, good-natured enough not to take offence. Frances, notwithstanding her pre-occupation, laughed at Victor's mimicry, forgetting – momentarily – whatever had disturbed her. The young ladies were entranced. Walter had to confess, despite himself, that Victor was a most engaging raconteur. He could engender an air of expectation, an edge of danger, which he played like a master.

Walter was excluded from the circle of the young. They had stationed themselves on the veranda and he could see them through the open door, gathered round Victor while he himself sat at tea in the living-room between Mrs Erskine and Helmina. Emily Farborough was explaining the work of the mission to Harold Stanbridge, Father Charles engaged with the Reverend Butler on the matter of irrigation furrows and packstone walls. Walter was referred to every now and then to pass an opinion on one topic or the other but he had half an ear on the nonsense going on on the veranda and from the corner of his eye saw Victor stand and stretch and heard him say, 'Come along then and I'll show you,' and he led his troop of followers down into the garden. The voices faded as they flocked round the side of the house. The clock on the mantelpiece struck five.

Helmina looked enquiringly at Walter. 'Evensong?' she said softly.

'I'll go across now.'

'Shall I come?'

'Benedict can help you for the moment, Mr Brownley,' said Emily, catching their words. 'I shall need Miss Smythe with me. Helmina, dear, ask Nowasha to bring more hot water.' She turned back to Mrs Stanbridge.

Helmina went obediently. Walter excused himself, shaking hands with the gentlemen, bowing to the ladies, taking his hat from the side table: duties to attend to, thank you for a marvellous day, safe journey back. All the preliminaries to farewell.

'Butler,' said Father Charles, 'I wish for your sake you had an assistant like mine at Debe Nek. He has taken the burden. I hope you shall never be enticed to leave and go recruiting, Brownley, despite Mr Stanbridge's persuasive arguments.'

Walter laughed. 'No, sir, my recruiting is of another kind.'

'And how successful he is!' said Emily. 'If one earned earthly riches for it, he'd be a prosperous man indeed.' It was a rare and warm salute. Walter caught Helmina's eye and she smiled up at him.

Walter went down the steps into the early evening shadows and he walked towards the church along the grassy track beyond the hall. He pulled out his pocket hymnal, thumbing through it, humming a snatch of tune here and there to help

161

him decide which to choose for the service. The little children who had been watching the festivities scuttled from the grassy bank outside the garden and trotted after him. He gathered quite a flock of them as he went and he turned and spoke to them, bending down to each one. They moved in close, a whisper of a smile passing between them because his Xhosa was still so bad and a small voice among them imitated something that he said and there was a ripple of fluting merriment. Walter laughed himself and ran a hand across a round, rough head, touched a small shoulder and an arm and sent them gently home, for the smoke from cooking fires was beginning to rise among the huts behind the church. He watched them go, the wind fluttering at the thin shirts and pinafores and he breathed the dust and woodsmoke of the dusk. A moment of respite as the sun lay down the last long rays across the edges of the hills.

He went into the church. Like a cave, it was deep in gloom. The lead struts of the rose window were a subterranean web, netting the blue outside. Above the altar, the small brass lamp, suspended on a chain, glowed red. His feet made little sound. The matting whispered with its own secret life as he passed along it. At the chancel steps he stopped and listened. He could hear voices in the vestry. The door stood ajar. A chink of light slanted down across the floor, fingering the base of the pulpit.

There was laughter and then faint, panting notes, labouring out: Abide with me . . . with me . . . with me. Brompton's musical-box repeated and repeated the phrase.

There was the sound of scuffling and the light lurched back through the gap in the doorway. Walter heard Crispin say, 'Leave it, Vic. I want to fix it. It will harm it if you play it . . . Please.'

'Oh come on, Crispin' – Victor humouring him – 'one time won't matter.' The activity subsided and the notes began again. 'He was as mad as can be,' said Victor. 'They found him naked in the forest and gibbering like a monkey. I believe he was *thakatha*'d. His servant hocus-pocused him. What did you tell me about the servant, Crispin? Tell them what he said. Something about crocodiles and *mshologus*.'

'Leave it, Vic,' said Crispin.

'Go on,' said Victor with a laugh. 'Can you imagine? A little naked man running about with a gun! I'm sure he kept on his dog-collar for the sake of modesty. Crispin here said he nearly shot old Brownley. That must have shaken him. Brownley couldn't knock a fly off the end of his big nose if he had to!' Laughter and shuffling as they pressed closer round the table. 'Tell them how it was, Crispin.' There was a touch of impatience in Victor's voice.

The young girls rustled expectantly. 'Go on, do!' cried one.

'Be a sport, Crispin,' said young Butler.

The notes scratched on, jerking out.

Walter pushed open the vestry door. The occupants turned, startled. The candle flame guttered in the draught and sent the shadow of Brompton's musical-box up against the wall, the notes crackled and died.

Walter could hear his own voice, far off, disembodied, the words of another man: 'What are you doing here?'

'Just having a look at the musical-box.' Victor's tone was light and crisp. He lowered the lid.

Walter could have turned and torn down the church with his bare hands for the rage that rose in him but his voice was steady when he said, 'May I have a word with you alone?'

The others left, mutely, led by Crispin. Walter did not look at Frances as she passed, although he heard her hesitate at the door. It closed behind her and Walter said, without taking his eyes from Victor, 'Is it necessary' – ice and fire: he could barely hear his own words against the tumult of his blood – 'to make light of someone else's pain?'

Victor picked up a candle-snuffer lying on the table and murmured something, almost smiled, 'Isn't that a touch dramatic?' He looked up at Walter.

'You, sir,' Walter's voice was low, 'play games with people that show an arrogant disregard for both their privacy and their dignity. I've seen it in every dealing you have with those less advantaged than yourself. Hubert Brompton was my colleague and I will not stand by and watch him treated with disparagement. You are neither my business nor my concern, but your carelessness is offensive.'

163

Victor was tapping the snuffer against his palm, half seated across the corner of the table. He straightened. He stood a head – more – taller than Walter and glanced down at him and then he said, with a small, derisive smile, 'Is that all that offends you, sir?'

How the blood betrays, marching up the neck and across the cheeks and through the ears, announcing itself. Walter could feel the heat rising. Poised, they stood, Victor and he. Then Victor shouldered his way past, opened the door and was gone. The draught blew out the candle that stood on the table. The little grey tail of smoke hung suspended in the dark.

He would make no sound. He would stand quite still. He would take no harmless vase or book or chair and vent his anger on it. Still. Still. And a great silence in the church beyond the door. He walked towards the table and touched the musical-box. How clear its shape, how sure the strong, crafted lines of its sides. He opened it and waited. Its voice was still.

Frances waited in the side porch of the church. Victor, striding out across the yard, caught sight of her, turned back and said, glancing swiftly around, 'Come to the stables with me.'

She shook her head.

'Why?' He looked at her. 'Are you afraid of what he will say?' He gestured with his head towards the church. 'I'll break his bloody neck before he speaks to me like that again.'

'What a hero you are,' said Frances with a small twist of her mouth.

Victor recoiled. 'What's the matter with you?' he said and she saw that the colour in his face was high.

Repenting, she touched his arm briefly but her voice was small and distant. 'Not now, Victor,' she said and she stepped back from him and walked away. She did not turn to see if he was watching. She had almost reached the orchard when she heard the angry clang of the stable yard gate. She listened, breathing deeply and then she turned and ran back towards the church.

Walter Brownley was standing by the pulpit, reading. He wore his cassock. He stood small and slight and dark with the

164

sanctuary light shining dimly above his head. He turned a page and set the book down, face first on the bench and opened the hymnal. He sensed her or he heard her step and he looked up. She waited in the aisle and he said, his voice reaching her, soft though it was, through the quiet space, 'What is it?'

She stood mute, her eyes on the matting. She could hear the brisk sweep of the robe against the pews as he passed. He stopped a pace or two away, the hymn book in his hand and she said, 'I'm sorry about the musical-box,' keeping her face averted. That was not what she had intended to say at all. Ever since she'd seen him climb down from the cart on his return from Mbokothwe she had wanted to run to him, stand safe at his protective side and say a hundred things, exhort him – just by his presence – to wipe out, expunge, or return to her what she had lost. But the words remained leaden inside her, unable to escape, forming and re-forming and dying as she began to utter them.

Still he stood, looking at her quietly. 'Is there something you wish to tell me?'

She said woodenly, the little words limping out like the notes of the musical-box had done, 'I don't think Victor intended to make fun, but if we did, I'm sorry.'

He glanced at the book in his hand. 'It won't be mentioned again.' The silence, the restraint, and yet the question hung between them: what happened when I was gone? 'What has upset you?' he said at last.

She stood painfully. Then she looked up at him. Such eyes he had. To see such eyes look back so steadily. Frances could not hold his gaze but, as she drew her breath to speak, the church door opened and Benedict came in, followed by Helmina and a file of students from the boarding-house. Seeing them, Walter Brownley said to her, quite calmly, as if he knew she could not turn to face them, 'Go to the vestry, and see if you can find my music. I think I left it on top of the dresser. Miss Smythe?' – he hardly missed a beat – 'would you play the hymns in Mrs Farborough's place this evening? Let me just help find the music. I've rather scattered it about.' Then he turned and Frances could hear him following her. He went swiftly to the dresser in the vestry, took a key from a drawer and opened the side door. He held it for her. She slipped past him, looked back. There was no need to speak. Then he closed the door behind her and was gone.

To be isolated with oneself, to stand in fear of one's own solitude, to look at the thing that walks within one, unable to break free: Frances had not dared think about what she had done until now. She had fled from it. She went back to the house and held herself in check through the farewells of the company and the tedious arrangement of the ladies in their traps and as soon as the last horse had gone along the drive, she excused herself. She could no longer sit in the living-room and sew, pretending that nothing had happened, or play bagatelle or read or talk to Miss Smythe or Crispin. It would have been a relief to stand, announce herself and say, 'I went to Victor's room the other night. Now you know, so punish me however you will.'

But her father had simply kissed her and her mother had said, pleased that her day had been such a success, bending from her usual restraint, 'You suit that muslin very well, dear. I shall send for another catalogue and see if there is a pattern like it. We could sew something new for the summer.' Crispin looked over at her and smiled and returned to the wood that he was carving, wresting from it the shape of a man or animal or bird, skilful and patient with his simple tools. She hesitated when she heard Walter Brownley's voice in the porch but she listened with a sinking heart to his retreat as he walked away towards the curate's lodge without coming in.

Victor only returned when she was already in her room. He went down the passage, paused a step outside her door. He laughed at something Crispin called from the living-room and made a remark about the beauty of the Misses Dohne. Her mother said, 'Go on with you, Victor!' and her father called, 'God bless, all', as he went to his study for an hour of work.

Frances undressed and put on her nightgown. She hung her clothes in the wardrobe. She went to the washstand and brushed her teeth and cleaned her face and she lifted the edge of her curtain to see if the window was closed. She blew out her candle and she lay in the dark on her back with her eyes open and she stared up at the ceiling. The tears came then, hot and silent. She restrained herself from curling up, from hiding her body in shame. She lay flat and still and felt the tears creeping down her temples and into her hair. She let them run.

When Victor had found her in his room, her fear and her imaginings had been banished as he had reached for her. She had gone to him, sensing the triumph of that strange new power in her that made him supplicant before her, abject almost: she could have had her foot upon his neck. Oh, how she felt that power! To see him so! She had kissed him tenderly then, lightness and triumph in her touch. And love. She bestowed it generously. And magnificence. That, too.

Then they were gone. And only fear was left.

That such certainty should spawn such fear and such regret! No penance, promise nor self-recrimination could change it now.

Reckless – fearing uncertainty, fearing loss, fearing a lifelong exile at St Matthias – acquiescent, too, to some inescapable and unnamed yearning, she had done this thing, knowing what its consequence might be. She knew about conception, pregnancy and birth. She had watched, daily, young heathen men and women walk in pride and near-nakedness and she and Victor had scorned and mocked Miss Smythe's sensibilities. Together they had once watched a bitch whelping, a new-born calf struggle from the after-birth. She had not flinched. One should exult in life, not hide from it. Victor had said that then and he was right: carelessly, they had overturned everything that they'd been taught, disbelieving it was sin.

And yes, she'd gone to Victor, knowing that she would – long before he had walked into his room and seen her standing at the window. Conspirators, her hand in his, her breath soft and shallow in her throat to hear the creaking of the roof, the shouting of the floorboards underneath their feet. There had been no fighting it. None at all.

At that moment she neither thought, nor feared. His embrace of her had been too urgent and the sudden pain too sharp and unexpected and the darkness of the night too great about them for the awesomeness of what she'd done to strike her. Only when they had both regained the present and the room around them seemed familiar again and she had heard him say, 'We are linked now, you and I, for ever,' did the realisation rise: she was tied to him by her blood, staked out by her sin, held captive through her own choice and will.

'Are you sorry for what we have done?' he had said.

'No.' She had only whispered it, searching for his hand as if to rediscover the familiar and sure.

'Do you love me?' He had said that too – he who never asked for anything but chose only to withhold or bestow as the whim took him.

'Yes.' The word had hung there and she had felt a great and sudden stillness – a great abyss of stillness as if, knowingly, she had walked into the night: 'Thy waste and thy desolate places and the land of thy destruction . . .' Those words had always stirred her with their grandeur and their loneliness. That was what she'd felt when morning came. Those empty places. That day and the ones that followed.

Frances ran the sleeve of her nightdress across her eyes, drew her breath. Drew it. Drew it. If she could lay that desolation down, unburden it at some quiet feet. And she said, the sob rising in her, 'Plotz? Oh, Plotz.' She turned her head into her pillow so none might hear her anguish.

And Walter, in his room, alone with his pile of books and his lamp and his pipe, took a mug from the washstand and set down a bottle of wine on the table. He had purloined it from the house – ah, yes, he admitted it quite candidly – and he proceeded to drink it all. He wrote a letter to Daisy while he drank and when he had finished, he sealed the envelope meticulously and propped it against his lamp. Ten pages, eleven pages. He'd lost count. It had been, in turns, both grim and entertaining. He stood and he said, 'I am drunk', and then he lay down on his bed and remembered nothing except waking sometime in the night and going outside and retching his heart out and in the morning he tore up the letter without reading it and he took Boggis and he rode him hard to the outstation at Chata to take a service.

Dead drunk, he'd been. For the first time in his life.

168

Chapter Eleven

The next day, when Walter returned from early service at Chata he went to the printing-room. He entered it with expectation, despite a raging head and persistent thirst, not wishing to be disturbed. This was a haven for good work and a place of retreat. Only Benedict was welcome here and he was eager to show him the parcel that had arrived while they were at Mbokothwe. It was from a printer in Grahamstown and enclosed not only a catalogue detailing the prices of the latest available print, but four blocks which he had ordered, engraved with scrolls, cornucopias and a simple representation of the church, copied from a photograph. The printer had included one depicting the rising sun and the words, 'May the sun never set on the British Empire'. Just the thing for the foot of the Choral Union Programme! Emily Farborough would be enchanted.

Benedict was waiting for him. He turned from the table and smiled, 'Good morning, sir.'

'Ah, Benedict, good morning to you. Let's close the door and get to work. So much has happened in the last week, I can scarcely remember where we were.'

Benedict showed him the sheets that had been printed before they went to Mbokothwe. Walter held one up and looked at it. 'Very nice, Benedict. The print is quite distinct and even. I think we have the consistency of the ink correct at last.'

Normal Training School:
Boarding fee £8 per annum
School fee 10/- per annum

Elementary School (Std IV and V):
Boarding fee £8 per annum
School fee 5/- per annum

'Have you started on the price list for the booklets?' Walter asked.

'Yes, sir, I completed it this morning.'

'Well, let's run it off now, shall we? Where is my copy of the text?'

Benedict took some handwritten papers from a drawer and then turned to the printer's tray.

'Preparation and Thanksgiving Offices, 1/- a dozen,' read Walter, consulting his notes. 'Vestry Prayers. On a large card, 4d. On paper, a penny.'

'I have tuppence,' said Benedict.'

'Make it one. Counsels for Communicants, 1/3 a dozen. Lessons from the Apocrypha, 6d each.' Walter looked up at Benedict and said, 'I'd like you to design the Choral Union Programme for me. Do whatever you like and set it as you wish. You may use these new decorations,' and he took the little blocks that the printer had sent from his pocket and laid them side by side on the table. He was watching Benedict's face as he lit his pipe. 'See what you can do. I shan't interfere.'

Benedict whistled between his teeth to see the little blocks. He took them to the ink stand and inked them and found a scrap of paper and pressed them down on it. And he laughed. 'Beautiful,' he said and sniffed the blocks delicately as though the smell of the ink was a delight. 'Thank you, sir.'

'To work,' said Walter, taking off his jacket and rolling up his sleeves.

They were absorbed, he and Benedict, oblivious of the passing of the morning, engaged in a communion beyond the price lists and the order for invoices that they had printed and parcelled up to send to Nettletons store and the little booklets they were preparing. Walter sat back and read from the proof in his hand, '*Wena wenziwa ngubanina*? Who were you made by? By God. *Upina u-Tixo*? Where is God? *Uyinina u-Tixo*? What is God? *U-Tixo ungu-Moya*. He is a spirit. *U-Tixo ukuzo zonke indawo*: God is everywhere.'

Indeed He was and it seemed to Walter that He had come to put them on the rack, to test them all: it was the lunch hour when Mzantsi came in from an outstation, riding on the mare, and went to Father Charles in the workshop and reported that an ox was dying near the fence, mucus pouring from its nose. Walter found Charles Farborough in the church on his knees. There was something in the way he was bent, a stoop to his shoulders that made Walter approach, put out his hand and say, 'Father Charles?'

'The rinderpest has reached us,' said the old man, tiredly. 'I have been looking for the signs these past months. How I prayed it would pass us by. There will be such a time of want.'

He stood and looked at the altar quietly. 'Will you go down to the house, Brownley, and ask Crispin to bring his rifle and send Benedict to fetch some men and boys from the lands. We will have to bury the carcass.'

Crispin brought his gun. The workmen fetched picks and spades. Walter went back to the printing-room. He tidied away the tools, set the papers on the shelves. He heard a shot. Flat, unexceptional in the afternoon with such a wind blowing, sending the windows rattling in their frames. He opened the door and walked out towards the group standing by the fence. Father Charles and Crispin stood watching as the workmen shouldered their picks, striking into the flinty earth. Nearby lay the ox, shot cleanly, its head thrown back, some anguished bellow stilled in its throat.

It took the men three hours to break the earth and lift the ox and fill the soil in. Father Charles, knowing the temptation to take the contaminated meat from the carcass, left Crispin to supervise the burial. He toiled with the field-hands, his head bent against the wind. Dusk had fallen by the time the mound was raised.

All afternoon as Walter and Benedict worked in the printing-room – Why am I a Churchman? *Yinina endibanga ukuba ndibe ngumChurch?* 1/4 per doz., all enquiries to Rev. W.J. Brownley, St Matthias Mission, Cape Colony – Walter heard the sound of the picks, prying at the earth.

The ox had stood there, in its aloneness, dying without struggle. It had not appeared – the harbinger of death and their destruction – bellowing and announcing itself for them to know the time had come. Thin, pathetic in its sickness, Crispin had shot it where it stood. What had Brompton said?

> And so shall be the plague of the horse,
> of the mule, of the camel, and of the ass
> and of all the beasts.

And as soon as the shot had echoed off, dully in the hills, it was as if a cold, urgent fear had seized them all, a frenzy of preparation to be away.

Within a few days of the shooting of the ox, a notice came to the Post Office, informing them that the roads would be closed to all traffic within a week. The boarders from the schools and the Training Institute were sent home. The nuns went with them, returning to the Mother House in Grahamstown. The classrooms stood empty. The workshops were abandoned but for Mr Groenewald and the old men. Father Charles and Walter went in to help whenever they could. The tinsmithy doors were fastened and a log rammed up against them to stop them from rattling in the wind.

Emily Farborough made a list of supplies needed in the house. Each person submitted their own. She and Frances compiled a notebook of wants. It would be entrusted to Victor to deliver to Dyer's in King William's Town on his way to the Grahamstown train.

Victor's suitcases were hastily packed, his room emptied, his boyhood things put away in the loft as if all sojourns at St Matthias were at an end. Arrangements had been made for lodgings overnight at the Stanbridges in King William's Town so that he and Crispin would be in time to catch the early train. Victor's suit, his hat, his shirts, his shoes were hastily prepared: a Victor-in-waiting hung stiffly in his wardrobe.

Crispin's school trunk was brought from the shed and laid in his room and Helmina took charge of it, bringing newly darned socks and lengthened trousers to pack in it. She put a sprig of lavender from the garden among his cricket togs and rugby boots while Emily fussed about the lists, drawing and re-drawing them, going through the minutiae of each day should anything have been forgotten. No one could tell how long the roads would be closed. There were so many hidden things to consider. Wine for communion, incense, candles in case the supply of sheep-fat should be depleted, paraffin and wood and meal and tea and washing-soda and soap and nails and screws and paper and ink and lime and seeds and hoes and feed for the horses and so much more. Cloth and needles, cotton and medicines.

She worked at the desk in the living-room with Father Charles on the night before Victor and Crispin went, a lamp burning between them. There was quiet, no one wishing to speak of a parting. Helmina drooped over the mending. Crispin sat near her, whittling away at his carving.

'What are you making, Crispin?' Helmina asked quietly.

'A little figure, but I'm still waiting to see what the grain decides it should be. I took the wood from the tree by the big pool.' He scraped with the knife. 'I wonder when I will be home again . . .'

'I will pray for you often,' Helmina said and the needle flew in and out of the seam.

'Six months is such a long time. Perhaps the roads won't open for a year.'

'Of course they will,' said Helmina. 'Do you think we could do without you for so long?'

'No one notices if I am here or not.' Matter-of-fact.

There was no wheedling for denial but Helmina replied, 'What a thing to say!'

'Victor will soon be at Native Affairs in Johannesburg.' He spoke softly. 'I would like to work with him. There is no use in my finishing school. What do I learn anyway? It's a caning every other week for blots in my books, no matter how hard I try.'

'Crispin,' Miss Smythe had turned her shoulder from the others. 'You must finish with school first. Then you may go where you choose.'

'Perhaps the mines,' said Crispin. 'Victor thinks that's a good idea.'

'Now why would you want to work down a hole?'

He laughed softly at her. 'Not down a hole! That's not what I mean. Vic was talking to Mr Stanbridge on Sunday and now he has an idea that one day we should both become recruiters for the mines and go all about the country together organising a team and signing up natives.'

173

'And here we believed Victor might be called to be a priest and instead he wants to be a sort of slaver!' She glanced across at Victor in the corner, near the lamp, his head resting against his hand, reclining in a chair, reading the Punch, his lids drooping now and then. 'I can see he's after empire-building of another kind.'

'It would be a good way to get about and see things,' said Crispin, crestfallen. He cracked his knuckles together. The sound was loud in the room.

'Crispin!' his mother looked up from her seat at the desk. 'Don't! You have learned it from the apprentices. They do it in church all the time and it is very vulgar.'

Crispin let his hands drop. He looked at them a moment. 'Imagine if I could have been a priest,' he said. And there was a warmth to his face – an odd, slow flush.

'Well,' said Helmina. 'The natives would have understood very well, every word you said. If I close my eyes when you are speaking, I can't tell you apart from Benedict or Tom.'

Victor looked up from his paper and regarded them. He smiled, as if to himself. Brief deprecation, concealed again as he subsided and yawned and returned to his occupation. Crispin, his eyes intent on Victor, half laughed – self-derogatory – as if he wished to retract his words and punish himself for having said them. Victor's glance had brought about the burning of his ears and he pulled at a lobe and bent his eyes to the carpet. Like a child, laughing in imitation of an elder, the smile had started in innocence, drawn in suddenly – with something of submission, with something of surprise – when he found that the mirth was turned against him.

Crispin stood awkwardly, and looked at his mother and father writing at the table in the corner and said, 'I'll just go over to the boarding-house and speak to Benedict.'

'I shall want to see if your jacket sleeves need lengthening,' said Helmina hastily, not wishing him to feel dismissed or scorned.

But he was gone before she could say more and the fly-screen across the door closed quietly behind him.

Helmina continued to sew, stabbing with her needle, wishing Victor was her victim, not the seam. She did not look up when he put his paper aside and left the room. She heard him step into the hallway and walk along towards the kitchen. The light in the passage wavered as his shadow passed across it. She looked up then and listened. She could hear the chink of cups. Frances was in the pantry preparing the tea-tray before prayers. Helmina snipped the cotton and tied a knot. Bold, provocative Victor. Snip, snip, snip. He could not hide it from her. Those looks! That careless, unconcealed bravado when he stood near Frances! She took up her reel of cotton and cut a length. She did not move from her seat. She did not go hastily after him. Let him trifle with Frances unhindered in the pantry. Let him. Frances, in her recklessness, deserved him. Helmina threaded her needle again. Cleanly, she thrust the cotton through the eye. Oh yes, Frances deserved him. And the sooner Walter Brownley saw it, the better.

Father Charles got up from the desk and took off his spectacles. He put his hand on his wife's shoulder and said, 'Leave it now, my dear, and let us have our tea. I shall help you in the morning. There will be time enough before Victor and Crispin set off. I'll just go across and call Brownley in to join us for prayers.'

He returned some minutes later, followed by Walter.

'Good evening, Mrs Farborough, good evening, Miss Smythe.' Walter put a bundle of letters on the table. 'Could Crispin take these with him tomorrow? I should prefer it if they were posted in Grahamstown.' He took a seat beside Helmina and smiled across at her. Leaning back, he looked about the room. He had not been in the Farboroughs' house for a week.

Frances entered with the laden tea-tray. She set it on the table and lifted the cloth off the milk jug. She murmured 'good evening' to Walter as he stood to greet her but she did not look at him and she retreated to the kitchen for an extra jug of hot water. She was some time about it. When she came back, Victor was behind her, walking closely, as if he had his hand concealed at her back and she confused as to where to look.

'Where is Crispin, Victor?' said Father Charles. 'Be a good lad and call him.'

So they drank their tea, each preoccupied with tasks not quite complete. Walter checked through his letters again. On top of them he placed a small parcel addressed to his sister Daisy. It contained a story for Miranda. 'Plotz and the Tale of Boggis, the Magical Unicorn.' His fingers lingered on the package: ah, Plotz, exiled to the lodge, almost dead for want of company.

Father Charles fetched his Bible and laid it on the table before him, choosing a passage. He looked up as Victor and Crispin came in and he said, 'There you are, then. Crispin, bring a chair for your mother. I will have her beside me. It will be some time before we have you all in the house together again and we shall miss you,' and he looked around at them and touched Frances's cheek affectionately.

Good and deep was the voice of Father Charles. Simple in his requests. No fervent supplications. No bargaining. He asked Godspeed on the journey to Grahamstown for Crispin and Victor. He said, 'May the Lord grant courage, not just in body, but in spirit; fair-dealing with all men; humility before God.' He opened the Bible and he read:

> See, I have set before thee this day life
> and good, and death and evil;
> In that I command thee this day to love
> The Lord Thy God, to walk in His ways,
> and to keep His commandments and
> His statutes and His judgements,
> That thou mayest live and multiply:
> and the Lord thy God shall bless thee
> in the land whither thou goest to possess it.

And when he had finished he shook Victor's hand, and Victor's eyes were upon his boots under the gaze of the old man, and then Father Charles turned to Crispin and drew his head in to his chest and there was a benediction in his fingers and he kissed Frances and Helmina and put his arm about Emily's shoulder. 'Good-night to you all,' he said. 'Good-night, Brownley, old chap, and God bless.'

Walter, due to leave before dawn for the outstation at

Gxulu, took his leave of Victor and Crispin on the porch. A perfunctory handshake from the former, a swift appraisal of his person, a cool goodbye, but Crispin walked with him to the lodge and said as he reached the door, 'I have packed the musical-box in my trunk, sir. I will repair it at school. We have a good workshop and more tools than here and the master will help me. I'll take it to Reverend Brompton when it's done, I promise.'

And Walter said, 'Thank you for going with me to Mbokothwe, Crispin. You are valued more than you can know.' And he took his hand in both of his and he looked at him and said, 'Book learning and accomplishment in the world mean nothing if you do not have compassion, Crispin. You have it in abundance – and the heart to stand steady in the sight of God.'

Walter sat a long time and smoked his pipe, a single candle burning to light his book. He went to bed after midnight and slept fitfully. Sometime towards dawn he opened his door and let the air in. He could see the grass stretching down towards the oak which tangled against the sky and, beyond, the bee skeps, squat and dark in the gloom. There was a waning shard of moon. Its light seemed grey and comfortless. He lay on the bed, awake, with heat in the throat and eyes rough with the need to rest. There was no quieter place than St Matthias at night. No sounds of men, no beast, no night birds calling. He could not hear the river as he could in times of plenty. The water was too shallow, too still, too listless to journey on. Palpable silence in that night, secret in its blood, secret in the heart of it: he did not leave the bed to scan the house to see if Victor's window was open, his room deserted. If it was, he did not wish to know.

Victor and Crispin left after breakfast, Benedict and Mzantsi accompanying them to bring the buggy back, laden with supplies. The luggage was brought by Kobus and Nowasha. Helmina followed, carrying a basket of food for the journey. Crispin, his hat pushed to the back of his head, was clowning to keep the desolation away. He kissed Frances for the third time, ran around her and kissed her other cheek again until she said, 'Oh, go on with you!'

177

He went to Helmina and kissed her too. She took out her handkerchief and said softly, 'Godspeed, Crispin,' and wiped her eyes.

His mother held his face between her hands. 'Work now,' she said, 'and I shall be proud.' And she looked at him and then she smiled, just a small softening of the sternness, and he turned to his father who took him to the buggy with his arm about his shoulders and saying nothing, but his embrace strong and firm.

Victor's farewell had been cheerful but perfunctory. He had come to Frances last of all but she could not look up into his face with her father and mother watching and Miss Smythe greedy with her eyes. She felt the pressure of his hand, his breath on her face as he bent to kiss her cheek. Then he was gone. He swung up into the driver's seat and shook the reins.

Mzantsi and Benedict and Crispin raised their hats, shoulders jostling, as the buggy spun out of the yard. There was Benedict, sitting in the back in his best jacket, his collar starched stiff as a curate's. He saluted, shouting something to the workers gathered near the forge. Jaunty, he looked, eager to escape, and a long road ahead.

It was a weary road from Rabula to Debe Nek and the fields were fallow round the homesteads. The wheels sent up dust to lie heavy on the bushes and the air was still and dry. Mzantsi slept, released from his duties. His face was soft, folded in on itself as he breathed.

Victor was preoccupied with thoughts of his own, driving the mules with some impatience. He said to Crispin, 'They'll let you out of school soon enough, you know. Play the dunce a bit this term and you'll be with me by Christmas.'

'I *am* the dunce,' said Crispin ruefully.

Victor waved the remark away. He said, 'What is needed are men who can speak the language. *That* you can do better than any. I'll talk to Mr Stanbridge about it and keep my ear to the ground and I'll cultivate the right people, you can be sure!'

Crispin said, 'Well, it will have to be on your own account. I won't get any references from the Head.'

'The devil take him!' laughed Victor.

Towards midday they came to the place where the road met the main route and Victor turned the mules south-east. A mile or two beyond, on the bank above a ford in a river, they came upon a tent. An idle wind slapped at the flaps which hung loosely at the entrance. It squatted like a vagrant, a small fire smouldering nearby. Beside the tent was pegged a sign:

Runderpest!
Pad Gesloten.
Road Closed.

They slowed their pace as a man emerged. He shambled up, like a creature from its den. He pushed his hat back on his head – a mane of grizzled hair reaching to the grime-rimmed edges of his collar – and he spoke, raising his arm to halt them. His words were heavy on his breath and there was a tremor in his hand. He said, 'Pull up,' and he pointed to a place where there was a hitching-post, made roughly of a thorn stake.

Victor drew in.

The man stood with his hands on his hips, thumbs hooked in his belt. He turned his head and spat a stream of tobacco-stained spittle. 'Rinderpest halt,' he said. 'Unharness your mules. They must go in the dip.'

'We were told that the roads wouldn't be closed for another ten days,' said Victor.

'No traffic after that,' said the man. 'This is a precaution. Where did you come from?'

'The mission,' said Victor.

'Then it's orders.' He jerked his head in the direction of the settlement. 'You are close to the kaffirs up there and they have got the rinderpest.' He gestured towards Benedict and said, 'Tell your boy to unharness.'

Crispin looked at Benedict and said in Xhosa, 'Hey, boy, unharness the mules,' and laughed and began to unharness them himself.

The man turned on Crispin. He said, 'Why are you and the kaffir laughing?'

Benedict and Crispin were both silent for the man was slow

179

and dull but the brandy was sharp in their nostrils as he came near.

'Do as he says,' said Victor, regarding the man as if he was contemplating putting his foot in his face. Together Crispin and Benedict led the mules to the dip. It had been constructed hastily beside the road, made of concrete and stones and stinking of carbolic. The mules balked and backed, jerking in fear as Benedict and Crispin tried to calm them. The man fetched a stick to drive them in, prodding them harshly, 'Camaaan, camaaan!' he shouted.

Hooves on stone, the grate and slip as they struggled to retreat, quivering legs and haunches, the incomprehension of slow animals, eyes turned back, snorting.

The man said, 'The old kaffir next.'

Benedict turned and looked at him. He said, 'Pardon?'

The man ignored him. He slipped his thumbs up to the inner edge of the greasy braces that held his breeches and addressed Victor. 'Tell the old kaffir in the cart to undress.'

'Why should he undress?' said Victor.

'He and your boy will both undress or I will undress them myself,' said the man and he laughed and the small stubs of teeth among the weed of his beard showed clearly and the tongue, like a sea-creature suddenly exposed, drew in to the darkness of his mouth and then he spat again and tapped the stick against the ground and stood there, with his legs apart, between the buggy and the dip.

Victor said, 'Why must they go in the dip?'

'Orders. All animals and kaffirs.' He took a piece of paper from his pocket, unfolded it and stabbed his finger at it. 'See.'

Before he could answer, Mzantsi climbed down from the buggy and he raised his hat respectfully and he said, 'Excuse me, sir. We are from the mission. I am the catechist at St Matthias. This young man is a student there. What is the need for us to go in the dip? We do not work with cattle.'

'So? This is a gentleman!' said the man and he swept his hat from his head and bowed. He wheezed with laughter. 'This is a gentleman that cannot go in the dip like all the other kaffirs. Other kaffirs aren't good enough for him any more. A wagon just went through the dip an hour ago and every kaffir riding in it. Quietly too, with no complaints!' He stepped up to Mzantsi who seemed to cower under the blast of his breath. 'Kaffir is kaffir however smart the waistcoat!' He hooked his fingers in Mzantsi's waistcoat and jerked. The old brass buttons flew off and his watch fell from the pocket and jounced on its chain.

Still holding him, the man took the stick in his hand and, squinting up at it in concentration, delicately lifted Mzantsi's hat by the brim. He lobbed it into the dip and said, 'Fetch it!'

'Leave him,' cried Crispin, springing forward, fists up. But Victor interposed between them, 'Fetch it yourself,' he said to the man, and cold, so as not to doubt him.

'Don't cause trouble, sonny,' said the man, looking him up and down. 'I have a gun and orders to use it if people disobey.' And he fingered his belt. 'I can also confiscate your mules and cart, so just tell these people to go in the dip. Quietly, see. Meek like lambs,' and his sea-creature tongue flickered behind his teeth.

'I will walk before you, *Mfundisi*,' said Benedict and deliberately he began to remove his clothes, his eyes on the man. He folded his jacket and his tie and his socks. Slowly he set his boots side by side and he laid his little hat on top of his trousers. He stood in his underclothes.

Mzantsi went behind the buggy and his breath was short and panting as he pulled off his shoes and his jacket. Bewildered – as though he had been kicked – he spoke no word but his lips moved silently and Benedict knew that he prayed.

The man came forward and the wheezing laugh was back in his throat and again, using his stick, flicking it gently as he approached, he lifted the edge of Mzantsi's undershirt and said, 'Off.' And he stood close and watched, his head thrust forward – a reptilian eagerness – as Mzantsi struggled from the undershirt. The man turned then to Benedict, but Benedict was already stripping.

Prodding Benedict softly with the stick, deliberate and probing, he said, 'Take off these pants.'

'I cannot go naked into that water. I will keep my trousers,' said Benedict.

'Off!' The man drew his hand towards his hip where his gun was thrust in his belt. Both Benedict and Mzantsi obeyed.

181

They stood naked by the buggy and the man jerked his head towards the dip. Then he picked up their clothes on the end of his stick and followed them. Victor turned away. Crispin averted his eyes from Mzantsi. Portly and abject, he half crouched, half waddled into the water. The man tossed their trousers and jackets, shirts and socks into the dip after them.

It was then that Klaus Otto's wagon came ponderously around the bend at the far side of the drift. Mzantsi stopped midway, froze as he saw the wagon creaking down towards them with the voorloper and the oxen and Klaus Otto's small gang of servants perched at the back of the swaying load. Benedict cried, 'Go on, *Mfundisi*!' but Mzantsi quivered there in his shame with the servants of Klaus Otto – gauche young heathen boys – staring unabashed at him and laughing. And Victor, despite turning away, had a look of fleeting amusement on his face but he walked off towards the wagon to hide it, strode across the flat stones laid in the stream.

Klaus Otto raised his hat. 'Morning, Mr Drake. I see they're wasting your time too, eh? There's another the other side of Town and the wagons drawn up for a mile.'

Crispin, paying no attention to the arrival of the other vehicle, began to wrench at the laces of his boots.

The man turned on him, 'What are you doing?' he said.

'If you dip them, you must dip me too,' said Crispin. He threw down his hat and his face was flushed and red.

'All right,' said the man, approaching closely. 'Take off your clothes, if you like. Let's have a look at you.'

Crispin flung his shirt across the buggy and was standing bare-chested in his breeches, wrestling with his belt, the man watching him, cunning in the eyes, when Victor looked round. He shouted, hurried back towards them. 'What are you doing, Crispin?' Half anger, half exasperation.

Crispin said, 'He made them strip and go through the dip, so I will as well.'

'Don't be an ass, Crispin,' said Victor. 'There's no point in flying in the face of the law. All natives have to go in and that's the end of it.'

'But why Mzantsi and Benedict?' he said.

Victor turned his back on the man and said in a low voice,

'You can't argue with this lout. He's drunk and armed. Let's get on with it and get away. We have a train to catch.'

The man was still standing close, staring at Crispin. Victor murmured, 'Put on your clothes, for God's sake. The revolting old faggot's enjoying this! I'd knock him down if it was worth the trouble.'

Crispin retrieved his shirt and pulled it over his head. Victor had taken charge. The man walked off and stood at the dip as Klaus Otto's voorloper and his other servants trooped through silently. Behind the buggy, Mzantsi and Benedict dressed in sodden clothes.

Victor swung up into the driving seat. He took the reins and the mules jostled under a brisk hand. Subdued, Crispin and Mzantsi took their places. Benedict pulled his hat down on his head. Silently, he followed them, his trousers clinging to his legs. They drew away. Victor raised his whip to Klaus Otto and guided the mules up the bank into the road. They drove a long time without any of them speaking. Then Victor began to whistle, urging the mules to a trot.

Mzantsi and Benedict sat at the back, facing each other across the luggage. Mzantsi looked at Benedict, scanned his face. He said, 'Our Lord tells us to forgive even those who deride us . . .'

'He was speaking of men,' said Benedict. 'We are only God's mules.'

'That is blasphemy, *mfan'am*.'

'Mules are denied manhood,' said Benedict. 'So are we.'

Benedict Matiwane had been reborn at the rinderpest dip. Baptised – not by fire – but by water and carbolic. He had watched Mzantsi, naked, crouching and shamed beyond his understanding, waiting for the pain of the boot in his back, the bullet in his side, the lash about his neck. Abject, they had stood together before a felon whose only power was the gun in his belt and the unwashed pallor of his skin.

No triumph, laughter, nor remembrance of times of innocence or hope could expunge this thing. Better to die like a dog than lay your naked shadow down before such feet. Better to have hyenas gorging in the heart.

183

Chapter Twelve

The rinderpest. Such devastation. Daily, the sky was scored
with vultures, turning on the wind. Daily too, the tribesmen
came, hungry and impoverished. An unseen curse had settled
on them. Emily Farborough, at the head of a battery of
helpers, made soup and bread. Straight-backed she stood,
immaculate, no trace of fatigue or distress. Doggedly she
worked.

No more red cattle were driven out to pasture. No sleds
were drawn along the dusty track by oxen, led by boys. The
wind sent dust spectres back and forth across the plains and
the roads were empty. Women hoed the fields. Men and children, bowed beneath another yoke. There were no oxen to
inspan for ploughing. The earth was broken into small uneven patches ready for planting.

Small settlements gathered about the mission lands:
shelters made of any detritus that the wind washed in. Sack-
ing here. Branches and fence poles there. Goats were tethered
to keep them from the gardens. Father Charles went among
the people daily and returned dust-laden at dusk. He said
tiredly to Walter, 'Here, Brownley, are our converts. They
sing a hymn for Jesus to get a slice of bread! I wish it was joy
and conviction that brought them.'

Meat disappeared from the Farboroughs' table and went
into the communal cooking-pot until it became unavailable
altogether. Miss Smythe held classes for the legions of children after her other duties were done. She told Bible stories,
interpreted by Nowasha the cook.

Emily sent to Grahamstown for clothes and Bibles but
weeks went by before requests were answered. She wrote to
Miss Prudieaux-Brune in England, asking help, but letters
lay sorted but unsent in small district post offices. Transport
was at a premium.

Father Charles sowed gardens of vegetables which the sun
dried thirstily. Then the locusts came and the gardens were
bare. He planted again: an old man stooping in the dust and

wind and heat. Emily worked at his side, impervious to defeat. *Laborare est orare*: the dictum remained uppermost.

Walter had not known hunger before and he had not seen it in others as he saw it then. It was a time of waiting and a merciless sky, white with heat, empty of rain. An inertia came upon the people and the journeys to the outstations made him sick at heart to see the want. How could he bring the sacraments to men whose mouths were parched for the taste of bread? How could he bring the message of God when the people did not have the strength to climb the hill to the chapel or the school or the small outbuilding where a service might be held?

It was with reason that the people called the plague *iTobiratyi*, the pride-breaker. Such was the curse. The people, Christian and heathen, came to Father Charles, asking help, but not even he could give them any comfort. Walter had met an old man on the path outside the mission, coming in with a small bundle of belongings on his back, an ancient, wizened pilgrim, seeking shelter. Walter had spoken with him, watching as he gazed silently along the track that he had trodden. And then he said, '*Zithi tu!*' and he wiped his hand across his mouth – a profoundly final gesture – 'the cattle are still'. And he turned unbent, despite his load, and walked on towards the mission.

In the years that had followed the opening of the tinsmithy and the carpentry and wagon-making shops at St Matthias, the mission had been almost independent. It was a source of pride to Father Charles. The Society for the Propagation of the Gospel had not granted an increase in its funding in that time for St Matthias was self-sufficient and thriving. So self-sufficient that the beginnings of dissent had been detected among the tinsmiths of East London. St Matthias's tinware was cheaper and better than theirs and provided unwelcome competition on the open market. Apprentices trained at the mission were in demand in town, and yet the merchants protested that priests should be engaged in spiritual matters, not in trade. Father Charles and old Groenewald took some satisfaction in their alarm and continued to produce.

And then the Colonial Government stepped in. Father

Charles showed Walter the letter, bringing it to the makeshift schoolroom which Walter was helping build among the shacks. He said, 'We've been told to cut back production at the smithy by more than half, Brownley.' No blame, no accusation, just his back more stooped than usual and, looking out across his mission lands, the far, patient blue of his gaze. 'Without the revenue, how will we make out? What about the lads?'

Walter turned with him and walked along the path, keeping step beside him. The little smithy, way off among the trees, the late afternoon sun washing soft sienna tints across its walls, seemed so small, so harmless. What of Tom and Reuben and Sonwabo and all the boys that worked with laughter and with song through the long afternoons after lessons? Besides providing training and labour for the people, the revenue funded building repairs, the purchase of implements, salaries, a hundred other things.

'The SPG will not give us more funds to make up the deficit,' said Father Charles. 'I sometimes wonder if it isn't better to be an unproductive mission like Mbokothwe and throw ourselves on the mercy of the Bishop.' He took his sun-helmet from his head and brushed his hand across his thick, close-cropped hair.

Father Charles seemed momentarily lost in some reverie and then he turned back to Walter and he said, 'It's not the only letter I have received today. There is also one from the Dean. He has suggested that all the missions in the Diocese have a Day of Humiliation service for the rinderpest.' He felt in his pockets. 'Here,' he sorted through the contents – pipe, prayer-book, papers – 'read this.' Walter took the letter from him. 'The Dean says,' Father Charles's voice was even, 'that the rinderpest is a blessing to us all as it will bring the heathen to the mission and make them receptive to the Word of God. He says we have much to be thankful for and that we should take it as a sign from God that the door is open to us to preach to a humbled and more submissive congregation.' Father Charles turned and stared at the abject little settlement below and then glanced at Walter. 'I believe the Dean has not served in the field himself, Brownley. Indeed no.' He seemed to purse his mouth, hidden though it was in the short vigorous grey beard. 'But there' – with half a smile – 'what would I know of the business of his cathedral?' He patted Walter's arm. 'I am riding out to Rabula now and will take evensong at The Hoek on the way home. Would you see to the Scripture class for me? I won't be home till after dark.'

'Of course,' said Walter.

'There is a parcel for you at the house. It came with the letters from Grahamstown. And there is also a notice from King William's Town to say that the rinderpest inspector will be here this week to inoculate the cattle. Please ask Mzantsi to tell the catechists to announce it at the outstations. We must bring in as many cattle as we can, although I fear we might be too late. I believe that the treatment is hopeless if a beast is already infected and that it can be a carrier for some time before the symptoms show. The letter says that there has been trouble at Peddie because animals that appeared healthy before the inspector came, have been dying since and word's been put about among the tribesmen that the Queen wishes to harm the black man and that the serum causes the disease. I don't know what we are to do if the same happens here.' Father Charles settled his helmet on his head and started away.

'Safe journey,' said Walter and he turned back towards the school building where women were smearing mud on the walls. He stood a moment and watched them, then he glanced away towards the yard where Father Charles crossed beyond the church, taking the path to the stables. It was clear that his back caused him pain for he walked as a sailor does, with a rolling gait, favouring the right side. The punishment of long hours in the saddle, of rising before dawn to make his visits to the outstations, of working in the sun and wind and heat and eighteen hours on Sunday, was exacting its due. He was an old man before his time.

Father Charles disappeared behind the quince hedge and Walter examined the spidery hand of the Dean's secretary on the pages that he held. He smoothed them, holding them in his shade, away from the glare of the sun, and read.

A blessing indeed! How could the rinderpest and the starvation and the want be a blessing? A blessing for whom? He would have liked to have taken the Dean from his dinner in the Deanery in Grahamstown and to have left him unattended among the hovels in the gardens at St Matthias. He would have liked him to see the women, listless in their exhaustion and their hunger, suckling children at sapless breasts. He would have liked to have invaded the sanctuary of that gentleman's study with the dust and flies and stink that pervaded the mission yard and shown him the fear in the eyes of the young and the resignation in the faces of the old. 'Day of Humiliation' be damned! This grovelling was Humiliation enough. This insidious, creeping despair and watching the skies for the first signs of locusts and watching the river for the last signs of water and the carcasses of cattle, bloated and obscene, lying in the fields! He would like to show the Reverend Dean all of it, to make him know *iTobiratyi*, the pride-breaker, for himself.

At noon Walter went down to the Farboroughs' house and knocked at the front door. Nowasha let him in. She was laying the table for lunch. There was a loaf and a bowl of broth. These simple things set on a plain white cloth. The basket of lush wax fruit on the sideboard looked strangely decadent.

Emily Farborough came from the living-room. 'Mr Brownley?' she said, beckoning him. 'The post is here and there is a parcel for you.' He followed her down the passage and waited at the door as she searched her writing bureau. 'I have been doing the accounts this morning,' she said, 'and the price of horsefeed has risen wickedly. It was five or six shillings a bag in January and the statement from Dyer's puts it at two pounds now!' She took up her spectacles and scanned the account. 'The horses will have to be retired at this rate.'

She pointed at another piece of paper and looked over at Walter. 'There is a circular from the Diocesan Offices. Do you know, only the smallest percentage of missions can expect help from the SPG now? What are we to do with the work in the smithy so reduced? And yet I see that we are still expected to contribute to the General Purposes Fund from the offertories as if we didn't have enough to see to ourselves. I do believe a lot of blockheads find high office in the church! We need at least two thousand pounds to set things straight, but we might as well wish for two million for all it will help. I have told the Dean before that a quarter of Mr Farborough's annual stipend is spent on feeding the horse which is essential to his work but he cares not a whit, nor that the students can barely see their books at study-times for lack of light.'

She picked up a parcel and handed it to Walter. It was weighty and wrapped in worn brown paper, dog-eared from handling. His fingers explored it expectantly. Three small books and a heavy, knobbly lump: Ottley's 'The Great Dilemma', 'Practical Reflections On Every Verse of Scripture' by 'A Clergyman', Benion's 'Cyprian' and a few pounds of Bevier Sol Fa print for choir sheets. Dearest Daisy. She could always be relied upon. It would be a treat to open it.

'And as if this is not enough to try the patience,' continued Emily, unaware of his preoccupation with the parcel, 'I have had a message from Mr Mzantsi that the teacher at the school at Nolovini is ill and that there is no one to replace her. Do you have any suggestions? It is too far for such small children to walk down here and there are dozens of them besides. Still, I really feel that the routine must be maintained at the outstations if we are not all to sink with the rinderpest.'

'We are stretched here, Mrs Farborough,' said Walter. 'Already the classes have doubled in size. I fear poor Miss Smythe and the other teachers are exhausted.'

'It would only be for a short time.'

'What about me, Mother?'

Walter and Emily turned. Frances stood in the doorway. 'I can't just sit here taking part in the sewing classes and helping with the music lessons if there's something more urgent.' She came into the room and looked at her mother earnestly. 'I could teach at Nolovini in the mornings and help with the music in the afternoons.'

'It's too far and you would be alone,' said Emily. 'It's unthinkable.'

'You did it when you first came here,' said Frances.

'Yes, but that was different.'

'Why?'

'Well,' Emily searched about, 'I was older than you.'

'No, you weren't. Not more than a year anyway.'

'But I was married.'

'Miss Smythe isn't married and you were prepared to send her.'

Emily hesitated. It was not a matter of age or of marriage. It was a matter of vocation.

Frances said, pressing her case, 'And anyway, those children are taught in Xhosa and none of you speak it nearly as well as I do.' There was no false pride. It was the truth. 'I'm the only person for the task!'

'We couldn't spare a horse and it is too far to walk.'

'It's no more than two or three miles,' said Frances.

'I could take Miss Farborough on Boggis or accompany her on one of the mules,' interposed Walter. 'Leave her there, do a tour of duty and fetch her back at dinner time. I could adjust the services at the outstations to ensure I was near to Nolovini at the correct hour.'

How formal he sounded, how businesslike. He held the parcel against his side and did not look at Frances.

'Do let me, Mother, please do. I'm useless sitting here. You always wanted me to enter into the spirit of the mission. Well, here's your chance to see that I can.'

'I shall speak to your father,' said Emily and she glanced from one to the other.

'Thank you,' said Frances and she kissed her mother lightly on the cheek but she sent Walter a strange, small, questioning look and went away.

As Walter walked down the path towards the curate's lodge he saw her through the window of her father's study, foraging energetically in the box of mission books, her sleeves rolled up to her elbows.

And so began the journeys to the outstation at Nolovini. Walter insisted that Frances ride Boggis and he took the mule, but when the mule went lame, he walked at Boggis's side, his hand at the bridle, trudging up the steep path to the high grassland above the mission grounds.

'And when I am an old man' – he had written in his journal one night – 'when I am an old, old man, God spare me, this will be the time that I'll recall. This time and the great wide sky and the burnt brown grass and Boggis plodding up the track to the outstation on the hill, standing with its mud-baked walls and the children waiting at the door, marooned in a vast dry sea of nothingness, always waiting . . .'

And he would leave her there among them – fingering her dress, hands tugging at her sleeves – and ride on, just he and Boggis on a path across the hill to some neighbouring settlement, riding in a wide circle about the school as if he were enclosing it in a magic ring to protect the place where she was, no matter how arduous the detour. And he returned at midday, fearful always, when the low building came into sight that it might stand forlorn and empty and she might not be there, but spirited away, snatched by some dark sorcerer. And he would stop and listen for voices, raised in song or chanting or, on nearing, catch the quiet shuffle of bare feet as the children bent above their slates and she walked among them or sat with a child in her lap that was too hungry and listless to listen.

And there were days too when Boggis had to be rested and they walked, setting out at sunrise, she in her cape, pulled up against her cheeks and her hands tucked into her pockets. She strode like a boy beside him and their breath tangled before them in wisps in the cold morning air. And sometimes they sang rhythmically, chanting nonsense poems that he taught her to keep their steps from flagging, and sometimes they sang other songs – soft and low – that they'd rehearsed with the Choral Union. And sometimes, too, they walked in silence and heard only the brush of their feet in the dry grass, or she would skip up beside him and ask for a story, just as Miranda might have done.

'What story?' pretending impatience.

'Plotz and the green lion.'

'Why not Boggis, the magical unicorn?'

And then they would come out of the shadow of the valley and up onto the free, wide edge of the slope below the school and she would call to the little children, huddled together for warmth, waiting for her at the classroom door. How her voice changed when she spoke in Xhosa, how the pitch deepened and rounded! And beneath and within it, an echo of warmth, stripped of the drawing-room detachment that he knew. No schoolgirl voice this. No prim, colonial conversationalist. This was surely how she spoke in her dreams, full and soft with laughter.

And in those morning rides Walter put aside all thoughts of rinderpest and famine – just for an hour as the sun rose and the last star faded – because the stretch of valley, between the mission and the school, was an enchanted place. Only he and Frances and Boggis and the bush birds – the shy and the secretive – came here. How Frances's mood changed each time they entered this no-man's-land beyond the river. None of the fretfulness or impatience she displayed at home were evident, none of the sombre preoccupation of the days since Victor had been gone. Here, they had a language of their own: a Plotzian language, devised and developed as the time went on. This place was the transitional territory for Frances-of-the-mission and Frances-of-the-little-school. Here, too, his priest's vestments were carefully stored in the saddle-bags and he walked freely in riding breeches and boots with his jacket slung from a finger across a shoulder, an explorer, an adventurer, Plotz in search of an enchanted land.

Here they spoke of everything. Everything, but Victor. Everything, but of the evening she had come to the church to seek him out and Benedict and Miss Smythe had interrupted and the opportunity had passed. That moment, so nearly known, lay between them. What had she wanted to say that she could not say now? He had broached the subject – oh, so tentatively – but she, like a small buck sensing danger, had retreated into banter, laughing at his earnest face, running up the slope ahead and plumping into the grass to wait for him as he prodded the lazy-footed Boggis up the track.

She had sat close to him as he rested there with the reins looped loosely in his hands and Boggis, with his knowing eye and drooping lip, an intermediary in their jokes, addressed by both as if for an opinion or a comment. How warm, how familiar was Boggis's scent and the tug of grass as he pulled at it and the unashamed gurglings of his stomach and the soft dusty shade he made as he moved about them.

How easy then it should have been for Walter to have put out his hand and taken up her fingers and held them in his. He had gazed at them often, right there, within an inch of his grasp and the word waiting, poised. 'Frances?' Just her name – Frances – and she would know. And yet, he'd dared not do it. She might retreat, recoil at the unfamiliar sound of it in his mouth, recall – swiftly – that half-contemptuous expression that he knew too well, that flint-eyed cool. So, instead, he'd stretched and said, 'Come along, Mrs B. Your pupils are waiting and this lazy animal will think he has no work to do. Besides, why should he have breakfast when we've had none ourselves.' He had stood and swatted the dust from his breeches and given her a brisk foot-up into the saddle and marched ahead, whistling.

'When I am an old, old man,' he had written in his journal, 'I will remember what a coward and what a fool I was. Bloodless. Half the sense of Boggis! Less of a man than a mule!'

And he remembered too the sudden quiet that always came on Frances as she reached the mission grounds when they returned at noon and that she always walked ahead a little and that her voice, when she turned to say goodbye at the garden gate, would be light and brisk again. She would go, small and solitary, up the lawn towards the house among the trees and leave him staring after her, no longer Plotz, magician and explorer, but Walter Brownley, priest.

The rinderpest inspector came. He arrived one morning, riding a grey, followed by a flock of sheep and a herder. The strange cavalcade entered the yard and the sheep, frightened by the mission dogs, huddled up against the wall of the church and pushed into the porch and stared with pale, vacant eyes.

The mission cattle, which had been kept close to the gardens ever since the outbreak of the plague, were kraaled beyond the church, well away from those which had been brought in from the outstations by the catechists. Thin, sunken-eyed, hides scrofulous from drought and dust, they milled about. Mzantsi stood vigilant among his little herd while Father Charles greeted the catechists, going among them, thanking them for bringing in their cattle. Animal-husband-men all, they smoked their pipes and exchanged news. The Christians from the homesteads around about came in groups, driving their herds before them. None of the heathen came. There were no red-blanketed men, marshalling their slim-horned cows.

Benedict and some of the other students were called to assist and bring ropes from the shed to hold each beast as it was inoculated. A restlessness and anxiety seemed to take the herd as strangers went among them. Somewhere, penned alone, the bull bellowed. The mission workers stood about, the old men murmuring among themselves, watching anxiously. Some way off, on the veranda of the schoolroom, stood Kobus's daughter, the ubiquitous broom resting against her shoulder.

A table had been brought from the shed and set under a tree. The Government inspector placed his bag upon it, opened it and extracted a number of phials and a battery of syringes. There was quiet in the yard. The old men drew together, watching. The students turned and looked, the banter dying down between them. No one spoke as the stranger walked down towards the makeshift shelter where the sheep were penned. Father Charles puffed at his pipe.

The inspector's assistant caught a sheep, held it deftly between his legs, immobilising it. The inspector bent to it and drew a phial of blood with his needle. He crossed to the cattle kraal, indicated that an ox should be brought. It was held, backing and balking. The sheep's blood was injected into its flank. The inspector took a small bottle from his pocket, filled the syringe and injected the other flank.

Through the long hot hours of the day he moved slowly but tirelessly from sheep to ox to sheep again, the sun flashing on the bright, cold metal of the syringes. And people came to watch, drawn as if by some strange sorcery, from the huts and houses, from the garden and the workshop.

It was Benedict who asked the question uppermost in all their minds. He said to Father Charles, 'Why is the inspector taking blood from the sheep and giving it to the cattle?'

'He is giving them bile from dead cattle and then blood from those that have had the rinderpest. The blood and bile are injected into the sheep and carried by them. It doesn't keep unless a living animal can be used to transport it.'

'Why do the sheep not get the disease?' asked Benedict.

'I don't know, lad,' said Father Charles. 'The mysteries of nature and of science are beyond me. There's a man called Professor Koch who has devised this and the Health Inspector, Dr Turner, says that it is the only way to stop the disease.'

Benedict turned and looked back at the watchers. 'I do not think that there are many who will understand the idea of mixing the blood of sheep and cattle,' he said.

'The treatment has been very successful in some places. Sadly, the heathen tribesmen resist it. We will have terrible difficulty ridding ourselves of the sickness if all the animals in the Colony are not inoculated. People will simply have to act in good faith.'

'This way, it is sure the cattle will not die?' Benedict looked sceptical.

'There are no certainties,' said Father Charles. 'But they will have a chance.'

But over the weeks that followed, they did die. In their hundreds. Except the mission cattle. Except those in Charles Farborough's personal herd which had been kept apart ever since the ox had been shot by Crispin near the fence. The mission people were silent and there was a strange brooding over St Matthias.

Father Charles tried to explain it. The inspector had said that cattle could have the disease for some time without showing the symptoms, that those that had been in contact with contaminated animals were at risk, that isolation and inoculation before a single beast in a herd had contracted the plague was the only sure prevention. And yet, there in the church on the Day of Humiliation, how could it be explained to the men and women sitting in the congregation with his own cows grazing quietly in the pasture below the curate's lodge?

Father Charles said to Walter as he stood beside him at the altar, assisting in the service, speaking softly and with resignation, 'I'd sacrifice our herd, every beast it in, each last beloved one, not to see the scepticism in their faces.'

He turned to the congregation:

Oh God, why hast Thou cast us off for ever?
Why doth Thy anger smoke against the sheep
of Thy pasture?
Remember Thy congregation that Thou hast
purchased of old;
The rod of Thy inheritance,
which Thou hast redeemed; this mount
Zion, wherein Thou hast dwelt . . .

Walter listened as he spoke the psalm and heard the break in
the old man's voice:

Forget not Thy poor for ever.

Outside, the crows would still be feasting, capering through
the glut of death.

Chapter Thirteen

There were a thousand people in the church at St Matthias for the Day of Humiliation service. More gathered under the trees that lined the avenue leading down to the porch. They came on foot and on donkeys. They came from Rabula and Chata and Gwili Gwili, from Nolovini, Sidenge, Tyume and Gxulu.

Even the heathen came in their ochred blankets, carrying their fighting sticks and the women, turbaned, bead-decked, and the maidens and the young men. A solemn gathering outside the church under the trees, the shadows deep and blue in the shade and the air hot and still at noon. Any ritual, any obeisance would be observed to whatever god might hear them: some power beyond their own was needed to relieve them of the scourge.

Walter, a pace behind Father Charles, followed the procession moving up the aisle: the choir and the deacons, the catechists and readers and Benedict leading, holding the cross before him. How the voices of the congregation gathered, rising, as if they had swelled from under the feet of the worshippers, full and deep and solemn and a sudden stillness in the avenue where the tribesmen waited, listening to the unfamiliar words.

The choir moved into their stalls and Benedict mounted the steps. He paused a moment and Walter came up and stood beside him. Beyond, the altar was clean and bare but for the cross and candles and the little lamp above, red with the flame of God. They turned aside and took their places, waiting for Father Charles. Benedict stood stiffly, drawn into himself, his eyes cast down. He gave no sign that he was listening but for the small tightening of his mouth as Father Charles began the service: 'Almighty God, unto whom all hearts be open, all desires known, and from whom no secrets are hid . . .' Woodenly, he stood. He made no response to the recitation of the commandments and he stared before him as if in some sharp and painful reverie.

197

'Thou shalt love the Lord thy God with all thy heart, and with all thy soul, and with all thy mind: This is the first and great commandment. And the second is like unto it, Thou shalt love thy neighbour as thyself. On these two commandments hang all the law and all the prophets . . .'

Benedict looked up then and caught Walter's eye. Walter inclined his head enquiringly but Benedict remained oddly aloof, shifted his gaze to Mzantsi, standing with his hands folded across his cassock, beard jutting fervently as he prayed, his head thrust back, his eyes closed. He regarded him a moment and then seemed to retreat from him too. He gazed again at the floor.

Walter went forward to read the Epistle and Benedict stepped down beside him to translate. Again his voice was wooden. He dropped his sentences at their ends, leaving them expressionless. Walter heard the sound of Mzantsi's robe as he turned briefly to look at Benedict.

When he had finished Walter returned to his place. He remained distracted by Benedict's preoccupation. He followed his gaze, discovering the focus of his attention. There, at the back of the church, among the menial girls of the mission, dressed in the oldest print, in german-cloth and calico, the badge of the St Agnes Guild pinned to her pinafore, was Kobus's daughter, Dorcas Pumani. He might have guessed.

Standing among the devout, how different she was from when he had met her. How different from the girl he had first seen speaking to Benedict near the mission gate, plucking at the Xhosa harp cupped against the curve of her naked breast – the ochred drape of her shawl, the soft, wild darkness of her eyes.

She had been at the mission ever since the time of the *umngeni* battle, when he had returned from Mbokothwe, laundering clothes in the great cauldrons behind the school and, in the absence of her father at the initiation lodge, taking care of his hut beyond the vegetable gardens. Still, she went home often, for Kobus Pumani's kraal was not far from the mission or the school at Nolovini, set against a hillside, looking down towards the river. He had seen her walking in her long skirts, moving swiftly up the path towards the ridge. The quiet obedience of the girls in the school was not hers, the prim, downcast looks of those in the sewing-room or in the laundry.

Walter had seen Benedict meet her sometimes and had smiled to himself to find how frequently Benedict had made it look like chance as he sauntered past the yard gate or took the path behind the boarding-house and though Benedict was allowed to speak no Xhosa to her, Walter had heard him often enough, quietly, in the recesses of the printing-room or secretly behind the buildings where the washing lines were strung between the trees. He'd seen them there amid the white cotton and the linen sheets, she with soap suds to the elbows. He had seen them exchange glances, and the flash of laughter as they parted.

She resembled her brother Sonwabo very closely. Her face, like his, was small and beautifully moulded. It was as if the high contour of the cheek could be bruised with the touch of a finger, so fine and unblemished was her skin. She moved with grace and candour and when she prayed she knelt with her hands folded calmly before her or fingering idly at the badge of the Guild of St Agnes at her throat.

It was to him that she had come, not long after he had first seen her, and asked him if he would accept her into the church because she wished to *gqobhoka* – break through – and become a Christian, feeling the need 'in her heart'. Walter had agreed, knowing well enough what it was that stirred her. Emily and Helmina had rejoiced at yet another convert and found a heap of faded clothes to hide away her comeliness.

The Consecration was nearing an end. Father Charles began the Lord's Prayer and the people joined him, the voices a distant murmur echoing in the nave but Benedict, kneeling beside Walter, stared ahead.

Walter knew the moment that had brought the change. He felt both helpless and responsible. A week before, he had gone with Benedict and the rinderpest inspector to the homesteads round about the mission. A strange white man with a flock of sheep wishing to inoculate their blood into the herds would be viewed with the gravest suspicion. The rinderpest inspector had welcomed Father Charles's suggestion that Walter and Benedict accompany him, speak to those who might be reluctant and encourage those who wavered. Benedict was known to the people, Walter a familiar sight on his horse, even to the most conservative tribesman. They had started at Emtwaku and ended at Nolovini, at the kraals that surrounded Frances's little school.

Among the homesteads that they had visited was Kobus Pumani's. It was a Saturday and they had come upon Dorcas and her mother in their field, hand-hoeing the small, sun-leached plot. Stripped to the waist, an ochred skirt about her flanks, bending and rising, wielding the hoe deftly, the sweat gleaming on her back, Dorcas had broken the earth while her mother worked beside her, loosening the bigger clods. It had been a shock to see her dressed like a heathen girl after the demure garb of the mission, the neatly plaited hair, the button boots that were too big for her. Watching her here, her vivid grace and strength as she laboured, her mission name, chosen for her by Helmina Smythe, had seemed suddenly absurd to Walter. No doubt she had another – meaning 'the awaited one' or 'child of the stars' or something equally evocative of the season of her birth.

Clearly confused by their sudden appearance, she had barely raised her eyes to greet them and only her mother had come forward hesitantly, following behind as they rode into the yard of the homestead.

Walter had not visited this kraal before. It was marked 'heathen' on the little map he had been given long ago by Emily Farborough but Benedict had pointed out the hut of Kobus's great wife, the mother of Tom and Reuben, and that of the second wife, the mother of Sonwabo and Dorcas. They had dismounted and tethered their horses near the byre where the aloe flowers were still red among the curved blue-green armoury of foliage.

Kobus's first wife had emerged from the house and regarded them with unconcealed suspicion, scanning the sheep that waited on the slope below.

Everyone at the mission knew Kobus's first wife. She appeared sometimes, vociferous and commanding, when Kobus had not been home with his wages. Her voice carried across the river and the gardens and there were jokes among the old men about hiding him in the vestry, for it was known that she would not enter the church and had a fine contempt for the mission girls who had no knowledge of harvesting or hoeing or the making of sorghum beer.

Walter had seen her appraising Benedict shrewdly as he dismounted. She'd asked, without preliminaries, why the *mfundisi* had brought a flock of sheep to her kraal.

Walter had explained and Benedict had translated and she had kept her eyes on Walter as if Benedict was some incorporeal voice. As they had spoken, Kobus's second wife had entered the yard and stood at a distance, listening unobtrusively to her co-wife.

Walter had ended by turning to each of them, encompassing them both and saying, 'This is the only way to fight the *iTobiratyi*. Those oxen which have had the disease but have not died in the plague are costing thirty pounds each in King William's Town. This is money that none of us can dream of. We have no way to replace the animals we lose so we must take this chance to treat our cattle with medicines that will keep them healthy.'

She had listened and the other wife had listened and Dorcas had approached, having drawn a shawl about her. She'd stood bare-legged with the hoe crooked in her arm and her face grave and Walter had seen the smallest glance pass between her and Benedict with something of fear and something of reproach as the inspector and his uniformed assistant had brought the sheep into the yard.

In the byre had been a heifer, a cow and a calf. The inspector had glanced at them and said to Walter in an undertone, 'Don't look too good to me. I wouldn't be surprised if they aren't brewing something between them.' He'd turned to Kobus's wife and asked the whereabouts of the rest of the herd.

'They are in the veld.'

'Will you bring them in so we may treat them?'

Kobus's wife had looked at him a minute. So eloquent was her stare, Walter had almost laughed. She'd made a noise in her throat and said, 'No. They are the cattle of my husband and strangers may not go with them into the cattle kraal.'

'It's the same with all of them,' the inspector had said im-

201

patiently. 'It's an impossible task.' He'd addressed the woman in a brisk voice and gestured to Benedict to translate so that there could be no mistake. 'It is the law,' he'd said. 'You will fetch the other cattle in. I do not have time to waste.'

Walter had approached Kobus's wife and spoken quietly. 'We are not strangers to you, Mrs Pumani. You know us well enough. Your husband has been at the mission many years and your sons were in our care before they went to the initiation lodge. Even we have had our cattle treated in this way. I have no doubt that Kobus would agree to this thing if he were here but we cannot wait for him to come back with the boys because, already, this disease is like a fire, it sweeps in and eats everything. Unless we meet it with a fire of our own, it will not shrink before us.'

It was then that Dorcas Pumani's mother had spoken. She had said, 'These are my cows in the kraal. This cow and its calf and the heifer from last year. You can give them the medicines.' And she walked towards the kraal gate.

Walter had not understood the words of Kobus's senior wife, was unable to grasp the meaning of the sharp, vindictive diatribe, despite the hours that he had spent with a Xhosa grammar open before him.

Dorcas's mother had responded calmly, 'My ears do not hear you. These are my cows and I will allow the treatment.' And she had stood unbowed with a quiet defiance in the face of the other woman's anger.

Kobus's first wife had stalked inside her hut and as she did, she'd thrown a look at Benedict so malignant, Walter had felt the hairs rising on his neck. No one had moved. Only Dorcas had looked at Benedict and Walter had seen the fear tremble in her face.

'Get on with it then!' The inspector had rattled the poles of the gate impatiently.

Dorcas's mother had lifted them down as Dorcas walked away to call the herder and the cattle in.

She had come back to the mission on Sunday evening, wearing her clothes from the poor-box. She had attended evensong and she had been at her wash-cauldron the next day but she had not sung as she worked and though Walter had seen Benedict speak to her briefly, she had turned her face from him and he had gone away.

When he had come to the printing-room Walter had said, 'Is there bad trouble at the Pumani house because of the inoculations?'

Benedict had answered, 'Cattle are a sacred thing, *mfundisi*. And they belong to the head of the homestead. The cattle kraal is not a place for strangers. We should not have gone in there.'

'Are you a stranger to them, Benedict?' His voice had been even and unthreatening. He'd wished no sense of prying to intrude. 'I know it is a house that you might visit often in the time to come. One day soon, you might be calling there to speak to Dorcas's father.'

'All the cattle were treated against the wishes of the wife of Pumani.' Benedict had flashed him a glance – the challenge was implicit – and he'd said, 'If they die, what then?'

'Half a million of the Colony's cattle are dead already! How can it be your fault if theirs go too? How can that change things for you and the Pumanis?'

Benedict's smile had been sardonic. How great and sudden the gulf between them! It had yawned at Walter's feet. There were issues here that he could barely guess at: customs and traditions far beyond his grasp. What could he know of ritual and of bonds of blood, of the sanction of the shades or of a boy, who – having been abandoned – had none? Trying to compensate for his inadequacy, Walter had stepped closer and put his hand on Benedict's shoulder. Benedict had not looked at him but he'd said – a certain resignation in the words – 'Their cattle will die. This I know.'

And they did. Within four days of the inoculation, the cow died, and then the calf and then the heifer. And after that the other cattle in the herd began to sicken.

Walter wished that there was something he could say to Benedict as he stood beside him at the altar, something to confirm the laws of probability, of cause and of effect, and though he knew that Benedict would examine and accept – intellectually – any explanation that he gave, the issues here transcended cattle and their ownership, their inoculation or their dying.

He could not have guessed how deeply or how far. That afternoon, standing on the hillside watching the inspector go among Pumani's herd, he'd smoked his pipe and thought of other things. But as he'd ridden away, he'd heard, echoing in the quiet of the afternoon, the doleful lamentations of a cow. The crying of the cattle in affliction: voices of the shades, risen up in vigilance about them, an augury of things to come.

The congregation gathered in the aisle, moved slowly up towards the rail for communion. Emily Farborough played softly at the harmonium, Helmina at her side, turning the pages.

Father Charles went down to the communicants, Walter beside him. They moved back and forth along the line, bending to each, Walter with the chalice in his hands. He did not count the numbers that he served but he saw that Benedict did not come to kneel among them, that he sat unheeding in the choir stalls alone. And Frances was not with them either. He could not even see her in the church.

Frances was working in the school at Nolovini when she heard the shots. The children looked up from their slates in alarm and she went to the door and gazed out across the slope, listening. Three, four, five. The intervals between them were regular. Six, seven. Then silence. A flock of hadedah ibises cried a warning as they flapped across the open ground and into the cover of the trees.

All morning the shots rang out. They were distant and regular. There was nothing random about them. It was as if each found its mark. To close out her own anxiety and the sound of firing, Frances gathered the children about her and she told them a story, defying all instructions to use only the Bible. She told them of the *zimuzimu* cannibal that had captured a girl as she gathered clay from the riverbank, listening all the time for the sound of hooves. Why did Walter Brownley not come? The sun was approaching its zenith. She could not send the children home unless she could be sure they would be safe.

'*Kwasukasukela*,' she began, feeling the sweat creeping down her sides. 'There was once a little bird that could lay sour milk,' and the children huddled closer, drawing in around her, eager for the familiar words.

She spoke, but she did not heed her own voice for she listened expectantly. There was a pattern. The shots followed each other in grim procession and then there was a silence for a long time until they began again at some other place. They came closer and she went again to the door to locate them, but the curve of the hill and the clumps of bush and trees blocked out the nearer homesteads. Still, behind the shots, the flat finality of their sound, she could hear the lowing of cattle, the distant disturbance of their hooves.

The sun was way past its zenith. The children were tired. She could see now the hunger in their faces, the listlessness in their eyes as she spoke to them. None complained. They sat patiently in the heat of the little room. She watched them and her eyes felt heavy, hot behind the lids, her arms and legs limp. If she was hungry, there were those at whom the pangs gnawed more relentlessly. If she were weak, there were those near weeping in their need to be revived.

The firing began again. This time it was very near, the sound rattling the door and the panes of the window. It came from just below the ridge, no further than the Pumanis' kraal that she passed each morning when Walter Brownley brought her up to school. One of the smaller children started to cry. Frances picked him up and set him on her lap. She held him, her hand cradling his head against her chest. They sat in silence. Frances began to count the shots again. One, two, three, four. The bellowing of cattle was distinct. Five, six, seven, eight. A woman's voice, carrying across the ridge. Nine, ten.

A fly made slow circles about the room. Round and round it droned, clung momentarily to a face, an arm. It blundered away, rising to the rafters. The voices of the cattle died with the shots. The woman was no longer shouting. The gun was still. Frances waited and the little children waited, their eyes on her face.

He came at last. Frances heard the ring of Boggis's bridle.

205

She set down the child and hurried to the door and opened it. There was Walter Brownley urging Boggis up the difficult curve at the lip of the hill. She glanced about anxiously as if the school might be surrounded by hidden gunmen and she ran down towards him. She reached his stirrup and put up her hand to the pommel and said, 'Who is shooting? I've heard gunfire all morning and no one came.'

He looked down at her and his face was grimed with sweat, his clergyman's collar streaked with red dust. 'I came as quickly as I could.' He dismounted and turned and looked at her closely, keeping his hands at his side, 'Are you all right?' he said. 'You are very pale.'

'Who is shooting?' Her voice caught in her throat.

'The inspectors are back,' he said. 'They're killing all the sick cattle. Government instructions.' He lifted the reins over Boggis's head and led him up the path. 'The repercussions of all of this will be awful. I was down at Emtwaku after I left you this morning and the people are very sullen. The inspectors were there yesterday and there are carcasses everywhere. It's carnage.' He scanned her face again. 'You must have been anxious about the children.' He did not expand on his own anxiety for her, but said, 'They're busy at Pumani's kraal just now. I don't think there's a beast left in the herd. Kobus will be devastated.'

'What shall I do with the children?'

'You can send them home. They were packing up to go across to Chata. There'll be no more shooting here today.'

The children went. They in their pinafores and winter jackets, as if blown by the wind, like a flock of little birds, seeking the shelter at the edge of the trees below the hill. They did not sing and they did not run. They went unobtrusively, the older children vigilant, keeping the smaller ones among themselves, carrying the young.

Walter turned into the schoolroom with Frances and watched as she gathered up her coat and books and set them by the door. She said, 'My father is holding a service here tomorrow before school. I said I'd prepare the room and I forgot to ask the girls to help me. We just sat and listened to the firing.' She went to a wooden cupboard in the corner and opened it, bringing out a set of cloths and a simple wooden cross and a pair of wooden candlesticks.

'Shall I arrange the seats?' said Walter.

She nodded and turned back to her task and the silence was sudden between them. She laid the cloth on the table. The children had embroidered on it *God is Love*, in Xhosa, in brightly coloured threads. She placed the candlesticks on either side of the cross and surveyed it, her back to him. Walter pushed the wooden benches into place. There were only four of them but lined there before the little altar, the room was transformed. There was a stillness and a sanctity and the light lanced down through small holes in the roof, stippling the whitewashed walls, trembling on the dung floor, laying medallions of pale gold abundantly across the altar, illuminating the cross. He stood, waiting for her to speak. She remained standing with her back to him. He could see how she drew up her shoulders a little as if marshalling herself. He said, 'What is it you wish to tell me?'

'There is nothing.' Her voice was thick and swallowed away and she turned and looked at him a moment. And she contained the tremulousness in her face and set her mouth.

'Whatever has happened,' he said quietly, 'it doesn't change what you are or how we feel about you.'

'Yes, it does,' she said and she looked down at her hands, and then she went to the door and picked up her books and her coat and she gazed out a moment at the hillside and he saw her blink swiftly – once, twice – and she said, 'I'm so tired and hungry I could cry.' And she opened the saddle-bags and slipped her books inside.

Walter closed the door of the room behind him. 'I'll help you up,' he said.

'May I ride in front of you?'

Without comment, Walter mounted the horse, leant down, put his hand under her elbow, steadied the toe of his boot in the stirrup and braced himself as she sprang up. He took the reins from her, drew them in, turning Boggis, then allowing him to choose his own path with the extra load.

Frances seemed limp, balanced precariously and unheeding between him and the pommel. He held the reins in one hand and linked his other arm about her, holding her steady against him. Her temple, brushing his chin every now and then as Boggis stepped along the uneven path, was hot. He raised the back of his fingers to her cheek, touching it briefly, 'Are you ill?' he said.

She made no reply but settled closer into the crook of his arm. She did not speak all the way to the mission, rousing herself only to grip the pommel as he dismounted at the drift and led the horse up the bank into the gardens of St Matthias as they came in view of the house.

He led Boggis all the way to the drive in front of the veranda and he lifted her down and set her gently on her feet and said, 'Bed for you, my lass. You've got a fever.' He smiled down at her, feeling still the heat of her under his hands and he searched her eyes a moment until she withdrew quietly and walked up the steps into the house, bumping her coat along the ground behind her.

He stood with Boggis and he heard Emily call from the study, 'Is that you, Frances?'

He could not hear Frances's reply.

'There's a letter for you in your room. It's from Victor. Bring it to me when you've read it – I'm anxious for his news.' A pause. Then, 'Frances? Are you ill?' The sound of footsteps. 'My dear child, whatever is the matter?' The front door closed – a solicitous hand shutting out the draught.

Walter walked away, a greater weariness than he had known in months dragging at his feet.

Chapter Fourteen

'I look forward to taking up the post that has been offered to me in the Transvaal. It will be better to be in Johannesburg than Grahamstown. There is more money to be made and if one is ever to have influence, one must be in the biggest centre. There is talk of moving into a house with some of my old chums from school and I must say that the idea appeals to me. They're capital fellows and I shall enjoy being with them. Since we last saw him, Charlie Fraser has joined the Native Affairs Department up there and Sonnie Hook is attached to The Corner House. They are very keen for me to join them. I will be an assistant to Mr Warburton, the Cape Colony Representative in Charlie's outfit . . .'

And so it went, full of news, full of plans. Frances accepted that Victor would assume that others might read the letter but all that he said that might have held a personal note for her was, 'How I wish I was lazing down at the river now, instead of in this dusty office! We all had good times there but I suspect I shall not be seeing St Matthias for some time unless I am called for any unexpected reason . . .' He sent his regards and he signed his name with a flourish. 'Yours ever, Vic.' After weeks of waiting – just that and nothing else!

Frances read it three times and then she took it to her mother, dropping it onto the pewter tray that Emily kept for her correspondence, and said, 'Victor's going to Johannesburg' and went back to her room. She undressed and got into bed, unable to stop the bout of shivering. The sheets were cold, the pillow crisp and chill against her cheek. Her mother and Helmina came, bringing extra blankets and a brick warmed in the oven and wrapped in muslin for her feet. Helmina pulled up a chair and sat beside her, her embroidery in her lap, watching her face anxiously.

Frances slept and woke and slept again. Half dozing, half dreaming, trying to grasp the motive in the letter and why he had addressed it to her when it was so impersonal, so clearly intended for them all. Victor only wrote to the family when he had something to tell – like when he had been made Head of School or when he was elected as captain of the rugger side. This letter had been sent, not just to inform them he was going to Johannesburg, but with another intention. Had he reasoned that in sending it to her, she, and not her mother, would reply? Was he asking for her reassurance that his next great game would not be thwarted by the consequences of the last? Perhaps it was implicit in his words: 'Here's hoping you're in the best of health. I think of all of you at dear old St Matthias. Do send me news' . . . A convivial, expectant tone.

Ah, if she replied, how she would have liked – at that moment – to withhold the crucial information that he sought! *He* had not waited through days and weeks as she had waited, fearful and wretched. He had not wept in the privy on a windy afternoon – grit in his mouth and in his eyes from a ride in a gale from Nolovini – with weary relief to find that they had been reprieved, exempt, for the time, from what they'd done. And yet, she'd wept as well, with an inexplicable sense of loss, that that great triumph, that fierce surrender to the dictates of her heart, that instant of potential procreation had been barren, rendered suddenly so small and shameful. She had hidden away to wash her linen and she had cried for the emptiness she felt.

So, he was going to Johannesburg: a huge maw to suck him in, to sink him in the bowels of Babylon. Did this mean that he would not return? What hold would she or St Matthias with its dusty yard and its shack-filled gardens and its decimated herds have for him? A vision of the women of Johannesburg wavered before her: parasolled, tight-skirted, beautiful beyond imagining.

When Helmina Smythe had gone away, thinking her asleep and closing the door softly behind her, Frances fetched her writing paper and her envelopes and her pen and she sat up in bed, despite the weight of her head, her burning eyes, the cold that seemed to have invaded every bone, and she wrote to him. Punctiliously she told him the news of the last month. She wrote about the cattle being shot, describing the scene from her classroom and the sound of Kobus Pumani's cows bellowing from below the hill and the devastation that awaited him on his return from the initiation lodge. She described the destruction of the tribesmen's herds, the corpses in the veld, the hours they worked to bring relief to hungry people. He might be seduced by the glamour of Johannesburg but she would not let him forget the reality of St Matthias. She wrote without sentiment, with a brisk pen. 'I am helping at the school at Nolovini because the teacher is too ill to continue. Mr Brownley takes me there before sunrise sometimes and fetches me back at noon.' Here she hesitated. The journeys to Nolovini had nothing to do with Victor. She turned the pen around in her hand. If he read about them, something of them – of the long, cool slope leading from the river, of the quiet songs as the sky faded pale and green above the hills – might be destroyed. Anyway, why would he want to know except to smile disparagingly at it all? She began a new paragraph and she wrote, 'At present I am ill myself so I don't think I shall be going there again for some time.' And she left it at that. He could think what he liked when he saw those words.

'No doubt Johannesburg will suit you very well. I expect we shan't be seeing you for a long time. Let us know your address so I can send you a birthday wish . . .' What nonsense it all was, writing such empty platitudes and his birthday months away! And he would know – he too – by her crispness and the carelessness of her phrasing that she was angry and hurt. Was there no escape from the confusion of their games?

That letter, that careless letter, was put by Helmina on the hall table for posting a day or two later. She looked at it a long moment. She had been present when Emily Farborough had read Victor's news out after dinner and she'd wondered if something more personal had been secreted among its pages that Frances had withheld. Even if it hadn't, what had Frances said in her reply? Helmina was touched with a small, cold finger of foreboding at the news that Victor was going to Johannesburg. It was so far away. There would be so many temptations before him, he might forget the mission and Frances. Helmina, acute in her watchfulness, had been lulled into some complacence towards the end of the holidays, aware of Victor's absorption in his pursuit of Frances. He had stalked her like a hunter. And then something had changed. Not in Victor, but in Frances. Some discomposure, some fretfulness had replaced her usual impetuosity. She brooded when he wasn't with her, was secretive and irritable. When he had left for Grahamstown, she seemed impatient for letters and preoccupied with thoughts she would not share.

Then the teacher at Nolovini had become ill, Frances had taken her place, despite Helmina's requests to Emily to reconsider, and she had gone each day, unaccompanied by anyone but Walter Brownley. How many times Helmina had lifted the edge of her curtain and seen them walk out in the early morning, crossing the lawn and the gardens beyond and disappearing down towards the Mtwaku and the drift, the horse on a leading-rein between them. Helmina fought valiantly with the small, shrewish jealousy within her. She prayed about it, she practised endless mortifications to punish herself – but it was impervious to her efforts. It remained, waiting to rise and overcome the best in her.

She looked at the letter and she held it in her hands and she turned it over. Then she placed it quietly on the table and walked away, cursing herself for her scruples.

It was Walter who took it to the post at The Hoek when he went to take a communion service in the village. He, too, looked at that letter, as Helmina had done, wishing to open it and read it and drag from it some reassurance that he feared he might not find. He had stopped on a curve of the road just beyond the mission, out of sight of the church, and taken the post from his saddle-bag. He had rifled through it and when he came to Frances's letter, addressed in her untidy, boyish hand, he had held it irresolutely. It was fat. It was heavy. What had she said? Did she speak of their journeys to Nolovini? Was she amusing or disparaging? What endearments had she used? Did she speak of the thing that troubled her? If she did, what was it? Holding that letter, Walter knew that the answer to his questions was here. Here, in this stiff cream envelope. Easily accessible. If he knew the truth, he would swear before God that he would not misuse the knowledge. If

Victor and Frances were lovers – there, he had said it – he would walk away and never say a word of his regret, never seek her out again, accept that he had lost his right to hope. If he made such a covenant with God, if he vowed discretion, wasn't it in the interests of them all for him to learn the truth and be done? He pushed his thumb under the edge of the flap. He stopped and put the envelope away from him. A letter was a sacred thing. Besides, he didn't want to know. Not at such a price. He tapped the edges of the letters together on the pommel and slid them into the saddle-bag and when he reached The Hoek he went to the post office and pushed them across to the clerk with a finality that bordered on relief and paid for the stamps out of his own purse and watched them disappear irretrievably into the depths of a postal sack.

He should have buried it. With some ritual precision he should have destroyed that letter: burned it, thrown it in the river, trampled it underfoot – Boggis would have been a worthy ally – or left it to decay beneath some bush. A greater service he could not have done himself, or Frances. A greater service he could not have done the people of the valley or the mission at St Matthias. Frances, ill in her room, locked away with her own preoccupations, had sent the letter out. Walter had taken it, and, because he was an honourable man, he had not read it and even if he had, he would have put it aside, perplexed at its triteness. There would have been nothing in it to persuade him to withhold it. Its import – then – would have eluded him.

That letter went on its journey. It reached Victor in Grahamstown two weeks later. His vexation at Frances for not telling him the thing he wished to know made him careless of the other news. But he kept it anyway and he read it again, idly one lunch hour, and sat back in his chair and scanned the ceiling and then he took a pen and paper and he wrote to Klaus Otto, the transport rider, and he said, 'I have just heard that many of the people at St Matthias have lost their cattle during the rinderpest. I am aware that labour agents for the gold mines are taking advantage of the losses in other districts to recruit boys and I am anxious that they should not stake first claim in an area which is of particular importance

213

and interest to me. I think, through the unique experience of having been raised at St Matthias, that I could gain the confidence of the local natives and – even if the beginnings are small – secure a steady supply from the area. I am aware that, at present, you are not engaged in recruiting but would consider it a privilege if you would work as an agent with me and, in the course of your own activities – with which I do not think such an arrangement would interfere – engage labour from the St Matthias area for which a capitation fee for each recruit would be paid. There is resistance among the natives of the Colony to working in the mines but, under the present circumstances, the offer of cattle advanced now against the promise of labour in the future, is difficult for men to resist. Many have no option if they are to subsist at all.' His strategy was simple, his terms reasonable, his proposition for protecting the interests of the recruits against the unscrupulous depredations of other agents, unimpeachable.

Victor ended his letter by saying, 'We must begin somewhere and our choice of the first recruits is important if we are to gain the confidence of the community. I have heard that Kobus Pumani, who works at the mission, lost all his cattle in the rinderpest plague. It would be particularly well-considered to enrol his sons, Tom, Reuben and Sonwabo. They will have influence with newly initiated boys, among many others. Old Pumani will be perfectly amenable to pledging them if the offer of cattle is attractive enough. Make it so.'

It was Frances's letter that had suddenly recalled for Victor the conversation he had had with Harold Stanbridge all those weeks ago, aroused him to the notion that the time to branch out – within the constraints of his position in the Native Affairs Department – had come. The unexpected opportunity was too good to miss. Only as many recruits as he could handle would be engaged. Klaus Otto certainly took no risks and stood to gain a fair amount from capitation fees. The only outlay on the venture, for the present, was enough money for a half dozen salted beasts to act as first inducement to Pumani. This he had – a legacy from his father – but the means of employing it needed to be learned. So he took his hat and on the way down the High Street to post his letter, he called in at an office on the floor above the draper's shop. He took the stairs two at a time and tapped at the door with the head of his cane. Obeisance to an established agent would have to do for now. He stood in the dusty vestibule and waited. The door opened and he stepped inside.

Frances was ill for a week and in that time Helmina went instead to Nolovini. Walter took her as he had taken Frances, walking out in the early morning as the sun was rising and riding back at midday when the children had been dismissed. He did not mount behind her when she rode the horse. He walked at its side instead.

They spoke of this and that and as the days went by Helmina's awkwardness passed. She told him of her childhood in Grahamstown, of the old house just beyond the boys' Cathedral School in Huntley Street where she had lived, of nursing her mother, of her death, followed by the long and tedious journey to St Matthias. In turn, she drank in eagerly his tales of St Augustine's in Canterbury, became acquainted with his tutors and his fellow students: Rodbard and Taberer and Clarke and Jones; the curate Bates in Calcutta, dear old Brereton in East Africa and more. In quiet moments she assembled faces for them, histories and homes. Should she ever meet them she would know them, find acceptance with them for having entertained them all so often in her thoughts.

They spoke, too, of the mission. Once Walter Brownley said to her, unexpectedly, as they trudged up the hill above the river, 'What do you think will become of Benedict?'

She turned and looked at him. 'What do you mean?'

'Do you think he will take Holy Orders?'

'That is Mrs Farborough's dearest wish. I know he has the abilities. Why, when he was a child he was the cleverest little fellow imaginable.'

'A vocation?'

'What do you believe?' She had retreated then, afraid to commit herself in case he should think her foolish.

'There is such an anger in Benedict at present,' he said. 'But he will not speak. I thought he was writing articles for the mission newspaper but, although he has been working relent-

215

lessly, he has submitted nothing. I have a feeling he is sending his work elsewhere. To *Izwi Labantu*, perhaps? He is a great admirer of Mr Soga. I have subscribed to it to circulate among the students but I cannot for the life of me follow the Xhosa myself. I saw an article written by someone called Matiwane.'

'It's not an uncommon name,' she ventured.

'It was about the rinderpest. I asked him about it but he was evasive with me.'

'Surely, you are the best of companions,' she said. 'I always thought you were completely in his confidence.'

'We have been in matters of work and the printing-press,' said Walter. 'He has a real feel for editing and laying out a paper. But recently . . .' He shook his head, and they had trudged on.

Searching vainly for a suitable rejoinder, Helmina said, 'He would look very well as a priest. I am sure that he would have a following.' Walter did not comment. She continued, a little lamely, 'You should ask Crispin or Victor when they are here. Crispin knows him better than any. Even Frances . . . Goodness, the games they used to play as children! The hours they spent together fishing in the irrigation furrows or collecting those giant earthworms for which this area is so famous!' She made a small face, said, 'Frances had no sense of delicacy then. It's as well the boys were sent off to boarding-school.'

It was the only time that Helmina had mentioned Frances during their rides to Nolovini, though her presence between them was palpable. Helmina had no way of banishing her or of claiming this unexpected intimacy with Walter as her own: there – always there – as if she dogged them as they crossed the hill.

Helmina said, stumbling on, 'Mrs Farborough has always had hopes for Benedict and even more for Victor. She dearly wishes that he'd be a priest and run the mission when Father Charles is too old. She would not want to relinquish her own place here. She would like St Matthias to remain in the family, so to speak. She has hopes . . .' She left the comment hanging, waiting, but Walter did not say, 'Hopes of what?' and she sat rigid as Boggis plodded on.

'If any has a vocation, it is Crispin,' he said suddenly.

Helmina glanced at him. 'I'm interested to hear you say that,' she said. 'It's what I thought myself – but there, it's impossible. He just doesn't have the ability as a scholar.'

'There's no lack in his understanding,' said Walter.

'It's his letters,' she said. 'He muddles them dreadfully. I had the greatest difficulty when I first taught him for he wished to write with his left hand and my predecessor had insisted he use his right. I don't believe it did him any good and now he doesn't know which to choose. It was all too late to start again.'

'You're very fond of Crispin, aren't you?' said Walter.

'Yes, I am,' she said. 'Ever since he was a small boy. He has a generous nature.' How stiff her words, how they belied the unreserved warmth and concern she had for Crispin.

'He's very fond of you as well,' said Walter. 'You hold a special place for him.'

Helmina smiled. Walter would have liked to reassure her of her worth but she hurried on, saying, 'He will end up such a vagabond, going about the country transport riding or joining the army or something heroic like that. And yet, he's a homebody. I never knew anyone who loved a place as much as he loves it here. There's not a tree, a bird, a heathen or a Christian boy that isn't a friend of Crispin's. He was such a happy child until Victor came.'

'Victor?' Walter knew his tone was wary. It was not just Crispin whose happiness waited tenuously on Victor.

'Mrs Farborough has never known the extent to which Victor has influenced the children,' she said. She paused, as if afraid that she had gone too far, then hurried on, saying, 'Victor used to play so many games with Crispin and Frances. He'd dare them to do things that were reckless. I used to dread his coming for the holidays. He'd climb trees far higher than was prudent, scale the rock-face down at the river to get birds' eggs. He did it himself, of course, but he made Crispin follow every time, though he was still so small. Crispin never said no. I know that he was terrified that if he failed, Victor would taunt him – not bullying – just ignoring him enough to shame him into trying again. It was a matter of honour to perform well. Victor is still Crispin's hero. Just as he is Frances's. Whatever he asks of her, she does. Whatever he wants, she gives . . .' and she broke off there because the colour was high in her face and she dared not look at Walter Brownley, knowing why he searched his pockets for his pipe and why he filled it with such care.

He said, 'I think she might be too strong a character to listen to Victor always.'

'He holds over her – he always has – a most extraordinary power,' she said. If she was to speak, she must say it now. 'And yet' – she chose her words – 'I suspect Frances has an even greater power over him. I have often wondered if Victor really cares for anything. If he does,' she paused, 'it's for Frances.'

Walter said nothing. He walked beside her, drawing on his pipe, and he had reached the school with some relief and seen Helmina Smythe inside. What had she been trying to tell him? Did she know – had she seen – more than she'd admit?

He rode away, going from kraal to kraal, at the Bishop's request, to take a register of communicants. Statistics dictated that the number should increase with every year but, looking through the ledger, it was clear that they were falling off. Increasingly, he found that kraals he visited were inhabited by women, children and the elderly. The men had gone. Sons and fathers – an inexorable drift – finding work in ports and inland towns: East London, Port Elizabeth, King William's Town. The cattle kraals were empty, the fields were bare, the sky was merciless and the dust haze hung on the horizon like a shroud.

What would he write to the Bishop? 'My Lord, herewith the register of communicants at St Matthias Mission. It is not for lack of zeal among the catechists or clergy that these returns reflect decreasing numbers. There are numerous factors to consider . . .'

Rinderpest, drought, the land allotments fixed by the distant acts of Colonial Government? Or was it that the tribesmen here had simply found the God that they had brought was wanting? If the stars in the sky were the cattle of God – as Frances said they were – why did they shine so abundantly in the dark? Herds and herds of them, grazing pastures deep in space when the cattle of the men on earth lay in hollows, dongas, ditches, bloated and decaying? Surely, if God was the loving and benevolent Father that they preached He was, for each of the oxen that died on earth, He would, in His compassion, extinguish, one by one, the stars that crowded His celestial kraal and multiply their herds below.

As he rode from homestead to homestead, his passing punctuated by the baying of dogs, Walter turned over in his mind what Helmina had said. She was right about Crispin having a vocation. It was only a Crispin, who had lived here all his life – a strange mixture of heathen, Christian and pantheist – who could understand the underlying rhythms. The capriciousness of seasons, the inconsistencies of men, the mythologies which lay in the heart of these hills would not shake a faith which sprang, not from the sermons of other men, not from the intellectual exercise of study and debate, but from some primal and instinctive harmony with God. That was the vocation that was needed: some consciousness, some certainty, some quiet beyond the inconsequential beavering for registers of communicants and letters to the Under-Secretary about the discrepancy of the various names or the weeding out of heathen practice that sent men like Brompton to a hell that might have been devised by Lucifer himself.

From kraal to kraal across the hills he went, Boggis with his ears half turned back as if to catch his words, should he suddenly speak aloud. He met Helmina later in the afternoon and they retraced their steps and came out on the lip of the slope above the river. Walter looked down at the path. He could see the tussock and the little bush beside which Frances had sat in the early morning with the first rays just touching the tops of the trees, her cloak pulled about her shoulders and her hands, waiting in her lap, curled in against the cold. That enchanted place, pale now in the lambent light, the grass dusted with late seed. He recalled suddenly Helmina's words '. . . I suspect she has an even greater power over him.' Victor was not the only victim of her witchery. His only hope was to return this hillside to its own reality: a slope of grass, drought-infested. Disinvest it of its magic and put her aside.

And yet, when he'd left Helmina Smythe at the door of the

Farboroughs' house and taken Boggis to the stable, he found Frances sitting on the edge of the food trough, a scarf wrapped round her neck – the only concession to the fact that she'd been confined for a week – waiting for him. She bounced down and put her arms about Boggis's neck and rubbed her cheek against his hairy, dusty face and said, 'Dearest Boggis, did you miss me like I missed you? Goodness, look at the rheumy old eyes!' Walter took the bridle to the tack-room and caught her peeping at him but she withdrew, laughing, and addressed another comment to Boggis, saying – brazen creature – 'Did Mr Plotz have a happy time with Miss Smythe? Does she mean to take my post for ever?' Saucy then, an edge of impudence: 'You must beware of her, Boggis,' she rubbed the horse's nose, 'she means to make a prince of Plotz.'

'Why should Plotz prefer to be a frog?' Walter did not take his pipe from his mouth as he spoke and he heaved the saddle onto its mounting and drew up the stirrups and pushed the strap through and looked across at her as she stood in the doorway. She must have read those eyes, for she looked away and smacked Boggis on the rump to send him off and wiped her hands against her skirt, inspecting them, her head bent from him.

It was then that he should have closed the tack-room door. No more Plotz, the amenable buffoon, the fairytale frog, entirely-in-your-power-to-dismiss. No hat in hand, no wry, diffuse, comic wit, no precise, avuncular voice, no restrained assistant priest. It was the time to show her.

And instead he readjusted that saddle and took a cloth and wiped it down. He said – he might as well have croaked – 'Should you be out in the cold?'

She shrugged. 'I've been cooped up for a week and I've run out of books.'

'I'll bring you some after evensong.'

'Not Mr Brightman's Liturgies. And absolutely no Latin.'

'Get along with you,' he said. 'If you're looking for romances, you'd better apply to Miss Smythe.'

She hesitated then and she turned, her head on one side, 'Can I go back to Nolovini with you tomorrow?'

'If you're well enough.'

'I'm well enough.' And she was gone, a half skip as she went down the path towards the house and the light sudden and bright up above the trees.

Walter walked down to his room to collect his Bible for evensong and select, from among his small library, something for Frances. He looked through his books, taking two a little ruefully – she was capable of both but was unlikely to feel inclined to either – and went to the table to refill his tobacco pouch from the jar. He turned to the little window and looked out.

The sun had already gone below the ridge and one of the herders was bringing in the mission goats, whistling as he swung down the road behind them. Beyond, on the slope above the packstone kraal, a figure moved swiftly up towards the boundary fence. It was Benedict. He went through the dusk from bush to bush – now exposed, now obscured, now quite clear against the hillside. He climbed diagonally towards a clump of wattles where the people from the hills around often came to gather wood. Fallen logs and trampled saplings marked its perimeters and the ground beneath the trees was bare and sandy. Another figure detached itself from the gloom of the grove and walked towards him. It was Dorcas Pumani, carrying a bundle of kindling. Together they turned and disappeared into the trees.

Walter gazed after them a minute, then he took up the books and left the room, disturbed. As he crossed the yard, the bell rang out for evensong. The light of the candles was caught, pointed and pooled, behind the uneven glass of the windows of the church and he could hear the scrape of benches and the low sound of voices. He pushed open the door.

There was a quiet busyness about the nave. The old men sat together in the front pews beside the children and Emily Farborough was looking through her music at the harmonium. Helmina and one of the young mission girls were handing out the hymn books.

The recesses of the church were empty and dim, touched only by the glow of the altar candles, the light from the lamp. And there, within, was gathered the small community of worshippers: the cleaners, the hostel cook, large and sombre, her shoulders draped with her widow's tippet, the lame man from the forge and his wife, his five little sons, the simple girl who cleaned the church, polished the pews, stacked the prayer-books on the shelf by the door. There were a dozen children – orphaned or abandoned or donated – clad alike from the mission-box, small legs dangling over the edge of the benches, Nowasha presiding.

One – no more than five or six – glanced up at him from the corner of her eye. Up and then away and pulled in, by some slight, nervous mannerism, the sides of her nostrils, and laid her hands neatly in her lap. He looked at her small head, so poised on the tiny neck, observed the groove of the nape, hollowed between the sinews made strong from carrying aloft the burdens that he knew she was obliged to bear each day – a can of water, a log of wood, a bowl of meal. When the first hymn began she sang in a high, husky voice, offered with no consciousness of self, taking pleasure in the music.

A strange gathering – as if each had taken refuge here, thrown up in their separate lonelinesses from a wider world: widows, orphans, the homeless or inept. Only a few among them were part of a family, were linked by ties of blood. A little band of the displaced, waiting out their hours between these benedictions, gathered here to fill that space – that evening space when the end of work creates a sudden time of desolation – to carry it into their hours beyond these walls.

Despite the life-affirming hymns, the warm community of sharing under the candles' yellow glow, they – almost all of them – were denied the expectation of fulfilment and of joy beyond the confines of the church. The familiar words of the prayers, the benediction, could not dispel the pervasive sense of loss, the deep constraint, shared by the people in that congregation. Only the little children sat content and sleepy – all those emptinesses as yet unknown – while out beyond their reach, beyond imagining, somewhere in the grove of trees beyond the mission yard, Benedict was celebrating life.

And how could he, Walter – he, who longed so much for that great celebration for himself – call it sin or deny to Benedict the right to seek it in the name of love?

222

Chapter Fifteen

It was spring when Tom and Reuben and Sonwabo Pumani returned to St Matthias. They came across the river, striding through the shallow water at the drift. Each wore a strip of cloth about his head. Their legs were long and naked and they walked without constraint or fear of admonition. They had been cleansed of all such notions. Initiated, they were men.

Behind them, watching from the bank, stood the young heathen of their age-set. Shoulder to shoulder, they waited silently as the apprentices crossed the Mtwaku. A reed-warbler called from the undergrowth: *mvi, mvi, mvi, vityori, mvi, mvi, mvi.* As if it were a signal, as if the words of the bird had been determined as a sign between them, the members of the initiation lodge on the far bank turned away. The grass heads parted as they went, fell back as though they'd never been that way at all. When the stillness returned the reed-warbler began to call again, *mvi, mvi, mvi, vityori, mvi, mvi, mvi.*

Emily Farborough, walking down towards the church from the school with Helmina, saw them crossing the pasture below the house, moving swiftly in their near-naked, savage elegance, accompanied by Benedict and a gathering of mission people. She stopped, shaded her eyes with her hand and gazed towards them. Ah, she could see it, even from there: the depravity, the lazy sensuality. They moved up the slope through the open grass, careless of modesty, passed below them, going towards the carpentry shop where Father Charles and old Groenewald were working with the students. They kept in step beside each other, led by Benedict, the ochre of their blankets bright despite the deep shifting shade of the trees in the yard.

Emily turned to Helmina and she said, 'I must find Mr Mzantsi. He will have to take these boys into his care. Their influence, right now, could do incalculable harm.'

Tom, Reuben and Sonwabo Pumani were reclaimed. New jackets were found for them; trousers, boots and shirts. Repossessed of raggedness, they seemed to shrink within them. Mzantsi took their fighting sticks, banishing them as if he were divesting their owners of a sorcerer's accoutrements. Each evening he sent Benedict to bring them to prayers in his house and he sat at the table in the middle of the spartan little room, the Bible open before him, a lighted candle at his elbow. It threw into relief the shadow of the cross upon the wall.

Each evening it was so. Sometimes, accompanied by her brothers, Dorcas Pumani came as well, the windows closed against the night, closed against the familiarity of the dark, closed against the stars. She came so that she might stand at Benedict's side without fear of censure, so she might walk back to her father's hut with him, his steps light at her heel.

And what of Kobus Pumani? Before he had returned to the mission he had taken the path up the hill towards his homestead, his voice great in greeting. He saw first the emptiness of his fields, for the rain had not come and clods of dry soil awaited the first falls of spring. Then he saw the cattle kraal and he saw the earth in it was brushed bare by wind, unmarked by hooves. There was a stillness about his home as if some great bird had swept away what lived there with the shadow of its wing.

His first wife came to meet him. Only she. She told him what had happened, how the shots had rung out in the morning and the cattle had cried out in the kraal where strangers had entered, pushing in where the shades of his ancestors resided, and when they had gone and the cattle were all dead a stillness had fallen on everything and a greater stillness had fallen in her heart to see it.

And he asked why it was that no one had stopped those men, for indeed he would rather have seen the carcasses lying in the veld than to have strangers enter into his kraal and kill his cattle so that their blood stained the ground red as the aloe flowers that had bloomed about the byre.

And the first wife said, 'It is the mother of Sonwabo who allowed them in. Because of the blackness in her heart and the jealousy that grows in it. It is she who allowed these strangers in.'

Kobus spoke few words to his second wife, the mother of Dorcas and Sonwabo. He listened to no reason, no deputations that he should speak to Benedict Matiwane on the matter of the blood of the sheep and the men who had shot his cattle. He took no heed that it was her cow and her calf that had died first. He would hear nothing of the law.

He left her and he went back to the mission and took possession again of his broom and swept the yard, while the old men with their sacks gathered up the leaves that he had marshalled into piles. And he brooded on the loss of his cattle. And then, one day, Klaus Otto's servant came and Kobus went with him to The Hoek and saw Klaus Otto's horse tethered to the rail outside the store. They spoke, standing there beside that shop and Kobus went away again, thoughtful, stooped, as though the shades were waiting at his back.

In early summer the roads opened again. And yet they were empty but for a few wagons that trundled the steep incline towards the Donsa Pass. Sometimes cattle were driven by, salted beasts that had survived the plague. Klaus Otto passed once or twice, accompanying such a little herd, not stopping at the mission but the cattle going straight ahead and the herder brisk with his whip and his whistle clear in the summer air. Walter remembered how he had watched them go, how he had admired the red flanks, the slim curved horns, the aesthetic of the aloes and the cattle and the rock of the hillside and the line of the voorloper's great looped whip against the sky, little knowing whose they were or what their destination.

The tribesmen went back to their lands. They ploughed by hand, wielding the hoe, and those who had an ox might hire it out to those who had the funds to pay. The first rains came and the settlement about the mission emptied slowly. The small structures remained for a time, the haunt of bush-fowls. People carried away their planks and poles, women bearing them on their heads, crossing the drift and the steep path beyond the Mtwaku. Some stayed. Old men, old women, little children left in their care. Emily Farborough still went among them with the Bible and her cauldron of soup still steamed under the pepper tree beyond the church.

When the school and the Training Institute closed for the holidays Walter returned to the printing-room. He walked up towards it from the lodge, eager to see what Benedict had done, free at last from choir rehearsals, suddenly unburdened from glee evenings, concerts and prize-givings. Benedict opened the door and ushered him in.

He was back. He stood and looked about in quiet satisfaction. 'Sit, Benedict, sit. Don't let me disturb you,' he said. 'I've been looking forward to this moment. I've had more than enough of concerts and duets and the Holy Nativity! If I have to watch another child dressed as a wise man in a table-cloth and curtain cord, I shall wish him to the devil.'

Benedict laughed and turned back to his work. Walter watched him a moment and then he said, 'Have you been submitting stories to *Imvo Zabantsundu* or is it Mr Soga's new paper that you favour?' Benedict did not look up and Walter continued easily, 'You are quite entitled to make comment elsewhere, you know. Besides, both are very good publications and reach far more people than our little effort. I suppose it's a matter of choosing between Mr Jabavu's policy or Mr Soga's, although I can't really express an opinion when my understanding of the Xhosa is so limited. I wish I could read it with more ease.'

Benedict flicked his tongue across his lip and half smiled down at his hands.

'Well,' said Walter, taking up some printed song sheets and glancing through them, 'I hope they're paying you for your troubles?'

'Yes, sir,' said Benedict. Then he looked up at Walter and he said, 'I thought you might be offended.'

'Because you chose a Xhosa paper over mine?'

'Yes.'

'Why should I be offended?' Then Walter laughed. 'Now I can be the only contributor to the St Matthias Echo without having to watch my back for my energetic competitor!'

That was not the issue, he knew, and he could see the flush behind the dark skin. Benedict was making a stand on his own

behalf. And so he should. He said, 'St Matthias is very isolated, Benedict. You will learn a lot from contact with others. I
am glad you've had such success.'

'I would like it if you did not speak about it,' said Benedict.

'What's there to be ashamed of?'

'Mr Mzantsi says it is wrong of me to go to another paper. I
think he does not like Mr Soga's ideas. He thinks them
dangerous. He calls him a "modernist" and he said Mrs Farborough would be angry that I spent my time on work for
someone outside the mission.' He paused. 'The sponsorship
from the lady in England . . . I cannot offend her.'

Walter shrugged. 'As Miss Prudieaux-Brune cannot read
Xhosa, I am sure she will remain in happy ignorance. Do not
send her a translation, that's all!'

Benedict said ruefully, 'I would rather Mr Mzantsi did not
translate for Mrs Farborough. She might misunderstand my
meaning.'

'Write for yourself, Benedict, not for Mrs Farborough or
anyone else. Still, I won't mention it if you'd prefer me not to.'

Oh, he knew Emily Farborough's opinions on this, her ideas
of the 'dangerous precedent'. She had expressed her opinion on
the crop of publications coming from other centres often enough. She had said something disparaging about 'natives in
spats' and the worldliness of the Xhosa editors. He had pointed
out – politely – that these men were all mission-educated, the
best students of their generation, but she continued in the belief
– irritable that he should contradict her – that all publications
should come from the mission stations themselves, carefully
supervised by the clergy. 'They'll be spreading sedition soon
enough,' she had said. 'Look at Fini in Mount Frere, inciting
the natives to ignore the poll tax. He has been given unpre-
cedented prominence in native papers. And the debate on the
vote and the Union of Native Vigilance Associations! It's a
hornet's nest they're stirring up! What next?'

Benedict had not shown his article on the dipping at the
rinderpest post to anyone at St Matthias but his piece had
brought sharp reaction from readers and the editor had devoted an editorial to the subject in the next edition. 'Another
Damascus', submitted by a young correspondent from the

district of King William's Town, was commended highly and other contributions were invited.

With some of the money he'd received, Benedict had bought a small gift of lace for Dorcas Pumani.

December came and Crispin returned home. He brought his trunk and his cricket togs, his old rugby ball and his bedding and all the paraphernalia of four years at boarding-school. Like the apprentices who had returned from the initiation lodge, their adolescence behind them, Crispin appeared, trailing the accoutrements of boyhood. They lay in disarray on the back porch, Emily presiding over them, Helmina in attendance, while Crispin – released from school for ever – took to the hills with his shotgun and his hunting-bag. His sports pictures, books and albums, his rugby cap with its tassle and braid and his blazer, brushed and folded, were packed into his trunk. This last remnant of his school-days was hauled up the ladder into the loft and laid in a corner:

C.W.S. Farborough
St Andrew's College
Grahamstown

So it lay, a sprig of rosemary Helmina Smythe had tucked inside the blazer crumbling and fragile in its musty folds.

Anticipation of Christmas, of evenings gathered round the piano or riding with Crispin and Frances and Helmina to the Ndwandwe stream, or of playing tennis or croquet with guests from The Hoek or King William's Town, was short-lived for Walter. Father Charles came to the printing-room one afternoon and said, 'Brownley, it's time Mrs Farborough had a change of air. I have been hesitant to suggest this, but I've decided that I should take her and the family to the coast for a few weeks. I am sorry to leave you in charge over Christmas but it seems sensible to go while the students are away. I shall write to Grahamstown and ask if there is anyone who could be spared to assist you.'

Walter heard his voice, agreeing to the necessity of the jour-

228

ney, demurring on the matter of an assistant, laughing away Father Charles's concern that he might be lonely or that Christmas might be dull on his own. 'I shall manage admirably,' he said, busy with his pipe. 'Mzantsi will help with the outstations, I am sure. You need a rest yourself and a spell at the sea will be capital . . .'

Father Charles might as well have clapped him in the stocks and when the old man had gone, Walter took a shovel and dug alongside the mission workmen who were repairing an irrigation furrow, ignoring their astonishment at his appearance or the energy with which he attacked the task. When he was done, he flung down the spade and went home to bath. The water that Nowasha brought was cold but he did not notice. He had set himself a two-hour exercise in Xhosa after dinner and declined an invitation to join the family at prayers.

They left within the week. He knew Helmina had asked if she might stay but Emily Farborough had insisted that she accompany them and she had packed her small bag and taken her leave of him after tea on the eve of their departure. She had spoken as if she had been sentenced to imprisonment. She lingered too, impervious to Frances's quick glance of dismissal, when Frances had come out onto the veranda to say goodbye. And so Frances had only said, crisp and detached, 'I'm sorry we won't be here for Christmas, Mr Brownley. I expect it'll be horrid on your own.' She had stood awkwardly a moment and then Helmina had ushered her away before she could say more or he reply.

The next day, he left before sunrise for Sidenge and when he returned that evening the house already had a deserted air about it and the wagon shed stood empty.

The Keiskamma River Mouth: he invented some vague and exotic stretch of coast to which his mind turned every now and then. Wind-swept sand, low bush, an ocean deep and treacherous, a margin of black, barnacle-encrusted rocks. Just before Christmas week, Victor would come and walk with her on that beach and hold the shells she'd gathered and burn his skin brown in the sun and bleach his hair gold . . . Walter did not think further. There were articles to write, six services on Sundays and a double burden at the outstations. Mzantsi was an old man. Despite his assurances to Father Charles, Walter did not expect him to take on extra work. He approached Benedict instead.

Benedict obliged without complaint and saddled the mare every other day to ride out to Rabula or Chata. Sometimes they went together, visiting the sick or those too old to come to service, carrying the chalice in the saddle-bags. And Benedict did well, taking the lesson, leading the hymns and the prayers without show, but with authority.

Walter said to him one morning as they rode to a distant homestead, 'Have you considered taking Holy Orders, Benedict?'

'Once,' said Benedict. 'I wanted to do what was expected of me.'

'What are your plans, then?'

Benedict rode for some time. Then he said, as if he were repeating something he had said before, 'St Matthias is the place where I live. I have no means to support myself.' He paused, added with resignation, 'Teaching perhaps.'

'That is not your vocation either?'

'No.' Benedict stared ahead. 'There is other, more important work to do.'

'Teaching is the noblest profession.'

'I am not a noble man,' said Benedict and Walter almost laughed to hear the old gravity in his voice.

'Then?'

'There is something beyond here,' Benedict said. And he let his eyes sweep the valley about them. 'But I have no means of finding out what it is.' Then he urged the horse ahead a little. Walter let him go. He had been allowed a confidence beyond what Benedict might normally have offered and he let it lie, aware, as the days passed, that Benedict worked long hours, late into the night in the printing-room, the little candle flame steady behind the panes of glass. Sometimes, even when Walter rose at three or four in the morning to go to Donnington or Donsa, he saw it burning like a distant beacon in the dark. Passing by the printing-room – unobtrusively, unwilling to intrude – he sometimes saw a figure, ardent at the writing table or lying prone on a crooked arm in sleep.

230

The Farborough house was closed. Only Nowasha went there to clean and dust and hang out the rag rugs in the sun when the bergwind blew. The curtains were drawn across the windows. Once, Walter went in when she was busy about her work and told her that he wished to practise the piano. She left him in the living-room and he took the stool to the instrument and sat before it.

He played quietly, not wishing to invite the curiosity of passersby. The music echoed up and down the small white room and the light drifted in, lapping at the edges of the blinds. How strange to come into a house when those that live in it have gone. It was full of empty sounds and sudden silences. He looked up at the array of photographs on the top of the piano.

Frances stared back at him from a silver frame. No more than eleven or twelve, Crispin by her side. He was dressed in a suit, the same quizzical half smile on his face that was so endearing and familiar. And Frances, goffered and starched, was arranged like a little doll on a chair with the drape of a curtain behind her, her face so grave he had laughed quietly to himself to see it so. The eyes gazed back, innocent of him, innocent of his absorption: Frances in another place, a world long before he knew her. Her hair was lighter here, loose about her shoulders, not tied back to reveal those delicate ears, the fragile length of neck he knew so well. Victor was here among the pictures too. A face like his had surely been conceived as the prototype for heroes. There was an empire in his gaze.

Scanning the portraits and cameos ranged before him, their subjects – suddenly – were like the characters in some distant myth, some legend he'd imagined or created, players in a game that he'd invented in his head. Only the wind tugging at the trees outside the windows seemed real and the sound of the field-hands singing in the yard.

It was a long and weary time and the heat and sudden storms of summer made the journeys to the outstations unpredictable and tedious. Walter kept an eighteen-hour day, driving off the loneliness with work. If he stopped his labours he would take a sheaf of paper from the store and write to Daisy or Miranda. He composed a Christmas story late one night on a sudden inspiration. Re-reading it, he knew that it would make his sister cry and laugh and cry again. She'd write to him in turn – long and lovingly – and though he'd hold the letter dear, it would not salve the hollowness he felt inside.

On Christmas Day he took an early service in a full church, Mzantsi and Benedict assisting, and he hosted a tea for the mission workers and watched as they cooked a sheep on an open fire, and then he saddled Boggis and rode to The Hoek to hold communion at the church in the village and afterwards went to the Nettletons for dinner. He played charades with the Misses Nettleton and sang carols round the piano while the children dropped off to sleep by the fire and the old man told stories of the early days in the valley when he and Father Charles were young together. He rode home alone as midnight chimed: just he and Boggis and the stars shining as they might have shone on that distant night to bring the shepherds from their sleep; just he and Boggis and the road white and gleaming as a river. So beautiful a night. So still and awesome in the moonlight. He reined in and, turning in the saddle, scanned the whole horizon and the trees, dark on dark, clustered in the folds of hills. The sharp promontory of Kaboosie mountain thrust up against the sky, the Southern Cross dipping in above it like a ship anchored in a limpid sea.

Here, in times gone by, he would not have felt alone. For here was God, dependably beside him. He listened, waiting. Was He there, somewhere in the quiet of that night? No wind. No sound. Then Boggis snorted, impatient for his stable.

Walter leaned forward and patted his neck. 'There, old man,' he said. 'Just you and me, after all.' He rode on, paused to open the mission gate. Carried on the night air, he heard – not hymns, not carols – but voices chanting somewhere: soft and plaintive in the dark. Voices and a Xhosa harp. Such ancient harmonies, such yearning in those notes. He went on alone towards the curate's lodge.

Just before New Year, Mzantsi came to Walter in his study and said, 'Kobus Pumani has spoken to me, *mfundisi*. He feels it in his heart.' He demonstrated by placing his hand on his breast and closing his eyes. 'He wishes to be baptised. He wishes to *gqobhoka*.' There was no scepticism in Mzantsi's face.

'Do you think he is sincere?'

Mzantsi folded his hands then and said, 'We pray daily for conversions.'

'Nevertheless . . .'

'Will you speak to him, sir?'

'I do not know that I can always follow him,' said Walter. 'Will you come with me and tell me what he says, so I am clear?'

Mzantsi nodded. 'I will bring him to you.'

Walter walked thoughtfully to the printing-room. He said to Benedict, 'Mr Mzantsi has just told me that Kobus Pumani wants to convert.'

Benedict did not look up from the type he was setting. 'I have heard.'

'Why do you think, after all these years at the mission and such an inveterate old heathen, that he wants a change?'

'He says he feels it in his heart.'

'Do you know what this means?'

'Yes,' said Benedict matter-of-factly. 'It means he will have to put away one of his wives. One is less trouble than two,' and he flashed a glance at Walter.

'Is this what Dorcas believes?'

'She has been baptised. What can she say about it, except be glad?'

'The Church's teachings are very clear on this,' said Walter. 'Polygamy cannot be tolerated.'

'Yes,' said Benedict non-committally.

'And yet, it's a terrible thing to put away half of the family. I can't quite accept that. What will happen to Dorcas's mother?'

Benedict shrugged. 'Sonwabo will have to work and provide for her.'

Walter looked at Benedict. 'How does this affect the way Dorcas feels about her faith?'

'She will have to accept it,' was all he replied and again Benedict had closed him out.

Walter pressed on, 'And if you marry Dorcas, is it you who will have to care for her family?'

He had gone too far then and he cursed himself for Benedict

233

said, 'If *you* marry soon, sir, you will not have to pay *lobola* to Father Charles.'

There was nothing that Walter could do to conceal the discomposure in his face. Nothing to ease the sudden heat. He had asked for it, intruding as he had. How foolish to think his carefully concealed secret did not shout aloud every time he turned his eyes to Frances or mentioned her name. Miss Farborough indeed!

Benedict almost smiled, but then he said, marshalling respect and courtesy, 'I have no cattle, sir, and no means of getting them.'

'Surely *lobola* isn't necessary for a Christian?' said Walter, covering his discomfort with debate. 'It seems to be a form of barter for the bride.'

'No,' said Benedict. 'It is a thing of the ancestral shades. It is given in deference to them. It is not payment for the bride. It is a gift given in respect for her and for her family. It is an insurance that she will have that respect at all times.'

Walter drew up a chair, sat back in it and said, 'The Church's view on ancestral shades is that the worship of them is a form of idolatry.'

'Then it does not understand,' said Benedict. Walter waited. 'We do not praise people just because they are dead. What is the use of that? Why should a man look for goodness and bravery, for wisdom, for all those things in life, if there will never be reward after death? It is men who had wisdom and courage who are powerful among the shades. It is they who are remembered in their families.'

Walter thought a moment. He said, 'There is a passage in the Bible that echoes the very thing that you have said. Let me see . . . I can't even recall where it comes from.' He spoke slowly, hesitating, then finding the words, '"Let us now sing the praises of famous men, the heroes of our nation's history, through whom the Lord established his renown, and revealed his majesty in each succeeding age".'

'That is how it is,' said Benedict, 'through each succeeding age.'

'And *lobola* is tied then to the shades and their wishes for the happiness and safety of their daughter?'

'That is so.'

'Tell me, Benedict,' said Walter. 'You have lived only at St Matthias and been brought up a Christian since birth. Who has given you this insight into the shades?'

Benedict did not answer directly. He said, 'You live alone, Mr Brownley. You have no family. Is God close enough to make such things unimportant to you?'

Walter looked into Benedict's face then and he said quietly, 'No, Benedict. To my great regret, no.'

Benedict inclined his head.

Walter had never thought before of Benedict's sense of self or that he might experience a painful isolation – not just from any knowledge of his family or forebears but from the people around him. If, like so many at the mission, Benedict was dispossessed, he was fighting still, and valiantly, for an identity. He sought no panaceas, asked no absolutions when he failed. He worked, he read, he wrote. He kept his own counsel.

Walter found himself saying, as he walked up towards the chancel in the empty church to prepare for his Scripture class, 'And I gave my heart to know wisdom but in much wisdom is much grief and he that increaseth knowledge increaseth sorrow.' Such a dictum from Ecclesiastes might deter a lesser man. But not Benedict. No, not he. How much better – in pursuit of truth – to challenge grief and sorrow. How much better than to hide away for fear of hurt.

Chapter Sixteen

Frances waited restlessly for Victor. His arrival would send away her discontent, the aimlessness of wandering about the beach. She could not understand herself. Holidays at the coast had always been anticipated by both Crispin and herself when they were younger with an enthusiasm which broke into near-hysteria as the time approached. The Frasers would be there and the Stringfellows with their multitudinous children and the Hooks from Kei Road and others that they had met every third Christmas for as long as she could remember. But now – disconcertingly – Frances thought of home and the little school at Nolovini, lingering about them in her mind as if she missed them. She who had always wished to escape! It was absurd. After all, here was company, here were parties and games and excursions and her only duty was to enjoy herself and to entertain the guests! Even the church services were held on the veranda of the old house with only a candle to decorate the table. No sermons, no choirs, no psalms, and the sound of the sea surging on the beach just beyond the edges of the lawn.

There were bonfires on the sand in the evenings and a little boat to row on the lagoon from which to see the world turned upside-down in the water with bird-flight ruffling a long pathway right down towards the bar where terns and gulls were gathered. There were walks in the dune forest and quiet places to read a book sheltered from the wind. There were picnics near the rocks where the low tide left pools filled with urchins and periwinkles, and laughter and teasing as they all practised for theatricals to be staged under the milkwoods on Christmas Eve.

Here was dear, handsome Charlie Fraser with his pranks and his jokes and Sonnie Hook and Crispin running wild and free into the waves and her father without his clergyman's collar sitting on a deckchair on the sand, his handkerchief knotted at the corners and set on his head and his reading spectacles rimed with saltiness from the air and her mother beside him, her rigidity blown away with the sea wind. These

236

were the things so long anticipated, so well remembered and yet – despite herself – Frances felt restless and aloof.

Victor would soon be there. He would send away – by his very presence, the excitement of him and the old familiarity – the odd, uninvited silences in her mind, the unexpected discontent with the sand and the sea and the silly games that they played. He would drive away the inexplicable need to climb up through the dunes where the soil was pale beneath the tangle of undergrowth and sit in a hollow and listen to the sea alone, with no one blundering after her.

But he did not send these things away. He made them worse. He seemed invasive, no matter where she went.

He arrived, striding up the path, exploding into the house, full of affability and lightness, seeking her eagerly. No discontent in him. No restlessness that he did not mean to overcome with her and oh, how he followed her, all but bullying her to make a time alone, despite the dozens of admiring children and eager friends that abounded wherever he went.

He took her rowing in the boat on the lagoon, guiding it close to the reeds, almost out of sight of the watchers on the beach, and he rested the oars and he bent forward and he kissed her: a kiss – his hand deft about her – presumptuously exploratory and rash. Oddly out of humour with herself and him, aware that Crispin and Charlie were fishing not far along the bank, she put his hands away from her, laughed to mollify him, said, 'Miss Smythe brought Daddy's binoculars to the beach specially to keep an eye on you!'

Still, amidst all the company, he found small opportunities to trap her: a breath against her cheek, the expectant pressure of his thigh against hers as they sat at table, another kiss snatched as she came from the pantry with the dinner plates, all but upsetting them on the floor. If she kept him at bay, it only seemed to amuse him to see it and urged him on to reckless activity. The landing of a fish, the rowing of the boat, his arms pulling at the oars, lean and strong and his face honed by the wind, became a proffered challenge. He was waiting. Expectant. She was torn between guilt because he had the right to expectation from her and irritation with herself for wishing – so bewilderingly but so fiercely – to withdraw.

237

On Christmas morning she awoke early and she heard the oriole dropping nectar notes in the summer air outside her window and, beyond, the lazy sigh of the sea. She lay and listened as though the sounds were the prelude to some enchanted tale and she thought suddenly of Walter Brownley, far away at St Matthias. So clearly did she see him, it was as if he had put out his hand and touched her. She could feel that hand against her cheek, the cool, strong fingers that had felt her skin the day that she'd been ill at Nolovini. She could hear his voice: 'There was once a man called Plotz who set forth on a journey to find the great green lion . . . He did not go alone. His companion in his trials was one named Boggis, a fantastical, magical unicorn . . .'

She had never heard a voice like Walter Brownley's. There was no edge to it, no suddenness. Its notes were deep and quiet with an undertone of laughter. Not the strident kind, not the sudden rushes and guffaws of Victor and Charlie Fraser and Sonnie Hook playing cricket on the beach. Another laughter from another place.

She ached to go home. All day, some small melancholy nudged at her despite the Christmas festivities. And that evening, when just the family had gathered round the table for dinner and the candles had been lit and the windows left open to a full moon shining on the sea, she had sat with a small desolate quietness inside her while Victor, pouring yet another glass of wine, his face flushed, searched for her hand under the table. He said – a rejoinder to some remark of her mother's – 'When Frances and I are married we'll come here every Christmas and invite you all and things will be just the same as they are now.'

And her mother said, 'Indeed, sir, are you not making assumptions? I don't recall that you have asked her father yet . . .'

'Or me,' said Frances, trying to withdraw her fingers.

Victor only laughed and held them more confidently. 'That's a little detail that I overlooked. May I see you after dinner, sir?' He bowed to her father and her mother said, 'Get on with you, you scoundrel. Why would I let my daughter run off to Johannesburg with you?' But she looked at him fondly, her head inclined.

There was a small expectant silence and then Helmina simpered and said, 'A Christmas engagement. What a happy idea!' And Crispin knocked over his wine and was sent for a cloth to wipe it up and only her father sat silent at the head of the table and then he said – almost severely – 'Where is the plum pudding?' and it sounded so incongruous, they all laughed.

Helmina ran to fetch it, as if ready to make a triumphant bonfire of it, and Victor turned to Frances and gazed at her with such a mixture of certainty and of possession that she looked away – no retreat – so he should not see the expression in her eyes.

As she stood at her open window later that night, the candle extinguished, she heard her mother's voice, low but clear, carrying from the porch, 'Charles, you know it's what we've always wanted. Frances may be young but Victor is going to Johannesburg and could change his mind. There will be so many temptations. Why didn't you agree at once?'

And her father said – distinctly she heard it and she could feel the slow, limp sting in her limbs at his words – 'Because she's not in love with him, that's why.'

Frances stood in the lee of the window, stunned. Stunned by the sudden, awesome truth. Her father must be wrong. She *was* in love with Victor. She had been all her life. She had followed him when she was small, played his games – his wonderful, brave, terrifying games – bled for him, dared for him, done anything he asked. She had covered for him when he'd gone out at night in later times, not knowing what his assignation might have been, but glad to be a part of his conspiracy, entranced by the intrigue. And then . . . then she'd gone to him. Yes, she'd gone, flouting family and God – for Love. Why else would she have dared so great a sin? It was only here, now, that she felt a distance from him with all the people, all the watchers, eager with their eyes and their tongues. It was only a temporary ill-humour that she didn't understand. It would be different when they were married, when they had a house and a smart little trap and neighbours in a town.

And then her mother said, 'They've been destined for each

239

other all their lives, Charles. Being "in love" is hardly a consideration.'

'It is for Frances,' her father said. 'Oh, it is for her. And who are we, my dear, to decide on destiny? That is God's prerogative, not ours.'

He must be wrong. Such thoughts were treachery to Victor and to her childhood and to everything she knew. If he were right then there'd be no absolution for her sin. She could not hold up 'Love' in mitigation for her act.

Relentlessly, she sought out Victor on the beach next day and beckoned him behind a rock and said, 'When will you speak to my father?'

He glanced over his shoulder to see if anyone was watching and he said, 'Come into the dunes with me. After lunch. Go straight along the beach. I know a place that's safe and I'll wait for you. Listen for me. I'll whistle. Turn up then and be careful no one sees you.'

'I will not come into the dunes with you, Victor, and I'll not be called for like a dog.' Her voice was steady and cool. 'Not until you have spoken to my father properly. And not after that either. You must wait now.' And she looked into his face. His eyes were narrowed against the sun and there was salt on his lashes. A fleeting exasperation crossed his mouth, 'But I love you,' he said. 'Isn't that all that matters?'

'I would have thought so,' she replied. 'But I was wrong.'

He did speak to her father and he was given leave to ask again when he had been in Johannesburg six months. Frances waited for him on the back porch, standing very still in the shade of the tangled creeper that grew up the trellis, hearing the cicadas shrieking in the bush beyond. At last he came from the living-room and he found her where she waited and he kissed her without speaking. He kissed her like a lover, claiming his right, lingering at her mouth, uncaring that anyone should see. She let him, acquiescing quietly to his explorations, an ineffable sadness in her touch.

The Farboroughs came home in January. Benedict had brought a telegram from The Hoek and Walter took it down to the house and spoke to Nowasha. The doors and windows

240

were opened and a team of young helpers arrived to clean and dust with her. Walter sent Benedict to Nettletons to collect supplies. The Sunday gloom that had hung over the mission for a month was suddenly lifted. He whistled as he went down to the printing-room.

The evening before their return he sat on the veranda of the lodge and smoked his pipe. He laid his books aside and he did not write a letter or bother with a sermon. He watched the sky and the moon rising pale above the river. He could hear the water somewhere in the dark, unwinding between the trees. Frances would be here tomorrow. Here. Back at St Matthias with her light, quick tread and her gruff little laugh. Would Plotz be resurrected? Or would she have forgotten him?

For the moment he did not try to imagine where she'd been or what she had done or what might have passed between her and Victor. He went to bed and lay on his back in the dark with his hands behind his head and looked up at the ceiling, at the fleet shadows of the trees on the far wall and his gown hunched against the back of the door. He thought of her. Lying there, he thought of her – daring to – knowing the folly of such imaginings when tomorrow she might dismiss him with a gesture. The Frances of a moment such as this was a creation of his own, just as Plotz had been, dangerously removed from reality.

Yes, and there was Victor, looming at her back, romantic as a gladiator. Heroic Victor. Epic Victor. And there *he* was: small, wiry, hair like a goat's – so she'd told him on a trip to Nolovini without the slightest hint of shame – and, oh, those eyes! Black as raisins, briar-brows above! And such a nose! He touched it gingerly in the dark. Victor had once said he could pass for an itinerant smous with a feature such as this! At least, like his chin, it asserted itself on his face! He laughed. 'Bloody fool,' he said before he fell asleep.

Crispin arrived first. He rode into the yard and there was a shout from the apprentices. They went to greet him, crowding the horse, their voices loud and full of laughter. Crispin swung from the saddle and the hands were upon him in greeting, and the heads were bent in towards his, listening to him

241

as he spoke. He came down the path towards the house with a cavalcade behind him and the ribaldries going back and forth among them and Mzantsi waddling after, calling greetings.

Walter came from the office and met Crispin in the path. There was a light in his eyes and his face was burned brown by the sun. He seemed taller and bigger than when Walter had last seen him.

'Crispin, old man,' he said, shaking the proffered hand. 'It's good to have you back again.'

'Not for long, Mr Brownley,' said Crispin. 'I've enough time to visit the old places, then I'm off again.'

'So soon? Where are you going?'

'Vic's got a post in Johannesburg with Native Affairs and he's arranged a place for me as a clerk and an interpreter in his department. These fellows are coming with me. Kobus signed them up with Mr Otto while we were away and they're ready to leave,' and he put his arms around the shoulders of Tom and Reuben and Sonwabo and they made a comic drilling action as if they were boring a rock-face.

'All gone at once,' said Walter, his attention half on the road beyond the fence, waiting for the wagon. 'The place will be empty soon.'

'It's all to be arranged,' said Crispin eagerly. 'It'll be a great adventure!'

They heard the wagon then and the dogs began to bark and Walter felt the slow pulse in his throat and he hooked his finger into his cleric's collar and eased it. Thank God for its armoury right now.

He did not look over in the direction of the wagon turning down the avenue but up at the trees tossing in a light wind and following the antics of the lads as they capered off towards the gate. Mzantsi was saying, 'The Lord be praised, they're safely home!' But he hardly noticed him.

There – the clang of the gate, closing behind them and the sound of the oxen snorting, drawing breath to smell their own pasture, their own stretch of veld. There was Father Charles in his white sun helmet and Emily Farborough beside him and Helmina Smythe, leaning forward eagerly and waving, fluttering her hand, and her bonnet all awry.

There was Frances. He took a breath. Steady on, old man. Shake hands with Mrs Farborough first. 'Mr Brownley, how good to see you.' Then Father Charles. Ah, to feel the firm grip of the old workman in his touch.

He helped Helmina down. A smile trembled on her face and he returned it. 'I'm so glad to see you,' he said to her. And he meant it. 'It's been very solitary here.' The flush was bright on her skin and she went to Mzantsi, greeting him enthusiastically to hide her confusion.

Walter turned from her to Frances.

She was bending down in the wagon, searching for something among the boxes and he went to the side and looked up at her. She turned her head and she said, 'Mr Brownley,' and she looked away and back again quickly from beneath the brim of her hat: a small, secret glance of gladness. He put out his hand and she took it. Those fingers locked a moment into his and then they were gone.

He was aware of her all through the activity of the day, the unpacking, the toings and froings from the wagon to the house and from the veranda to the garden, and when Emily sent a note for him to join them at dinner that evening, he dispatched Nowasha's little granddaughter with his acceptance. He saw her scampering back to the house with it. Meanwhile there were consultations with Father Charles and Mzantsi, registers to go over and mission business to discuss.

The old men and a dozen supplicants and well-wishers waited in the yard to welcome Father Charles home. Walter accompanied him as he went among them and took a seat near the church wall. Walter saw him touch the worn stone as if he were greeting an old friend and listened to the slow, beautifully enunciated Xhosa as he spoke to the gathering.

When Father Charles was finished, he walked with Walter to his office and he closed the door at last and said, looking about at the warm, shabby room, 'I am glad to be home.' He smiled at Walter. 'I missed your company more than I can say.' He bent and opened his drawer and scratched about, searching for something. From beneath a sheaf of papers he drew out an old pipe triumphantly. 'Ah,' he said. 'I was right! Oblige me with a bit of tobacco,' he said. 'My wife will be busy in her house for an hour or two. Let's have a pipe and I shall blame it all on you. She scolds constantly about smoking which is the very devil of a penance.' Walter, with a sense of conspiracy, offered the tobacco pouch. Together, slowly and in silence, they performed the ritual they had shared so many times: filling and lighting their pipes and having them burn satisfactorily before they leaned back in their chairs and began to speak.

And as they sat, Walter heard, far off, Frances calling to Nowasha. He looked at his hands and her voice drifted out somewhere in the garden. Father Charles cocked his head and smiled. He said, 'The change has done them all the world of good, but they were restless in the end. Frances wanted to get home. I hardly expected it of her with so many youngsters about the place. Oh, we had a good time walking by the sea. And how I did enjoy the books you lent me. Such companions! Mrs Farborough was quite competitive with them for my attention. She will tell you herself. Helmina enjoyed them too when she wasn't wandering about on the shore collecting shells. There wasn't much new company for her, poor girl.' He looked about the room again, with satisfaction. 'Despite the work awaiting me, I'm pleased to have my own study back. There was no escape from young people and busy women where I was and I look forward to a bit of peace!'

'Were there many visitors?'

'A number of families take their holidays there. We had friends down from Fort Beaufort and acquaintances from Kei Road were staying nearby. You know the Frasers, of course, but the Hooks and the Stringfellows were there as well. You have heard us speak of them? And then Victor came for Christmas. As you know, he has been offered a position with the Native Affairs Department in Johannesburg, as assistant to the Cape Colony's Representative. He was recommended by a friend of his mother's and he has been brought to the notice of Sir Godfrey Lagden. I have no doubt he will make a great success of things, despite the troubles in the Republic at the moment. He is eager for adventures! At any rate, the indications are that he is destined for great things. The interest of the gentlemen concerned is a feather in his cap – which sits rather tightly on his head at the moment – but who am I to question his enthusiasm? Victor has always been ambitious and has a talent for being noticed.' He inspected his pipe and said, 'No doubt you've heard that my dear wife believed he'd take Holy Orders and continue the work at St Matthias.' He looked up. He regarded Walter steadily. 'Our hopes so often outdistance us. You will agree that Victor was not made to be a clergyman. He will do very well in Government or quasi-government.' He paused. 'He has always had legislative instincts.'

Walter was silent.

'He has arranged for Crispin to go with him,' continued Father Charles. 'Crispin's knowledge of Xhosa will ensure his success. I doubt there's a colonist that speaks it better than he. I don't know that it's right for Crispin but he insists it's what he wants. Tom and Reuben and Sonwabo are going too. I believe they were recruited by Mr Otto, although when, I cannot say. Has he mentioned recruiting to you?'

'No,' said Walter. 'I didn't know he was involved. It must be something new.'

Father Charles puffed a moment in silence. 'So, Brownley, our young men go out. Isn't that why we trained them? At least they're not a lot of prodigals.' He glanced at Walter. 'How can we keep them here when the smithy is closing down and the cattle are dead and the land of every family has been so depleted? But I wish Victor had thought of some place else. Johannesburg sounds like a veritable Sodom and Gomorrah. Crispin is unprepared for living such a life and Victor . . . well . . .'

Father Charles tapped his pipe at the edge of the table and looked into the middle distance. The silence was sudden. He cleared his throat. 'About Victor. When we were at the sea we spoke a lot. He had plans . . .'

There are times when interruptions come as if the gods – taking pity – send a momentary reprieve. Walter knew that Father Charles was choosing his words with care, that he had something to say that was significant, and that it involved him in some important way. But Mzantsi knocked at the door just then and stood on the threshold, full of gladness to see

245

Father Charles, reiterating his delight at his return and announcing, before Walter had had a chance to speak, that the newest candidate for baptism was Kobus Pumani. Father Charles had glanced at Walter for confirmation.

'It's true,' said Walter, without conviction.

'Well, good heavens! What next!' Father Charles rose and invited the catechist in and asked him to explain the sudden change of heart.

He listened to Mzantsi's words and then he said, 'Kobus has two wives. What will become of the second?'

'She has left the homestead already,' said Mzantsi. 'Kobus tells me she has returned to her own people. He says that she was glad to go.'

'And the boys are accompanying Crispin to the mines. Does the father agree?'

'Oh, yes. He has been speaking to Mr Otto every time he has passed,' said Mzantsi. 'He has all but ordered them away.'

'It's very sudden,' said Father Charles. 'Really, I don't wish to doubt him, but I wonder what has caused the change?'

'Divine intervention,' said Walter drily.

'Indeed the Lord works in wondrous ways,' Mzantsi said, his face solemn.

Father Charles exchanged a glance with Walter and Walter turned to the window and stood at it, his hands behind his back, rocking thoughtfully from heel to toe from toe to heel. His mind wandered from the conversation. He did not follow what Father Charles and Mzantsi said. The garden in front of the Farboroughs' house was empty, but already washing fluttered on the line and the banksia roses were in bloom across the fallen oak. Somewhere there. Somewhere.

'Well,' said Helmina, lifting Frances's clothes out of the portmanteau and laying them on her bed. 'When are you going to announce it? How long is it to be a secret?'

Frances pulled the skirts from the top and turned to the cupboard to hang them. She said, trying to keep the irritation from her voice, her eyes straying to the window, 'Announce what?'

'Goodness, Frances! I thought when someone decided to become engaged, it was a cause for celebration? You behave as though you despised the idea!'

'Of course I don't,' said Frances, closing a drawer of her dresser with some force. 'Victor had had far too much wine! He was only teasing. Father didn't take him seriously.'

'My! But you're insulting! He was as serious as ever I've seen him,' retorted Helmina. 'If you were my intended, miss, I'd box your ears!'

'How could he marry me now, anyway?' said Frances hotly. 'Do you expect me to live in a house with Charlie Fraser and Sonnie Hook and a whole lot of other fellows?'

'Really, Frances, you are vulgar!' said Helmina. 'A pledge is a pledge, nevertheless.'

'What pledge?' Frances rounded on her.

'By your conduct with him, Frances,' said Helmina. 'Don't think I haven't seen you! I trust that you haven't been trifling with Victor all these months simply to discard him?'

'Of course not,' said Frances, with a tight edge to her voice. 'It's a matter of economy, that's all. He is speaking to my father again when he is settled and I'd rather nothing was said about it now.' She swept the rest of her belongings into her dresser and lifted the carpet-bag. 'I'm taking this to the loft,' she said. And she left the room.

She climbed the ladder and took the carpet-bag to the corner. She sat on the edge of Crispin's trunk, waiting quietly in the gloom. The wind was nudging at the corrugated roof. It complained softly. Frances leaned her arms on her knees, listening to the old familiar sound, trying to remember all the times that she had hidden here when she was small, but the festivities at Christmas kept intruding in her thoughts.

She had been glad when Victor went, he and Charlie Fraser and Sonnie Hook leaving just before the New Year, riding in a little troupe along the road, turning to wave as they'd reached the bend. The holiday had ended with their going, the remaining week occupied with packing up the wagon, walking desultorily on the beach, the gathering of young children listless from too much sun, and only Crispin glad of the time to fish alone.

Frances had gone with him sometimes, happy in the quiet companionship. And if they had spoken, they had sometimes talked in Xhosa as they had when they were children and did not want an eavesdropper to understand. It had always been the language of comfort for them both, the language that had soothed tears or hurt, murmured by Nowasha in the nursery, arms rocking, hands cradling; of little rhymes, of little games and when they had knelt side by side at bedtime, it was in Xhosa that they had prayed until their mother had forbidden it. Still it was their secret cipher and they had used it then, as if needing to reassert its meaning between them before the time should end and some long separation engulf them both.

And Crispin had said on the last evening as they had walked back from the rocks, his rod across his shoulder and a quiet sea breathing on the sand and a flight of cormorants strung out just above the first faint swell, 'I don't think we will ever be here again.'

'Victor said we'd come every Christmas,' she had said.

He had glanced at her then. 'I know.' He went on a pace or two and then he'd turned and he'd seemed to look at her and all of the sea behind her and all of the sky above and the house with its lamp set on the table on the veranda beckoning to them in the dusk and he had said – that inimitable word – 'Kanti . . .' And even yet . . .

Frances came down from the loft, stepping carefully, for the ladder was leaned precariously against the wall. She did not return to the house, but walked out across the yard, past the stunted oak at the back gate. There were goats browsing in the thorn bush beyond the fence and she could hear the bees, going back and forth from the skeps, laden with pollen. She took the path beside the curate's lodge. She counted the doors of the house. One, two, three, four. The fifth was open. The curtains at the window breathed in and out in the afternoon breeze.

She stood at the fence, waiting. She heard him come out onto the veranda, stand a moment. She heard his step on the path. She knew that tread. Firm, quick, one step just a little heavier than the other. He stopped. She did not turn around. She heard him cross the grass, approaching. He reached her

at the fence and she looked round at him. And then she stood
again with her hands on the top strand of wire facing out into
the thorn-scrub and the pasture.

'Mrs B?' Ah, so tentative.

'Mr Plotz?' Softly now.

He put his hand over hers. She did not move and then she
turned her fingers in, curling them within his palm. She stood
beside him with her hand in his, her head close to his
shoulder. He dared not move in case she might recoil and run.

'I missed you,' he said. Just a breath: the words were lost in
his throat. She did not speak but crept a little closer, as if
tucking down in comfort at his side. He smiled then and no
one saw his eyes: so great a tenderness. So great indeed. The
goats beyond browsed on, oblivious.

That a moment so important should be so transient, so
ephemeral: it was with expectation that Walter went to the
Farboroughs for dinner that evening. Near midnight, he had
all but fled from the house.

He was welcomed by Father Charles at seven, brought to
the living-room and drawn in among the family as though
they all had missed him in their separate ways. Frances, unobtrusively, had brought her stool quite close to his chair, and
sat not far from his knee, watching the fire. It might have
been midsummer but a storm was building up above the
Amatolas and a sharp, cold wind was blowing.

Father Charles fetched the sherry from his study, Helmina
played a tune and all the faces turned to him had seemed –
each one – suddenly so dear, so familiar, he felt he'd been
reprieved from exile. They all talked at once, telling him
about the beach, the enormous fish that Crispin caught on
Christmas Eve, the Frasers and the Hooks and how, next
time, they would not leave him here but take him too. So
much content within that warm, fire-shadowed room, only
the wind outside, tearing at the trees.

She was so small and beautiful just there beyond his reach,
she with her tawny hair and her green eyes and her hands
linked about her knees: those hands that he had held in his
that afternoon, which she had placed in his in trust and quiet.

He wished that he could reach for them again and breathe the scent of her as he had done so briefly – so completely – before she'd gone away, without another word, and left him standing on the lawn, the conqueror of worlds.

There was no striving for attention at the supper table but a happy sharing of a meal, enjoyed by all, and a companionable silence every now and then, and the gravy steaming in its jug and even Helmina induced to have a glass of wine, and Father Charles saying to his wife, 'These are beans from your garden, my love. I'd know their flavour anywhere.'

Emily smiled and touched his arm. 'Indeed, my dear, they're not. Nowasha purloined them from Mr Mzantsi without permission so you're dining on stolen fare.'

'Will you play and sing for us after supper, Mr Brownley?' said Frances. 'We've had no music for a month.' She inclined her head and looked at Walter and she seemed to gaze at him for an eternity. He could not turn his eyes away and he heard Father Charles's voice somewhere at a great, great distance saying, 'Join me in a glass of port, old man? Shall we celebrate a safe return? Port but, sadly, no cigars . . . what do you say, Brownley?'

He shook himself from her, turned, 'Port? Yes . . . thank you,' and he folded his napkin and then unfolded it again, aware – suddenly – of the scrutiny of all of them. 'Music, yes. Why not?'

He only glanced up, daring no more, when she went from the room, following her mother and Helmina, her silhouette slipping swiftly past the light of the hall.

He sat with Father Charles and Crispin in the dining-room and the decanter was passed between them. He watched the port rise in the glass, tipping to the rim. Diamonds and rubies in the candlelight and the trump of thunder way off across the hills.

Father Charles cocked his head and listened. 'Rain at last,' he said. 'Praise God for that.' Again – a deep, heraldic peal.

Walter sipped his wine and Crispin said, turning to his father, 'When did Klaus Otto start recruiting?'

'I have no idea,' said Father Charles.

'When I spoke to Kobus this afternoon about Tom and

Reuben and Sonwabo working on the mines, he said that Klaus Otto's coming was the will of God and that they would return with enough money to buy herds of cattle and make him a rich man. It was like a pantomime. And all the time that he was speaking, he was looking at me from the corner of his eye, watching me.'

'He's an old rogue,' said Father Charles. 'I shall have to speak to him about his wanting to *gqobhoka*. He likes to put on a show, especially if the audience is good. I need to know that he's sincere.'

'Sonwabo's too young to send to the mines, surely,' said Walter.

'We should keep him back,' said Father Charles. 'He's never been a strong lad.'

'Kobus wouldn't hear of that!' said Crispin. 'Vic should have him as a houseboy instead. I wonder what Frances would say if Sonwabo turned up to cook for them.'

Walter's glass did not move in his hand. No tremor touched it. He placed it on the table before him, an eternity to set it straight upon the cloth and watch the candle flame's reflection settle steady in its heart. He did not raise his eyes. But he knew he did not breathe and when he did, he took it quietly and long, and he said – his voice calm and even, 'Is Miss Farborough going to Johannesburg?'

There was a silence and he looked up, quick enough to catch the admonishing glance that passed from Father Charles to Crispin and to see the flush at Crispin's ears.

Father Charles cleared his throat and he picked up his table napkin and wiped his mouth with a sort of brisk resignation. He said, 'Victor has asked for her, yes. But I have told him to wait a while. They're both too young. Too young, both of them. So nothing shall be said for the time.' And he did not look at Walter and Walter was grateful for his consideration and Crispin, wanting to make amends for his indiscretion said, 'Let's have a song, sir. I'll tell Frances to choose the music,' and he went from the room.

Walter's legs moved. He set his chair precisely in its place. He turned from the table and Father Charles ushered him through the door, a hand lightly at his elbow as if to steady

251

him. They went down the passage and the walls seemed to tilt towards him and the thunder was near, as if it might invade the house. He wished it would – and strike him down. Curse himself for a fool! Fatuous, deluded fool!

Father Charles opened the door of the living-room for him and he went inside and the heat of the fire seemed to rush at him. Frances looked up from the piano where she sat with Crispin at her side. The smile hovered a moment, then faded. Her eyes darted from him to her father and back. But he said – and his voice was masterfully deceptive – 'Shall we have a duet to start with? Will you join me, Miss Farborough?'

He played. He did not know how. And she played beside him. So distant, so far, as if plains and ranges and rivers and deserts had arisen between them. Their fingers moved across the keys, side by side, now up, now down and never touching. He watched them, mesmerised, and when the final chord was struck, Father Charles called 'Bravo!' and she rose and went to sit in the recess by the fireplace without a word.

Piece after piece he played and then Father Charles sent Crispin for the Bible and Walter did not hear the words that were read: his arm in the breach, keeping the tide from sweeping in to overwhelm him. It required all his strength to stand in stillness in that room.

And as Father Charles spoke the Lord's Prayer and they murmured it with him, the rain came. Loud and sudden on the roof. They paused, looking up: a moment of silence for its long-awaited benedictions.

'A last tune before we all retire,' said Emily unexpectedly. 'I'm glad to be home.' And she stepped across and put her arm in Father Charles's and he placed his hand over hers and looked down at her. There, the first cracks threatening to open to the flood. Walter leaned across to take his hat from the table. 'What will you have, Mrs Farborough?' he said.

'The Corelli,' said Frances from her shadowy retreat by the fireplace.

Cruel she was. Cruel indeed to choose this piece, knowing how to turn the knife. He went to the piano, placed his hands above the opening chords. He played: minor key, phrasing impeccable, a melody to sear the heart. And when he had finished, there was quiet in the room and the rain held a moment in abeyance. He stood and closed the instrument and said goodnight. He could hear his voice, addressing each in turn. And then, Father Charles was at his side, ushering him to the door and Helmina was fetching an umbrella from the hall. He took it from her without a word and turned away into the rain.

Chapter Seventeen

And so the rains came and the foundations of the mission buildings were lapped with mud. On two occasions, Walter had had to spend the night in isolated kraals because the drifts were up and the Amatolas were dark with wet forest and mist hung in the ravines like subterranean smoke. On another, he had lodged with a trader up the Donsa, spending five days in his house, impatient to be gone and Boggis bent under wet sacks in a leaking stable and no way to send word of his whereabouts.

So it was that he was isolated in some watery eyrie thirty miles from the mission when Crispin and Tom and Reuben and Sonwabo left St Matthias in the company of Father Charles for Grahamstown to catch the train to Johannesburg. If there had been a cavalcade setting out as there had been on the day they had gone with Kobus to the initiation lodge, he had not seen it. He had known nothing of their departure.

He had to wait an extra day after the sun appeared for the rivers to subside a little before he could attempt the journey back, riding Boggis hard, taking routes above the confluence of streams, wading drifts, exhausting both himself and the horse before they came across the ridge and saw the mission far below.

When he had stabled Boggis and fed him a bucketful of bran and meal, he hurried down to the office in search of Father Charles, but he found Emily Farborough there instead, working in the half-gloom on the account books, a watery sun glimmering at the window.

'At last!' she said, rising. 'I was beginning to be anxious. Mr Farborough left on Monday for the SPG meeting in Grahamstown. He was loath to go before you were back but Crispin and the apprentices had to catch the train to Johannesburg and couldn't wait.'

'What a rain!' said Walter, taking off his jacket and laying it over the back of a chair. 'I would have liked to see the lads before they went but there was nothing I could do. I was marooned and I was more impatient to get away than was polite. I'm sad I've missed them.'

'All the rivers are up,' said Emily. 'Mr Farborough would have abandoned the idea of going at all if he hadn't wanted to see Crispin safely away and if the new Bishop hadn't been expected. I know he was most curious to see him. If the rain holds off he should be here in a week.' She glanced out of the door. 'It looks rather forbidding over the Kaboosie and I have just sent Frances and Helmina and Benedict in the trap to The Hoek to collect the post and deliver the needlework to the Ladies' Guild. The order was long overdue, but now I'm worried about the drift.'

'I'll ride into the village and accompany them back if you would like me to,' said Walter.

'If they're not here by dinner time, I'd be grateful.'

Walter left her and went down to the curate's lodge. His boots were damp and cold and he needed a change of clothes. Nowasha saw him and before he had unpacked his bag she was tapping at the door with jugs of hot water, warm with the smell of ironstone, and a child dragging the tub behind her.

Left to himself, he listed the tasks that needed attention, updated his register, washed and shaved, keeping Frances from his mind. In the time since he'd played the Corelli in the living-room and plunged out into the rain, he'd forbidden her his thoughts. Cast her out. He fought himself with an iron will. And yet she'd haunted him, silent and spectral in his sleep and in his consciousness. He took clean clothes from the cupboard, shrugging his damp coat over them and went to the church in search of Mzantsi, marching remorselessly through puddles and mud eddies, not looking across at the house or letting his eye linger at her window. Such foolishness was past. He was a middle-aged priest, dry as a stick and busy as the Devil himself. He consulted his pocket watch. The candidates for baptism should be awaiting him. No doubt Mzantsi would be there to translate when his Xhosa faltered, book in hand, his surplice starched and ironed and smelling of the cupboard in the vestry.

Six aspirants were sitting in the pews, Kobus Pumani among them. The old men, like acolytes about a priest, turned to watch Walter's approach. Mzantsi was not there. The vestry was empty and his robe still hung in the cupboard. Walter took the instruction book from a shelf and brought a small upright chair into the church. He placed it before the old men and sat on it, facing them. He said, wearily, 'Let us pray,' and led in the Lord's Prayer, the Xhosa easy at last in his mouth, '*UBawo wethu osezulwini . . .*'

He opened the little book that he and Benedict had printed for their instruction and he began: 'Who is God? *Ubanina uThixo?*'

They sat in the church before him, humble to instruction, old men all, wrapped in shabby overcoats, gathered about Kobus's tall figure. Kobus kept his eyes closed as if Walter's words had to be dissected without distraction. Walter glanced every now and then at the inscrutable face. Was he listening or was he in a trance? He needed Mzantsi at his side to clarify his stumbling Xhosa. The gloom in the nave loomed and faded, loomed and faded as rain clouds gathered in again and a strange green light seemed to lap along the aisle. Walter went to fetch a candle so that he could see the pages of the pamphlet better. He wondered irritably where Mzantsi was, but the old men only shrugged when he asked. It was as he was returning from the vestry with a candle sheltered in his hand that he saw him, through the open door of the church, bent against the wind, hurrying past, his hat clutched against his chest, his coat tails leaping up and out as if trying to hold him back.

Josiah Mzantsi went in the wind, down towards the Farboroughs' house. He went with a purpose, ignoring the small restraining voice in his head. The evening before, he had seen Dorcas Pumani – despite the fine drizzle – walking down to the river. She had gathered sticks as she went and she had stopped and gazed expectantly up the slope towards the mission grounds. Then her stance became relaxed and quiet as if she had seen the thing for which she searched. She had become self-absorbed, resting her arm on the upturned bundle of wood that she had been collecting and staring off in the other direction.

256

And out of the trees that grew along the banks of the Mtwaku had come Benedict Matiwane, sauntering down towards her as if he were to pass her by with no more than a greeting and yet, as he drew level, she had laid the bundle down and fallen in step, seemingly without an exchange, and they had walked together towards the trees, moving fast, strongly mounting the slope. They had gone among the foliage and Mzantsi, standing quite still, his hat in his hand, had turned from the sight of their retreat with a shuffle and a lurch. He had stopped, put his hat upon his head and pulled the strap below his chin. A lover's tryst, flouting the rules of the mission: they were posted in the hall of the boarding-house. They applied still, even though Benedict might have passed his final examinations, even though Dorcas Pumani was only a mission worker, not a student:

> Article 3: No boy shall go beyond the Boundaries of the Mission
> Lands at any time or be outside the walls of the Institution after the last bell rings . . .
> Article 11: Boys are strictly FORBIDDEN to join the girls in their walks.

There was no doubt about their intentions. This had been prearranged and they were there in the twilight, where none could see them, exposed momentarily in their deceit to his hidden scrutiny. Mzantsi knew the implications of their hurried disappearance, the last backward glance as they entered the trees. Something of the meeting, the languid, unsurprised turn of Dorcas's head as Benedict had passed, had shouted the intimacy between them. *Umetsho* or worse. Mzantsi felt as though Benedict had betrayed him, overturned each lesson he had taught, each plea he'd made for purity and right-thinking, each sermon, each catechism, each evening prayer that they had shared.

And yes, too close, too well remembered had been the spectres of his own youth: the sudden taste of it, the shadow of it sunk too nearly in his flesh.

He had turned from his purpose, hesitating, glancing now

at the place where they had gone and back at the old grey church among the trees. He did not know what to do, on whom to call. Father Charles was in King William's Town to meet the new Bishop, Mr Brownley had not returned from the outstations for five days and the river surged across the flat-lands. Drifts would be impassable and mountain paths wet and treacherous. Who knew where he might be?

Mzantsi had looked down towards the Farboroughs' house, wondering. He had not wished to speak to a woman on matters such as these, but the rules were the rules. He was their custodian. He could not see them broken flagrantly, almost within sight of the boarding-houses.

Avoiding the church, he had returned to his cottage and closed the door behind him. He'd eaten a meal which had been prepared for him by the mission cook, washed his plate and gone out into his backyard. His chickens and his veg-etable garden provided pleasure and comfort when he felt alone. He had gone to the fowl-run and bent and peered in-side. He had names for his hens, just as a herdsman might have had for his cows: the red one, the guinea-fowl, the little dun. Ten fowls. Eleven.

One had been missing.

He'd cast about, searching under the hedge, calling softly, 'kip-kip-kippie-kip', but nothing came. And in the earth, where his cabbages were planted, was evidence of the soil having been disturbed and smoothed again, brushing out the traces of a thief.

One had gone, maybe two.

This had been his sanctuary, a place where little children came with buckets to water his plants and where only Nowa-sha was allowed to take an offering for the Farboroughs' table under his eye. Someone had been here. Someone had come and taken from him, unannounced, not trusting to his gener-osity to give if he were asked.

He had gone inside and closed the door and lit the candle and looked out of the window, peering into the misty twilight. The reflection of the flame had wavered in the pane, flaring momentarily across the shadow of his face.

Once he had had a wife. Large, simple, shielded by her

piety. She would have been vigilant of his little plot, she would have put the fowls to bed and shared the cabbages with those that might be needy. She would have filled and lit a lamp and opened the Bible and sung a hymn and given him counsel. He knew then that the comfort had not been in the words she read but in her presence there. Now she was dead. Fifteen years or more had passed and still the night assailed him, despite his prayers.

He had sat at the table and put his hands before him. He had pushed aside the matter of the chicken. He'd thought of Benedict – out there in the dark, there in the wattles with the girl – flouting all the rules. Since the time at the dip, Benedict had become inaccessible, defiant even. He did not come voluntarily to matins and evensong with the old eagerness. He had to be summoned. He sat in the printing-room until late at night, no longer a companion, a man to whom he could impart all the wisdoms of his life.

It was the girl. Since she had come to the mission to work in the laundry and care for her father's house, Benedict had been preoccupied and distant. Ah, Mzantsi knew that girl: the quick, youthful strength in her walk, despite the demure cast of her eyes and the slim, severe cut of her skirt, despite her badge of the St Agnes Guild at her throat. He saw the piety at her devotions in the church and the modesty with which she sat in the sewing-room, instructed by Miss Smythe, but he knew the sudden candour of her glance and the small, defiant set of her chin.

All night he had debated the matter. Small, dark offerings in mitigation, remembrances – so many – of the slights, the humiliations, the emptinesses. His and Benedict's. On and on. But when morning came he had closed out any scruple that the night had brought him, pushed aside his reservations and taken himself and his resolve down to the Farboroughs' house. He would not shrink from his pledge to God and to the mission. He took his hat, ignoring any lingering doubts, closed his door and set his face towards the church. He did not go inside. He hurried past, knowing that a class was waiting. He ignored this duty for another that was greater. He went down the path towards the gate of the Farboroughs' garden and he opened it and went through, treading softly on the gravel path between the beds of flowers. Ragged crows tossed across the sky above him in the wind. He went, a lonely old man in a black alpaca coat.

Seated next to Benedict as he drove the trap into The Hoek, Frances turned and glanced at Helmina with her cape drawn around her and her nose red from the freshness of the wind and she said, 'It's going to rain again.'

'Then we'd better just deliver the sewing while Benedict is at the post office and not stay for tea at the Nettletons,' said Helmina. 'The water at the drift is up enough without more rain.' She glanced down at the mud spattering out from the wheels of the trap, holding herself steady against the seat. 'I wonder where Mr Brownley is,' she said. 'He's been gone so many days, I do hope he hasn't had an accident.'

'He's probably fallen off a cliff along the Donsa,' said Frances, knowing Helmina's intention and goading her. 'Or drowned. Can he swim?' She made a small face. 'Englishmen never can.' And she turned her back on her companion and looked out across the hills. She'd show none of her own anxieties. She began to chant a Xhosa song – just a snatch – to annoy Helmina and she took up the package that Benedict had placed between them on the seat and read the address written on it, *The Editor: Izwi Labantu*, and shielded it under the folds of her coat from the random drops of the rain, speaking to Benedict in Xhosa in a loud, conversational way, knowing that Helmina could not understand.

A mile from the village they came upon Dorcas Pumani walking in the road. She turned, startled at the sound of the wheels, stepping off into the grass at the side of the track.

Frances told Benedict to stop. 'Hello, Dorcas,' she called. 'Would you like to climb up? Where are you off to in the rain?'

Dorcas hesitated, shifting the basket that she carried from one arm to the other, smoothing the cloth that protected it with her hand.

'There is room for you,' said Frances, indicating to Benedict that he should help her in.

Benedict looked at Dorcas and she glanced back at him reluctantly.

'Come along, do,' said Helmina. 'The rain will be back any time and we shall all be soaked.'

Benedict clambered down and took the basket from Dorcas. It seemed as though she did not wish to relinquish it and she shook her head imperceptibly at him as he placed it in a corner. Frances looked back at it curiously. It contained a cabbage wrapped in a cloth. The feet of a chicken stuck up, the toes curled in against each other.

Silently Dorcas climbed in and settled herself with the skirt of her dress tucked up beside the basket. She placed her hands demurely in her lap. As they started away, Helmina said to her, 'Why are you walking out in this weather? You will catch a chill from wearing damp clothes.'

Dorcas looked at her uncomprehendingly, then averted her eyes, ignoring the scrutiny.

A half mile from The Hoek, with the houses plain among the trees, Dorcas suddenly leaned across and told Benedict to stop. Frances said, 'What is it?'

Dorcas licked her lips and glanced at Benedict and then she looked over towards the roadside. Frances followed her gaze. A woman waited there, sheltering by a bush.

Small, bent in, her shoulders covered with a sack, she looked up hesitantly as the cart drew level.

Frances stared. She said, 'Who is that?'

Dorcas did not reply but Benedict said, 'It is her mother.'

'Her mother?'

'Yes, Miss Farborough.'

The trap stopped and Dorcas climbed down. Benedict handed the basket to her and Frances greeted the old woman. '*Molo, Mama*,' she said.

'*Molo, nkosazan*'.'

Such a face: sunken at the cheeks, cadaverous, the eyes deep in the sockets of her skull. She had something of Dorcas in her, something of Sonwabo in the curve of her cheek and the line of her lip and something too of age and death, a sack held in a claw of hand, the sinews lying taut along its back.

'You are Dorcas's mother?' said Frances.

261

'*Eeehe.*' A sigh more than a word and the eyes shifting to her daughter. 'That is so.'

Frances said, 'Where do you live?'

The woman indicated a hut far up a hillside. 'I stay with other people . . .'

Frances followed her gaze. A rash of huts, little shelters like the ones that had been built around the mission at the time of the rinderpest. Half-constructed dwellings, hidden in the bush, the detritus of a town, creeping from its edges, from the fences and gardens and the dusty street of the village.

Helmina said softly but impatiently, 'Come away, Frances. We will be caught in the rain if we don't hurry.' But Frances ignored her.

Frances said in Xhosa, 'I see that you are suffering, mother.'

The woman regarded her a moment and then she opened the sack and revealed the contents. Roots. Leaves. Berries. A concoction of twigs. 'This is the food I must eat,' she said.

'Why?'

'Why?' Frances saw the tired, patient depths within the blackness of the woman's eyes. She waited.

The woman said, 'Pumani has put me off to *gqobhoka*. He has taken cattle from the transport rider, Otto, in exchange for my son, Sonwabo, but he has kept them for himself and discarded me.'

'In exchange for your son?' Frances regarded her with bewilderment.

'For all his sons, because his great wife has bewitched him.'

'Come away, dear!' Helmina was peevish, not understanding what they were saying.

'Tell me,' said Frances and she climbed down beside the woman so she could see her face directly. She could feel the wind coming then, a wet, warm wind and drops began to splash in the mud about her.

'The cattle were gone in the *Tobiratyi*,' said Dorcas's mother. 'All of them shot.' And Frances heard again the strange explosive ringing in that little schoolroom at Nolovini all those weeks ago.

'And then the man came – after that he came, some time

262

after all the cows were dead and the heart of Pumani's wife was set against me because I had let the white man put the blood of sheep in the veins of our herd and let him enter the byre – and he told Pumani he would bring cattle if he would send his sons to the mines when he called for them. And Pumani said yes. He said yes in his greed and because the woman that is his wife has *thakatha*'d him with thoughts of oxen and of bulls and because she wanted his heart to turn against me. He did not ask me. Sonwabo is my son. He is my only son. But Pumani said yes, he will send him and his brothers, those sons of his other wife, when the man Otto asks for them and when the cattle come. They will work and he will have his herd. He was glad to do this thing and never thinking to know my wishes.'

She paused and clutched the sack more tightly about her shoulders. 'Those cattle came,' she said, 'those ones that took away my son, Sonwabo. They are up at Nolovini, where my homestead was. And after that Pumani says he will *gqobhoka* and I must go.' A shadow crossed her face. 'He is afraid of the anger of the shades for what he has done, knowing he is wrong,' she said. 'That is why he came to the *mfundisi* and asked to *gqobhoka*, knowing that the *mfundisi* will tell him he may only have one wife. This is the thing Pumani wants to hear. Now I go like a pig that must dig for its food and my son is gone and the cattle that were paid for him grow fat in the kraal and the cattle that my father gave to Pumani are all dead.'

Frances stood with her coat whipping round her legs and Dorcas silent beside her with the basket at her feet. Without turning from the woman, Frances said, speaking in English, 'Benedict? Is it true about the cattle?'

And Benedict said, 'Pumani has cattle. They were brought to him by Mr Otto some time ago.'

'Where did they come from?'

'I do not know,' said Benedict.

'Have you told my father?'

'What is there to tell?' said Benedict. 'Kobus Pumani's cattle are his affair. How should I know where they come from or why?' He cracked his knuckles, said flatly, 'If he wished to be baptised, we are supposed to rejoice with him.'

263

'Why didn't he make provision for Dorcas's mother?'

'It is Dorcas who cares for her.'

'With what?'

'With what she can find,' said Benedict and he glanced away uneasily.

Frances looked at the basket at Dorcas's feet. She changed to Xhosa then, so Dorcas could understand her words. 'Why didn't you tell my mother? Why didn't you ask for help?'

'What help is there for the second wife of a Christian?' said Benedict, answering for her.

'Frances!' said Helmina. 'Whatever are you talking about? Get in at once.'

Frances ignored her and said to Dorcas's mother, 'Come with us now. We will take care of you.'

The woman hesitated. Dorcas shook her head. Benedict was silent.

'Benedict,' said Frances. 'Dorcas's mother must come back to the mission and we must find a place for her.'

Benedict said, 'And what will Kobus say?'

'I don't care at all what Kobus says!' said Frances angrily. 'She cannot be left to starve.'

He said in English then, and softly, 'She will be afraid of *thakatha* from the first wife and from Kobus.'

'I know that,' said Frances. 'I am not foolish. It's a fine thing to become a Christian to put off your wife and sell your sons and then indulge in *thakatha*!'

'Frances,' said Helmina. 'I must insist you get in. We'll catch our death of cold.'

Frances took the old woman's arm — all but imperiously — and made her climb up into the trap. Dorcas followed. Frances took the basket and tipped it over the tail-board. The cloth fell off and a cabbage rolled into a corner. A black and white fowl lay inert.

They proceeded in silence along the road. Frances did not look at Helmina, heedless of her anger and affront. The old woman sat crumpled, Dorcas at her side. Benedict turned into the road that led between the houses. He drew up outside Nettletons and got down to secure the horses to the hitching-post. Helmina lifted the sewing parcel from the floor. She said, 'I shall speak to Mrs Nettleton and I shall wait indoors until the rain has passed. I trust you will come in and say good-morning.'

Frances did not reply. She sat where she was and she picked up the package that lay on the seat. She looked at the address again and then she turned to Benedict and said, 'If you want anything to write about to this newspaper that you're supplying, Benedict,' and her voice was clear and even, 'write about cattle advances. Tell the editor how a man pledged his sons to labour in exchange for cattle. And then, tell about how the man became a Christian so he could put off his wife to starve in good conscience because she objected to what he'd done. Tell them that. I am sure it will make excellent reading.'

She looked at Benedict then. Straight in the eyes. The restraints fell away a moment before custom reasserted itself and she withdrew. She turned from him and jumped down from the trap and walked briskly through the Nettletons' gate and down the path to the front door.

'We cannot go back in this rain,' said Helmina, standing on the Nettletons' porch and closing her umbrella decisively.

'It won't clear.' Frances was impatient. 'We've got no choice.'

Helmina's cheeks were bright. 'Frances, really! How can we drive in a downpour? And how can we ask the Nettletons to have us with such a crew of people? As if Benedict weren't enough!'

'Exactly!' said Frances. 'That is why we will have to hurry.' She went out onto the verge and climbed into the trap and said to Benedict, 'Please ask Mr Nettleton for a few meal sacks from the store. We'll return them next time we're here.'

'I'm not driving back to the mission looking like a washerwoman with a meal sack over my head!' said Helmina, following irritably and muddying her hem in a puddle.

'Please yourself,' retorted Frances.

'Frances!' Helmina's voice shook. 'Why are you so rude?'

'Oh, do come on!' cried Frances in exasperation. 'Or the drift will be flooded and we shan't get through.'

She did not speak on the way back to St Matthias and she

did not wish the rain away. She sat with the meal sack around her shoulders and water streaming in her face. She paid no attention to Helmina who complained about the ill-effects of such exposure and kept her eyes ahead, watching the road between the drooping ears of the reluctant horses.

As they reached the mission gate Frances clambered down to open it and she glanced up at Helmina. 'We're home,' she said, for Helmina sat with her eyes tightly closed as if the rain stung her skin. Her hair was wet, plastered against her skull. She looked as though she had been crying. Beside her, Dorcas's mother crouched among the sodden sacks clutching the basket with the cabbage and chicken, but Dorcas sat upright, unflinching in the rain, beautiful as sculpted wood, the drops sliding from her hair.

As they drove into the yard, Frances saw her mother standing in the porch of the church with Mzantsi by her side. They stood expectantly and her mother raised her umbrella and stepped out, hurrying towards them, calling, 'Mr Mzantsi, ask Mr Brownley to send Kobus out to see to the horses.'

Benedict drew the trap up under the trees.

Emily turned to Frances and surveyed her, saying with some exasperation, 'Why didn't you stay at the Nettletons? It was foolish to come back in this.'

'There were too many of us,' said Frances, alighting.

Emily looked into the trap. 'Where has Dorcas been and who is that woman?'

'Dorcas's mother. We found her,' said Frances. 'She is starving. I couldn't leave her.'

'Dorcas,' Emily said, enunciating with care and surveying her mother and the basket in her arms, 'you will go and change and ask Nowasha for some clothes and food. Then you will come and speak to me at the kitchen, do you understand?'

Dorcas nodded silently and climbed down, helping her mother.

'Helmina and Frances,' continued Emily, 'go and put on dry things or you will both be ill. Benedict' – there was no softening here – 'you will come to the house at once.'

Frances glanced at Benedict but his face was closed and impassive.

It was then that Kobus emerged from the church with the old men. Frances heard his voice, heard it and the tone of it and turned and stared. He was looking at Dorcas's mother and loud was his cry!

And Dorcas's mother stood in stillness with the rain running from the sack at her shoulders, facing him. With a curse, Kobus turned and plunged away behind the church.

Frances followed Helmina as she half ran, half crouched with her sack. She let her go ahead and walked upright, not heeding the puddles, for the rain was warm and cleansing. She reached the garden gate and looked back a moment at the church. The old men were standing in the porch with Dorcas and her mother. And there was Walter Brownley among them, listening to their words. He was back. Thank God, he was back. She ran inside then, stopping only to discard her boots on the porch.

She went through the kitchen, pulling off her cape. The kettle was steaming on the stove and she warmed her hands at it. She fetched a mug and poured a little water. The warm, metallic taste was comforting. She heard her mother come into the house through the side door, leading Benedict to the study. She leaned against the rail where the dish towels dried, glad of the heat.

She could hear her mother's voice, reaching along the passage, quiet now, now raised a little. She went to the door and listened. She walked towards the study, her stockinged feet making no sound. She heard the words quite clearly and she went closer, bolder now, unafraid to be an eavesdropper.

'Benedict' – and Frances could hear the authority in the tone – 'Mr Mzantsi has reported to me that you have been meeting Dorcas down by the river. There are others, when questioned, who have seen you too.'

Benedict did not reply.

'You know the rules of the Institute.'

'Yes, ma'am.'

'It is a question of morality.'

Silence.

'Do you deny it?'

'No, Mrs Farborough. I have met Dorcas, as you say.'

267

'And flagrantly broken the rules?'

'Yes, ma'am.'

A pause. 'Have you no sense of propriety, Benedict? Miss Prudieaux-Brune has sponsored you right throughout your education. You are like a son to her, though she has never seen you. What shall I say to her when I write my monthly report? That you have been, not just disobedient, but immoral? That you have met a young girl in secret places? Are the consequences of those meetings yet to be seen?'

'There will be no consequences,' said Benedict.

'Indeed?' Her mother's phrasing was heavy with innuendo. 'And how many abandoned children do we have in the orphanage and how many in foster care? Do I need to remind you of your own beginnings?'

'I am reminded every day, ma'am,' said Benedict, and Frances did not doubt the look that would have crossed his face, and she could feel the ice and fire of it marching in her own blood as she stood and listened.

'And so,' her mother's voice was low now, 'am I to understand that that heathen vice that shields you from "consequences" is practised, here on my mission, within sight of my church?' The rain had started softly again. It fell gently on the roof. Frances came closer to the study door. Her mother said, 'Benedict, I thought, I prayed, that you would be the first – after Victor – to take Holy Orders and assist Father Charles in his work. What decay has set in, Benedict, while we have been looking elsewhere?'

Silence again.

'This is not the only matter,' she said. 'Mr Mzantsi tells me that a chicken has been stolen from his fowl-run and cabbages from his garden. It is evident that Dorcas is the culprit.'

'Her mother is starving.'

'Is that a reason to steal? She could have asked me. I would not have denied her.'

'She was afraid. She did not wish it to be known that her mother was close by. She fears her father and the powers of his other wife.'

'It is theft, none the less.' Frances heard Emily's step as she crossed the floor. She drew back into the shelter of a doorway.

268

Her mother continued, 'Dorcas will have to go. She cannot create a precedent at St Matthias. Adequate arrangements for her mother and herself will be made as soon as possible. I shall see to it myself. Until that time you may not speak to her or have any contact with her at all. Miss Prudieaux-Brune may not wish to continue with her sponsorship of your studies and, if that is the case, we will have to review your position as well. In the mean time I have asked Mr Mzantsi to take you into his house. I am told that passions are something that tempt all young men and I am prepared to give you an opportunity to redeem yourself.'

Again, Benedict made no reply.

Emily's voice rose then and Frances could hear by her tone that she was bringing the interview to an end, the *coup de grâce* poised. 'You will be forbidden to take Holy Communion until I am satisfied that you have purged yourself of the wickedness of the last few weeks.'

Frances stepped back into the living-room and listened as Benedict walked away down the passage. She heard the side door open and then close quite firmly behind him: a moment's stillness and the roof creaking under the fingers of the rain.

She walked towards the study then, step by step, unwavering. She stopped at the threshold of the room and she said, 'Mother?'

Emily turned sharply from the window.

'If you wish to know about depravity you should not be speaking to Benedict. If you wish to know about theft, the matter of a cabbage and a chicken are nothing in comparison with cattle bribes and labour contracts. If you want to know about sponsorship that makes slaves of people, like Miss Prudieaux-Brune has made of Benedict, then ask Kobus Pumani how and why Tom and Reuben and Sonwabo were sent to the mines and decide then if you still care about a cabbage and a hen.'

Her mother regarded her a moment, her head rigid. Then she said, in a quiet voice, 'Frances, do go and change. You'll catch cold and be in bed again.'

'Don't you hear me?' Frances could feel the heat rising and the tumult pushing at the doors.

'You are not permitted to speak like that,' said her mother, marshalling the authority of years to stand like legionaries at her back.

'I will speak as I wish.' Frances went on inexorably. 'Klaus Otto advanced cattle to Kobus so that he would promise his sons for recruitment.'

'I believe that is a common practice,' said Emily, 'and I disapprove of it as much as you.'

'It's no use disapproving!' said Frances. 'You have to do something! You should have seen what Dorcas's mother was collecting to eat. She had a bag of roots. That's all! It's easy for Kobus to say he wants to be baptised. If he put off Dorcas's mother, he had no need to worry about whether she'd agree to Sonwabo going to the mines or not. It wasn't her concern, and now she's no longer his.'

'Frances,' said her mother impatiently, 'I fear you are meddling. Kobus sincerely wishes to be baptised. Mzantsi has questioned him at length and is convinced of it. He was wrong not to provide for his wife but we will rectify that as far as we are able. The church is very clear about polygamy. As to the cattle advances, I think that you are being naive. I am sure that it is practised everywhere. At least one can assume that Klaus Otto will take care of the interests of those he might recruit. He's a very pleasant man. Better him than someone unscrupulous.'

Frances felt her heart striking at her chest. She took a breath. 'And yet, despite it, you are sending Dorcas away for stealing a cabbage and a chicken?'

'I am sending her away for a crime far greater than that.'

'And you are banning Benedict from Communion.'

'I despise an eavesdropper.' Emily's voice rose.

'I'm glad I heard the things you said, for now I know that you care nothing for Benedict's feelings nor his needs.'

Emily gazed at Frances and then she said, 'Be silent,' and her eyes went beyond her to Helmina standing hesitantly in the doorway.

Frances glanced at Helmina and turned back to her mother. 'I will not be silent,' she said and the rivers rising. 'Do you think I don't know why you are punishing them? Do you

270

think I have lived here all my life and learned nothing, seen nothing?'

'Frances, hush.' Helmina twitched at her arm from behind, urging her away.

'You cannot conceive of his sin,' said Emily briskly. 'It is heathen vice of the most vile kind and I will not pollute my mind nor yours by mentioning it.'

'*Umetsho*,' said Frances defiantly.

Emily stared. With triumph, Frances saw the slow revulsion in her face, as if her mother, looking at her, was regarding something strange and frightening. Emily was silent. Helmina did not move. 'You think that Benedict is full of darkness and depravity?' Frances paused. 'It's not only Benedict who has done wrong' – there was no stopping the words now – 'nor Dorcas. It's Victor and I. If you drive them out for what they've done, then you must drive us out as well . . .' and her voice wavered and cracked.

Emily's face was ashen. Mechanically she picked up a half-finished kneeler from a chair. Her voice trembled. 'Helmina dear,' she said, not looking at Frances, 'I don't know what these girls are about, but I have had to unpick this work. Would you give it back to Rosamond and ask her to start again?'

Frances stood, gulfs opening before her. Then she turned and walked away.

She went to her room and closed the door and stood in the centre of the rug. She wanted to tear her clothes from her and trample them, to overturn the furniture, to crush the little china jug of flowers to clay, to splinter it like an eggshell between her fingers. She wanted to shout so that she rattled the window-panes and the plaster fell down, but she stood quite still, the rage – and its futility – welling in her. If she stayed in this room with the demure, the familiar and fragile things around her, ambivalence might seize her. Fear. She might capitulate before the spectre of her guilt, her sin. She might lie down on her quilt and weep and wait for retribution. God might come and exact a due – 'violence covereth the head of the wicked and the prating fool shall fall . . .'

She had chosen the text herself. Had some guiding hand

271

directed the choice? Satan perhaps – the familiar subject of childhood castigations? The words on that ill-considered sampler seemed prophetic. A full confession would be exacted. An indemnity required, forced contrition, payable to God – as represented by her mother – over years. It would suit her mother very well. She would send her away to marry Victor as she'd always wanted. And Victor and she could remind each other – in perpetuity – of their mutual carelessness. They could maim each other daily in remembrance of it.

Still wet from the journey in the trap, her clothes cleaving to her skin, Frances went from her room into the silence of the house. She walked away: down the steps of the veranda, out across the yard, along the path past the orchard and the stables. She ran, knowing her purpose. She did not look up at the familiar – the kindly – head of Boggis ruminating over the stable door. She went to the church and let herself in. She walked down the aisle, her steps rustling on the matting as she went. She walked, knowing God was watching her, the red light in the sanctuary flickering in the gloom. She paused at the altar-rail and she looked up at the cross on the cloth and at the flowers that Helmina had arranged; the purple furred heads of irises and the daisies, the small yellow hearts, fringed with white, pure and fragile in the green light. She went to the vestry. She closed the door behind her.

He was there, in his cassock, and he turned to her, startled by her step. An eternity to see that face, looking back at her, standing upright and inviolable in his parson's robe. She reached for him. Just that. No more.

So many years to wish for something and so much pain in finding it. He held her as she cried, his face bent to hers. 'They will send me away,' she said, drawing her breath to weep again, and as she spoke he could feel that the dark was rising, some inexorable blackness washing in around him. 'Help me.' Her hand reached out for his.

'How?' His eyes were steady on hers.

'Undo my sin with Victor.'

'By compounding it with another?'

The sob was swelling in her throat.

'I love you far too much for that,' he said.

In quietness he held her. Steady in the shield of his arms. He let her cry unhindered. With need, with sorrow and with loss. He held her still when all the tumult of her tears had gone. And the portraits of Father Charles and the Reverend Greenstock looked gravely on and a row of candlesticks sent their shadows, side by side, lancing up against the wall.

Chapter Eighteen

Emily Farborough went to her rose garden. She closed the little gate knowing she could count on no intrusion. This place was hers and it was sacrosanct. She walked between the plants. They had recently been pruned and the grass between them was swept clean of leaves and twigs: Kobus had been busy that morning as he'd been instructed. She could not have visualised, as she had indicated where she had wished him to work, the changes that the day would bring.

She sat on a wooden bench in the small summer-house in the shadow of banksias growing so profusely about it – the first that she and Charles had planted so many years before – and looked across the garden. She remained straight and still with her hands in her lap, tutored to restfulness. She wept quietly. But for the steady course of tears across her cheeks, she gave no sign of weeping, she neither drew her breath nor sobbed. She wept more restrainedly but no less deeply than Frances did at that moment in the vestry. And she wept alone with no one's arms to comfort her.

Emily could admit to no confusion. She had to keep the vision of her own vocation clear, against the tumults of her doubts and the exhaustion that her dedications caused her. To admit doubt was to presuppose defeat and God would not have dealt so cruel a hand.

To allow a doubt, to explore it even, would be to question God. 'Put your life in the hands of the Lord and He will reward you richly.' She had done that and now, it seemed, reward eluded her.

She had bargained with God in those first weeks at St Matthias so long, long ago. She had pledged to dedicate the life of her first-born to Him in return for a safe delivery. She had promised it in the months of waiting and in the hours of fear and pain when, at last, her time had come. She could make no greater offertory as she lay in a lonely and terrifying labour with the heathen bush streaming in the hot wind, a breath of pestilence outside her window. She struggled hour after hour, hour after hour through a night, a day, a night, fighting with each breath to reach the end. She had said, 'Thy Will be done' when the midwife had stood quietly beside her and her assistant had hurried away her stillborn son. She had turned her head aside and held her grief with dignity. But God had demanded more than just a life, He'd demanded two.

Against all instinct and with no prayer in recrimination or self-pity, she had buried her second son as well. She had had no expectations and she'd made no pacts with God when Frances was born. She had arrived in winter, in the early dusk of evening. Her cry had made the midwife smile and say, 'Here's a lusty one, Mrs Farborough. My, what a pair of lungs!'

And then, not long after, with the waning of her youth, there was Crispin. He was too late to match her early aspirations, too placid to rekindle ardent hopes. Nowasha had taken him and put him to her own abundant breast. He had dreamed his first two years away, strapped to her back, lulled by the soft harmonies of her voice, unresponsive to any other.

Despite her detachment from her children's world, sacrificed to the demands of her mission work, its punishing hours, Emily had always supposed herself their shield, the buffer set against the unknown treachery beyond the gates of St Matthias.

To be a missionary had been her choice and one to which – in consequence – Frances and Crispin had been born. Her vocation was their inheritance. She had nothing else to give. It was her duty to ensure that they might live and grow without the knowledge of the compromise her choice had been. Faith must be planted firmly – brighter, stronger than her own – lest they imbibe her doubts and have no means to fight them. She did not wish for them – because she loved them – the aloneness of that battle.

And now, despite the years, despite her well-learned restraint, despite having banished shows of tenderness that might soften their resolve, she had been repudiated. Frances had faced her not only with contempt but as though she were a stranger. She had spoken as if the only tutors in her life had been the very things that Emily herself had fought to conquer,

275

as though the spectres in the black, malignant bush that clung to the edges of the mission lands, had claimed her for their own. Why had such a madness arisen to challenge her when Charles was absent from her side? Oh, for the unobtrusive vigour of his faith! The certainty and trust!

For Charles there seemed to be no battle for that certainty, no dyad and no doubt. She had marvelled at the prodigiousness of his work: the wagons and the ploughs, the tinware and the carts that went out in such abundance. His contentment and his joy were in the companionship of his men in the workshop, in bringing in the harvests from the lands, in the produce of his gardens watered by the furrows he had made of river stones. In thanks for all of this he brought his workmen to the church with him at evening, offering up their labours at the close of every day. Simple, reverent praise of God – another workman in the sky, another man who shouldered a hoe, who drove a cart and laid his burdens down to rest at night. Charles did not bargain with God. He exacted no debts, asked no favours in return for labour. He thanked Him for the sun and the rain and only prayed – in times of need – that He might stand by all of them.

Emily had often been impatient with Charles's lack of evangelical zeal, his preoccupation with the simple tasks he set his men. She had always striven for a wider vision for the mission, a goal just beyond the immediate grasp, beyond yet another wagon, another brickfield, another load of tin mugs. She argued for a more far-reaching spiritual and educational thrust where the principles of all that she had ever valued would be embraced and nurtured. She strove for victory over the insidious darkness. If this were not attainable it would make a jest of all her life and of the faith she had sustained with so much pain. She could not allow such a possibility and she had raised her children to serve as she had served and championed Victor, drawing him to her cause, to soldier faithfully on her behalf when it was clear that Crispin could not follow where she led. She had set herself this task with dedication and with pride and if warmth and compassion had been lacking in her dealings with them, she had reserved as little for herself.

And now, Frances and Victor – in whom she'd placed the greatest trust, the repositories of her dearest hopes – had betrayed her. At every level they'd betrayed her and made a mockery of all that she held dear. She sat dispossessed in an isolation and an aloneness beyond any that her husband or her children or any at St Matthias could comprehend. None were held in bondage as she had been. None yearned to be released as she had done. None knew the fear that had stalked her in all the years since Charles had brought her here.

Emily looked up and saw Helmina at the gate. She beckoned to her and Helmina entered the garden. She came down the path between the roses and hesitated a pace or two off, letting down her umbrella slowly and shaking it out. She raised her eyes to Emily's face and then looked away. Emily made no apology for her distress. She said, 'Helmina, come and sit with me a moment.'

Helmina closed her umbrella and leaned it against the seat. She sat tentatively, twisting her fingers in her lap.

'How could this have happened?' Emily's voice was steady.

'I don't know, Mrs Farborough. Victor is very reckless . . .'

'It is Frances who is headstrong.'

Helmina did not reply.

'Why did you not warn me of what was happening?'

Helmina was at a loss.

'How long have you known?'

'I don't think I *knew*,' Helmina said, the heat burning low at the angle of her jaw. 'I was never certain. It was just something about Victor . . .' She sent away stray wisps of hair with her fingers. 'And once, when you were at The Hoek, Frances ran off to meet him . . . It is difficult to say.' She was silent then, not trusting herself to speak, aware of her inability to distinguish between what she had visualised so often and what she had really seen. Her extensions of those looks of Victor's had occupied her greedily – those moments when she'd watched him rest his eyes on Frances and sensed the small, unconscious swallow, secret in his throat, like a dog waiting to be fed. She said, 'They have been so familiar with each other all their lives, one might miss the signs that one would see in others.' And she cast her eyes down then, away

277

from Emily's gaze. No, she had missed none of them. None. And those she had not seen, she had invented. She could feel the tears herself, crowding in behind her lids. How closely and how damningly she faced her own deceit.

'Of course,' said Emily. 'Why should you have been aware of it any more than I. Perhaps I did not want to see it. I have always believed that Frances was destined for Victor. It's what I wanted. Perhaps it is my fault that this has happened.' She sighed. 'Perhaps, indeed, it is. I placed too little restraint on them from the start.' She was silent a moment, then she said, 'Frances cannot remain here. I expected too much in believing she might withstand the wild influences and the isolation.' She said bleakly, self-deprecatingly, 'I have bred a nest of heathens and idolators without knowing it! She must go to Grahamstown at once. She's defiant and angry. The society of other people will do her good. It will steady her. Victor's mother will have her, I know, and the sooner we prepare for a wedding, the better, despite what her father believes.' She drew her breath. It was still unsteady. 'I wonder if I dare tell him the truth. It will break his heart.'

Helmina could feel the perspiration at her lip. Unobtrusively she wiped it away. 'When will she go?'

'Without delay.' Emily rose. 'Will you find one of the herders or field-hands and send him to the house? I want someone to take a cable to the post. I must tell Mr Farborough to wait for me in Grahamstown. I'd like him to be there when we arrive and then we can settle things and return together.' She touched the cuffs of her sleeves and rearranged them. 'Ask Nowasha to fetch Frances's trunk down from the loft. We will pack at once.'

Helmina went and she dared not say a prayer of thanks: retribution surely lay in wait and her shame was heavy at her heel as she walked away.

Emily did not watch her go. She stood and turned her face to the sky. It seemed so distant and aloof: the stillness of the clouds – so far, so far – as the twilight crept in among the gathering squalls.

She reached the garden gate and closed it behind her. She could hear drops falling from the trees – random beats on the gravel drive, startling in the silence. Her step was even as she mounted the veranda steps. She went inside the house, walking slowly down the passage. She stopped at Frances's door, drew her breath in weariness, touching with the tips of her fingers at the edges of her eyes. She composed herself, knocked gently, almost tentatively. She waited for the turning of the key.

Walter had let Frances go. He had let her go out into the afternoon and he did not follow her. He sat at the table in the vestry in that green gloom with his hands on the table before him. He did not move for a long time. Then he stood slowly and took off the cassock and hung it in the cupboard and closed the door.

He had let her go when her tears had subsided and she had moved away from him and had stood with her back to him. He had listened as she spoke, with the calm of subterranean water rising against the raging in his heart to reach for her again, to sweep away right and reason. But instead, he had said – quietly, measuring his words – 'I cannot offer you an escape, Frances, just because you need one now. In time you would feel trapped again but when you've found out what it is you really want, I'll be here.'

And so she'd gone. Out into the restless rain of the afternoon and the vestry was filled with the presence of her and of her words tramping through his mind: words of self-recrimination, the heroes of her childhood crumbling about her. She was a gatherer of icons and portents, the player in Victor's games of honour, the witness to unknown tragedies. He'd heard her out. And then she'd said, 'I went to Victor's room with him . . .' He waited and she'd faltered on, 'as if I were his wife,' and her hand had searched for his as though she were drowning.

She'd asked for a redemption but he could not play the part of that redeemer. In the tumult of retreat from what she'd done, he could not stand protector at her back. This was something she must do alone. Complicity would not exorcise the thing from which she fled. It would compound it. He would not have her turn in time – he could see that slow, sad smile of dismissal – recalling Plotz to shield herself from the blazing truth of his eyes and exempt him from the debt that she'd imposed so recklessly, resurrecting the sawdust mannikin to taunt him: not when he had tasted her tears on his lips. He would not be a source to her of either self-recrimination or regret when she had time to look back and reflect.

But – if he could have acquiesced, if he'd surrendered to the tide, he would have taken Frances to the sanctuary of his room, obliterated from contention the memory of what she'd done before. Oh yes – and he'd have shown her love as she had not conceived that love might be. And then he'd lie beside her in the quiet of the dark, shield her tenderly, listen for the small, strong beating of her heart.

Instead, he'd stood aside and made her walk away.

He went from the church, letting himself out of the side door. He took the path to the stables, heedless of the mud eddies, hearing only the sighing of the sky: a great burgeoning of rain, sweeping in across the hills. He stood, his face raised up to it and he tasted salt in the drops that coursed across his cheeks. He reached the stable and opened the door and Boggis turned, nostrils dilating softly at the scent of him. He reached for Boggis, resting an arm along his back. He leaned his face in weariness against the sheltering neck.

And he had never known that Frances had gone to her room and locked the door and taken off her drenched and muddied clothes, leaving them on the floor, and lain on her bed, in the dim, blue shadow of the walls, with the rain drumming at the roof and wept for him in yearning. But he did not know. And if he had, how could he have gone into that house, set in armoury against him, Victor shadowing his back, and shown her?

And so she went. Within a day she was packed and the trap was prepared for her departure. Walter watched her from the door of the printing-room as she walked towards the church in her travelling cloak, her mother and Helmina at her side, ushering her in through the porch. He stood waiting for her to re-emerge and when she did, she hesitated and she looked across at him, mute, her small face pale beneath the brim of her hat and he went towards her, there under the scrutiny of her mother and Helmina Smythe and he took her hand – a brief salute – and her eyes darted up a moment, seeking his.

She was gone. And the sound of the gate closing out the trap lodged in his head as he turned away and returned to the printing-room. He worked all morning, Benedict at his side, and neither spoke though both had things to say to make the print lie idle in their hands. He went out into the afternoon and he saddled Boggis and rode to Nolovini with a package of booklets for the teacher and when he returned he pitched a few cricket balls to the students on the rain-sodden field, glad of the strong rush of air in his lungs and the brisk wind.

He answered a note from Helmina asking him to join her at supper in the house. He went, afraid – for the first time – of his own company. But to sit at the table with Frances's empty chair opposite, to feel something of her in the room, hear her voice, plunged him into silence. He answered Helmina's enquiries but he did not hear his own words. When the meal was finished she brought him the Bible and asked him to read the evening lesson. He opened it randomly at Kings and he began:

> But he himself went a day's journey into the
> wilderness, and came and sat down under
> a juniper tree: and he requested for himself
> that he might die . . .

'That is a rather gloomy verse,' said Helmina bleakly.

'I'm sorry,' said Walter, closing the book and putting it on the mantelpiece. 'I've been gloomy enough company myself.' He mustered a smile. 'I'll think of something more hopeful for tomorrow's reading so let's leave this now, shall we?' He rose. 'It's been a long day.'

Unobtrusively, Helmina slipped the chess-board that she had taken out in expectation, back into the bureau drawer. Walter saw her and he said, 'I'd like a game some other time, if you still feel inclined.' It was a small offering, but it sufficed. Helmina smiled back at him and showed him to the door.

'Weather's clearing,' he said, looking up at the sky.

'Good-night,' she said. 'Until tomorrow.'

'Good-night.' And he turned from her and went swiftly down the steps into the dark.

Some time after she had gone to her room and was preparing for bed, Helmina heard footsteps on the gravel of the kitchen path. She listened, her comb poised above her head. She leaned across and lifted the edge of the curtain. She drew back silently for Walter Brownley was standing in the yard looking over at the house. He remained quite still. It seemed to Helmina as if his stillness held arrested some terrible anguish: a cry, a howl. He had taken off his cleric's collar, his shirt was open, his neck pale. He stood in a strange kind of nakedness without that collar and she felt a sudden shame at seeing him – as if she had blundered on some secret: it was Frances who had sent him out like this. Helmina let the curtain fall: how closely love and bitterness stand skin to skin. How interchangeable. She sat, as taut, as still as he.

So the days went by and Frances was gone and within a month of her departure he was gone himself. When Father Charles returned from Grahamstown, Emily at his side, he called Walter to his study and after he had greeted him in a spontaneous embrace of welcome and affection, he said, 'If I weren't a servant of the church, Brownley, I'd have taken a cudgel to the Bishop and knocked a hole in his unheeding head!'

'Why, sir?' Walter felt the alarm in his voice.

'I've a letter for you. He wants to send you to Mbokothwe.'

Walter stood, wordless, his eyes fixed at Father Charles's watch-chain.

'God knows how I argued and bullied for him to leave you here,' said Father Charles, 'but he said you were ready for a mission of your own and he could offer any number of new incompetents to encumber me. He is quite determined that you're the man for Mbokothwe. I should not have sung your praises so loudly and my wife should have been positively barred from his company. If she had, you might have been quite safe.'

'Mbokothwe?' Walter said mechanically, gulfs, chasms and abysses opening before his feet.

No exile, devised by God or man, could have been more absolute for Walter. And yet, there was one more devastated even than he: Helmina Smythe stood stunned when he told her the news, a subterranean creature blinded by a blaze of white, arctic light. Small and bitter were her words with God, bitter as her self-recriminations. Maimed to the core of her, she sat alone the day he rode away on Boggis into the berg-wind morning, leading a laden mule. With something of resignation, too leached and weary for despair, she abandoned hope and laid it down and turned her back on it.

Chapter Nineteen

Journeys. And the tap of the wheels of the train, days across the Colony, nights across the Orange River Republic. Days and nights, days and nights and a doom in that countryside. Each river is a Jordan, its crossing a passage to an underworld. Those grey or green or mud-brown waters, the repository of the destinies of men who have passed this way before. There are those who have returned and there are those who have not.

The trains disgorge their men, workers all, ragged in exhaustion, the lines stream in towards the transit camp. There, the touts and the labour-thieves and the purveyors of bogus contracts wait at the edges. Inside is Officialdom, sleeves rolled up, world-weary, pen and stamp poised against the tide of migrants. This way, boy. That way, boy. Stand naked before the medical officer so he may look you over.

'Old natives this side.'

'Sick natives that side.'

'Strong boys here.'

'What is your name?'

'My name is Sonwabo Pumani.'

'Sonny is it? Sonny-boy? Yes. This side, Sonny-Boy. Next.'

Here is Tyamzashe and Gxowa. Now they are Fokisi and Ma-British. 'This side. This side. Here by One O'Clock and Four O'Clock and Blessing.'

'Where is your pass?'

'Which is your chief? Which your district? What is your father's name?'

'Have you been here before? Which recruiter? What rate of pay?' Stamp, stamp, stamp. 'Next.'

The lines go on and on.

'How old are you, boy?'

'It is the Time-of-the-Great-Drought.'

Pause. 'Too young.'

'Send him to Mostert's farm to work off the contract time.'

'Those recruiters at Lady Frere must look out for the law – they'll be caught. The fine's a hundred pounds for under-age.'

'Pass cheats from Pretoria will be caught. Deserters will be jailed. Sick boys to the hospital.'

No one comes from the hospital alive. It is the prelude to the grave.

One. Two. Three. Send them to the M.O.H. One. Two. Three. Four. This lot's for Mostert's farm. 'Why did your father send you when you're still a *kwedini*?'

'He owed the storekeeper.'

'He owed on cattle.'

'He owed on maize.'

He owed all his life.

And the trader calls the debt in and so the sons are sent away too young and children who are still hanging at the mother's breast are pledged already for a future time. He'll send for them one day and sign them up. Oh, one day soon he'll remember what is owed and call them in.

There are foreigners here. They speak a language that none can understand: there has been a crop failure in Portuguese East Africa again. Fathers, grandfathers, husbands of women many years past child-bearing. 'This way, boys. Look sharp. Watch out for the Egyptian at the Kaffir Eating-House. He'll take your money and steal your pass.'

Sonwabo stands quiet before the medical officer.

'Circumcised. He can't be under-age.' Stamp, stamp, stamp. 'Next.'

And so to find the scattered clothes and to look about for Tom and Reuben and the others from Rabula and The Hoek. And watching him, the compound policeman with his policeman's cap and stick and jacket and his policeman's eyes. Sonwabo turns away.

There had been a man on the train who had said, 'The mine police are Zulus. You must fear them.' This is what he'd said and in the night the wheels had turned and turned, churning out across the veld: they are Zulus . . . they are Zulus . . . they are Zulus . . . on and on. They are Zulus . . . the jackals of the compound, the lackeys of the camp *induna*, he who is the great hyena, he with sloping shanks and eyes that gaze, half-sunk in darkness.

Sonwabo feels those eyes from a distance, those small hyena

eyes and he takes his clothes and covers himself and walks away and still he knows, those eyes are watching him. Even in the open air with the heat to fill and dry the lungs, they watch, they follow. Beyond the walls, the winding-gear of the mines, like the skeletons of beasts that have died of plague, claw the sky.

They are called before the compound supervisor, standing ragged in the open ground between the living-quarters. Here he comes, in his shortness and his stoutness, and surveys them all and calls the *induna* and the policemen to gather near him, like ticks beneath the tail of the bull. He speaks the language of this place. At first, it is difficult to follow for it is something from which all the wisdom and the thought of speech has been taken and it knows its voice only in commands: Here, boys for surface work; there, boys for underground. So Tom and Reuben stand to the side where the underground workers are herded. It is for underground that they signed the paper with the white man Otto. It is for underground that Sonwabo signed the paper too.

But Sonwabo hesitates. If there is to be a choice, even if the pay is less, he will take the surface work. Anything to avoid pushing his way into the stomach of the earth, into the suffocating dark. He can feel it, even there, standing under the high pale sky, as he'd felt it once, locked in the vestry cupboard so long, long ago where Victor Drake had shut him in. Small and terrified, he'd lain, cramped and airless in his own oozings, until Father Charles had found him and lifted him out.

Standing there in the compound, under the eye of the manager and the *induna* and the policemen with their cudgels tucked beneath their arms, he can feel the dark on dark pushing in against his eyes and chest as he had felt it then and no sound but the marching of his blood in his ears. If he goes into the shaft his innards would desert him, spill themselves about him and leave him empty. There, in the tunnels where the faeces lay about on the ground and the shift that was to work eight hours stayed fourteen, sometimes fifteen, lashing without pay, issued with 'loafer's tickets' if the hammerboy's holes were not deep enough, muscles tearing with fatigue, hunger

286

gnawing like rats in the stomach, his eyes would be blinder than if someone had taken a stick and gouged them out.

The *induna* approaches and appraises him. Slow, expansive, a look is cast back to the manager who nods – a brief, smug interchange. The *induna* says, 'That side,' and prods him to where the group of surface workers wait.

Sonwabo is separated from his brothers. He is taken with others – young as he – to a room which has a mud floor and a brazier and rags stuffed into the gaps between the roof and the walls where the tongue of the wind creeps in at night and licks at their very hearts until they are raw with the cold and with shame.

It is there, in the days that follow, that this *induna* takes Sonwabo's book of shift tickets and holds it in the maw of his great hand with the counterfoils as yet unmarked and says, assessing him as a predator might assess its prey, 'It is I who will mark this book for work and for food.' He flips the tickets between his fingers, caressing them. 'You will bring your things to my room,' he says. 'I will lock them up very nicely with mine. Here can hang your coat, here your pants. Here you can leave your goatskin bag.'

Sonwabo obeys and there is an apprehension in his stomach, a warning murmur in his blood. What is wanted of him? The policemen accompany the young boys to their quarters. And they are festive. And lewd. Cajoling and insinuating. They are bartering for boys.

Here is food.

Here is drink.

Both are offered and in their hunger none of them refuses.

Here is my room. And the policemen laugh – for it is just a den, boarded up against intrusion in a communal barracks.

Here you will cook and clean and sew when your shift is done.

Here you will be rewarded with our favour.

And they are rewarded.

Time after time in a brutal dark.

And in the hours before the dawn Sonwabo lies in stillness, the air of that little den so fetid he might be prisoner in a stope behind a wall of rock and all around the concrete bunks lie tiered in two, each like a coffin, waiting for a corpse. Behind his locked lids Sonwabo might recall, grasping at it – so far in memory and in time it might elude him – the sanctuary of St Matthias, safe in the fold of its valley, and the low hills, rank on rank, closing it away. And searching further he might find a bird – its words, the scale of its whistle. If he should purse his lips in their dryness and try to whistle he might touch that note: *unomanyuku*, the warbler, calling, calling.

> *Nomanyuku! Sikuphe inqhaka?*
> *Nomanyuku!* May we give you milk?

But here no bird sings to herald the first light of morning, no girls raise their voices in a chant, accompanying their work, no children play, no fires are made with fragrant logs, smelling of sap, released in warmth from the heart-wood. No. Here, in the damp, urine-stained gloom of the compound rooms is the sound of men asleep and the sharp smell of braziers. Coal embers watch with the cruel gaze of unlidded eyes, whispering among themselves in the half-dusk of a perforated bucket in the centre of the room.

What do those ember-eyes see when the night comes to revive them from the soft, grey heedlessness of day? They burn: the gaze of the All-Devourer.

It was Crispin who found the truth. He blundered in unwittingly late one Saturday afternoon. On an unexpected and urgent errand to the mine compound where Tom and Reuben and Sonwabo lived, and having to wait around for the supervisor to return from a cricket match, he went in search of them, hoping to find them off duty somewhere among the compound huts. His task, as a junior clerk and interpreter in the Cape Colony Representative's Department in the Office of the Superintendent for Natives, was not arduous although he was called on at all hours to deliver messages or clear up misunderstandings but – between tasks – there was often time, awaiting a dispatch or a sheaf of forms, to talk to workers, exchange greetings, listen to the conversations of the men standing at the shaft-head at the end of a shift.

He walked down the dusty path from the supervisor's office towards the compound huts. He turned aside at the gate and spoke to the guard on duty. Beyond, a concourse of mine workers, many dressed in tribal regalia, were proceeding across the open place between the buildings. Among them were four or five young women.

Crispin stared and he said to the Zulu policeman at the gate, speaking in Xhosa – no syllable mispronounced, no word wrongly intoned – 'What are women doing here?' and a smile to hide his surprise.

And the policeman laughed and gesticulated lewdly. 'These are not women. These are brides. Boy brides. *Bakhontshana,*' he said.

Among them was Sonwabo, little carved wooden breasts strapped to his chest and at his side the compound *induna,* looming greatly above the crowd.

Crispin watched the throng disappear into a room, the door choked with revellers, and he turned away. Disturbed, he went back to the compound supervisor's house and waited on the veranda steps until he came and he said, his voice measured and his eyes elsewhere, 'Is there a party in the compound, Mr Oosthuizen?'

'I expect it's a brides' party,' said the supervisor.

'A brides' party?' Crispin did not look at him as he spoke.

'You'll get used to these things.' The supervisor shrugged. He said, 'It's a year's hard labour for anyone caught, but that doesn't stop them.'

'Caught?'

'Sodomy.' Oosthuizen took a cigarette from his case and tapped it on his thumb. 'We wink at it,' he said. 'It keeps the police in control of newcomers. Divide and rule. Besides, if you let the old *induna* have his bride, he'll do as you say and no questions!' He looked out across the garden. 'The younger boys are got up quite prettily and they don't seem to mind. At heart they're all savages, you see. We don't condone it, but we keep away when we think there's a brides' party on the go. It's only when the missionaries come in and interfere that we make the right noises. It's the least of the things you'll see while you're here.'

Crispin moved from foot to foot and the supervisor continued, contemplative as he smoked his cigarette. 'The police boys might rule by fear but they're good to their *bakhontshana*. They give them sweets and tobacco and little treats. Besides, it keeps the money in the compounds too because they spend in the shops close by. I've an interest in the store near the gate myself and the turnover's so good with miners buying extra food and the old men getting presents for the "brides" to oblige them that I'm making a tidy profit. The more they spend, the less they have to take home, the longer they stay. It suits us all.'

Crispin rode home on his bicycle through the windy afternoon, seeing the spokes racing and feeling the tyres bouncing on the dusty corrugations and when he reached the house that Victor shared with him and Sonnie Hook and Charlie Fraser, Victor did not seem to want to hear what he was saying. His attention was diverted by the others coming in from Saturday sports, flinging their jackets down on the bench in the hall and calling for the servant to bring beer. So Crispin held his tongue in the odd conviviality of the evening with the dark just beyond the railings of the veranda and a myriad moths, pale and drab as mine-dust, looping in the dusk above the grass, and Sonnie saying suddenly, as he deftly tossed an empty beer bottle from hand to hand, 'Let's go to Frenchfontein to Sylvio Villa!' He looked over at Charlie and Victor. 'Just for a lark, Vic. What do you say?'

And Victor glanced at Crispin, standing beside him, and said easily, 'Take Crispin,' and he folded his arms with a half smile on his face. 'I've been invited to the Chief's for dinner.'

Sonnie raised his glass. 'High places, Vic? Or is it the pretty daughter who begged the old man to send the invitation?'

'Is there a pretty daughter?' said Victor lazily.

'As if he hadn't seen!' said Charlie and he winked at Crispin but Victor rose and stretched and yawned and frowned at Charlie, with a secret shake of the head and a glance back at Crispin. There was a small silence and Crispin cracked his knuckles and stared off into the garden.

'Well, let's go to Sylvio's for a drink anyway,' said Sonnie, opening another beer. 'Shall we take Crispin?'

'Crispin won't like it.' Victor started for the door.

'He will if we hold his hand,' said Sonnie. 'How about the Sylvio Villa, Crispin?'

'What's the Sylvio Villa?' said Crispin.

'A sporting venue,' said Sonnie.

'An Initiation Lodge,' said Charlie, pleased with his own inventiveness.

'Go on, Crispin. We'll look after you.' Sonnie went indoors for his jacket.

They went together, out into the evening, walking a while then taking a cab, high-spirited, and Victor accompanying them, elegant in his evening dress, shepherding them, leading them along the pavements of the town to the lanterned doorway of Sylvio Villa. Victor mounted the steps to the hall and led them to the parlour. They were greeted by a woman who looked them over briefly but candidly. She smiled at Victor. Little pointed teeth in the parted petal-lips. Victor nodded to her, ordered drinks, lit a cigarette, while Crispin stared about the room, rubbed his hand across his hair. Swallowed. He glanced up and caught Victor's eye. Victor smiled – both affectionate and amused. Crispin knew that expression. He'd been recipient of it as a child when Victor – sudden with largesse – had presented him with his precious rugby ball and allowed him to play with it all afternoon.

Charlie thrust a tumbler of gin into Crispin's hand. 'It's all they've got,' he said. He raised his glass. 'Buck up, old man. You're about to enter the Gates of Paradise.'

There were men. There were girls. Smoke and noise and the woman who had greeted them went about the guests exchanging a word here and there. There was a small, flamboyantly dressed man in a floral waistcoat sitting at the bar with whom she conferred every now and then. Miners and clerks and shopkeepers. Gentlemen and rogues. Girls in ripe-coloured dresses, bows and feathers. A matron with a small cigar. Someone ruffled Crispin's hair. He turned, startled. White arms, black eyes. 'It's a very handsome lad,' she said, addressing Victor. She called for more gin.

They drank and the piano played on. Sonnie and Charlie

were there, sitting at the table. They seemed to loom and recede, loom and recede before Crispin's eyes. Victor had disappeared.

'Where's Vic?' said Crispin, starting up.

'Never mind Vic,' said Charlie, disengaging himself from among taffeta and lace.

Crispin peered round. There – Victor was standing in the doorway calling for his coat and hat. He was speaking to the hostess. He glanced across at Crispin, raised his hand, grinned. The hostess smiled and ushered him out. Crispin half rose to follow.

'Hello there, Crispin,' said Charlie. 'Not so fast. Vic's off to dinner and we're not invited.'

More gin, more piano and the black-eyed lady stood behind his chair and leaned across his shoulder and said, pulling gently at his ear, 'You're to come with me, laddie,' and she glanced across the room at the hostess who inclined her head, affirming something and then turned aside and spoke again to the small man at the bar.

Crispin was led obediently away, down a passage and up some stairs, and the sweat jumped at his lip and along his back. He wiped his sleeve across his face. The woman turned to urge him on and the feather in her hair was unaccountably like the one Benedict always wore in his hat. Crispin watched it, mesmerised, fighting nausea and the gin burning in his throat. She ushered him into a little bedroom. She turned and surveyed him when she'd closed the door, her hands on her hips, and said, 'There, lad, you don't look as though you know what's expected of you.' She laughed – just a little laugh, half motherly, not unkind – and he could feel the floor floating slowly from beneath his feet and the room tilting all around him in its meanness and its shabbiness.

'I don't have any money . . .' he began.

'Your elegant friend in evening dress took care of that,' she said. 'Pity he was in such a hurry. Perhaps you'll bring him here another time?'

Crispin nodded, staring at her as she raised her skirt and stripped off her stockings. He saw that they had holes in them, darned with a little bit of thread in the wrong colour and momentarily, sharply, he saw Helmina's fingers darning, taking up little stitches, catching them together.

He swallowed and stared at his feet. The music from the room below came up through the boards, the voices far away, like sudden gusts of wind. He heard the bed sigh and creak as the woman sat on it. He looked up and she smiled and put out her hand to him and said, 'There now, sweet-'eart. There now. Come and sit awhile beside me and we'll talk first, shall we?'

And when he went down again, alone, closing the door behind him with the hollow sound of the water jug disgorging into a basin following him like a voice down the empty stairwell, he stopped at the landing where the stairs curved to the vestibule below and he thought of Sonwabo, his face so clear, so close. Sonwabo, somewhere in this same town, in this same strange, fetid dusk, with his little carved wooden breasts and his strings of beads adorning his neck. And did some voice lisp at his ear, as it lisped at Crispin's, gloating at his shame?

Crispin stopped and leaned against the wall to steady himself, for a nausea from the gin was rising in him again and the wrung-out weakness in his limbs had not abated. He peered over the banisters into the hall below, holding onto them with both hands, not moving, for he did not trust his legs to carry him further down the stairs. There was a man beneath. He could see the crown of his head, the place where his hair was thinning – a miner, perhaps, for he was thickset, dressed neatly but in workman's clothes. He was talking to the woman who had greeted them and her voice was raised and petulant as if she were summoning another by her tone.

She said, 'This is a private house, sir, and the right to come in is reserved.'

The little man in the flamboyant waistcoat who had been sitting in the parlour appeared suddenly, alert as a ferret. He said, 'I'll take this one, Mrs de Lacey. Go back to the guests.'

The woman stepped aside but she did not retreat to the parlour. The small man turned to the newcomer. His voice was low and brisk but Crispin heard his words. He said, 'I'll have no missionaries here. You may take your tidy little pamphlets and leave the premises before I have you thrown out. I've warned you before.'

''Tis the Lord that should be warning *you*,' said the miner, and his eyes blazed beyond the man and swept about the hall and up the stairs. He stared straight at Crispin, standing in the shadow. 'Lads like him,' he said and flames dancing in the air. 'Led to ruin and damnation. Young women brought under false pretences to this town! Florists and milliners and laundresses indeed! We know their trade – every one of them!'

He remained looking up at Crispin. 'What's your father, son? A miner like meself? A clerk perhaps? I'll wager he's an honest working man as cares for your mother and brings home his pay, every penny. Does he know where you are tonight?'

Crispin did not move and the heat was rising in the pit of his stomach, the gin, in a wave, coursing before it.

The miner turned and left the house, shouldering a way out as if pushing back some pestilence clinging at his heels. He did not close the door. The small man in the waistcoat darted at it and pushed it shut, uttering a curse. 'Keep them *out*, Marie. Out! Out! They'll ruin the business,' and he disappeared into the parlour followed by the woman.

Crispin descended to the hall and sat in the stairwell, his forehead on his knees, leaning his back against the wall. The black-eyed woman came down, freshly rouged. She did not see him. She went into the parlour and he heard her voice. After some time she came back, accompanied by a large man with mutton-chop whiskers and a limp. 'This way, 'andsome,' she said and she ascended the stairs again. Crispin heard the uneven clump, clump of the man's gammy leg on the bare boards. He heard the wheezing breath, the shuffle as he fumbled with his coat at the landing. Clump. Clump. There – they were at her door. It opened and closed. Clump, clump, clump. Then silence.

Sonnie and Charlie came down at last, laughing and pushing each other, boys triumphant after a joust, neckties awry, hair on end.

'Ho there, Crispin! Will you have a drink?'

Crispin shook his head.

'Looks a bit the worse for wear,' said Charlie. 'Take his arm, old man.'

Crispin did not remember the journey home, except that Sonnie and Charlie were singing in snatches and once they lifted him shoulder-high as if he were a hero. He remembered pulling away from them and heaving up the gin in a gutter and hearing a hymn being sung where the lights of the Villa lay splashed on the dusty pavement and saying, 'Who's singing?' and Charlie replying, 'Only old David Evans's Holiness Mission trying to frighten the whores out of their stockings.' And then he'd said, 'Where's Vic? Call Vic.'

'Vic's at the right side of town, old man, eating roast beef and tickling Miss Warburton under the dinner table,' said Sonnie expansively.

And for some reason, inexplicable to him, Crispin shouted, 'Damn Victor to hell! Damn him!'

And Sonnie and Charlie shouted too, 'Damn Victor to hell,' and laughed and whooped to bring the neighbourhood dogs out in a frenzy of barking.

Crispin fell asleep in the cab and tripped on the step when they reached home. He was dragged into the house and thrust through the door of his room. He staggered to the washstand and threw up again and again. Gin and bile, over and over, the bed dancing on the floor as if the devil had given it legs.

As the first pale light of morning rose across the roof-tops he awoke and turned and dozed and slept again and there was Sonwabo, bowed under his beads with his little wooden breasts dangling on a string against the hollow of his chest and racked with weeping. And there was the woman with the black eyes and the white flesh bearing down on both of them. She was sinking her teeth into his skull. He could hear the breaking of the bones. He could feel her sucking out his brains, licking at his cranium. He shouted himself awake.

He peered around, shaken, the sweat cloying at his neck. Victor was sitting on the end of his bed, eating an orange, sucking the juice from the pulp of skin and watching him.

Chapter Twenty

A copy of the Government Proclamation, 'The Disposal of the Property of Lunatics' came in the first post that Walter received at Mbokothwe. The Dean sent it with a letter of instruction and Walter unfolded it and laid it on the table in the little living-room of the mission house and weighted the corners with the teapot and the ink-well. He read it and he laughed and he could hear the sound of his laugh recoiling from the dim rafters of the room.

'A Governor's Pleasure Lunatic is a person,' explained the Dean solemnly, 'for whose detention the Governor is authorised to grant an order. Further, the Court directs and authorises any curator to dispose of the lunatic's property, perform any contract relating to the property of the lunatic entered into by the lunatic before his lunacy . . .'

Walter put the letter down in exasperation. Who was the lunatic indeed? Here he was, standing at the brink of idiocy himself, curator of a Governor's Pleasure Lunatic. And yet, the dementia seemed to belong, more properly, to the authors of the proclamation or to the Dean. It was preposterous! He picked up Brompton's photograph from the bookshelf and looked at it. Aloof, yes. Distant. But no lunacy, no darkness, was evident in that calm, triumphant gaze. He walked about the room. The neatness of the furnishing, the punctiliousness of the papers, filed and dated, the clothes folded in the cupboard, maiden-like in the precision with which they were put away, belied any incipient madness. Or was such order a desperate gesture against the encroaching chaos?

Walter returned to the letter. 'Please dispatch Reverend Brompton's belongings to the above address in Grahamstown,' wrote the Dean. 'It appears that he has no close living relatives. I suggest that small personal effects be donated to the servant that he kept. Church registers and account books and anything pertaining to the mission may be retained at your discretion . . .'

It was a sad task.

Walter was methodical. He emptied the cupboard and drawers, packing their contents as neatly in the trunk as Brompton might have done. It is the small, concealed things that give – so often – the measure of a man. In a box was a set of cuff-links, a stock pin and collar studs. Beautifully engraved and polished. In another, a nail file, a little silver mirror, a jar of hair pomade, a mourning ring and a coin case. A small bottle of cologne. So neat, so precise, so well preserved. A copy of The Land and the Book: Ecclesiae Sancti Pauli Cath: Lond: Eleemos: Hubert C. Brompton, 1877, First Religious Knowledge Prize, was set among his treasures.

Walter found an embossed letter-book. It was half filled with copies of correspondence, dating three years back. My dear Clarence. My dear Pole-Carew. Dear Mr Palmer. My Lord: a stream of correspondence to the Bishop, enough to occupy an evening of reading.

Walter took the book to the table and turned the pages by the light of a candle. There were columns of figures, percentages, every permutation of the statistician. Mission and offertory returns were recorded. There were no intimate letters, none that seemed to be written to members of his family. No communication with a mother or a sister or a friend. But there were letters to colleagues, factual and brisk:

'My dear Roberts . . .'

'My dear Mr Tilbury . . .'

'Dear Mr Daunsey – At your suggestion, I have planted a field of maize. Alas, the locusts came.'

'There is rust . . .'

'There is black-spot . . .'

'There is hail . . .'

'My horse had glanders and I had to shoot it. It is a pity for it was a good horse. I have bought another from a native headman nearby but it has proved to have an uncertain temper. My servant, Pusey, says it is bewitched . . .'

'There were only three at Matins this morning. Perhaps things will improve. I believe there is some influence at work in these parts with which I must acquaint myself . . .'

The dates between writing became longer. May, then October, then March.

'Dear Henderson, I have had no reply to my letter which I believe I sent in September last. I am anxious to hear from you'.

'My dear Bates, did you receive my letter? It is two years now since I wrote and I am concerned that my correspondence might have gone astray . . .'

'Dear Sir, I am posted at a very isolated station in Kaffraria and am anxious to have communication with anyone engaged in the mission work of the Society for the Propagation of the Gospel. I seem to have lost contact with old colleagues . . .'

These little messages going out across the world, like a lantern's beam, glimmering fainter and fainter in the gathering dark.

The pages became empty, letters trailed away, half finished. Silence in those tissue-leaves. Walter laid the book in the bottom of the trunk and took the pictures from the walls and stacked them on the table: the Queen with her garland of roses, the etching of Keble, the London Street complete with barrel-organ.

Walter found Brompton's Bible in the bedside pedestal. It was inscribed:

Presented to Hubert Carey Brompton
on the occasion of his ordination
to the Office and Work of a Priest
in the Church of God in the Cathedral Church
of St George, Grahamstown, on June 5th 1890,
by Allan B, Bishop of Grahamstown

Nine years to destroy so much hope, so much promise. So short a time, indeed, to eliminate a dream. The Governor's Pleasure Lunatic was now confined to a box, roped and ready for transportation to the nearest station.

He folded Brompton's shirts and his trousers and he wiped

298

his boots. He packed them with the pictures in between, the Queen covered over with silk underwear, the dandy's little box of cuff-links and adornments at her chin. The jar of pomade, the razor, the container of salve he gave to Pusey who parted his hair down the centre of his crown and came in at meal times to lay the table, smelling of brilliantine and bear grease.

Walter had nothing of his own to set on the empty shelves except his books. He had purchased nothing in the time that he had been at St Matthias. No picture, no memento adorned the walls. There was only his journal and a letter-book, as yet unused, that he had bought at Stutterheim on his way to the mission.

Perhaps, some years from now, some young curate, fresh from St Augustine's or from Oxford, would come and pack away the trunk marked Walter James Brownley, according to the Proclamation of 1899 of the Cape Colony Government and stand – curious – with his letters to Miranda and to Daisy in his hand, explore his journal and feel foreboding at his back to read sane, prosaic words, belying the creeping malaise, the insidious madness seeping in. 'I am sitting at Brompton's table and the fire is no warmer than when I visited here all those months ago. The tea is better though. I bought a good supply from Nettletons before I came away from St Matthias. I have a tea-cosy made for me by Helmina Smythe. It is a rather doleful object, but it keeps the pot warm enough. Pusey is here. He materialised from the bush when he heard the cart and took up residence as if he'd never been away. I was ready to dispatch him without further ado. But there is something about him. Something so eternally tragi-comic in his face, so dependent in his demeanour – though I know, if my predecessor is to be believed, that he is a veritable sorcerer – I can't dismiss him. Besides, no sooner had I taken the stuff down from the cart than he had extracted the tea and made a pot and presented it to me ceremoniously, rigged up in his frock-coat and buttons. How could I protest? No doubt he will be the cause of my going mad, but I intend to challenge myself and him. Under the circumstances, there is nothing else I can do . . .'

There is nothing else I can do . . .

Nothing, indeed, but to work titanically in the months that followed. He rose at four and he slept near midnight. He ploughed and sowed out in the sun and in the cold wind of that first winter. He built the fallen sections of the church and he repaired the windows and he restored the broken boards of the floor. The people came. One or two. Four or five. A woman. A man. A family destitute from the rinderpest. Another, dispossessed of land. The crop failed. He sowed again. Hail destroyed the vegetable patch. He sent for seeds and planted out the seedlings, covering them with straw and grass to protect them from the wind.

Boggis was there, bad-tempered at the sourness of the pasture. He took up a mule-like stance by the fence and disdained the attentions of any passersby, but he remained Walter's confidant, the companion on rides to distant homesteads, dependable and slow.

From Pusey – at last – Walter learned to speak Xhosa. Day in, day out, he spoke it until he all but forgot that it was not his mother tongue. He did not open his own beloved books in the evening but goaded himself to hours of studying grammar and setting himself exercises. He wrote to Benedict and had him send copies of every issue of *Imvo Zabantsundu* and *Izwi Labantu* that he could procure. It was from the perusal of these newspapers and the columns – oh, how many hours to decipher the complications of idiom, phrase and construction – that he learned most about the hostilities mounting in the Transvaal, Jabavu's pro-Boer stance and Soga and Rubusana's hopes that the Imperial Forces would bring matters to a swift end, extending the voting rights of the Colony's Africans to their brothers in the Republics. For Walter, the issues became not so much a matter of British citizens' grievances and Boer suspicions in the Transvaal, of gold or government, as they were in the colonial press, but a matter of whether the Cape African Franchise would be left intact and how a British victory would affect such rights. He became an avid follower of the editorials in both papers and he wished that Benedict was there, that he might have discussions with him. He longed for his little press – oh, how he wished for it – so that

300

he, too, might write and send his offerings out. It was with pleasure – and envy – that he received a bundle of pamphlets and the St Matthias Echo from Benedict. He had started a small, vigorous tradition of his own, contributing regularly to *Izwi Labantu*, disseminating information among the educated, like himself. Walter smiled to think how the old Albion might wheeze at its own exertions. Benedict gave opinion on the vote, the place of the black man in the impending war, and Walter wrote back, applauding him.

August came and hostilities seemed inevitable. Buller was on his way to Natal, Johannesburg was being evacuated, the mine overlords long gone to the Cape. A steady stream of townspeople left daily in wagons and trains. He read, with fascination, an account in *Imvo* of how J.S. Marwick, the Government Superintendent of Natives, had led a column of Zulu mine workers on foot from Johannesburg to the Natal border, ensuring their safe return through Boer lines. Scores joined the march. Bandits and desperadoes, the displaced and desolate. Some were co-opted along the way by troops, others died, others marched south, singing, Marwick at their head.

Where was Crispin? Where were Tom and Reuben and Sonwabo? He read that some workers had been forced by the Boers to stay on the mines, unable to escape, keeping production to a maximum to fill state coffers and help the war effort. Martial law was enforced. Repression was brutal, wages twenty shillings less than in the preceding months. And where was Victor? This was something he did not allow himself to think of often. Perhaps he was in Cape Town ensuring that his fledgling empire came to the notice of the great and influential. Perhaps he had joined the Imperial Light Horse and was on his way to the front. Perhaps he was in Grahamstown. With Frances.

In his little house, like a fishing boat beached on a reef, Grahamstown seemed so distant to Walter, a rumour far away from the stillness of those plains. No sound of guns came on the wind. No troops passed by. There was no watch in the night, no hidden fires, no guard to challenge stealthy footfalls in the dusk.

The post was erratic for the mail trains had stopped running. The feast of papers and pamphlets disappeared. The letters from Father Charles and Benedict became a rarity. Walter was marooned on his abandoned hillside. Supplies were scarce. He felt the want and daily there were women and children at his door, thin and secretive as shadows, waiting in patience for medicine, for a bowl of meal, an infusion of tea made from the dregs in the pot. Waiting, always waiting. He turned none of them away, went hungry himself, hoarded forage like a miser so that Boggis might not sicken. He worked and worked and worked. And rarely prayed.

He had not realised it. He stood one twilight at evensong, with the wind blowing red grit against the walls, pounding them, an assault of the elements, and he knew, standing there in his cassock with his hands peaked before him and a small congregation at his back, Pusey vigorous with the incense and making the chain clank against the receptacle, that he had been barging at God, suffused with anger and exhaustion. The realisation made him angrier, and that most unacceptable emotion – cynicism – lurked in his heart. He stood in desolation at the altar-rail with his back to the shabby pews, more desolate than he had been the night he'd watched outside the Farboroughs' house and stared at the empty window of Frances's room.

After dinner he took his empty correspondence book and he wrote to Frances, but when he had finished the letter, he failed to tear it out and fold and stamp and send it. It lay unread against the copy at its back, withering for want of a recipient: 'This is a place where a green lion might live. I know he is here. He has a lair in the fold of hills behind the church. I sometimes think I hear him roaring in aloneness in the night. I know a lion does not roar. It grunts mightily, dredging up its heart . . .'

Grahamstown was a millennium away. Continents across an ocean could not be further. There she would be busy with her wedding plans, gathering her trousseau and visiting young ladies in the town, playing the piano in the evenings to Mrs Drake. No Corelli for her, oh no. It would be 'The Village Blacksmith' or love poems in melody, full of sentiment. She would write letters in the early afternoons to Victor, on a bench perhaps, in some fragrant, walled garden – he had seen them at the backs of white-faced houses. She'd be a frequent visitor to the haberdasher's and the milliner's. Frances choosing crockery and linen and deciding on the edging for her bed-sheets! He put his pen away. He closed the book. He placed it on the bottom shelf to gather dust and cobwebs. Damn Frances. Damn God.

He turned out the post-sack each month, searching, despite himself. Pusey always watched him, impervious to his impatience.

Frances cursed her trousseau, labouring at it every day under the fond eye of Mrs Drake, stitching with needle-roughened fingers. She scorned a thimble and was careless with the cloth. She had always hated sewing. The novelty of Grahamstown, being taken about to tea, turned like a doll to be admired or criticised by the town's matrons, the shops full of things she had never seen before, had palled. The walks to the High Street, glancing at the little houses along the way and imagining which she would like to own, had become an empty game. Their doors stood too close together, their shutters blocked out the air. They peered from behind their fences, like so many Helmina Smythes, conferring together. There were no blazing aloe fences, no strange spur of the Kaboosie rising in the distance.

St Matthias was receding. She wished it away in desultory activity, suppressing any intrusive thoughts of her meeting with Walter Brownley in the vestry. He had sent her from him and, in defending Benedict, her angry announcement had bound her to Victor unconditionally, made her prisoner in his mother's house. She had made the choice herself. There was nothing she could do to change it.

Victor's mother was full of small surprises – here a little treasure of her own, given to adorn a new home, there a sheaf of recipes to be studied and absorbed: the dishes Victor most enjoyed. Even the engagement ring had been chosen by her – on instructions from Victor – selected from her own plush-lined box. It was a square-cut topaz with a small diamond on each side. An old, old ring, belonging once to Victor's grandmother Drake, a relic of some distant union. It hung about Frances's finger, placed there without ceremony as if it had legitimised her sin.

She had hoped vainly, when she came to Victor's mother's house, that there would be something familiar that might obliterate the knowledge of the past few months and reinstate the Victor of her childhood. His cricket togs, his rugby cap. Even an old toy with which she might identify. They were there, in almost every room. But their placings and the things among which they lay, were strange. There was nothing of happy recognition in her discovery of them. They were insignificant against the weight of his father's presence. It pervaded the house. Frances looked often at the ornamental ribbons, the dress sword, the portrait – the aloof, effete profile of Victor's father, a man from a long-gone age. The mourning of the drapery, the heavy swags of the curtains, the solemn texts and twilight landscapes hung on chains from the picture rails among the regimental mementoes, made it a shrine to his memory. No wonder Victor had feared the presence of his father in the dark of the night, looming greatly among these relics of war.

She noticed that there were no tokens to commemorate her own kindly uncle but for a small photograph on the writing bureau. And though Victor's mother might call herself Alice Farborough, and though she might have been her uncle's wife for longer than that of Claude Drake, she had styled herself the widow of the hero of Ulundi.

All of this, Frances knew, would belong to Victor and herself in time. This, and the abundant legacy her uncle had bequeathed. The furniture, the books and the arsenal in the locked gun cupboard, would be transported to Johannesburg, along with Victor's mother. Her expectations were clear. 'You are so young, Frances,' she had said. 'I could be such a help to you in domestic matters. It takes years of management to understand the workings of a house, the treatment of servants, the correct attitude to the garden boys. You surely won't be speaking to them in that heathen tongue of theirs? It will encourage familiarity. Don't use it, dear,' – gently chiding, for she had heard Frances in the kitchen with the cook – 'it quite upsets the order of things.'

Woodenly, Frances stopped speaking to the housemaid, distanced herself and kept away from the scullery. She retreated to the music-room instead and spent time sorting the unused sheaves, finding little to interest her.

Following her one morning, Victor's mother brought her needlework and settled herself in the window-seat and said, 'Do play for me, Frances. I hardly ever hear a note. Victor's father had a superb voice and he accompanied himself. We had such grand times together.'

Frances searched for something she might know and stumbled through a few unfamiliar pieces and then she laid the music aside and played from heart. She remembered more than she had anticipated.

'Don't stop,' said Victor's mother when she came to the end of her repertoire.

Frances hesitated at the keys. A minor chord, the first four or five phrases of the Corelli. She drew back and rested her hands in her lap. Mbokothwe. So far away. What was he doing? Riding somewhere on Boggis? Busy with his beloved books, smoking his pipe?

'What is it, Frances?'

Frances fought the constriction in her throat, 'Nothing, Aunt Alice. I was just remembering the horse at home. Isn't that silly? I don't know why I thought of him. He was such a donkey!' And she was saved by the housemaid coming to the door and announcing callers – so many callers, so many indeed, come to see the little country cousin Victor Drake had decided to marry – and she hurried from the room.

She poured the tea and passed the plates and when the precentor's wife complimented her fleetingly on the locket that she wore, she said – and her voice seemed to come from a distant place – 'It belonged once to a Mrs Brodowski. She had a monocle that magnified her eye enormously and she wrote metaphysical poetry and rode in a dogcart decorated with plumes.' The silence that followed was a triumph. Plotz would have laughed out loud to have seen their faces.

She looked at all of them ranged in front of her in their stiff discomfort and she brazened out the disapproval of Aunt Alice's glance, almost laughing with a small, bitter twist to

305

her mouth. She had bound herself to this! In one moment of anger and impulsiveness, in defending Benedict, she had announced her fall and assured her future among people such as these. Of what use had it been? Dorcas had been sent away to Fort Beaufort with her mother, into domestic service with some connection of the family's. Kobus had been reinstated at the mission. His first wife had been brought down, a neophyte for the St Agnes Guild, redirecting her natural ire into uncompromising piety while their cattle grew fat on the hills. Benedict lodged with Mzantsi and her mother had written that he 'progresses very nicely. There is a new quiet about him which encourages me to think that he may consider Holy Orders after all.' Benedict to the church, Frances to the marriage-bed, harnessed to the round of calls, the small talk of the parlour and tea with Aunt Alice and her acquaintance. Oh, for Nolovini and the stretch of grass leading up to it! Oh, for the little school and the children drooping over their slates and the ring of Boggis's bridle as he came over the lip of the hill!

Aunt Alice said nothing after the incident at the tea-table. Frances waited to be summoned but her aunt had remained silent. No doubt she had been warned by her mother not to test her temper! A girl who could sin so brazenly had to be handled with circumspection. Nothing must jeopardise the impending wedding. She sent Frances out to the post instead, with a parcel and a bundle of letters to mail.

Frances marched down the road towards the High Street. She ran her umbrella along a paling, making it ring and breaking the tip off the shaft. She poked it belligerently at the ground, twisting it round, her overcoat flapping about her skirts. She reached the post-box and looked at the envelopes, pushing each separately into the slot. One addressed to her parents, one to Victor, an assortment from Aunt Alice to relatives and friends.

Her own letter to Victor was not long. As the months passed, they had become shorter, almost peremptory in their description of events and yet, in tone, as familiar as if she had been writing to Crispin. But the war was imminent and arrangements had been postponed and Victor was writing of enlisting in a corps being recruited on the Rand, rather than come home and marry her. He was secure, now she was in his mother's house. His letters were filled with instructions and complacence.

She turned away and stood on a corner, looking along the road. It was the dinner hour and the pavements were empty but for housemaids gathered on corners and a group of women burdened with kindling and wood, trudging down the street. Frances could hear the beginnings of their song, knowing the words herself, knowing them in her head, high and plaintive, and the stands of wattles on the slopes near St Matthias clear before her eyes.

She followed them a little way, listening unobtrusively, and then she wandered down Bathurst Street, past the shop fronts that seemed to slide, side by side, towards the dip, and rise again with the long undulation of the hill. She idled at a pawnbroker and second-hand dealer's window, pressed her nose against the glass. There, among the pots and boxes of books and hastily exchanged trinkets, was something so suddenly familiar, that she rubbed her finger against the glass where her breath had misted it and stared. She pushed open the door of the shop and went inside. A small bell tinkled. The man behind the counter, recumbent among the pages of his newspaper, looked over at her.

She pointed to the window. 'May I see the musical-box?' she said.

He nodded and she bent to it and touched the lid. She could see it in Crispin's hands as he had worked on it. She could see him with his head inclined and his tongue edging along his lip in concentration. She picked up the box and set it on a chair. She did not open it. She crouched before it, looking at it. Here was a place where Crispin must have fashioned a little sliver of wood to staunch a split in the inlay; there, the corner worn and the veneer – irreparable – chipped away where he had smoothed it with the tender buffing of a fine file.

The man said, 'Came from Fort England where the mad people are kept.' She glanced up at him. 'It's a good piece.' Frances saw him appraising her, weighing up what he might ask her to pay.

She crouched down and she opened the lid. She waited. She heard the faint whirr of the mechanism. She smiled, knowing Crispin had worked many hours at school with the master, reconstructing it. The song was faint but true, only here and there a small disharmony. 'Abide with me, fast falls the eventide, the darkness deepens, Lord with me abide, when other helpers fail and comforts flee, Help of the Helpless, Oh abide with me . . .'

The man was watching her. 'There is someone else interested in that box,' he said. 'If you want it you had better take it now. I was expecting a gentleman to come back for it.'

She was silent and he continued, 'An orderly from the hospital brought it down. Asked a tidy price for it . . .'

'I don't have any money,' said Frances. 'May I take it and pay when I have . . .'

'I don't extend credit.'

Frances held the box as if shielding it from his indifference. It was Brompton's box. It was Crispin's.

It was Walter Brownley's box.

He had stood by it in the vestry and she had heard him say to Victor in a voice to still the sea, 'Do not make light of someone else's pain.'

She hesitated and then she pulled off her ring, the blood hot at her ears with outrage for what she did, and she said, 'Will you hold this ring in place of the box until I have the money to pay for it? Fair exchange. For ten days? A week? After that you can sell it if I haven't paid.'

The pawnbroker looked at the ring and he glanced at the hand from which she had drawn it and he brought the ring to the door of the shop and examined it in the light. Frances said peremptorily, 'I'll have a receipt, please,' and she waited while he wrote it in his little book and made her a copy and he was silent as she took the musical-box and settled the handle of her umbrella over her arm and walked out onto the pavement.

It was only as she started up the street that Frances realised what she had done. But she did not hesitate, she walked briskly back to the house with the musical-box tucked under her arm. She went inside and up to her room, closing the door firmly so no intruder might tap at it inquisitively and she laid the box on the table, opened it and listened to the soft notes, a little yearning voice in the quiet of that room. Trancelike she listened, until the light faded outside the window and then she closed the lid and lifted the box into her lap, holding it against her, smoothing her fingers across the contours of the wood.

Chapter Twenty-One

Johannesburg was emptying. Already Sonnie Hook and Charlie Fraser had gone back to the Cape, en route to Natal. There was talk of forming a regiment recruited from those who had left Johannesburg. Influential men – Reformers – like Aubrey Woolls-Sampson, Karri Davies and Charles Mullins had been planning for weeks. Volunteers from the Cape were already bound for Durban to swell their numbers and Victor was impatient to be away to join them.

According to a letter from Charlie Fraser, there were already half a dozen of their old school friends in the corps, Grahamstown boys all, and anxious to get to the front. But Victor was caught. Elevated to the sudden heights of Mr Warburton's desk, deputising in order that his senior might accompany his family to the safety of Cape Town, Victor could not leave for the Colony until instructed.

It was the eve of Mr Warburton's departure for the Cape when Victor was called to quell a disturbance at the mine where Tom and Reuben and Sonwabo worked. For Victor it was a crucial coincidence of timing.

The mine manager, anxious enough about the turmoil in Johannesburg, had arrived himself at the Native Affairs Department and asked for Mr Warburton. He had a strike on his hands. At such a time, when most reasonable people were packing their bags and heading south! He wanted the Right Man to deal with it. Damned Colony natives! Always the most trouble! Always the most independent! Always intractable!

Mr Warburton, he was told, was at luncheon at his Club with a number of important officials and colleagues from his own department. Final strategies had to be planned before the exodus from the Transvaal could be achieved. A note was sent. 'Dear Mr Warburton, Excuse me for appealing to you at a time like this but I have an ugly situation brewing at the mine. There is a group of Cape boys with a trumped-up case against a ganger whom they assaulted severely this morning.

They refuse to go back to work until their complaints are heard . . .'

Victor, sitting at the far end of the table, saw his chief glance at the note brought by the Club Secretary and rub his finger across his brush moustache. Then Mr Warburton looked up and beckoned to him, excusing himself and rising from the table. Victor followed him across the dining-room. Mr Warburton handed him the note without explanation and Victor read it.

Victor looked at him enquiringly and Mr Warburton said, 'I'm relying on you to deal with this disturbance swiftly. Call in the police if necessary. I'll await results with interest. Here is an opportunity to triumph,' and he took a slip from his notebook and wrote, 'I am instructing Drake to deal with the matter – a competent speaker of the native tongue, my brightest rising lieutenant.' He dispatched the note with the Secretary and Victor was sent, without his lunch, back to headquarters.

The import of what Albert Warburton had said was not lost on Victor. He went from the office, pulling his tie straight, setting his chin and calling for Crispin. He needed an interpreter that he could trust, should his Xhosa falter.

They drove to the mine and called at the manager's office. Victor was ushered in, introduced to Oosthuizen, the compound supervisor, and various minor officials and was offered a chair, centre-stage. Crispin stood quietly to the side, watching.

The manager outlined the case. 'We have a shift of Colony boys sitting in the compound yard. They won't move until we have acceded to their demands. We'd like you to get them back to work.'

'What are their demands?'

'Firstly, that the ganger on their shift is dismissed for beating up of the boys. Secondly, that the loafer's tickets that this man has given should be reviewed. Thirdly, that the native that was causing all the trouble should be given meat rations again.'

'Why was the boy beaten?' asked Victor.

'Insolent sod,' Oosthuizen, the compound supervisor, interjected. 'He was a surface worker but he gave the *induna* no end of trouble with his insubordination so I had him sent underground. It seems he didn't like it much in the shafts,' and he exchanged a smirk with his staff. 'What did he expect if he was coming to a mine, I ask myself! At any rate, he complained about feeling ill all the time. Probably been drinking. The drinkers are always malingering. So the ganger became impatient and showed him a fist. And quite right too.'

'However,' the mine manager resumed, 'not content with a bit of discipline, the team leader, encouraged by the trouble-maker's brothers, hit the ganger and all but broke his neck.'

'And the issue of the meat ration?'

'The *induna* is in charge of stamping meal tickets,' the compound supervisor said. 'In order to discipline the boy, he stopped his meat ration but, when that didn't work, I decided to send him underground. If we don't keep a tight rein on discipline, we'd be sunk in a week.'

'And the loafer's tickets?'

'Loots, the ganger, is strict on loafing. If the boys slacken and don't drill the required depth, there's a loafer's ticket waiting for them. It moves them along, I can assure you. We've had boys here three months in excess of their contracts because of loafer's tickets. They're an example to others of how *not* to work at a mine!' And the officials smiled among themselves: some small, exclusive exchange from which the uninitiated were excluded.

'Does this Loots give them regularly?' asked Victor.

'He's strict,' said Oosthuizen non-committally.

'Stricter than most,' the mine manager conceded. 'In fairness, I have had complaints before.'

'May I speak to Mr Loots?' Victor said. 'I would like to hear his version of the story.'

'It's the natives who are your concern,' the compound supervisor said hastily, glancing at the manager.

'I think it would be inadvisable to listen to one version,' Victor was firm. 'Only a word.'

'Send someone for Mr Loots,' the manager said. 'I hope he is well enough to speak to Mr Drake.'

Oosthuizen, the compound supervisor, was eager to fetch him himself. From the window, Crispin saw him speaking emphatically to the ganger as they returned across the yard towards the manager's office.

Loots was a big man, his jaw stained purple where the fist of the team leader had caught him. He eased himself through the door in his bulk and belligerence and stood, waiting to be questioned, his glance sliding to the compound supervisor's every now and then, as if for direction.

'Mr Loots,' Victor said, 'I am the Cape Colony Representative of the Native Affairs Department. I believe you have had some trouble with Colony boys on your shift.'

'Bastards, all of them,' Loots said, and his words thick where his tongue had been split against his teeth. 'I've been a ganger for ten years. I know my job. My boys listen to me. If they don't, they get the fist.'

'Is that so?' Victor said. 'Assault is common practice with you?' A pause. 'However, that aside, why did you hit this particular man?' Victor turned to the compound supervisor, 'What is his name, sir?'

'Whose name?'

'The worker who has been assaulted.'

'Sonny-Boy.'

'Who?'

'He is known here as Sonny-Boy. I think his name is Pumani.'

'Pumani?' Victor repeated and he caught Crispin's eye a moment. He half laughed, a small snort of derision. 'Sonny-Boy, is it?' And he all but dangled the name in the air before him.

The condescension was not lost on Oosthuizen the supervisor, and he glowered at Victor but Victor ignored him and continued, 'Why did you hit him, Mr Loots?'

'He was lazy.'

'Lazy?'

'He was sent underground for causing trouble and he was always complaining about being sick, so I gave him something to be sick about. I won't have loafers on my shift. Any boy that's ever worked with me knows that. This boy comes to me and he says he has had enough – and in English, mind, giving himself airs. Get a kaffir who's lived near a mission and you have trouble at once! He says he's had enough. He complains about loafer's tickets – I gave him three in a row, lazy bastard – and about meat rations. I expect he thinks he's underground for a picnic, and so I thought I would teach him a lesson. I didn't know his brothers were on the shift too and they started to shout and then the team leader – also Cape, and a native whose hide I've been after for a long time – hits me. There I am, without defence, with a lot of mad kaffirs in the shaft and lucky to get away with my life.'

'Perhaps he was speaking the truth about being sick,' Victor said. 'Why should you disbelieve him?'

'These niggers are always saying they are sick. You should go down the mine yourself,' and he cast his eye over Victor's immaculate suit, 'and smell the stink of all their sickness.'

'This man had had no meat. No wonder he was weak.'

'That's his problem with his *induna*. Not mine. He was a surface shift boy.'

'Why was he sent down the mine?'

'To discipline him.'

'And you were asked to make sure it happened?'

'What happened?'

'That he was disciplined.'

The man looked confused then, trapped. He said, 'I don't know what you mean.'

'You know quite well,' Victor said. 'Answer the question.'

'I know who the trouble-makers are.'

'Answer the question.'

'Yes.'

'By whom?'

'Mr Oosthuizen, the compound supervisor, told me to take no insolence,' he mumbled. Victor turned and regarded the supervisor a moment, a fleeting glance, the slightest lift of his brow.

'Thank you, Mr Loots,' Victor said distantly. 'You may go.'

Loots went with an air of self-righteousness and grievance, nursing his bulk and some injury greater than the assault to his person. Crispin watched him with apprehension but Victor paid no attention at all. He took up his hat and, rising, said, 'Well, let us speak to the men in the compound.'

'The case seems clear-cut to me,' the compound supervisor, Oosthuizen, blurted out, standing between Victor and the doorway. 'I'd dismiss the trouble-makers, order the rest back to work and fine them heavily if they disobey. It's the only language they understand.'

Victor made no comment, nor even exchanged a glance with Crispin. He walked with the manager, affable and relaxed. Crispin could see that he was enjoying himself.

They followed the manager to the open place between the barracks of the compound where the miners were gathered in the yard, shoulder to shoulder, side by side. Victor stood a moment and regarded them. Then he greeted them cordially, his pronunciation almost perfect, gaining the attention of the watchers at once and leading his entourage – with the air of a visiting headman – to take his place on the office steps with the manager of the mine beside him and Oosthuizen, the compound supervisor, calling for order.

Crispin stood unobtrusively behind Victor, his hat in his hand, and looked among the throng for Tom and Reuben. He searched a long time. And as he looked, a man stepped forward from the crowd and identified himself as Mayekiso, the team leader of the shift. He spoke, he said, on behalf of all of them, and on behalf of his brother Pumani who was even now in the hands of the doctors who were stitching his face.

'One of the three sons of Pumani of Qoboqobo?' Victor interjected, naming the district of St Matthias. And the miners exchanged glances, wondering that this man should know the place even of the newest and the humblest recruits and the team leader said, gravely, 'It is he.'

'Continue.' Victor listened as the team leader spoke, his head half cocked, as though he were reaching for far-off truths. Crispin interpreted in an undertone. Victor, despite his fluent replies, declaiming in Xhosa, sweeping broadly with his arm and throwing his voice, was often unable to capture Mayekiso's idiom and nuance as accurately as Crispin and he listened more to Crispin's words than to the team

315

leader, although he gave no indication that his attention was divided between them.

The complaint, the team leader said, was about the white ganger with whom they worked. They would not go back underground unless he was dismissed. He was a cruel man. He had said he would stop their meal tickets because they had objected to his treatment of Sonwabo. It was unjust. Besides, he gave loafer's tickets almost every week. There were men whose time had long expired but who could not fulfil the number of shifts for which they were contracted because this man was so free with loafer's tickets. A loafer's ticket simply cancelled the shift just completed if the hole that a worker was required to drill for the dynamite was not deep enough.

'How can a man drill a hole,' the team leader said, and indicating the size with his fist and his forearm, 'if the first few hours of the shift are spent in lashing – clearing the rubble from the day before – and the labour not counted for the wage?'

These were the things that a ganger could do to enslave his team because he was a god when he was under the ground. He could take your work. He could take your food. He was like a thief that a man does not see but feels in the heart, making the blood grieve.

Victor said, 'Why was I not called before, if this man is the cause of your complaint?'

The team leader replied. 'We did not complain,' and his voice was brisk, 'because, although we have been told we may go to the inspectors at the Native Affairs Department, we cannot leave this place without a permit. It is the *induna* who does not like this thing called a permit. He is jealous with it. He keeps it hidden from us all. So we cannot speak.'

And there were murmurs from the men and the *induna*, standing off with the police at the edges of the gathering, seemed to dismiss the words as a man flicks grains of snuff from his sleeve.

'But today you have complained,' Victor said. 'What is it that has awakened your anger?'

'It is the small flea on the dog that will send it to madness at last,' the team leader said, and there was a sigh of agreement among the men. 'The small flea, burrowing to the heart of the dog.'

'And what was the flea upon the dog?'

'This man Pumani was one that did surface work,' the team leader said. 'He was chosen for it. He was glad to do it. But there was a disagreement with the *induna* and the *induna* stopped his meat tickets. He had him sent underground.'

'What was the disagreement?'

There was a silence and there was a hush and the mine police hovering at the edge of the gathering had their truncheons alert in their hands because the miners knew that to speak now of the *bakhontshana* would bring another storm, like the voices of sorcerers gathering in the night, swift and vengeful.

'Leave this one,' Crispin said quietly at Victor's shoulder.

'Why? We must have the truth.'

'You will have it. But don't talk of it here.'

'So,' Victor said and a touch of irritation in his voice, almost ready to take issue, 'there was a disagreement between the *induna* and Pumani?'

'That is so.'

'But it is not their disagreement about which we are arguing here?'

There was a silence and the workers shifted and the compound supervisor took out his handkerchief and wiped his face and settled his hat more carefully on his head. 'Not here,' said the team leader.

'If you have brought no complaint about the *induna*, then I shall speak about the ganger.'

And the men subsided as though a danger had passed and settled and watched while Oosthuizen, the compound supervisor, swatted at flies with an expression on his face that showed he was pretending to be elsewhere but was not, for the sweat was standing at his neck and creeping through his shirt.

The team leader said, 'Sonwabo Pumani was sent underground when it was not his task to be there. He is not a man who works in the shafts.'

'The *induna* sent him underground to punish him?'

'Yes. It is the *induna* that spoke to the supervisor of this

317

compound. It is the supervisor, Oosthuizen, that told the ganger to take Pumani on his shift.'

'The authority of the *induna* is a strong and important matter,' Victor said cautiously. 'The *induna* is there to keep order in the compound as does the headman of a district. He expects to be obeyed.'

'If a headman is unjust, the anger of the people will follow him. The anger of the shades will brood at his back.' The team leader cast a glance at the police standing round the *induna*, gathered in their uniforms, ranked against their men. He paused and the threat seemed implicit in his stance. Then he turned back to Victor and he said, 'There are some men who can work in the stomach of the earth and there are some who cannot. Sometimes, when a man is a child, a thing comes to his heart or his spirit that he fears. This man, Pumani, feared to be closed in the dark. It was like a madness with him.'

Crispin watched Victor when these words were said, standing upright as a soldier and remembered Sonwabo screaming, the whites of his eyes showing and the spit bouncing from his lips as he was carried to the vestry and Victor saying, half in laughter, half in exasperation, 'I'll lock you in the cupboard, you insolent little beggar!' So long ago at St Matthias. So long, long ago.

'He was sick with it,' the team leader said. 'The sweat was standing on his skin like dew on the grass before the sun has risen. At the end of almost every day that he worked, Pumani was given a loafer's ticket. And this is because he is kept longer lashing stones than any other man so his strength is gone when he comes to drill at the rock-face. And his blood is finished because he has had no meat.'

'So many days this happened,' the team leader said, and a hush in the compound courtyard and far away a mule braying to intrude its noise, 'that he was finished and it is then that his brothers came to me and said, "This is Enough." And Sonwabo Pumani himself said, for all to hear him, "This is Enough. I will die like a dog and I will be glad to have rest. Have they not killed me already with their words and with their deeds? I am sick now. Soon I will die and be glad."' The team leader paused. 'The white man took Pumani by the collar and he hit his face against the rock. He said, "If this boy is sick, I can always make him sicker." He beat his head again and again against the rock, not hard enough to hurt the bones but hard enough to make the skin cry out and weep blood for its pain. The ganger says then, "I will send you to the *induna* and you will go in the stocks and he will decide when to release you," and Pumani says, "And then I will surely die."' The team leader looked round at the men gathered about him and he said, 'And he will die indeed.'

He will die.

He will die.

He will die.

Like a lament, the words were taken up by the men gathered in the courtyard, hovered in the mouths of the watchers.

Victor was silent, as if listening to the closing lines of a litany. He glanced at the *induna*, standing there among the policemen with their truncheons and their polished buttons, and he turned his eyes to the compound supervisor. Victor waited for the silence to grow and then he said, 'And so you hit the ganger? You punished him for what he had done to your brother?'

'I hit him,' the team leader said and there was a touch of scorn in his voice as if he had demeaned his fists. 'It was clear that he would kill Pumani for no reason, when he had said simply that he was sick and that he was hungry, and when there is a snake swallowing a chick, do you let it do so while the bird is still crying out in the snake's mouth for mercy? So I hit him,' and the team leader made a sound – like that of striking a dried-out gourd with a stone – and said, 'I took him up to the surface. He is not very much hurt. But Pumani – he is in the hospital and though he is alive in his arms and his legs, he is not alive in his spirit.'

'What a lot of bosh!' the compound supervisor interjected. 'I should have charged them all with assault!'

Victor said smoothly, his voice rising above that of the supervisor's, 'We will confer, the managers and I. We will speak of this matter. I have heard the words of the man Loots and I have heard the words that you have said and I

319

will weigh them in my hands. It is good that I have been called, for a man may not strike another without justification.'

Victor stood a moment in silence, his eye sweeping them all and then he turned briskly and walked to the manager's office, followed by the senior mine officials and Crispin. The door was closed behind them and he laid his hat on the table and said, careful with his words, 'Victimisation gives a bad name to the mines. It is a very delicate matter. I am satisfied in my mind that Loots is blameworthy and I would dismiss him if I were you. If you can't agree to that, I would have him disciplined and transferred to another mine.'

'Steady on, Drake,' the manager said. 'It's not such a simple matter.'

Chairs were drawn up, tea was brought. The workers, sitting in the yard, sang songs, the chant low and continuous outside the fastened windows. The deliberations took two hours. Victor proposed a hearing for Sonwabo, once he should be well enough to speak. He demanded a review of the loafer's tickets issued by Loots and a reinstatement of meat rations. He suggested an official apology from Loots or the management on his behalf. The compound supervisor's face was flushed, each word of Victor's eliciting a muttered 'bosh' under his breath.

'Mr Drake,' the mine manager interrupted, raising his hands, 'Mr Drake' – and a touch of asperity – 'you are going too far! Such lenience would be deplorable! You are acceding to every whim! We have to maintain discipline on this mine. The status quo. To give the nigger an inch is to commit suicide, no less. Mr Warburton, I know, would consider this extremely rash.'

'I am the representative of the workers from the Cape Colony,' Victor said. 'They are under my protection and I am not leaving here until justice is done. Those were Mr Warburton's instructions and I will honour them.' And so lofty was Victor's voice and so commanding his eye that the manager might well have imagined him in possession of a house on Parktown Ridge among the magnates.

The manager said, as if suddenly aware of some impending need to be conciliatory, 'Of course, justice must be done, but to dismiss a ganger publicly will give the natives all manner of airs. We shall have a strike for every harsh word they hear!'

Victor said, with an edge of disdain, 'Inconsequential demands will be treated as such. Your workers know it. Their own tribal councillors would out-debate all of us on important matters and dismiss what is trivial with the contempt it might deserve.' And he spoke in a way to make the manager adjust his tie and be busy about his cigarette case. 'You will agree' – and none would have disagreed with Victor then and Crispin wished that he could have laughed when he saw the face of the compound supervisor as if his very eyes were breathing fit to burst – 'that the victimisation of workers by gangers must be kept under very strict scrutiny. I would be failing Mr Warburton and my duty to my department if I closed my eyes to such abuses.'

Victor clearly liked the sound of his sermon but he kept a rein on the pomposity that was creeping in and he said, less loftily, engaging each man's eye a moment, 'There have been enough rumours of brutality for us to take any such reports very seriously indeed. As I said, I strongly suggest that Loots be suspended or transferred. It will be an act of faith in your workers and such a gesture will reap more benefits than you can imagine. You are as aware as I am that a mine can rise or fall on its reputation. Once a bad name is earned, it is very difficult to change it. I have boys through my hands daily who refuse to go here or there and it is the very devil of a job to persuade them.'

'Nevertheless, dismissing a white man on demand from a bunch of natives could create a dangerous precedent,' the mine manager said, mustering some resistance.

'Not at all,' Victor replied. 'In this case, the timing couldn't be more fortunate. If we're not all mistaken, we're about to engage in war and I cannot see this mine being open much longer but, when it's over, we want our boys back, with as many friends and relations as they can bring. I really consider that it would be wise to play this little matter with tact and take care not to scare them off. Besides, you cannot deny that their complaints seem reasonable. Clearly Loots had no justification for such harsh treatment or for denying Pumani food.' Victor took a cigarette from his case and glanced round at the others. 'If you agree to my suggestions,' Victor said, pressing his argument home, 'you'll have them back to work and singing within the hour.'

The compound supervisor, Oosthuizen, looked sullen but he said nothing. He glanced every now and then at his senior, waiting. The mine manager said, 'I do believe it is a precedent but I cannot deny that the timing will make it possible to accede this time.'

His concession was grudging. Victor did not allow him to waver, however. 'Reinstatement of meat rations for Pumani,' Victor said, ticking items off on his fingers. 'Loafer's tickets given by this particular man reviewed. Cancelling a percentage of the loafer's tickets will go a long way to reminding the workers which mine has given them a measure of freedom and you will not have lost on production – it's all water under the bridge. Both parties stand to gain.' He paused. 'Transfer of Loots.'

The mine manager stood a moment in silence, weighing up the options. 'We'll try it,' he said. 'But I'll be calling you back to answer for it if we're plunged into insurrection in the future.' He half smiled and shook Victor's hand.

Victor went out, leading the entourage. There was a murmur of expectation, a rumble from the workers.

The manager addressed the crowd, retrieving his authority. He spoke without conviction. 'Meal tickets are yours again.' He hesitated and looked back at Victor. Then he said, his voice rising, 'The loafer's tickets given by Mr Loots will be reviewed and if necessary, cancelled.' Cheers and the sound of laughter. 'Mr Loots will not be working on your shift again.' They rose, jubilant, drowning out the rest of his words. He stepped down and Victor, quietening them, said, 'I am glad to have met the men of my place – the "homeboys" of my Colony. *Salani kakuhle*. Stay well.'

Victor departed like a prince leaving an outpost in which loyal subjects cheered his path. Crispin caught Tom and Reuben's eye, exchanged a greeting, a word of future meeting, and followed Victor to the trap, taking the driver's seat and hastening the horses away from the compound gate.

It had been a triumph. But the self-congratulations were short-lived. Within a fortnight the victory had been overturned.

Chapter Twenty-Two

Two weeks later Sonwabo was arrested by the police for sodomy. Oosthuizen, the compound supervisor, and Loots, the ganger, had tipped them off. The interrogation was short. Loots told them Sonwabo had admitted, there in the stope, that he was an *nkhontshana*, that he had paraded it, taking whoever would have him, that he wished for surface work so he could be an *nkhontshana* again. What can an *nkhontshana* do there in the earth, when his work is at dusk in the compound?

The police spoke to the *induna* in front of the compound supervisor Oosthuizen. Did Sonny-Boy solicit?

Yes, he did. You can see by his eyes that he is an *nkhontshana*. You can see he is a boy who wishes to be given the favours of a girl. Such lewdness, the way he goes about! The compound supervisor has suspected it. The *induna* has suspected it. Neither would allow such filth in his compound if he could stop it but the men who are susceptible are not easy to find.

Laughter and the glances of the policemen as they hovered about Sonwabo where he stood in silence in the compound supervisor's office. The police were sent to the place where Sonwabo kept his things. With the help of the *induna* they found the little wooden breasts Sonwabo used to entice men, hungry for their wives. He was taken away without being allowed a word beyond having said – in truth – that he had been an *nkhontshana*. To extract such words was easy. Few men, whose faces have been sewn together with a blunt needle and a careless hand, will dare deny the accusations of the police. He did not even see his brothers when they took him. He was not given time to say goodbye. Someone saw him going with the police and that was all. His brothers heard it when they came up in the cage from underground.

Tom and Reuben Pumani applied to see Victor Drake at the Native Affairs Department. Their permits to leave the mine were not forthcoming. When, some days later, Crispin came

324

to the compound, they saw him and called him and went a little way across the yard with him and squatted down near the fence and – looking always for the compound police – they told him that Sonwabo had been taken to the jail. And they told him why. Crispin listened and when he had heard he rode away and took the news to Victor.

Victor said, 'Goddamn the infernal boy!' He walked around his office, pushing papers and chairs about the place, venting temper. 'They've done it to get at me! That's all! And they know I can't do anything about it!'

'Why not?'

'Because the law is very clear on sodomy, Crispin,' said Victor. 'I avoided the question so carefully – on your insistence too – and they've caught me! I could strangle that fat compound supervisor!'

'I knew, if you said anything, the manager would turn the matter round and send Sonwabo to jail. The ganger would have been forgotten or they'd have said he had good reason to hit him. You'd have got nowhere.'

'Well, we're rather clever after all!' said Victor, half cuffing Crispin and laughing. 'I never thought of that!'

'I tried to tell you when I saw the wedding with Sonwabo and the *induna*, but you wouldn't listen. It's all much more complicated than you think.'

'So it is.' Victor reached for a cigarette. 'Whichever way you look at it, they've caught us.'

'What are you going to do?'

'I might get the sentence reduced,' said Victor. 'But the Zarps aren't going to be too sympathetic to deputations from an Englishman at this particular moment and especially not when it comes to immorality. You know what the Boers are like? I doubt I'll get anywhere. It's bad luck but there is really nothing else that I can do. At least Loots is gone. They were pleased about that.'

Victor stood and took his jacket from the back of the door. He was impatient to be off. He said a little flippantly to hide any hint of self-importance, 'I've got a meeting with some fellows from the Chamber, so I must go.'

Bright young men have a way of being noticed by the

powerful. Victor had been seen. Besides, he played cricket. He was the best fast bowler on the pitch that season. He was Claude Drake's son. His name was mentioned often – in memoranda and at dinner tables when the port and cigars were handed round. Victor Drake's star was in the ascendant. He was not going to lose his chance.

Crispin heard him walking down the passage, his cheery greeting of the clerks. He heard him whistle as he passed the window on his way to catch a tram. He sat in Victor's chair, with his hands on his desk and he thought of the compound where he'd just been, squatting by the fence, away from the ears of others and listening to what Tom and Reuben had said.

It was the truth indeed that Sonwabo was the *induna*'s *nkhontshana*. There was nothing he could do once he had been chosen, a gift given by the compound supervisor – by a silent nod of acquiescence. Oh, they had known. These things were not secret among men in that place. They had seen the wedding. They had watched him go in silence to the old *induna*'s place. Not speaking. No. Not laughing. Just doing this man's bidding like a dog. This matter of the *nkhontshana* weighed on him. It made him heavy. The *induna* became angry because Sonwabo was not glad with the favours that were shown him. He was not grateful that he was the most favoured *nkhontshana* in the compound. He was not filled with awe at the power of this great *induna*.

Sometimes, Sonwabo refused to be obliging. Then the *induna* would not stamp his meal tickets. Often, Sonwabo had been hungry and Tom and Reuben had shared their food with him but what is the use of meat when it is a piece the size of a bird's egg? The *induna* discovered that they were feeding him and so he set his police to watch and he said he would take the food of all of them or send them away to another compound and keep Sonwabo for himself. He could do this thing, being as powerful as a hyena is among a pack of jackals.

So they stopped giving Sonwabo their meat but the *induna* discovered that being without his food did not make Sonwabo any sweeter in his temper or more willing with his favours. He said he would send Sonwabo underground because he knew –

as a hyena knows when it smells fear – that Sonwabo was afraid of the stomach of the earth.

And he did. He asked the compound supervisor to do this thing because it is known that the white man and the old *induna* are brothers in their secrets and their schemes. The white man, Oosthuizen, will keep silent about the *bakhontshana*. The *induna* will keep silent in his turn about the dealings of the white man in the store and in the selling of illegal liquor. Both grow fat and contented in their silence. And the ganger, Loots, is in the hand of the supervisor – even he – for there are profits to be had where other men might fear the law. These things are far beyond the matter of Sonwabo. Every man knows this. But each man keeps his silence because, at his back, is another who keeps silence for him too. So it is.

And Crispin had said, 'Why then did the ganger strike Sonwabo?'

And Tom had said, 'He was told to treat him like a dog. And he was angry that his strength was finished and he was angry that Sonwabo fears so much to be in the ground. He vomits and he sweats. In his anger, this white man says that surely Sonwabo is a girl. He says he cannot drill a hole because he is an *nkhontshana*, not a man. He says this, knowing the shame that these words will bring. This is a thing that the man, Loots, likes to hear. It is a thing of power for him. It is a blade for his knife.'

Crispin had listened, squatting in the compound with the wind fretting up and down the dusty yard, the winding-gear a Calvary against the sky.

Sonwabo had been sentenced to a year's hard labour for sodomy. It was a charge seldom brought against the *bakhontshana*, but, if pressed, the law had to be upheld. Victor was angry. He raged at the snub, aware that the arrest had been devised to humiliate him rather than to punish Sonwabo.

'What rotten luck!' he said to Crispin. What rotten luck indeed. 'Still, it was a victory over Loots for the boys, let's face it. We've created a precedent which will serve them well.'

And which would serve him better.

He wrote a letter to the Governor of the jail asking good

treatment for Sonwabo Pumani, promised himself to follow it up with a confidential visit to ask for a reduction in time and then he had pushed the thought of Sonwabo aside. There was nothing more he could do until the law had run its course. Besides, there were more pressing considerations. War was imminent. There had been news that the British Cabinet had decided to send ten thousand men to defend Natal, should the need arise, and Victor was awaiting instructions from Mr Warburton regarding the repatriation of workers from the Cape Colony. As it turned out, there were none. The High Commissioner, from the distance of Cape Town, ignored their plight as well as Mr Warburton's deputations. They must make their own way as best they could.

Victor went to the compounds to speak to the managers, the bearer of official news that amounted to a betrayal of the people in his care. At their mine, he sought out Tom and Reuben Pumani. He brought money for them and had written a letter which he hoped might assure an easier passage home. Under the circumstances, it was the best he could do. But they were not there. The workers that shared their shift said that they had gone. Absconded. They had deserted a week after the arrest of their brother, Sonwabo. Victor went away – vexed – his victory spoiled. If they had disappeared into the labyrinths of the settlements around the town, he would never find them. He saw no point in trying.

But Crispin tried. For days and days he rode his bicycle about the streets. He spoke to people, asked directions, listened to the words of men in compounds and on corners. But even he could not find them.

The trains were full. Mine workers and artisans, shopkeepers and domestic staff were travelling on foot, in wagons, carts, any conveyance that could be procured. The house was empty with only Crispin and Victor coming home to it at night and the passage echoing with the sound of their feet.

Crispin, despite Victor's insistence, would not leave. Intent on a mission of his own, he searched the compounds, spoke to miners, asked vagrants, prowled the roadways, looking for Tom or Reuben Pumani. No one had seen them. Their names were unknown in this town. They had disappeared without trace.

'I can't leave until I've found Tom and Reuben,' Crispin said. 'Nor can I go with Sonwabo still in jail. I will have to see them to the border and be sure they have a place on a train.'

'Do you want me to book a carriage for their exclusive comfort?' said Victor flippantly.

Crispin glanced at him, half frowned, almost puzzled. 'What else can I do? I will have to take them with me.'

'And ask for a commission for each of them in the Corps? Oh, I'm sure the CO will be delighted to share the mess with them.'

Crispin cracked his knuckles. He had no repartee to counter Victor's.

'Don't be a fool, Crispin!' Victor said in exasperation. 'No one would accuse you of abandoning them! You have no choice. We're teetering on the brink of a war. The ultimatum's only days away. How can you be expected to wait around in the circumstances? You're jeopardising us both by being so stubborn.'

'You can go. I wish you would. I'm not asking you to stay.' And the flush was dark on Crispin's face.

'Be reasonable,' Victor tried a conciliatory tone. 'Sign up with me. Sonnie and Charlie are waiting for us to join them. The war will be over in a month and then we can find Tom and Reuben and make deputations for Sonwabo to our heart's content!'

Crispin was unmoved.

'I've even been asked by one of the senior officers to join him on a recruiting drive to the Colony on our way to Natal,' said Victor, trying a new strategy. 'He's heading for Grahamstown to inveigle some more of the old school chums to come with us. I'll put in a word for you, Crispin. You can see Frances and encourage the lads to swap their school-books for a Lee Metford.'

'I'll wait.' Crispin made for the door.

'Listen, Crispin,' and Victor strode after him and pulled him round by the arm, and ready to strike him, he was so angry, 'Tom and Reuben have run off. They've deserted!

They are not concerned about waiting for you! They might be in the Colony by now for all you know, getting fat at St Matthias. Why are you hanging about looking for them? No matter how unfortunate a business it is, there is nothing you can do about Sonwabo if he's in jail. The Zarps won't hand him over so you can take him home like a wet-nurse! They might just invite you in to keep him company! It's suicide to stay. Absolute bloody suicide!'

Crispin wavered. 'I'm sure Tom and Reuben won't have gone,' he said. 'They'll be waiting for Sonwabo somewhere here. I know them. They won't go without him. So why should I?'

'They've been gone for weeks! If they were so keen on waiting for him they'd have shown up here long ago. One of them would have been round scrounging for some money or a rail-pass. Haven't we seen it all before, for God's sake!' and Victor let him go, pushing him so that he jarred his shoulder against the door. 'It will look very poor indeed if you don't join up.' He tried a new tack. 'You'll end up being co-opted into some mine by the Boers and then what will people say? Crispin Farborough's mining for the enemy! It won't look too good on the record. Mr Warburton will take a very dim view of it. You can kiss your career goodbye.'

'There are thousands of workers with no transport home,' said Crispin. 'It's our responsibility.'

'You amaze me!' exclaimed Victor tiredly. 'It is the High Commissioner's problem, not yours. Are you looking to play the hero? Do you want to make a damn fool of yourself like Marwick is doing? He's planning to march all the Natal workers home through Boer lines! They'll die in the attempt or be massacred.'

'I wish I had half his nerve.'

'Well, show a bit of nerve and come with me. Do you think a handful of rotten, ignorant Boers can hold off the British Army for more than a week or two? You'll be back at your desk by Christmas.'

Crispin wiped his hand across his lip, avoided Victor's eye. 'Perhaps I'll stay then. It won't be long to wait.'

'My God, I don't believe it!' Victor raged, restraining himself with difficulty from laying his hands on him. 'All that talk about the army counts for nothing! You're funking it! That's it, isn't it?' He stared at him, examining him as if he were repelled. 'That's wonderful! That's marvellous! Imagine having to explain to people that my prospective brother-in-law did not wish to join up. And his excuse was that he wanted to wait around for a native sentenced for sodomy! Looks good! Sounds better!'

Crispin went to the door and opened it. He said, his voice half apologetic and his colour high and the sweat standing at his lip. 'I'm sorry.'

Victor turned on him. 'I'm ordering you, Crispin. And I expect to be obeyed. You'll pack your bags and be ready by tomorrow. We won't get out of here if we leave it a day later.'

'You cannot order me,' said Crispin.

'You're not twenty-one yet and you're obliged to listen to the more senior members of your family.'

'You're not one yet, Victor,' said Crispin and he closed the door quietly and went away.

That evening Crispin could hear Victor packing in his room. Later, he heard him going down the stairs, his step on the flagging of the porch. From his window, Crispin watched him walk down the path. He guessed where he was going. He saw him turn the corner of the street and disappear in the gloom. He wished he could undo the angry words. Victor *was* a member of the family and he might as well have struck him as speak the way he had.

If he followed, he could make it up to Victor, beg him to forget what he had said, drink the throat-numbing gin at the Sylvio Villa with him in some final gesture of friendship until his limbs felt heavy with its weariness. Then he could trudge upstairs to the room of the woman with the white arms and the black hair and the loose mounds of flesh and let her do with him whatever she liked. Crush his skull, sap his blood, suffocate him: send him once more to that extraordinary oblivion he'd never dared seek out again and which tormented him, despite all his resolve.

He sat on his bed, leaning his elbows on his knees. Far away he could hear the noises of the town and closer, the silence of the narrow street. So many houses boarded-up, so many lawns grown rank. Where were Tom and Reuben? Where had they gone? Victor was right: they had not waited for him; they had not waited for Sonwabo. When last he'd seen them, there had been reserve and distance in their eyes and they'd looked down and away when he had said goodbye. He had felt they'd watched him go without regret.

Crispin got up from the bed and wandered restlessly to Victor's room. He stood a moment at the door and looked around. It displayed no more comfort nor property than had the prefects' common-room at school. Punctiliously ordered, the suitcases were strapped and ready. Only his books and letters had been left in hasty disarray on the desk as if he had suspended his task on an impulse. A small picture of Frances stood among the papers. Crispin regarded it a moment and he said softly – suddenly – 'Don't do it', but she stared off to the right, unheeding, her head tilted in the way it always did when she was being stubborn.

Then, as if the words had been some treachery from which he had to flee, Crispin ran down the stairs, leaving the front door to bang behind him. He kept on running, the breath bounding in his chest, and he followed Victor, catching him half a mile or more from the house. Victor turned and looked at him, as if he knew the very words of betrayal that he had said. 'Yes?' he enquired distantly.

'I'll come with you,' said Crispin.

Victor looked down at him a moment and Crispin could feel the burning of his ears and his breath was still unruly. 'Let's have a drink on it.' And Victor put his hand on his shoulder and turned him down the street.

They returned late at night and supported each other up the path towards the front door. Comrades, they. Men going off to war, linked by the call of the bugle, the tramp of feet, the bones of the dead that had gone before. They sang, standing there in the hallway with their voices loud in the well of the landing and Victor, with his coat torn at the shoulder and Crispin with his boots undone. Regimental songs. Hymns: *Non Nobis Domine* and Crispin losing his way on the second phrase. So they sang the school song instead, to attention

332

against the balustrade with no thought of the incongruity in singing hymns when they'd spent a part of the evening at the Sylvio Villa. All was time-honoured in the ritual of preparing for war. Next week, next month, they might be dead.

'Five o'clock and we're away,' said Victor, lurching up the stairs. Crispin negotiated the flight behind him, reached his room and threw his clothes into his old suitcase. It had been his father's. The initials C.M.F were embossed on the leather. Crispin felt the indentation of the letters under his fingers. So worn with use, this bag must have gone with him to St Matthias as a young curate, carrying his few, humble belongings.

Packing it then, Crispin closed his eyes, feeling the room dip and sway, his clothes hanging loosely in his hands and St Matthias, so long suppressed in his thoughts, gathered up its images behind his lids: the red cattle grazing on the hills and the old grey church at the end of the avenue and the crowns of the yellowwoods up above the other trees, in procession, on the banks of the Mtwaku. And his father in his alpaca coat with his sun helmet and his clipped white beard and the droop of his deep blue eyes and the craggy hand which could sink peace to the very bones, by its briefest touch.

And Crispin knew what his father would have done. He would not have gone away and joined up. He would not have plunged his reason into darkness at the Sylvio Villa in cheap spirits and an unknown woman. He would have stayed. Because his first duty – apart from his duty to God – was to his brothers and his friends, his first obligation to those he knew and loved and whose welfare was bound to his own. Before Valour. Before Glory. Before Honour. He would have searched for Tom and Reuben. He would have waited for Sonwabo. He would have brought them home. Then he would have joined up. A soldier indeed.

Crispin took the rest of his things doggedly and put them in the bag: his razor and his brush and his carving knife and the scraps of wood that he had been working on and the little Virgin he had made and had not yet polished. Like Frances, she turned her face from him. Just the sad inclination of her head made him look away in shame. He closed her in the suitcase and he put it in the hall.

All night he lay, unable to sleep and the shadows of the street drifting across the ceiling. He tried to pray but the words got lost in the trudging of his thoughts. To go, to stay. To stay, to go. To go, to stay. Towards dawn he got up and went down to the privy in the yard. He stood in the sandy garden and looked at the sky, the pale dawn rising. No arguing against himself, no glib rationalising could change the truth. He went in and found a paper and a pencil and he wrote, 'I have made a mistake. I'm sorry. I am doing what I know is right. You are not to blame and you are not responsible for me. I don't want to join the Imperial Light Horse. Please believe me. You can call it funking if you like but it would be a sin of omission if I went with you. Good luck and all the best to Sonnie and Charlie. Yours ever, Crispin.'

Victor did not stir as Crispin dressed, nor when he took up his suitcase and quietly closed the door of his room. Crispin hesitated in the hall, ready to tear up the note on the table and plunge back up the stairs to wake Victor, knowing that if he did, Victor would have him down at Park Station and shouldering his way through the throng to the train before he could reconsider.

He went away, walking fast, carrying his suitcase down the street, heading for the centre of the town, losing himself among the dingy shops and sheds, never looking back to where the bigger houses stood in their deserted rows upon the ridge.

Chapter Twenty-Three

Victor came to Grahamstown. Newly initiated, he was a lieutenant of the Imperial Light Horse, travelling in the entourage of the good captain, his mentor. Sons of the town, welcomed gladly, admiringly, the task of encouraging men to join up triumphantly achieved almost before they had stepped from the train. They were irresistible. Down the railway line they had travelled. To Middelburg and Graaff-Reinet, to Cradock and to Bedford.

Victor, allowed home briefly to greet his mother, walked directly from the station. She saw him from her window and she called out, her voice tremulous, 'Oh Frances! Here is Victor! Here he is at last!' and fit to faint. Frances ran from the study where she had been attending to the accounts. She went to the front door to open it for him and she stepped out onto the veranda. There was Victor coming up the path in his uniform with his boots shining and his hair as groomed and gleaming as his buttons and his face grave and eager at once as if he had been looking for her and not looking, marshalling himself to match the distinction of his dress. Oh, Victor! The hero incarnate as she had always known he would be! Every fantasy, every foolish dream!

And she stood.

He reached the porch and he stopped and looked up at her and there was a moment of silence so complete, Frances could have grasped it in the air between them. Then he bounded up the steps to her and he put his arms about her and he kissed her cheek and held her away from him to examine her and she laughed and said, 'Goodness, Vic, what's all this parading? I thought you were the colonel come to visit,' and she touched her palm against his tunic. 'There'll be rows of ribbons on your chest before the year is out.'

His mother came through the door, a-flutter at the sight of him, claiming him from Frances and leading him in and calling, 'Frances, tell Ellen to make breakfast for Victor and be quick. Oh, Victor darling, let me look at you,' and tears

335

springing to her eyes, unashamed. 'You're the very picture of your father! Oh Lord, it is too much to bear!'

After he had eaten and laid his napkin aside and regaled them – full of stories, full of laughter – of the reception they had had along the route and mimicked the dignitaries of every town, he said, 'I'll be back for dinner,' and he looked at Frances like a triumphant boy.

He rose and kissed his mother on the forehead and turned to Frances. She stood at the far side of the breakfast table. She had busied herself with the salt cellars and he, a sudden stranger in his uniform and boots, and Aunt Alice – how she would have liked to beg her back – hurrying from the room on a pretext of calling in the maid to clear the plates when the dinner bell was squatting conspicuously on the sideboard. He came around to her and he drew her to him. She said, 'Wait, Victor, Ellen will come in,' but he, careless of intrusion, was hungry about her mouth.

And so he was gone and when he returned that evening Frances opened the door and said, half laughing and not sure where to rest her eyes, 'There you are, you silly old boy, looking so handsome and smart.' She stood aside for him and offered him her cheek. He reached for her but she took him by the arm and brought him swiftly to the living-room where his mother waited, impatient to see him and possessive of his time.

He poured sherry for himself and sat in the window-seat, his eyes resting every now and then on Frances as if to ensure she had not slipped away.

'Where is Crispin?' Frances said.

Victor put his glass down slowly and rested his arms on his knees and linked his hands. 'Crispin was going to join up with me and then he changed his mind. He was packed and everything and when I woke on the morning we were leaving, he was gone. He left a note. There was nothing I could do.'

'What happened?' said Frances and she could feel a small pulse beating in her throat.

'He felt he couldn't come with me,' said Victor. 'He felt obliged to stay in Johannesburg. He said in his note that he didn't want to be in the ILH. How did he put it?' Victor frowned, searching for the words. 'He said that it would be a "sin of omission" to go or some incredible notion like that.'

'Sins of omission,' said Frances softly, almost chanting the words. 'That's what Daddy always used to say to us – don't you remember?' And she looked across at him. 'He used to say that sinning was not about the bad things you'd done and regretted but about the failure to do what you should have done. Especially for others.' She looked at Victor intently. 'What omission worried him? Why did he write that?'

'Do you remember the boys from St Matthias that went up with him?'

'The Pumanis?'

'Yes. Those three, from the carpentry shop. One of them was put in jail . . . some petty squabble on the mine . . .' and Victor reached for his sherry again and drifted the liquid round the glass. 'Once he was arrested, the other two just disappeared. Crispin felt he couldn't leave until he found them, despite the war. He said it was his responsibility to see them to the border because he knew them. It was such a lot of nonsense because he had nothing to do with them really and they'd run off weeks before. I'm quite sure they're back at St Matthias by now and Crispin is roaming about Johannesburg and likely to be arrested by the Zarps. I don't know why he was so stubborn except that there's this other fellow from Native Affairs, from the Natal office, who marched a couple of thousand Zulus to the border just before the ultimatum. He even had to resign from the Native Affairs Department to do it because the powers-that-be wouldn't give him permission – and quite right. It was extremely eccentric behaviour. Yet Crispin sees him as a sort of hero. I wish I'd never had anything to do with those wretched Pumanis. At least I've learnt it's much better not to know the boys you get signed up.'

There was a small silence and then Frances said, her gaze steady, 'I thought Klaus Otto had signed them up.'

'Yes, of course he did,' and Victor's eyes slid from hers.

'Well then, why should it concern you?'

'Oh, it doesn't really.' He stood and stretched and refilled his glass and drank it down in a mouthful.

'He advanced Kobus cattle for his sons, that I know,' said

Frances, unrelenting. 'I've often wondered where he got them from, right after the rinderpest.'

'Cattle advances are common practice in recruiting. Everybody does it.'

'Do you work with him?' she said.

'Well, if I do,' and he turned to her and smiled, 'you can take credit for the idea. It was you who told me Kobus lost his herd. It was the perfect opportunity.'

Frances could feel the throb of blood marching in her head. 'And so you gave him money for cattle?'

'When the war is over and when I've established myself a little more and met the right men and done the right things, I'll build an empire in recruiting, Frances. A fair one, a good one. A recruiting monopoly where standards can be set to the best advantage for all, properly controlled in conjunction with the mining houses. There's too much labour stealing and too many unscrupulous touts and such a range of conditions in the compounds. All that can be standardised and kept under tight control. The natives need to know where they're going and what they're doing and who to turn to and who they can trust. I've been thinking about it for a long time. It'll be a great work. The mines will need more and more labour. They'll need men who can understand the boys, know the way they think.'

Frances almost smiled but her hands were damp in her lap. He saw her expression and he said, 'I've spent half my life at St Matthias. I think I'm uniquely placed to succeed.'

'It seems Tom and Reuben and Sonwabo have been a great success,' she said and her voice was small and flat.

'For every Tom and Reuben and What's-his-name, there are a hundred happy fellows and, besides, their problems didn't have anything to do with their contract.'

'It's rather like an omen.'

'You sound just like Crispin,' said Victor in exasperation. 'You two are as suspicious as a pair of red-blanket heathens looking for omens at every turn!'

'Well, if you say you know the natives so well, then you will understand why,' she said and the vision of Sonwabo Pumani's mother standing in the rain with the bag of roots

338

clawed in her hand and a lifetime of want hovering about her was sudden before her eyes.

And she had sent the letter.

She remembered it.

That trite and brittle letter, meant to punish him for carelessness, for having done what he had done and walked away, leaving her with the fear of discovery and consequence.

'Frances, sweetheart,' with a glance at his mother who looked from one to the other in both incomprehension and alarm, 'it's a matter that's very complex.' He stood behind her chair, drew his finger along her sleeve, cajoling. 'Trust me. It's for us. I've been working hard to make a place for us. Johannesburg is far bigger and the people I have met far more influential than you could know.' He leaned across her shoulder to look at her averted face. 'I'm onto something beyond your dreams.' He bent closer then, to find her eyes. 'I don't want to argue on my only night at home.'

'Of course,' she said, her eyes on the carpet. 'I was concerned about Crispin, that's all. I don't like to think of him alone up there.' She glanced at Victor's mother. She was watching her. Frances had dared to cross Victor. Her expression was diminishing.

Frances faltered. Then she rose. 'I'll just see to dinner, shall I, Aunt Alice?' she said. 'I'm sure you'd like a word with Victor on your own.'

She went to the kitchen door. Ellen was busy and singing about the stove. Frances slipped away unobserved, out into the garden. She felt heavy. Weary. Where was Crispin in that hostile town? How would he make out? So gullible, so ingenuous. And yet, if he had felt it right to stay, then it was right. Crispin reached into the heart of things instinctively. She wished she could salute him: she knew the price he must have paid defying Victor. Somewhere was a truth she could not grasp. All that she had known that was secure and safe, that was predictable, seemed to be receding. There was no one she could tell. Or ask. No Plotz to show the way.

She walked across the lawn to where the daisies glimmered white among the shrubs. She picked a little bunch for Victor's room – a small token to counter the emptiness she'd offered him. She stood in the dusk. Looking back at the house, she saw him with his back against the lighted window of the living-room. So broad at the shoulder, so slight in the hip, and his long, long legs; his neck, so much a man's, all the delicacy of its boyhood gone. She could recall it still, under the clasp of her exultant fingers when she had gone to his bed all those many months ago, the arch of it, bent down to her and the striving weight of him.

She watched him, standing there against the light, unaware of her. He put his arm up against the window-frame and seemed to be listening, his head inclined. The line of him and then the suddenness with which he moved away. She saw his shadow throw itself against the ceiling and the dip of it as it passed swiftly across the picture rail and the door loom out as he left the room. She hurried towards the house with the little bunch of flowers in her hand but he met her at the porch, almost stumbling over her as he walked out. He checked himself in mid-stride and he looked at her, full in the face, and she saw the bewilderment in his expression and the blood burning in his cheek at the curve of his jaw. He took her by the wrist and turned her back towards the garden and the posy fell on the veranda steps.

'What is it?' she said, afraid.

'Mother said you'd pawned the ring.'

The abruptness of the words made the act seem so bleak, so unspeakably callous.

'I can explain,' she faltered.

'Nothing can explain it.'

'I have it back.' She held out her hand but he turned impatiently from it.

'Why?'

She said, hating herself and his mother for their sly betrayals, 'I got it back.'

'You mean, my mother insisted you took the money to buy it back.'

'I didn't have any myself.'

'Then why did you do it?'

'Because I found Reverend Brompton's musical-box in the pawnshop and I couldn't leave it there. I couldn't. And I had nothing else to give.'

'You found Reverend Brompton's musical-box,' and the intended sarcasm did not hide the tremor in his voice. 'You pawned my engagement ring for Reverend Brompton's musical-box?'

'It wasn't your engagement ring! Your mother gave it to me with my mother watching. It's their arrangement, not ours! It's their vindication of all our so-called wickedness and sin. You didn't choose it. You didn't even put it on my hand. What sort of engagement is that?' And as she spoke she knew that she was being cruel and that her words were subterfuge for truth. She had pawned the ring because the box was more important and the box was more important – not because it had belonged to Hubert Brompton – but because, in her mind, it was Walter Brownley's. And he knew it.

He glanced down at the old ring on her finger, reinstated by his mother, and he said, 'We'd have been married by now if this war hadn't come along.' He could not look at her. He said, 'Do you want to call the wedding off?'

She saw the small muscles working in his face and she raged at herself for the cool distances in her head when she wished to reach for him and hold him, comfort him, recall a far time and weep for what was lost.

He waited for her answer and she said, 'I wish we were still small at St Matthias.'

'And could play games,' he said disparagingly.

She nodded, a half inclination of her head. 'Yes, even that. That's what we knew best. Before sins and wars and people being bartered for cattle and being lost.'

'And so?' He was waiting.

'What can I say?'

'That you have never loved me. Just say it and be done so I can go.'

'That would be a lie. I've never known a world without you. You were my life from the day I was born and maybe before.'

He could not bring himself to say, 'And now?'

Sensing it, she reached up to him and kissed his mouth very softly, a gesture of conciliation, and he took her hand with leaden fingers, as though it belonged to a stranger, not to someone who had come to him once, surrendering herself, caressing him, holding him about the neck with fierceness and with love. He stood there in the garden facing her and did not speak but looked out across the lawn, and when the dinner bell rang he led her in and pulled out her chair for her and was attentive to his mother and attentive to her. In his quietness and hurt, Frances felt an infinite tenderness for Victor. In his lieutenant's uniform, won at last – somehow at her behest, a consequence of their great game – he sat, the hero, the soldier, the true son of his father, and she knew that no defeat could ever come which would turn the blade as she had done that day. In doing so, she might as well have taken up that knife and turned it in her own heart – over and over – and bled beside him.

He was gone at daybreak, saddling up to ride out to Port Elizabeth to embark by sea for Natal. But before he went, he sat at the table in the kitchen as Frances made the tea, the soft green light of dawn only just bringing bird-song to the garden outside the window.

She stood quietly behind him and she put her hands on his shoulders and touched his hair and he pushed his cup aside and reached for her and she went to him, reaching for him too as if to capture, by their touch, something that was lost and for which both grieved equally. And Frances kissed him, feeling the sorrow in her throat, and saltiness about his lips as if they'd tasted tears. And then she watched him ride out into the street, while Aunt Alice cried, standing on the porch.

He went, mounted on the bay, the light nudging up above the hills. He turned at the corner and looked back at her. A soldier, he saluted her, his buttons flashing in the sun. She stood, the little wind tugging at her hair, intent on holding the fading sounds of the horse's hooves and far away, the chime of a bell ringing for matins in the town.

He was gone – the Victor of her girlhood – and the street was still and she turned her face towards the sky and saw a flock of egrets, flying in formation, lit white with early light and heard the sigh of wings. Heading east. Heading east and home.

The heroisms of battles are written of in later times, distilled to celebrations of the fine and tragic and remote. They become the property of those who did not fight them, find glory in the contemplations of those who were not there. The heroes are all brave and self-effacing, they are handsome, strong and proud. Legends are born of all of them. In the drawing-rooms of Grahamstown the most prosaic, buck-toothed boy became a prince! And Frances, because she was engaged to Victor Drake, was accorded a sudden glamour she did not want, became the reluctant symbol of some sacred trust among the women and the girls, of steadfastness and faith, as if, by this, they stood as guardians of their men against some distant fate, kept a constant little flame – a purity of remembrance – burning to their names. In the daily tasks of making bandages for the field hospitals and small sacrifices at meal times in the interests of selflessness and the war-effort, they honoured them.

It became quite tedious, all this maudlin self-sacrifice and stoic duty. Children were reminded, when they grumbled about their supper, that those besieged in Ladysmith with General White were reduced to rations of trek-oxen and hard biscuit and, later, to eating their own horses, the courageous beasts that had carried them to battle. Such stories were a popular adjunct to a Sunday meal when small boys were less than enthusiastic about sago pudding. Aunt Alice recounted them often enough when boarders from the preparatory classes at St Andrew's were sent down for tea at weekends and sat in some awe in the dining-room with the portrait of Victor's father on the wall and a photograph of Victor in his Imperial Light Horse khakis and slouch hat glancing at them – in passing – from the dresser.

The reality was different. Unflinching silence in the face of terror was expected. And glory was only gained by being seen. By leading the charge, by cresting the hill abreast, by standing steadfast – and observed – in the face of shells and bullets. By fixing the bayonet for the final charge and rallying to the call, 'Remember Majuba, lads!' with a howl to avenge it.

343

Victor knew it at Elandslaagte, his company – unmounted – flanking the Gordons and storming the hill into the teeth of General Kock's fire. He knew it on the scree-strewn slope, advancing without cover and the enemy unseen among the boulders of the higher ridge, and the Gordons going on, their kilts dragging with mud and their sporrans white-tailed targets for a marksman. On they went, up into the singing rain of fire, Colonel Chisholme leading, his red scarf tied to a walking stick, a small, jaunty flame in the distance while his men rushed up behind.

And all about a storm had raged. The great volcanic orchestrations of the sky diminishing the small strivings of men beneath, fighting for a thorny ridge in a vast, trackless landscape and the sound of the pipes of the Gordons rallying for the final assault lost in the growling of thunder, the march of the great battalions of clouds.

And there, as he reached the summit of the hill, blood and water sluicing to his very bones, Victor saw the little red flag of Colonel Chisholme lying in the mud and Colonel Chisholme beside it, eyes open, careless of the needles of the rain. Victor stepped around him, flew across the ridge like a gladiator, begging for a hundred Mausers to tear him apart.

On he went, racing to be first, Charlie Fraser at his side. Then Charlie fell as the bullets spun around them and Victor surged on, heedless of Charlie calling to him, heedless of the supplicating hand that reached to hold him back. Bullets struck sparks from the rocks and above, a great parade of clouds moved down the sky, and the light of late afternoon, livid with smoke and mist, broke through.

Jubilant men, helmets raised on bayonets, shouting victory out across the ridge: the Gordons and the Manchesters and the ILH cheering. And to the side, the drumming of the hooves of horses and the Lancers, moving out in pursuit of the fleeing enemy: some subterranean disturbance coming up through the ground, like an echoing roll of thunder to the sky which had given up its storm for light. The screaming of ponies and the sounds of retreat grew fainter and then the tired infantry streamed back, victorious, leaving the cavalry to finish the day.

It was then, the objective achieved, the ridge won and the Johannesburg Commando put to flight, that Victor returned, searching among the dead and wounded to find Charlie Fraser. Sonnie Hook was with him, crouching over him, protecting his face from the rain.

Charlie Fraser. Bold, energetic, schoolboy Charlie. He lay on the slope, a rock against his side and his hat upturned, like a busker's put there in the hope of coppers. Charlie, who had called the war a lark, who couldn't wait for the fun to start, who had dared himself to match Victor step for step, had been cut down before he had even made the crest of the hill, and the Boers an unknown adversary still. For him there'd be no moment held in memory of some deed, some fine and gallant deed, some act of heroism beyond the call of duty. There, within the first half-hour of the first battle, clean-bowled in the first over. Just another man lying on the field, just a name waiting to be listed.

Victor approached and looked down at him and Sonnie Hook shook his head, a slight shrug that seemed to send a shudder through him. 'It's over,' he said.

Victor stood in silence. He did not turn his eyes to see the remains of Charlie's legs, mangled out in boot and bone and mud. Charlie had called for him and he had not gone back nor gripped the hand that had reached for his. Invincible Victor, bloodied gloriously and his bayonet still shining in want of gore, had turned his back on him.

Victor squatted down beside him and he looked at Charlie Fraser – down and away and the mud and smoke black on his face – and he said, with a half shake of his head, 'Damned rotten luck.' And then he said to Sonnie Hook, 'Major Woolls-Sampson has been shot in the thigh and Captain Mullins has a chest wound. Were you there when he and Johnstone rallied the fellows? Good for the old school.' He gazed out beyond the hill to the plains below. 'Pity old Charlie wasn't there to see it,' he said, his voice quiet. 'Come on, boy,' he touched Sonnie's shoulder. 'Time to go.' And they stood and walked away. Nor did they turn again. Charlie Fraser lay amongst the rocks with his fellow dead, indistinguishable.

Victor got typhoid. To be ill was as bad as funking it. This was no bloody way to fight.

Where the victory?

Where the glory?

Where the medals?

He raged at himself between fevers, drenched with sweat and shivering in unwashed sheets, the battle continuing day and night, day and night behind his lids. He hovered now and then at the brink of some dim and beckoning oblivion. He drifted from a recognition of the endless murmur of the ward to some turgid place far off, as if fighting up from drowning, threshing with his arms. The distant boom of the Long Tom at Bulwana, the half-minute silence, then the sudden whine and explosion of its shells, did not touch him. Sometimes Sonnie came and stood beside him. He saw his face, lean and still, watching his. And then he went away again and left him to the dim green twilight.

Crispin had taken a room at the back of a Boer woman's house. She gave him tea and bread in the mornings and asked no questions. She was glad of the money. He worked in a mine, offering himself, searching among the faces for Tom and Reuben Pumani.

Among the miners there were those who had been left behind and those forgotten – abandoned by their recruiters – who'd been herded off trains by troops, forced at gunpoint back to the shafts. They were hungry men, trapped in the sewers underground. Sick men, some of them, frightened men, and those that did not care but worked and slept and worked again and lived time in a vacuum. Ghost people, waiting for reprieve.

Tom and Reuben Pumani were not at the mine where Crispin was employed. He asked among the workers if they knew of them, but no one did. They had not heard their names.

For weeks he worked, supervising lashing, drilling with the hammerboys, down in the dark of the earth. Irishmen, Jews. Afrikaners from the Cape. Englishmen, caught by inertia or circumstance in the trap of Johannesburg. Victor would have called them vermin. Funkers. Traitors. Crispin worked beside them: pimps and touts and carpenters, vagrants and transport riders left without a wagon; thieves and card-sharps and artisans who had been asked to stay or who had no interest in the war. Frenchmen. Germans. A stranger company he had not known. Displaced among a group of men who barely knew his name.

And in the darkness of the shaft or in the heat of the small corrugated room at the back of the Boer woman's house, airless and rustling with the secret foraging of insects, a deep despondency settled on him. Letters that he wrote would take so long to reach their destination, so long to gather a reply that, once he had sent his father word of where he was and why, he put his pens away. And when the letter had been posted, he was severed once again from all he knew. He was not Crispin Farborough here. He had no history. No family. The men he worked with were furtive, like himself, fugitive from the army or from the law, or from their families. And in all the confidential talk at the mine-head after shifts, there was a subterfuge – in the most affable, the most confiding – there was a shadow of deceit. 'So why're you here, boy?' as if he were to show a hand of cards. He shrugged and played the simpleton. He was here to find Tom and Reuben and Sonwabo. A reason as aberrant as any in the eyes of men such as this. And so he said, 'There was nowhere else to go.'

And then, one evening, walking home, the dust thick upon his skin and the other miners flowing round him, ebbing in and out along the street, with their ragged bags and tin food-boxes, he saw a group of men standing by a compound gate, singing. Instead of passing by, he stopped and watched them.

Among the singers stood the man who had barged his way into the Sylvio Villa and seared Crispin with his gaze: 'Does your father know where you are, lad?' And he remembered Charlie Fraser saying, 'It's only David Evans's Holiness Mission trying to frighten the whores out of their stockings.' Crispin stood and listened as they sang Revivalist songs. They were unfamiliar to him. His mother's impatience with any other church but her own, her condescension to Methodists or Baptists, her horror of any modern sect – her grudging admiration of the Scottish missionaries – had been instilled in him

347

and Frances since they were very young. Still, he did not move away. He watched them as they spoke to the mine's policeman who opened the compound gate and let them in. He stood alone in the street once they'd gone, waiting at the roadside, and listened to the faint singing in the distant yard, swollen now by other voices, a dirge lagging at the heels of brisker notes.

Some time later the group came out again and started down the street. Crispin went across to them, walking fast to catch them up and said, 'Mr Evans?' and raised his hat. 'May I have a word?'

The man who led, short and stocky as a prize-fighter in his miner's clothes and boots, turned and locked him in his gaze. 'Evans it is, and what can I do for you, son?'

So it was that Crispin joined the Holiness Mission. In joining it, he was able to go from compound to compound at night after the shift was done. Black with the dust of the shafts and only his eyes pale in his face, he went with them and stood with David Evans in the rooms and dormitories and compound yards: somewhere here – somewhere – would be Tom and Reuben and, if they were allowed to minister in jails, there would be Sonwabo. He would find them all.

When David Evans spoke, his voice shook with the kindled fire of evangelism. His hands reached out and up and trembled with the vigour of his words. 'Let us stand together in the great offensive against the entrenched powers of darkness in this land, that much "black gold" in the shape of saved and sanctified dark-skinned natives may be presented to the Great Retriever. Come, come to the table and seek a clean and purified heart.' There were faces turned to them from the shadows of the compound rooms and the table laid sacrificially, with cloth and candle and a Bible and a cross to keep away the brutal night and the darkness of the shafts and the hunger and the meagre food. No train, no road, no safe passage home and far away, dreaming in want, perhaps crumbling and gone, a hundred homesteads. The reality was the wind in the roof of the compound barracks and the stench of the yard and the man with the Mauser at the gate.

Crispin sat at meals with the mission people when the work

was done, in the little mission house and David Evans talked: of finding land to build a church – pushing the war aside – visualising days when thousands of men would return from scattered tribal lands to work the seams of gold. 'I believe,' he said, 'that the hundreds who have been brought here and who will be brought to mine and work, and to put off their ways of sloth and idleness, are brought here by the will of God, that they might hear our Gospel message and take that message home, like a tide flowing backwards whence it came.'

And Crispin listened but he could not grasp those words, and he could not say why he denied that they had truth in them. Did God put such affliction on a man to save his soul? If God, indeed, were a Great Retriever, why should He retrieve them in this way? There was greed in this doctrine. Another kind of greed to rule and to extract and to hold ascendancy. The truth was somewhere else and he could not grasp it. He wished he could believe what David Evans had said. Or even what his father said. Or gather comfort from standing at the table in the compounds after dark, listening to the congregation shift and stretch and then subside. 'Come to the table and confess and all your sins will be forgiven you.'

And still the sick lay dying and still the rocks crumbled and men came up with injuries that festered to their very bones and still the meal tickets went unstamped and the pay was given and then withdrawn in payment of debt or promise. There was no justice in it.

But he stayed, because he knew, soon enough, he would find Tom and Reuben Pumani. And he did. At the railway compound, on the outskirts of the town. And when they came to the table, a sudden look about them of the catechism class at St Matthias, and they said their names – unfamiliar though they were – he knew them instantly, by the very posture of their backs. He turned to them in quiet recognition and they looked back and then he went to them and he said, where others could not hear, 'I was waiting for you. Why did you leave the mine?'

'There was no one who would protect us from the *induna* and the compound manager. How could we stay after what was done?'

349

'I would have sent you home.'

'There was Sonwabo.'

'Why did you change your names?'

'We got new passes. It was the only way.'

'Have you heard of Sonwabo?'

'We have not seen him. We have been to the jail but they do not know his name and we were chased away.'

'I will go myself,' said Crispin, 'now that I have found you.'

And he went. A miner with no name, no nationality and the warders weasel-eyed to know why he was there. He came from the Holiness Mission, he said. He had a letter from the missionary, David Evans. He showed it to them. At last they let him in. He searched the records. No Sonwabo Pumani. No Sonny-Boy.

'Perhaps he is dead. There are many who have died. Some were let out and told to go.'

'With papers? With money?'

'Where will we get money for kaffirs?'

He looked in the records again. He went to the cells. No Sonwabo. No Sonny-Boy.

'How must we know all their names? The names were written but how can we tell if they are right? You get a native here with ten different names. So you choose the one that you can write. What does it matter? If he was here, he's gone. Most likely he's dead. We had enteric here.'

They were only prisoners.

They were only kaffirs.

Down the passages and past the buckets that stank of sewage and out into the afternoon.

All this time of waiting, knowing he was there. Then nothing.

'And if he is dead, then where is his spirit?' said Tom.

'And if he is dead, then how can we lead his spirit home if we do not know the place in which he died?' said Reuben.

'He will always be there, waiting for us to bring the *mphafa* branch to draw him back,' said Tom. 'His shade will never be at rest.'

'There is no such thing as a shade,' said David Evans in anger. 'There is no such thing as a shade in the scripture of

Jesus Christ our Saviour. The good will be raised up by the Lord with the just and the meek. And the wicked, the idolators and heathen, shall be cast out into darkness and eternal fire.'

But they knew, meekly though they stood, they knew indeed: his shade would never be at rest. Wherever it was waiting – in quietness or in anguish – to be taken home.

Crispin left the mine and went to work for the railways with Tom and Reuben, waiting out the time with them, glad to know that they were somewhere within reach even though they loaded trucks, enduring kicks and curses from the men in charge while he was cleaning engines and counting stock and saying nothing – for an Englishman was scorned above all else inside the yards. But he saw Tom and Reuben when the evening came and they all filed out beyond the gate and he often said, 'When General Roberts comes and chases all the Boers away' – speaking softly, in Xhosa, with the ears of the railwaymen about him – 'we'll find a place in the first truck heading south. The border and home.'

'The border and home,' they said.

The border and home. As if in passing out beyond this place they could undo the months that they had known, discard them, shrug them off like mine dust and be free.

The border and home. Sometimes they sang to think of it. Some little snatch of song and St Matthias and the hills above the mission where they'd hunted, vivid there among them.

Chapter Twenty-Four

The seasons at Mbokothwe did not drift into each other as they did in places with less harsh a climate. The first summer of the war was long and dry. The people of the district were brought to the brink of famine when the crop failed. By March many were surviving on roots and berries. Only then did a few unseasonable showers bring relief and a thin veneer of grass cover the sheltered slopes of hillsides.

Walter, the farmer, watched the barometer with an interest he had never displayed before. He measured wind velocity and cloud formations. He read articles on crop production and disease in plants. He hoed and sowed and harvested. His small vegetable garden struggled to thrive. It was laid out close to the house where he could irrigate it with water from his own eccentric water-furrow. He was a regular holder of work-parties and one of the women from a nearby homestead, famed for her sorghum beer, graciously agreed, for a moderate fee, to brew it in his backyard, lending a festive air to their labours when a school was being built or bush cleared for cultivation. The planting of crops, their reaping and enjoyment, would be celebrated in a traditional way.

And in time, Walter's church was full. He chose only the most rousing hymns, the most hopeful prayers. Those in red blankets who might attend out of curiosity, were never turned away. Walter preached in Xhosa, pretending to be oblivious of the amusement on faces when he made a mistake. He played cricket with his scholars, taught the rules of rugby to a small class of eager herders and experimented with trench farming.

He wrote to Benedict, asking if he would like to come and help him but Benedict replied that his duties with the printing-press were too arduous and there was a distance and formality in his words that saddened Walter. His letters to Father Charles were full of business and the replies he received were long and helpful in their advice on building, ploughing, seed varieties and the kind of doctrine he had found most useful in the early years at St Matthias. He rarely referred to his family except to say, in ending, 'Mrs Farborough, who is exceedingly well at present, sends her kindest regards. All at St Matthias wish you were here and we remember you daily in our prayers.'

He spent long hours with Pusey in the evenings and he wrote down all that Pusey told him. Of history, of custom, of music and chant, transcribing as best he could, without an instrument, the songs that Pusey sang. He asked him about the role of the diviner, recalling the accoutrements hidden in the thatch of Brompton's room. It was months before Pusey offered the information that his own initiation as a diviner was complete. Walter had shaken him by the hand and said, 'We are men of a similar profession then. There is much we might learn from each other.' It did not occur to him to preclude Pusey from participating in duties in the church and he did not care what the Dean might have said.

In time, Walter had been invited to witness a healing that Pusey had held at a far homestead. He had sat quietly in the shadows, intrigued by the ritual, weighing parallels, moved by the authority and the reverence with which Pusey conducted the ceremony.

He became a welcome guest in all the homesteads round about, his yard was always filled with people. The mission was a happy place to be and his small school flourished. But in the quiet of the night – so still, he thought he heard the voices of the stars far out above the hills – he was stalked by a need so great he learned to fill the hours of dark with work to keep it from consuming him until, at last, exhaustion overtook him.

But often, in the early hours, he might wake and listen, thinking he had heard a voice, that someone waited close at hand. A presence just beyond the door. He would take his letter-book and write to her, knowing he could never send the pages that he wrote. Her choices had been made for her and only she could change them if she wanted. Clearly she had acquiesced to her mother's wishes. And to Victor's. Perhaps they had become her own. It was implicit in her silence. For all he knew she could be married now and quite content. There was no reason to suppose she might have waited. Consequently, he had no right to communicate with her. And only because it was Plotz who composed the letters and Mrs Brodowski to whom they were addressed – and full of humour and stories and fantastical nonsense – that he would countenance them at all.

And so the months went by and news of the war trickled in. Sometimes he acquired an old newspaper. Sometimes a small corps of scouts or transport riders passed to be questioned eagerly. Letters had almost ceased to arrive. The railway line between Stormberg and Rosmead had been blown up and post had to come by sea and post-cart the long way round. Letters lay for weeks in depots, awaiting transportation. Events – Magersfontein, Colenso, Wagon Hill, the disembarkation of Lord Roberts in Cape Town, the relief of Kimberley and Ladysmith – seemed so distant when compared with the immediacy of his own struggles to secure water, to plough land, to teach the ever-growing number of children in his care, to build and sow and harvest. He felt besieged himself, there on his hillside: the distant silence of the plains was the unseen enemy encamped about him.

Summer became autumn and there was an early frost. In June, a fortnight after the event, Walter heard the news of General Roberts's relief of Johannesburg. He felt celebratory. Surely, this signified the ending of hostilities. He wrote to Daisy to share the news with her in a sudden surge of patriotism. Instead of sending Pusey, he would go to Stutterheim himself to replenish his stores. With some ceremony, he awarded himself a two-day holiday and packed his bag.

At the end of the week he set out, putting Boggis between the traces of the cart and leaving Pusey in charge of the mission. He borrowed an aged mare from the local headman and tethered it behind to help with the homeward trek. He spoke to Boggis as he drove, settling back into the quiet companionship of the old days and Boggis listened as he always had, turning his ears this way and that as if sifting the information and digesting only what he would.

'There will be post, old man,' said Walter. 'And, perhaps, a parcel from Daisy, although if she has baked a fruit cake it will be dust by now. I hope that there'll be a letter from St

Matthias. Not just the usual newsletters and papers but a little more perhaps.' And Boggis stumbled, jolting Walter and upsetting the angle of his pipe so he kept his musings to himself for a while. He made yet another list. Tobacco and a bottle or two of wine. Paper and a letter-book. Ink, nibs. A dozen delights to select among the seed and feed, the hoe blades and the candles for the church.

He camped that night at a stream, using an old tent Father Charles had once given him and building a little hearth for his kettle. He was away before dawn and reached the ridge above the town at midmorning where he drew the horses in to rest and to stretch his legs and tidy himself before descending to the outspan. Standing on the edge of the slope and looking out to where the morning haze hung thick with dust, he could see the road that dipped away along the deep green edges of the Amatolas, running west-south-west: to the Donsa, down towards the plains of the Tyume. To St Matthias. He turned from its beckoning and he went on into the town and drew up outside the General Dealer's and took Boggis and the mare to the trough for water.

A morning of business followed and he visited almost every shop on the main street and called on the Rector of St Barnabas. He was invited to return to lunch when he had attended to his purchases and he went back to the cart to supervise the loading of meal sacks and horsefeed.

He stopped in at the post office just before noon and was rewarded with a bundle of correspondence tied up with string. He cut it and spread out the letters on the seat of the cart. There were four from Daisy, one from the Bishop's secretary, another from the Education Board, a dog-eared, much travelled epistle from an old student friend, anticipating his own arrival in the Cape. A notice from the Temperance Society, a circular from the SPG, papers and a journal, and a gift from Miranda for an uncelebrated birthday, in the form of a Punch wrapped up with a note inside. There were three newsletters from St Matthias, printed and impersonal, with a note from Benedict apologising for having sent no papers but newsprint was very short and he had had to abandon the Echo for the time being. A page and a half from

Father Charles. He scanned the words, looking for her name, but it was not there. He put the letter away with the rest to be read at leisure. There was nothing else. He searched again. No, nothing else. Nothing at all. And there, as if anticipating his disappointment, his need for other news besides bulletins on the progress of the war and the drought and the locusts and the price of horsefeed, the wicked rise in the cost of paraffin, was Klaus Otto, drawing up in his transport wagon outside the Lutheran Church.

Walter started towards him eagerly and hailed him, knowing which road he would have travelled and knowing where he might have outspanned on the previous day.

Klaus Otto was glad to see him. He raised his hat and he climbed down and came to Walter, offering one big hand in greeting and in the other his tobacco pouch held out for him to fill his pipe.

'Mr Brownley,' said Klaus Otto. 'It's months and months!' And he pumped Walter's hand and showed him to his wagon to sit a while on a bench in its shade and he summoned his servant and told him to make coffee and he settled himself by Walter and smoked quietly, offering comments on the weather and the state of the roads until the mugs were brought, steaming and sweetened with a coneful of sugar each.

They talked of the war and they talked of the crops and Walter told him what he had been planting and building. A familiar repartee between farmers, whiling away their time at market and keeping a sharp eye on their animals.

Walter asked about Klaus Otto's family. His son was growing and another baby was on the way. The little house in the valley beyond Fort Beaufort already needed additions. Klaus Otto had a new air of prosperity and his wagon was smartly refurbished, plain but efficient.

At last Walter said – looking out across the square – and keeping his tone in check, 'Did you pass St Matthias yesterday?'

'Yes,' said Klaus Otto. 'I spent an hour or two in the workshop with Mr Farborough. I broke a pair of spokes coming through the drift. He helped me make repairs. We had a good talk, he and I. He's an old man now. The work is heavy for him but he told me an assistant is coming soon.' Klaus Otto glanced across his shoulder and down at Walter at his side. 'He spoke about you,' he said. 'He wishes you were coming back and he was impatient, *ja*, impatient I would say, that someone was being sent from England. Although he didn't say he wasn't welcome, I know the old man well enough to see he'd rather be without a stranger.'

Walter smiled. 'Is he in good health?'

'His back is troubling him. He walks as if there's a twist in it like an old tree feeling the wind.' Klaus Otto took some time tamping down the tobacco in his pipe and ruminating on what he had just said.

'Did you see anyone else?'

'Just Mr Farborough and the lady who teaches the native girls to sew. She brought us tea. She is very polite and pleasant.'

'Miss Smythe?'

'That's her.' And he made no further comment on Helmina although Walter saw her suddenly, vividly, with a small pang, walking across to the wagon shed with the old familiar basket and the bottle of tea and slices of bread fresh from Nowasha's oven, and butter sparingly spread, arranged on a plate and tucked in with a clean white napkin. She, in her serge skirt with her bunch of keys at her belt, and the morning sun shining right through her skin in its translucence and fragility, and finely lined about the eyes like delicate, middle-aged ladies in far away English parishes.

'And what has happened to the rest of the family during the war?' said Walter. 'The last time I heard of Crispin he was at the Native Affairs Department with Victor Drake but they must have come away before October when the fighting began.'

'Haven't you heard about Mr Crispin?' said Klaus Otto, suddenly confidential with news.

'I haven't had word of the family for months,' said Walter.

'He's working for the Boers!' said Klaus Otto.

'Surely not!' Walter almost laughed.

'I hear he was a plain ganger in one of the mines that was still operating and now he's on the railways.' He glanced at

357

Walter to see his reaction. 'It doesn't sound like the son of Mrs Farborough, does it?'

'There must be a reason,' Walter said. 'And a good one at that.'

'People in The Hoek have been talking and wondering why he didn't join up with Mr Drake. I didn't want to press Mr Farborough and seem inquisitive so I asked about Victor Drake instead. You know he went to the Imperial Light Horse with all those men from the Reform Movement in Johannesburg? He was with the troops at Elandslaagte in October. I heard from people in King William's Town, who have relations in the regiment, that Mr Drake is likely to be decorated. They say he was as brave and as cool as a cobra, as if he was daring the enemy to kill him.' Klaus Otto gave a small laugh. 'They didn't, of course, although he almost died of typhoid and nearly murdered the doctor for signing him off duty when he wanted to be up and fighting! He was caught during the siege at Ladysmith and I believe Mrs Farborough was sick with worry because they heard no word and for a time they weren't sure if he was alive or not. Rumours here and rumours there.' Klaus Otto called out to his servant and gestured that he should refill the mugs.

'I didn't know Victor was there,' said Walter. 'Of course, I have heard general reports about the fighting in Natal. Occasionally people pass by the mission who have some news. I've seen the papers sometimes. I had a set of scouts once, resting up in bad weather. Otherwise it's not easy to follow the progress of events. Not having an assistant, I cannot leave the station for more than a day or two. This war could drag on far longer than we thought.'

Klaus Otto said then, half in pride. 'Did the British think they could overcome the Boers so easily?'

'No doubt – with their usual arrogance!' Walter smiled. 'Need I ask where your sympathies lie?'

Klaus Otto relit his pipe and said, 'I'm the subject of a British Colony and I'm speaking to an Englishman! What can I say?'

'Why should the British expect good German colonists like you to love them?'

358

'At present I have no quarrel with anyone but locusts,' said Klaus Otto, swilling his coffee around his mug to catch the dregs together. 'I'm lucky I have the transport riding and now the recruiting to fall back on, although no one is being sent to the mines at the moment.'

'I heard that you were the man who signed up the lads from St Matthias,' said Walter.

'They were the first batch,' said Klaus Otto, 'and I had some success with boys coming in all along my transport route.'

'Does it earn you much?'

'It will.' Klaus Otto tugged at the edges of his beard. 'I couldn't have started without Mr Drake. That's why I don't like to hear about him fighting like a snake!' He laughed and took a nail to his tooth, extracting a thread of tobacco. 'I want him about to revive the partnership once the war is over.'

Walter said with care, to hide his surprise, 'I didn't know you were in partnership.'

'In fact,' said Klaus Otto, 'it's confidential really and I don't believe Mr Farborough has any notion of it yet, but Mr Drake works with me on the side, so to speak. When he heard about the cattle losses in the rinderpest he took his chances. He has money of his own, I'm told. Weren't his father and his stepfather rich men? He outlaid enough for me to buy some salted beasts and advance them against promised labour contracts. That old rogue at St Matthias – the father of those carpentry boys you had there – took some of Mr Drake's cattle and promised his sons. It would have worked well if those boys hadn't disappeared. The cattle were looking nice and old Kobus was happy. Nothing an old kaffir likes better than standing and admiring fat oxen and thinking of his sons coming home with their pockets bulging.'

'Disappeared?' said Walter, and the faces of the three clear before his eyes as if they'd been at his confirmation class the day before. 'I hope nothing has happened to them. They were the very best of lads.'

'The war again. I don't know. Too many natives up on the mines were caught without transport home. I had hoped Mr Drake would have seen to it that they got back safely. We want a reputation for being reliable, but something happened and there was word from Mr Crispin to his father that they'd absconded sometime in September last. I was hoping they'd be home to encourage others to follow them as soon as the mines reopen.' Klaus Otto sighed. 'Besides this, the only problem I have had so far is with that surly young kaffir that prints the accounts and the newspaper at St Matthias. I asked him if he'd like to be a runner for me.'

'A runner?' said Walter.

'Collecting names in districts and getting boys to apply for permits, making arrangements for the advance of the cattle. All the preliminary business. A runner can make things go very smoothly and earn a good bit himself.'

'What did he say?'

'If I hadn't wanted to avoid trouble with Mr Farborough and hadn't been in a hurry, I'd have pushed in his insolent face. He said he'd go to the devil before he'd sell his brothers for cattle, which shows just how ignorant these educated natives can be. It's fair exchange for labour. No one is made to sign up. It's not slavery.'

'The state of slavery is not always very clear-cut,' said Walter. 'Sometimes, it is forced on one – the only alternative to starvation and death. It usually goes by another name, but it is slavery, none the less.'

Klaus Otto shifted his great weight and tapped at the bowl of his pipe. 'Anyway,' he said, to fill the awkward silence, 'after that, I didn't want him as my runner, so I just left it there.' ·

'Isn't recruiting rather a conflict of interests for Victor Drake?' said Walter. 'I shouldn't think such activities would be approved of by the Native Affairs Department.'

'We all do something on the side,' said Klaus. 'Look at me. I'm supposed to be a transport rider and now I am a farmer and a recruiter as well!' And he laughed, with some pride. 'As for Mr Drake, he's really a passive partner. He only advances the money for the cattle. The rest is up to me. There's no problem. When he's ready he'll probably move over into re-cruiting full-time. There'll be money to be made after the war, if he will only take care of his neck! As you can see, I have a particular interest in it at the moment! The magistrate in King William's Town was telling me some time ago that Mr Drake is quite the young bull of the compounds. Last year there was nearly a riot over something but he calmed the natives without difficulty. Talks like a chief to inspire them or tells them stories in their own tongue to make them laugh. He rescued everyone from an ugly business and took the natives' side without losing face for the managers. You'll agree that I'd be a foolish man to lose my contact there. His name will be known everywhere.'

'Victor's empire,' said Walter.

'Pardon?' Klaus Otto looked at him politely.

Walter put his mug on the ground and made a little indentation for it at his feet, preoccupied by what he had been told. No wonder Benedict was distant and angry! He recollected himself and said to Klaus Otto, 'Did Father Charles say any more about Crispin?'

'I gathered, from the little he said, that one of those carpentry boys was in jail and that Mr Crispin wouldn't leave without him or his brothers. His father believes this is why he didn't join up. I don't see that he should have been looking out for them myself, but that's what he's done.' Klaus Otto was silent and gazed out across the square. Then he said, 'Is Mr Crispin a bit simple, perhaps?'

Walter suppressed a wry smile. 'No, Mr Otto, not simple. He has a different vision, that is all.'

'Well, it seems that this matter of looking for these boys was more important than the Boers or the army. We had a joke together, Mr Farborough and I, because he told me that not long ago he'd had a letter from his son out of the blue, saying he'd joined a Welsh sect preaching to the natives left in the compounds. Mr Farborough said he was glad his wife was away in Grahamstown because knowing that her son was working for the Boers was one thing, but his being part of another church would make it impossible for her to show her face to the ladies in The Hoek again!'

'I've never known Mrs Farborough to allow herself time away from St Matthias except under protest,' said Walter cautiously. 'She's not ill, I hope?'

'No. She's not ill,' said Klaus Otto. 'But she has been forced to stay in Grahamstown because of the railway line being repaired. Mr Farborough was anxious about her travelling by cart at this time with so much uncertainty. He said, though, that he was expecting her any day and looking forward to it except that he would have to smoke his pipe in secret again.'

'Why did she hazard a journey at all?' said Walter, knowing he was coming to the moment which had precipitated every word of this conversation. His palms felt damp on the knees of his trousers.

'She got a permit to travel up to Grahamstown to arrange Miss Farborough's wedding. It seems an odd thing to do at a time like this with Mr Drake still in the army and begging to be killed with all his wildness. Women are like that, I suppose. They never let the chance of a wedding slip them by.'

'I thought they might have married months ago,' said Walter and his voice was plain and steady.

'It was postponed because of the war, but Mr Farborough said his wife will not allow it to be held off a day longer than is necessary. They'll be married just as soon as Mr Drake gets a moment's leave. In the next few weeks, I should think.'

'At St Matthias?'

'In Grahamstown.' And Klaus Otto was silent for a moment and drawing at his pipe. 'I asked the same question,' he said, 'and the old man told me an odd thing. He said she had refused to come home and have the ceremony in the church at the mission, or to have him take the service. I didn't like to ask about it because I could see it made him sad. He just said she wanted the cathedral and the Bishop, no less.' And he shook his head and said, 'Each to his own.'

They turned to other things and talked about the merits of the stock up for sale in the pens, walked across to look at it and watched the heavy sacks of grain being loaded into a wagon and, as they spoke, Walter was entirely absorbed in what Klaus Otto had told him and he heard his voice replying or commenting at a distance from his thoughts. He thanked Klaus Otto for the coffee and invited him to call in at Mbo-kothwe if he should ever go as far afield on his recruiting trips.

362

He sent his greetings to Mrs Otto and he left good wishes for the birth of the baby. He tethered the spare horse to the cart and harnessed Boggis, caressing his lips and smelling the warmth of bran and oats, and feeling the soft probings of Boggis's nostrils searching his hands. 'So there it is, old man,' he said to him. 'Such an empire indeed!'

He went to the Rectory and he had lunch with the Rector of St Barnabas and his wife and then, when he had paid his respects to the Ladies of the Church Guild, gathered in the hall for afternoon prayers, and politely declined the Rector's repeated invitations to stay the night, he mounted the cart and he went from the town, up the ridge to the open country beyond. From the summit he looked back and he saw Klaus Otto's wagon lumbering slowly down the road towards the Donsa: St Matthias and home, and the sun catching the tip of the voorloper's whip.

Klaus Otto had brought news again, an unwitting emissary, delivering his message so prosaically, in that ponderous voice: Klaus Otto never would have seen the crumbling of the earth about their feet! Walter might well have divined it all before he had spoken. Crispin. Benedict. Tom and Reuben and Sonwabo. Victor.

And Frances.

Despite a dozen different imaginings, it was all so inevitable. So predestined. And he remembered what he had written in his journal on the first night at St Matthias all that time ago: '. . . there is an odd sense of predestination. It is strange how strongly I feel it. What it is I do not know but I shall leave before it takes me in. I shall leave before I am its victim.'

Walter travelled east an hour or two until after dusk and then he outspanned and set up his little tent in the lee of the cart and he hobbled the horses and gathered kindling and made a fire which glowed well for the wood was brittle with drought and the wind was only a small breath in the grass.

He made a meal, choosing new supplies. He ate fresh meat for the first time in weeks and made a pot of tea which was strong and sweet. Then he lit his lamp and hung it at the entrance to his tent. He fetched his letter-book, pen and ink and settled himself, hearing Boggis's gentle cropping somewhere nearby and the drag of the tether across the ground. He smoothed the first empty page and he wrote until the embers of the fire died away. He nudged at them with the toe of his boot to make them flare again:

The road from Stutterheim to Mbokothwe
13th June 1900.

My dear Frances,

If I were a poet I would write a poem to you because, somehow, farewells like this should be couched in language to address the heart. But I shan't, for I am far too prosaic an old cleric to attempt it and I fear you would laugh at my efforts! Only lovers may resort to poetry of that nature, without exciting derision. Consequently, I do not qualify to play the bard and your scorn is the last thing I desire. And having heard nothing from you since you left St Matthias and nothing of you until today, it may not even be appropriate to write at all – an intrusion on the distance that you have chosen to put between us. If it is, I apologise, but continue nevertheless for, this morning, I learned from our friend Klaus Otto that you are preparing for your wedding after all, and that, within the next few weeks, you will be married. Although I had often persuaded myself that you were long married, the conversation of this morning was the confirmation that I needed to goad me from an odd state of suspension into which I have fallen. Besides, I cannot let such news pass without acknowledging it and, in a sense, without taking this opportunity of saying goodbye to you: I may defer that reality no longer. Despite recent silences too deep to fathom, and memories of what was said when last we spoke too clear in my mind, I am your friend. As always. I think I have been your friend since you smiled at me at table on the night that I came to St Matthias and in some way earned your salute for taking Benedict's part. Do you remember? Probably not. But I do.

Before I came to St Matthias I was content, in my way, with my books and my music and my own company. My vocation was steady enough for my superiors to think me fit for service away from home. I believed I would not disappoint them – and then there you were, waiting to overturn it all, only happy when you were meddling with the hearts of others – as you meddled with mine! But I offer no censure in saying this, for my vocation is not your concern and it was not your fault for causing an enchantment – you with your buttermilk stars and your green lions and Boggis and Plotz and your magical unicorns! Do you think I ever would have invented them without you? The stories I once told to Miranda were thin and Plotz was a pale little mannikin in comparison with our creations. Now Plotz stands at my side, a constant reminder of my foolishness – and, grudgingly, I must acknowledge – my greatest happiness. And yet, I trust that when I leave this place, he will be content to bid farewell to me and stay behind. If he came to St Matthias searching for the green lion, he has found it in himself. I think this lion of his is nothing more than a great loneliness and, in seeking it out, challenging it head on, face to face in its own desolate place, he, at least, has come to know it calmly and if it's not quite tamed or slain, his attempt has not been without valour.

So it is that I must part from my comrade Plotz, and leave him with his lion for I do not wish his fate for myself. Remembrance of good things shared is better than the burden of travelling on together when the mutual need is gone. Besides, Mbokothwe will suit him admirably for he has bonds of sympathy with Pusey. They understand each other well for they are both figments of two strange imaginations!

Mandlankosi Jingiso – which is Pusey's real name – is no more Pusey than Walter Brownley is Plotz, except, of course, when they choose to be, which is, in itself, a complicated subterfuge. Pusey was created by poor Brompton to shield his heart from his own prying eyes, a panacea for some intolerable darkness. Now that he is dead, the name 'Pusey' remains as some odd relic of his pain. Plotz was invented by me for the same reasons. The only difference is that Plotz can disembody if the need to extinguish him arises, while Pusey exists – in the official registers and memoranda of this mission – the butt of jokes and Mandlankosi Jingiso is shackled to him quite against his will. He may be a diviner and a bard but he is also a vagabond-child, a flotsam thrown up by the tide of death of the great cattle-killing long ago, stockless and landless. In other circumstances, I suspect that Mandlankosi Jingiso would have been the progenitor of statesmen yet to be born.

In the peace of evenings such as this – which no longer fill me with the foreboding of dark forests and in which I no longer wait for the notes of the musical-box, that sad and solemn icon of poor Brompton's – I hear another music which I think you might have heard as well if you had been able to sit in quietness with me. How I would have liked to share it with you, and I sometimes delude myself – fatuously – that you would have been contented here with me. Then I remember – in time – that I have always been something of a frog and not the prince you wished for so ardently. I am not the bestrider of worlds as Victor is and I was not blessed by the gods at birth with so much charm and beauty. Still, I do not envy Victor: the breadth of the tasks he has set for himself, the complicated nature of their execution, would daunt most men. I heard to-day of his unflinching valour in battle. Such stories do not surprise me for I would have expected him to be fiercely cour-ageous and I salute him for it, though I fear for him and for those he touches: it is a burden to have been tutored for hero-ism, when one is so afraid of failure. The two, alloyed, can make a tyrant. Still, I have no right to judge him and believe that, with you beside him to encourage his talents and to tem-per his ambitions, he might become both greatly respected and successful. I wish it might be so – for both of you.

For a long while, I have known that it is time for me to go and I suppose that today, seeing the road to St Matthias as I drove into Stutterheim and speaking to Klaus Otto – who first brought me there aeons ago in another lifetime – I recog-nise, at last, that the moment has come. So, dear Frances, despite having made a garden here which yields abundant leeks and onions, carrots and cabbages, potatoes and beans, and despite having whitewashed a little house and built some extraordinarily quaint furniture (this was unintentional) and made of a derelict mission station quite a thriving and pros-perous place, boasting a growing community, it is time to find an energetic successor and move on.

It is strange that despite my early sense of deep displacement, the madness that seemed to pervade each shadow, I have grown to love these bald, sun-bleached hills, this high white sky and my sober little house with its dung floor. Long ago I saw you kneeling with delight to sniff the scent of such a floor but now, I fear, you would not approve of it, for I remember too that you said you would like an elegant stone house and a spider to ride in! No doubt, such riches will be yours before long. Still, it is some consolation to me that Plotz will be caretaker of my cottage and that I can leave my sentiment behind with him: I have no intention of breaking my heart for a hut in a landscape, as well as for one of its inhabitants.

I shall write to the Bishop and inform him of my intentions and I know that I will not have difficulty in securing some assistantship somewhere in England until I decide whether I will stay in the ministry or resign my office as a priest and follow some other course.

Even before I came to Mbokothwe, I suspected that my vocation might have been misguided. The realisation caused me some pain but I am neither the first man, nor the last, to discover a flaw in his commitment. Working with your father, witnessing the astonishing depth of his Faith, has made me understand, fully, what vocation means. Living at Mbokothwe has taught me how arrogance and ignorance divide us from our fellow men.

I came here filled with dread, beset by demons created from nothing but observing Brompton's own inner unhappiness, and discovered a community of people striving, each in his own way, to satisfy life's needs – both spiritual and physical. The people hoe, they plant, they till, they procreate, they laugh, they weep, they die, as people do anywhere. If they achieve peace and fulfilment through the church, or if they achieve it through reverence to their ancestral shades – or through both – it is their own affair. Who am I to judge? I have studied the teachings of the Church my whole life and have sought for the veracity in every word. And yet, something escapes me – not in the ministry of Jesus, not in all the great philosophies and wisdoms of the Old Testament or the

367

Gospels – but in what *we* have made of them. I think we have taught without either vision or true compassion and we have forgotten that God is Just far beyond our comprehension of the word.

And living here, the theology of these old hills has humbled me and yet confounded me. There is a truth and pattern that transcends my simple understandings but, being just an ordinary man, I know I cannot sublimate the loneliness which I feel so profoundly with self-imposed challenges that might lead me on to grasp their meaning. If I could, I would achieve some measure of the greatness that your father has achieved and I would be content to stay.

Although I shall pass through Grahamstown on my journey, I will not come to say goodbye. This is the admission of a coward, I know, but I could not see you easily on the eve of your wedding, and as I am leaving Plotz behind, I would find it hard to speak without him there to ease the way. Besides, I have no wish to recall you in any other place but at St Matthias, on the hillside across the Mtwaku and below the Nolovini ridge. That was an enchanted time.

Accept my farewells and accept my apologies for having gone away without a last salute or the grace to come and wish you joy in all you do. There will be no reminders of you where I am going – which is as well – and I shall ensure I take none with me. However, I have no doubt, little Frances, you will sometimes walk across my dreams.

If you do, step gently.

Walter.

And in the morning, when he met another wagon going into town, he handed the letter to the driver with a generous gift of tobacco and a half crown and extra money for a stamp and asked that he might post it. And so it started on its way to Grahamstown.

Chapter Twenty-Five

A man appeared at St Matthias. A traveller. He carried an old bag and wore a greatcoat, despite the unusual warmth of the June day. Helmina, walking up towards the school, the wind light and the Kaboosie a fragrant blue against the sky, saw him standing outside the printing-room, talking to Benedict. She gazed curiously as she passed by. When she returned, half an hour later, he was still there and Benedict was still listening, intent and silent.

She hesitated and then she went from her path and she approached them. Benedict turned, half startled and his eyes, looking back at her, had both fire and distance.

'Is there something wrong, Benedict?' she faltered.

'This man has brought news from the mines.'

'Tom and Reuben and Sonwabo?' said Helmina, breathlessly. 'What has become of them?'

But Benedict turned back to the man and he resumed his conversation in Xhosa as though she were not there. Helmina withdrew. She watched a moment from a distance, examining the messenger. He walked barefoot, round his neck were strung the tattered remnants of his boots and the lines of want were deep in his cheeks. She called, 'Benedict, bring the visitor down to the kitchen and I will get Nowasha to prepare some food.'

Benedict inclined his head but he barely glanced at her. She went away, hurrying, and she called for Nowasha, but no one was in the kitchen, and so she took the heel of a loaf and she cut a slice of meat from the small cold joint and she filled an old mug with milk and she carried them herself up towards the printing-room.

The man took them hesitantly and courteously but he ate with fingers reaching for the food, covetous to taste it.

'Where is he going?' Helmina asked and she could see that he was in a state of exhaustion.

'He is going up the Donsa,' said Benedict.

'How long has he been travelling?'

369

'Months. He was at the mine with Tom and Reuben,' said Benedict. 'He came to tell me that they are still in Johannesburg. But he does not know where. He came to tell me about Sonwabo.'

'Why?'

'He was in the jail.'

'What for?'

'I do not know,' and he looked at his hands. 'It is something he must speak about.'

Helmina said, 'If he wishes to stay here and rest a few days, I am sure that Mr Farborough will be happy to help him and to hear news of our boys. I will speak to him as soon as he returns from Rabula.'

She went away to find Emily Farborough and turned only at the orchard gate and looked back and there they stood, the stranger like an old brown bird in his rags, travel-weary, a sudden spectre from another world, to send a shadow nudging at her heart.

The stranger went with Benedict in search of Kobus Pumani. They stood among the old men and they spoke. The people of the mission gathered about them. The wife of Kobus Pumani pushed her way to the front and she heard the words he had to say.

He spoke of the time at the mine. He spoke of the ganger and of the wounds of Sonwabo. He spoke of the *induna*. They heard these things like the breath of something else reaching them from far away, a breath of something from under the earth where men are kept from the light. He spoke of men deserting from the mines, eaten up by hungry labour-touts offering better wages. This is where Tom and Reuben had gone, like others before them, walking from the compound without a backward glance and never returning. They were taken, the stranger said, by labour-thieves from other mines. They could disappear then, away from the wrath of the ganger and the *induna* and the supervisor and be given passes with names that were not their own. It was not too difficult to arrange.

And then the war came.

There were men, like himself, who had tried to walk. But for each that had crossed the border of the Transvaal, there were others left behind, in railway waiting-rooms, death coming to them stealthily at night, starvation reaching for them. He told of the men taken into the mines by the Boers and forced to work for half a wage, the sickness in the hospitals and the emptiness of the countryside and, everywhere, the fear of soldiers finding them and challenging their right to food.

The traveller went with Kobus Pumani to his house, Benedict and Mzantsi and the other old men following. They sat in the dimness of that hut and listened to his words, hearing them again, many times, so that they should not forget what he said.

'A jail is a place to die,' he said. 'It is a place to die as the hospital is a place to die. A jail is a place to meet with men that seize the spirit and bend it as they wish.'

This thing that had happened to Sonwabo. This thing.

'When the war came, the jail was opened and some walked out of there. And some were dead and others were herded into a gravel pit and the Boer soldiers shot across that pit, with the people in it and laughing to hear their screams. One man died, another was wounded. The rest must have madness in their heads from feeling these bullets hungry for their blood. This was the jail where Sonwabo was.'

'And where is he now?' Faces were turned to him and watching.

'I cannot say. I do not know.'

'This is the thing that will happen to our sons and the sons of our sons,' Kobus Pumani said. 'He is only here to show the way for all of them.' And he stood in silence, turned from them, a blackness in his face to feel the betrayal of cattle and of men about his heart.

Benedict went back to the printing-room, knowing he must write to Dorcas Pumani and tell her what he had heard. To offer her – in bleakness – what this man had told him and not to bring the words himself so that his eyes might engage hers with their truth! How would he tell her what had happened to Sonwabo, setting it in words on paper? How would he explain? She would turn away in bitterness to hear it read.

He remembered her in her pagan beauty sitting with her harp in the crook of her arm and the morning sun sheening her skin and the sound of her music, low and soft as bees drifting through the bush. And now, because of him, she was in exile, confined to some dark kitchen in Fort Beaufort, at the beck and call of maiden ladies, vigilant about her soul, free on Sundays in order to attend the church and visit her mother in the afternoon, bringing the little scraps and pickings from the kitchen that she would be allowed to gather, no doubt reminded constantly to be grateful for the benefit: a small enamel dish, packed with cold mutton fat and a rejected apple and a slice or two of last week's bread and crumbs of cake as a reward for meekness. This she must endure for him and he, unable to redress it, could not rescue her from its humiliation. He had no home, no money, and no power to change these things.

The face of Dorcas Pumani held grave and steady in his mind and the face of her brother, Sonwabo, moved across it, as if they were one.

And Tom and Reuben? Where were they? Where were they in that vast, unknown, hostile place? Why had they not come back, walking with the traveller? Was there some corpse in an unknown compound, an abandoned figure at the edge of a train track, a desolate stretch of veld which marked a final burial-ground?

Benedict stood and went to the window. He looked out at the cattle grazing in the pasture beyond the church. And he remembered the transport rider, Klaus Otto, who had stopped at the mission on his way through to Stutterheim a week or two before. He had come in search of him and found him in the printing-room, finishing an article he had been writing for *Izwi Labantu*. He had startled him by appearing – a great bulk in his doorway – and saying, 'Are you Benedict Matiwane?'

Benedict had nodded and come forward, enquiringly, and Klaus Otto had said, 'I was given your name by someone with whom I work. Would you like to be a runner for me? I am a recruiter. Do you know what a recruiter is?'

And Benedict's words had been terse, for Klaus Otto should not think him so ignorant of something that so closely affected his people. 'I know,' he had said.

'If you bring in boys for me and have them here when I pass, you will be paid a fee for each one. You would earn a lot.'

'And how shall I persuade them?' Benedict had said and pressed to keep the superciliousness from his voice.

'You will tell them about the mines and the wages – a shilling and more a day – and good working conditions once the war is over. I have this on authority from the Native Affairs Department. There is plentiful food and doctors if they are sick. I have a man who will go with them on the train to make sure that they arrive at the right compounds. I will have cattle to advance to their families and more in waiting for sons not yet ready to go. I have many cattle. If you work with me you will earn good money.'

'Why do you choose me?'

'I was told that you were clever and are known by the boys in this district. I was told that you'd be glad of money to set yourself up in independence.'

'Who told you that?'

'Someone who knows you very well.'

'Someone from here?'

Klaus Otto had inclined his head. 'And from high places elsewhere.'

Benedict had known then. Oh, he had known. And he'd set his chin and said, 'Mr Drake does not know me well if he thinks I would sell my brothers for cattle.'

After that, Klaus Otto had gone away and Benedict had watched his wagon as it climbed the hill. How could he work as a runner, a body-snatcher, going like a trickster among the tribesmen, deceiving them, dangling the dream of oxen and fat cows before them? He knew about the mines from what he'd read. The editorials were devoted to conditions in the compounds all the time. If indeed it had been Victor Drake – bending from high places – who had sent Klaus Otto to seek him out, how could he believe that just because he needed money to achieve his independence, just because he knew

Kobus would not part with Dorcas without a handful of high-born cows, that he'd succumb, grateful – grovelling even – to be a part of this? At the time, he had put the thought of Klaus Otto's proposition aside, but now he recalled his words as he watched the cattle, grazing at peace where the grass was rank and green and egrets spun about them with the lifting of wings. What more would be exacted from them all – for this?

All through April and May and into the first week of June, while her mother was in Grahamstown, Frances felt suspended in the midst of a whirlwind, anchored to some deep silence within, while all around her so much was active and busy. The house was always full of visitors. People came to see her mother daily and she, away from St Matthias, revelled in the role of gracious hostess. The talk was of weddings and of dresses and of flowers and the best housekeeping aids. The talk was of Victor. There was the endless chatter of women enjoying the prospect of claiming a part in such a joyous affair. Oh, they could just see the report in the Grocott's Penny Mail, 'Wedding Bells for a Hero of Elandslaagte'. And the bride so beautiful! Frances was caught in the inexorable progress towards that moment.

There were visits to the wives of other clergy, visits to the school and the Kaffir Institute to see the work being done, for Emily Farborough had St Matthias always in her mind and a day did not go by without her being aware of it, without her acquiring things within her limited means to take back for school or church or boarding-house. Frances saw how she enjoyed these daily excursions – almost with a gaiety – insist though she might that she was anxious to be home.

Up the hill to Mrs Mullins, down the hill to Mrs Wyche, a morning with Mrs Cornish at Bishopsbourne and her best hat out for the occasion! A concert at St Andrew's and the boys reciting stirring poems: the glories of war were not far away and the older fellows nudged each other and stared at Frances, the prize of a well-remembered hero. Sunday evensong in the Cathedral with the precentor preaching and his choir a gem, despite his five young sons in their choirboys' robes laughing in their pews and passing a startled tame mouse between them.

The roll of muslin in the work-room was waiting to be cut into a wedding dress. Frances did not approach it. So much whiteness and softness, in such abundance! Her mother and Aunt Alice – after some confidential deliberation, she knew – had decided that she deserved to wear it: a generous concession at the evidence of her contrition. Neither would ever have admitted to any subterfuge in choosing it. Frances, after all, was a model of propriety. Modest, quietly-spoken. Meek. Grahamstown had done wonders for her and the matrons of the town would never question the aptness of the choice! She would be a vision in orange blossom and lace! All that was needed now was Victor. Alive and in good health.

They awaited his letters greedily. Once Ladysmith had been relieved a great batch arrived together, the news spanning weeks: letters from the hospital bed, letters from the convalescent house, letters from the barracks. Each was a chronicle of daily events. They told of the actions, the shellings, the conditions in the town, the cricket matches with bombardments going on and the time the Boers had fired off a salvo with a Christmas pudding wrapped in a Union Jack with 'Compliments of the Season' tied to it. They told of Charlie Fraser's death.

After that, without being granted home leave, Victor had set out for Mafeking. He had been at Maritsane in the middle of May where Major Mullins had been so grievously wounded. He had written to tell of the skirmish and said he hoped – if Johannesburg was relieved within the next few weeks – to be home, at least by early September. His writing was cheerful and brisk, knowing Frances would feel obliged to show the correspondence to his mother. He avoided asking about the wedding, as if afraid to elicit information that he might not wish to hear. To Frances he conveyed his expectation simply, 'I think often of coming home, trusting you'll be there, as you said. Until then . . .', the hope implicit in the words.

September. September and the wedding. It seemed that there was nothing that could stop it now. After the honeymoon, Victor would return to Johannesburg and settle things and she would follow. No sooner had the word 'September' lodged itself in Aunt Alice's mind than she had started packing trunks. Each appeared from the loft like another small vessel in a great flotilla, berthed in the spare room and opened for its cargo. Frances left her and her mother to attend to them and retreated to the kitchen. She stayed there, helping with preparations for their meals and speaking in Xhosa – inconsequential talk – but reverting to the language of her childhood, uncaring if Aunt Alice or her mother should hear.

And Ellen, in telling her the doings of the town at her side of the hill, of marriages and births and the hopes of her children and the jealousies of her neighbours, never referred to the coming wedding or to Victor. Only once she said, 'For some, the heart can sweeten and grow content but some bury it at the gate of their father's homestead and walk away empty as a gourd and never return to find it.'

Her father's homestead. If she could have taken the cart and ridden out to St Matthias – oh so far across the dark hills – and seen it there among the trees with the road winding down and her father in the porch of the church, how she would have run to him with the dust at her heels and the smell of it sweet in her nose and her heart light-winged as a bird! It was bitter to think that she had forged her own exile so completely. To think that she had told him, in this house, before he'd left her there and returned to St Matthias – and with her hands in his and her eyes bent from his quiet gaze – that she had wanted this.

But he had looked at her a long moment and he had said, 'Do you love him, Frances, or is it the idea of him that you love?'

'What I did, I did for love,' she'd said, drawing herself up and facing him.

'And love was not enough.'

'I will find enough love.'

'Enough,' he had said, taking her hands in his again and touching her cheek, 'enough to seek the truth and to have the courage to recognise it and then to live by it even if it means that you must be alone.' And his eyes had held hers then, knowing well the thing she feared.

376

'What is the truth?' she had said.

'I cannot tell you that. Each man's truth is his own, more elusive, Frances, more mysterious than love. But fear can blunt the search for truth and needless guilt can damage love for ever.'

And she had put her arms about him and he had said, 'God bless, my dearest daughter. Use this time to think, make friends and be happy in the company of others. This is something you must do, for you have needed an escape too long and carried burdens that you did not need to bear.'

'I will miss you, Daddy.'

'And I will have you in my thoughts each day and wish you strength. I know that you will find it and discover for yourself what it is that you must do.'

No censure. No rebuke. No recriminations. He had offered freedom with a gentle hand.

Frances went from the kitchen, Ellen looking after her, and she ran up the stairs and opened the door to the room where Aunt Alice stood marooned among the trunks and she said, 'Where is Mother?'

'She is in the fernery, Frances, mending a cloth. It's the very thing for the wedding breakfast! Quite lovely! I found it among my linen. Do go in and see it. You will be enchanted!'

Frances hurried away, her steps light and firm as she went down the long passage to the end of the house and let herself into the fernery. She stood a moment and watched her mother stitching at the cloth and then she approached her chair, waiting just behind it, speaking softly, as though she might startle her with her words, careful that none might overhear. 'Can I come home with you next week?'

'You'll be back for your wedding, Frances. It's only June and there's still too much to be seen to. You can't leave Aunt Alice to it all. The end of August will be soon enough.'

'I mean for ever.'

Her mother looked at her sharply. She returned to her sewing, the needle swift about the cloth. 'I thought you had always wanted to leave the mission. That's what you said, Frances.' Then words to wound, 'What you did assured your escape.'

'Was it such a terrible sin?'

'It was a binding commitment.' Her mother paused, as if granting some remission, and said more gently, 'Sins that are repented of may be forgiven and yet, commitments must be honoured.'

'No matter what the cost?'

'No matter what the cost.'

'Even if neither of us wants it any more.'

Emily Farborough's needle was still. Her mouth formed words, but none came.

'It's my fault, not Victor's. He has kept his word,' Frances said, aware of the rigidity with which her mother listened. 'Please may I come back with you?'

'Why have you changed your mind?'

'I have no business marrying Victor, that's all.'

'Do you have no regard for each other after what has happened?'

'Of course we do. We always will. But if we marry, we will both be miserable.'

'How can you possibly be miserable if you care for each other?'

'I want to come home, that's all. I would like to work at St Matthias. I was happy there. I didn't know it until now.'

'Is there any other reason?'

'No,' Frances shook her head. 'No reason.' Emphatic. 'Just the rightness of it.'

'It's natural for a young girl to be a little afraid of marriage and want to retreat to girlhood,' her mother said. 'Even I had those fears before I married your father.' She almost softened. 'Moving to strange places is unsettling but such feelings will pass. In a month or two you will wonder why you were so foolish.' And the needle was busy again, stitching, stitching.

'I know I shall hate Johannesburg.'

'You will have a comfortable life and opportunities far beyond those that I have ever known. You should be grateful.'

Frances chose her words with care then. 'Have you ever thought that I might have my own vocation – for something other than being someone's wife and being comfortable?'

'What nonsense, Frances!' Her mother said. 'You simply

don't know what you are saying. Do you comprehend the difficulty and the heartbreak of working on a mission?'

'I have lived on one all my life.'

'And been shielded every step of the way.'

'Then why did you believe that Victor could have been a priest and married me and carried on with your work? Was that just a way to ensure that you would stay at St Matthias for ever, even when Daddy was too old to work? Did you want to run it your way, through us?'

'Frances!' Emily's voice had remained even but the tremor was there beneath the words. 'We have not disagreed since I have been here and I do not wish to argue now.' She put her hand briefly to her eyes. 'Please do not dissect the work I have done these past thirty years or my motives for it.' She paused, drew her breath, continued more evenly. 'I made a mistake in thinking Victor had a calling. I acknowledge it and I was wrong! But do not speak to me of vocations and St Matthias. You made your choice, in the full knowledge of what you did. You cannot simply sweep it aside now. In the eyes of this family, and more especially in the eyes of God, you are married to Victor already, and if you do not feel the same, then what you did was truly immoral and a graver sin than I believed you capable of committing.'

'You always say that *I* was immoral. What about Victor?'

'He is a young man. Young men cannot always be held responsible for their passions. It is foolish to believe they can and that is why it is so reprehensible to lead them on. I should have warned you, but I never dreamed it might be necessary. I blame myself more bitterly than you can know and I pray for forgiveness daily.'

'Do you really think that is the truth?' Frances felt the heat at her neck. 'Daddy would never believe that! He would blame us equally. And forgive us both and allow us the luxury of our own sins without taking them on himself to double our sense of guilt!'

'It was you who told him – in this house – that you wished to marry Victor.'

'I believed it then.'

'I wish,' Emily lowered her voice and the needle lay idle in

379

her fingers, 'I wish I had never told him what you'd done. I wish that I had spared him the pain of knowing.' The slow breath hovered in her words and Frances, knowing her intention – no matter how unwitting: extorting guilt remorselessly – fought the old, old anger and futility that rose inside her. She did not speak. She went to the window and looked out at the garden where Aunt Alice was cutting roses and putting them in a flat flower basket, moving desultorily from one bush to the next. As always, she was filling in her hours with gestures of aimless grace. Wandering from breakfast to tea, from caller to caller, carrying her losses and her ennui with her like some faint, sad music.

Frances turned her back on her and said, facing her mother, 'If I have no choice in all of this and I may not come home with you next week, then you will allow me to decide where I get married and how. If I am to marry Victor,' and she would not allow her voice to waver, 'we will do it here. If Aunt Alice wants the service in the Cathedral and the Bishop and the whole pompous chapter officiating, she can have it, for all I care. There's no need for either you or Daddy or anyone else from St Matthias to come. I would prefer it if you didn't.'

'You must be married from home,' her mother said. 'Your father would be devastated if he did not take the service. How can you exclude your parents or even think of such a thing?'

'I could not stand before my father and make untruthful vows. I could not insult him in that way nor shame myself – not after what he said to me before he left for home.' She held her breath, fighting tumult. 'If I must do this thing, then I will do it on my own. There is no need to explain it to him. He will know. As for the rest – you can say what you like. There is a war, after all, so there are dozens of plausible excuses for getting married here. The roads are dangerous, Aunt Alice can't be expected to travel, Victor has too little leave. Crispin's away. The expense is too great . . .'

Her mother continued with her needlework, her face averted. Then she said, 'I will speak to the Diocesan Secretary tomorrow. There will be no more delays with this wedding, no matter how unsatisfactory an occasion it turns out to be.'

Frances smiled – a small, painful smile – a counter to angry words. The real question in her mother's mind, Frances knew, was who would have married her if Victor didn't. Who would have had her after her shocking admission? No one, discovering her secret – no one desirable – would have wanted her. Any further delay was dangerous. The war might drag on and Victor might be killed. Then what would happen? A widow was one thing. A girl who had succumbed, quite another. That was how she would be thinking. That was how she'd always thought. Propriety above all else. Even if it compromised the truth.

Frances looked at her mother, there across the room, imprisoned by her fear and her implacable aloneness. Their eyes met. Her mother's gaze wavered – a moment of nakedness, a moment of bewilderment and doubt locked hastily away. Frances had never glimpsed her mother's heart before and she went to her and knelt beside her and took her hand. It rested in hers briefly and then it was withdrawn and the old restraint returned.

Quietly Frances went away. She went in lightness as if she'd laid a burden down and, when her mother left for St Matthias a few days later, she felt a momentary tenderness as she saw her board the train alone and turn and raise her hand in a gesture of truce.

The sense of parting – and of loss – had been profound.

June. July. The weeks passed and Aunt Alice, embroiled in the prospect of a move, was oblivious of Frances's retreat. Frances said nothing. There was nothing that she could have said that Alice Farborough would comprehend. There was nothing she could do until Victor came home. She allowed Aunt Alice her complacent twitterings about her expectations of Johannesburg, her feigned and happy exhaustions when she swamped visitors with a commentary on the multitudinous tasks that lay ahead and when they offered their assistance, she did not contradict when Aunt Alice said, 'Frances is so capable and willing, my dear, we will manage admirably together. But I shall call on you – oh, indeed I shall – if we should falter!'

Then Walter Brownley's letter came. It came in late July. The drawing-room was full of ladies, gathered about the tea-table, and a fire burned strongly in the grate and Frances was busy with the teapot and fetching hot water from the kitchen when she heard the thud of the post falling through the slot in the front door. As she passed through the hall she scooped it up. There was a letter from Victor, a catalogue for Aunt Alice and a large stiff envelope, fat with many pages. She set the pot of hot water on the floor and she turned the letter over to examine it. She felt the sudden slow constriction of her heart. She remembered that writing well. It was Walter Brownley's.

'Frances?' Aunt Alice's voice from the drawing-room. 'Where are you with the hot water, dear? We're waiting for our tea.'

Frances picked up the pot and went in and set it on the tray. She handed the letter from Victor to his mother.

Strange to see the possessiveness, the tenderness with which she took up the letter and to see the eyes of the others follow it into the workbasket at her knee. 'We'll read it together, shall we, dear?' she said, offering a little supplicating smile. 'We'll treat ourselves to it after dinner,' and a small inclination of her head to Mrs Wyche. 'Such an occasion to have a letter from Victor!' she said and she turned back to Frances and gestured at the envelope in her hand. 'What is the other post?'

'Just something for me from St Matthias,' Frances said and she slipped it into her pocket. 'And a catalogue from Birch's for you,' and she put it on the table.

So long a morning with the drinking of tea and the exchanging of news and the little wander about the garden for Mrs Stone to take some cuttings while discussing the treatment of boils! All this tediousness and the letter waiting in her pocket! Frances was half demented by the time the guests had left. But go they did, at last. She cleared the tea things with Ellen and then she escaped down into the vegetable garden, behind the screen of fruit trees, where no one would see her, despite hearing Aunt Alice calling her from the veranda. She took Walter Brownley's letter from her pocket and she opened it and smoothed it out in her lap and she read.

Each page. Each phrase. Each word. Three times she read

that letter. She could hear his voice. And she could see him clearly except that he swam and settled and swam again and she wiped away the tears that fell on the paper. She had not cried since she had stood in the vestry with him. Not a tear. Not a tear. Not a tear since she'd breathed the scent of his cassock – a touch of tobacco and shaving soap – and wet its front and all but wiped her streaming nose on it, had he not come to her rescue with his old handkerchief and mopped her up as if she were a child. With these words of his in her hands, St Matthias was at her elbow, achingly close, and how she longed for it! How she felt, suddenly, the desolation of displacement, the dislocation from all that was loved and familiar and right.

'Besides' – he said – 'I have no wish to recall you in any other place but at St Matthias, on the hillside across the Mtwaku and below the Nolovini ridge. That was an enchanted time . . .' She read the words over and over.

She wept for home then. She wept for her father and the creak of the roof of the house and the garden with its tangle of aloes and thorns and the roses in between. She wept for the wind in the high, high gums and the oaks with the new leaves turning in gladness to the sun. She wept for the dappled places hidden on the banks of the Mtwaku and the little school at Nolovini and the children chanting rhymes and the bell at evening and the scent of the church and the voices singing hymns in Xhosa – a reverence and warmth she had not heard since she had left, despite cathedral choirs. She thought of the curate's lodge with its steep slope of thatch shining silver-grey in the sun and the five small doors leading out into the cool of the veranda, and the grass stretching to the fence where she had stood once with her hand in Walter Brownley's and leaned her head against his shoulder in comfort and content to have him close.

And she had never known till now how much he had loved her. Not a game. Not a story. But a truth.

She turned to the first page of the letter and looked again at the date. It was six weeks old. Surely he'd be gone by now. Perhaps he had already passed through Grahamstown. What had she been doing on that day? What careless, thoughtless thing had she been doing when he had walked down some nearby street, to catch the post-cart to Port Elizabeth, unobtrusive in his parson's suit and hat with his old carpet-bag and pipe?

Frances had never wept as she did then. Not the storm of remorse and defiance and regret that she'd let loose in the vestry on that distant afternoon. Not the angry recriminations with her mother. This weeping was not pitiful or self-indulgent. This weeping was not even a catharsis of the heart. She wept deeply for her loss. For Walter Brownley. And for herself.

She had no business marrying Victor. She knew it and Victor knew it. And both of them were trapped: by their childhood, their families, the expectations, the much-vaunted 'destinies'. No wonder Victor had been reckless. It was as if he had defied that destiny and sought for her an honourable release. Courageous, sporting Victor.

She stood in the garden, between the gooseberry bushes in the sandy path and the little straggling rows of cabbages turning their faces from the wind and she thought – without retreating – of the night she'd gone to Victor's room. It had almost been inevitable. All games, all through their lives, had led to it. Everything had been a preparation for it.

A wondrous game indeed.

It had been done to bind: yet it had released her from him. It had freed her heart. If convention had not made it otherwise, it would have been the moment to salute his beauty as he had saluted hers – and generously – before they turned away.

Frances went towards the house, the cold wind tugging at her skirts. She took her letter to her room and put it in the musical-box. She washed her face and combed her hair and went away, not caring if the signs of weeping showed. She closed the door of the living-room behind her and sat at the piano. She put her fingers on the notes and she played the Corelli softly, hesitating here and there, but finding the tune, finding it and following it.

Victor's mother came hurrying in, letting the door swing back impatiently. 'There you are at last, Frances!' she cried in exasperation. 'I have been calling for half an hour and Ellen is looking up and down the street for you. Wherever have you been? Have you forgotten that we're dining with the Dean?' And she flurried Frances from the room and up the stairs to dress and Frances followed, acquiescent, oblivious of the pantomime about her, distant from it all, quiet on the Nolovini ridge.

Chapter Twenty-Six

First, the soldiers came.

They came in May. Johannesburg was relieved and the black mine workers, breaking out of the compounds, gathered in the streets of the town to cheer General Roberts and the columns marching in. They burnt their passes, building up a bonfire in the street. They danced on pavements, where they'd never dared to walk before. Tired men and jubilant. The Union Jack was raised, the Vierkleur torn down. Indeed, they all believed that the war was over. Surely, it was time to go home.

Crispin stood with the motley crowd watching the parade. Among shopkeepers and road-workers and black men come in from the shanty-towns and compounds, he sang 'God Save the Queen' as the Union Jack fluttered in the winter wind and cheered with the soldiers. The Guards Brigade marched past with the drums rolling and the Essex followed and the Eighteenth. Crispin watched them in their uniforms, shabby from wear, but laundered for the occasion, and the brass smart and polished.

He was glad Victor was not there to see him, dirty in his railway clothes, holes in his boots and thin from the labour and evenings spent without a meal in the fetid compound barracks taking prayers. He felt, too, the disdainful eyes of officers, scanning the crowd, guessing what they thought: such civilians were the flotsam of the earth, the rats come up from the sewer into the light. To have felt the fleeting contempt as eyes passed over him, filled him with a sudden shame. These men were veterans of nearly every battle of the war. Had he funked it after all? There was something simple and complete about a soldier's life and death.

The troops gathered round the Law Courts, Lord Roberts went in, accompanied by Dr Krause, detailed to hand the keys of the city to him, the formal act of surrender. The troops cheered again. Crispin walked away after a time, through the ebb and flow of people coming and going about the square.

The smoke from the burning passes drifted above the dusty streets. There would be trains soon. Trains and home.

The burning of the passes had been premature. The jubilant Africans were herded back to where they came from, the moment of euphoria passed. No man was allowed to go anywhere without his pass and those who had burnt them would have to work for the Military at the Ferreira Deep, breaking stones for road-making. Five shillings for a pass and days to work off the debt. How the gangs moved, wielding the sledgehammers, their labour closed away from the eyes of more hopeful men! A pass for five shillings. Five shillings for a pass. These were the words they chanted as they swung their hammers up and down, up and down, ringing the iron heads against the rock. The butt of a Boer Mauser was only changed for the butt of another gun, and the words of the soldier in charge were no different, only the accent in which they were snarled. And when the pass had been earned, the money for a train fare had to be found and a rail permit obtained. And how was a man to eat in between? The mines were closed, the stamps were silent, the unemployed thronged the streets. Crispin went to Tom and Reuben and he said to them, 'I will go to the people at Native Affairs where I was working and I will ask them for rail-passes. They will see from your contracts how long you were here and they will give me permission to get you home. I promise this now.'

Crispin went then to the Native Affairs Department to enquire about travel documents for Tom and Reuben Pumani. He walked among the throngs waiting to go in: to find some way of getting home or of obtaining work or of earning food or of tracing families; the hopeful and the sick and those who had been there so long, they had forgotten when it was they'd first arrived.

It was strange to walk up the steps to the familiar offices, see the desks there. Sonnie's and Charlie's and Victor's, and even his own, and only a small staff of hastily recruited men – some the elderly, retired from civil service posts, some mere boys – and the patient queues waiting in the yard for their attention.

Crispin stood in the doorway uncertainly. An old walrus who had once been the ferocious caretaker of the account books sat behind a senior desk. Mr Edgar Lemmer. He said, loud enough to stop all activity around him, 'Didn't you sign off here to join up, Farborough?' and he looked at Crispin's clothes sceptically and a touch of tension about his hairy nostrils to see his shabby jacket and worn shoes.

'I've got to get some miners home, Mr Lemmer. They've been here long over their contract,' Crispin said, approaching him.

'So they all say outside,' the walrus said, casting a baleful glance out of the window at the crowds waiting in the yard. 'Every last nigger says he's been here too long and enough trouble I have with belligerent boys when it's the recruiters to blame and not us. I've got complaints from the compounds about men demanding back-pay, if you please, and will I send a labour inspector to talk sense into them! Have they forgotten there's a war in progress? They'll be more trouble than brother-Boer in no time and we'll be locking ourselves in before long while they beat down the doors.'

'Is there a train going to the Cape that I could get them on?' Crispin asked.

'Oh, indeed? A train to the Cape?' He looked Crispin over slowly. 'Where have you been in between?'

'Working in the mines and on the railways.'

Lemmer contemplated him as if masticating the information. 'Since you aren't working here any more, why should these natives be your concern? You should have seen to them before you walked out.'

'It wasn't possible then.'

Lemmer said, a walrus-bark, 'Names?'

'Names?' Crispin repeated mechanically.

'Of these boys.'

'Tom and Reuben Pumani.'

A lackey was dispatched to look in the files. It was some time before he returned. He put the papers in front of Edgar Lemmer who cast his eye upon them. 'Absconded!' he said with some triumph, breathing heavily as if in search of fugitives. A fat finger jabbed at the lines. 'See. Here.' Another glance at Crispin's shabby clothes. 'Run off! There's a note from the compound manager. Deserted!' He closed the register.

'I have found them. They've changed their names.'

'Well, they should be in jail then, shouldn't they? It's an offence, you know it as well as I.' And a sniff and the skin of his jowls yellow with tobacco juice and his breath thick with its taint.

'Is no one being sent back home?'

'Bona fides,' Mr Lemmer declared. 'Only bona fides. There's martial law still, you know. And who's to work the mines if the Chamber opens them again, which it could any day? What fools we'll look sending all the boys at our disposal in the wrong direction!'

'I'll pay for them myself.'

Mr Lemmer drew himself up and his watch chain hovered at the darn in his black stuff waistcoat. 'Is this a bribe?' And the clerks watched furtively, papers poised in hands.

'No.' Crispin's face felt hot and he rubbed his hand across his hair, feeling the eyes of all of them inspecting him, no longer covert in their glances. A reprimand from the walrus was licence enough to stare. 'Of course not. I just want to get them home.'

'I'd like to send all the kaffirs home and never see another one for the rest of my life if I could!' Lemmer said and his moustache closed down across his mouth and his eyes scanned the audience. Those among them, who were within the range of patronage, smirked politely.

'Mr Drake was to have seen to it,' Crispin said.

'Oh! Mr Drake?' Exaggerated deference. 'Mr Drake is in the army, my boy, fighting for his country like most other young Englishmen I know,' and a glance about him at his younger staff – disparagement to wither – and back to Crispin. 'We'll see what Mr Drake has to say when he comes back.' And he proceeded to settle himself – a gesture of dismissal – taking his time to arrange his prodigious limbs.

Crispin turned away but he had not gone more than a block, when he heard footsteps behind him and there at his shoulder was one of the clerks from the walrus-entourage who said, 'The cost of two rail-passes, a pound on the side and I'll get them for you,' with his eyes all over the street and hovering at the gate of the Department building.

Crispin hesitated. He glanced at the clerk's face: small and pinched with a tooth missing.

'Cattle trucks, any day now,' the man said. 'I've managed it before. Often.'

Again Crispin hesitated and he felt the sweat at his lip. 'I haven't got that much.' He searched in his pockets.

The man shrugged. 'Can't help then. Need it in advance to fix it, see?'

Crispin counted up his silver and coppers. No dinner. Not tonight. Not tomorrow. It didn't matter. It was worth it. What he had in the box hidden under the floorboard in the room would be enough for this and his own ticket home. The man watched impatiently as he fumbled with the coins. 'When is there a train?' Crispin said.

'Tuesday morning. Maybe. From Vereeniging though. Get there early.'

'I only have eighteen and six on me now.'

The man pursed his lips. 'I'll take it as a favour.' Exaggerated reluctance. 'Bring the rest on Tuesday. One pound, one and six still owing, mind. I'll be waiting. Tuesday. Eight o'clock.' He took Crispin's money and slid it into his pocket and patted the flap. 'I must look sharp for the old man back there,' and he gestured with his head. Then he was gone, crossing the street and recrossing it and whistling as if he'd been on an errand to the teashop.

Crispin was at the station at eight o'clock. He and Tom and Reuben with their old bag, taken from the mission-box long ago – some relic of Miss Prudieaux-Brune's Benevolent Ladies – and packed with their few belongings. Crispin searched for the man from the Department among the people crowding the station and rocking the cattle trucks to push their way in. 'Wait here,' he said, 'and be ready to get in as soon as I come,' and he went all along the periphery of the station looking, looking. The man was not there and the travellers were jostling to get in.

Among the crowd was a large group of Sotho miners. He knew them by their dress. He wove among them, searching here and there for the man with the pinched face and his eighteen and six in his pocket. As he turned back towards Tom and Reuben, a trap, accompanied by a number of men on horseback and some mine police, entered the yard. Everyone turned to watch and the Sotho workers moved together defensively, suddenly silent. From the trap emerged two men, dressed in overcoats and large with importance and business.

One of them was Edgar Lemmer. The walrus.

Crispin backed, keeping his head down and moving into the shadow of the station building. The two men approached the Sotho miners, the compound police behind them. The rest of the gathering on the platform remained suspended, watching.

Edgar Lemmer and his companion planted themselves on the station step, in authority. The walrus eyes swept the crowd as if what they saw gave offence and Crispin shrank against the station wall, edging towards a white railway worker, dressed as shabbily as he, feeling less conspicuous by his side.

The official who accompanied Edgar Lemmer called on the Sotho mineworkers for their attention and they turned to him but they did not approach. They stood aloof and waited.

'Who is the younger man?' Crispin asked his companion and gestured with his head, his hat brim low across his eyes.

'The manager of the Vereeniging coal mine,' the railwayman said, picking his teeth. 'There's going to be trouble if he tries to stop the train. We've got orders to run on time.'

'Why should he stop the train?' Crispin barely suppressed the alarm in his voice.

'I heard that these mine boys are refusing to work. Some trouble up at the colliery. They're deserting openly. They're a lot of trouble-makers, these Basothos.'

The manager of the mine raised his voice, speaking pidgin Zulu, and there was a ripple of mirth among the other watchers, settling in to enjoy the spectacle. 'You will return to work immediately,' he bawled. 'I have Mr Lemmer from the Native Affairs Department with me and he has his orders to insist.' And the walrus wheezed at his elbow. 'You have no authority to go.'

The spokesman for the miners stepped forward unhurried-

391

ly and regarded the officials and the police for a moment. He was a small man, with the paler skin of a mountain tribe. A poised, ascetic face, eyes slanted, the mark of more ancient ancestors. He said, his voice respectful but authoritative, 'We were told that the fighting between the English and the Boers was over. This is what the recruiter said at the trading store at home. He sent us to Aliwal North. We waited there in hunger for three weeks. He had not found us rail-passes and he did not explain to us the reason for delay. He told us we would be paid one shilling and sixpence for each day we waited and that it would be given to us when we got to this mine. We used our own money to eat but we had so little that some became sick and died. We are men who honour our word, we signed with our thumb to say we would come. But when we came to your mine you told us you would not pay us this money for waiting so long for our rail-passes. We told you yesterday we would not work unless we were paid at once. This you refused to do and so we will go home to our wives and our children because you are not men of your word and the recruiter is a liar and we will not sign our names with him again.'

'If you leave,' the manager said, 'you will be breaking the law.'

'We have our rail-passes,' the Sotho miner replied. 'We came in hunger and we leave in hunger and there are those among us who will die before they reach their homes, but we will go and we will not return.'

'You are breaking the law and the punishment for that is jail,' the mine manager said, mustering a great voice. 'I am warning you very seriously not to break the law.'

'And you have broken your contract through the mouth of the recruiter that you sent. Yesterday, you yourself broke your word when you said that you would pay us and did not. We do not see that money in our hands. It is not we who are thieves and law-breakers . . .' and the sentence remained unfinished.

'I have a means of stopping you,' the manager shouted. 'You will relinquish your rail-passes now. You may not travel without them and I will not let you leave this station with them in your possession.' And he turned to the small contingent of mine police and gestured with his head, 'Take them,' as if anticipating resistance.

The workers looked at the leader and he withdrew his rail-pass quietly from the folds of his blanket and tossed it down at the feet of the approaching officials. A gesture of marvellous contempt and no expression on his face. The other workers followed his lead. Then he turned, raising his arm – a sweep of its robed length – and ushered his followers towards the train. Orderly, they climbed into the cattle trucks with the other workers. There was nothing the manager could do, with so small a contingent of policemen, armed only with truncheons and the adversary so unprovoking in its defiance.

The manager and Mr Lemmer conferred, the walrus's eyes going in every direction, gathering fugitives into the maw of his memory, to file them among his account books for future reckoning. Crispin saw a man called to the inner circle and then dispatched hastily and with an ostentatious furtiveness. He swung up into the saddle of a proffered horse and rode away, spurring it through the gate. The station-master was consulted, the guard beckoned. It looked as if the train would be allowed to leave.

Crispin glanced at Edgar Lemmer among his lackeys and he eased along the station wall towards the crowd pushing into the train. He found Tom and Reuben and he said, looking back now and then across his shoulder, 'The man who was bringing the passes is not here. He has cheated me,' and he saw the anxiety in Tom and Reuben's faces, just as they had seen the fear in his. 'Go among the Sotho workers. It is your only chance. They have given up their passes but the train is still leaving and I do not see what can be done to stop them from going home. Who will know you are not with them?' Again he glanced back at the officials, keeping his head down for the platform was emptying and he had become conspicuous. 'There might not be another train for days and with the fighting, the railway line could be blown up at any time.' And he emptied his pockets and he gave them the money that he had brought to pay for the passes and what he had saved to pay for food along the way. He said, 'Go well and take greetings to my father. I will follow as soon as I can.' He put out his hands to touch theirs. Held in Tom's was a small branchlet of an *mphafa* tree. Crispin looked at it a minute and then up at Tom.

'It is for my brother Sonwabo,' Tom said. 'It is all I can do to lead him home.'

Then they were gone, swept in among the Sotho miners, into the cattle trucks, disappearing into the dark of the carriages as the train pulled away.

Crispin heard the wheels gathering their strength to go and the creak and squeal of steel on steel. He turned to retreat.

A shadow loomed over him and his eyes were slow in coming up to look. The walrus stood before him: Mr Lemmer in his implacably black suit.

'Farborough?' A triumph in those words. Fat with malice.

'Mr Lemmer?' The sweat was like oil on him, cloying, burning his eyes and the pounding painful in his throat.

'It is fortuitous' – and Edgar Lemmer savoured the word – 'that I was called to deal with the desertion of the Sotho workers by the manager of the Vereeniging Colliery. I thought I might find you here. Two birds with one stone, what?'

The pause seemed endless and the sound of the train receding.

'Do not think I am unaware that you paid eighteen shillings and sixpence to my clerk as a deposit and in favour for two rail-passes,' and Crispin felt the morning wind about his legs as if it were fierce enough to knock him off his feet. 'He's canny at catching a briber. He has done it more than once for me.'

'I had no choice,' Crispin said, mustering some defiance. 'Those men were entitled to go home just as the Sotho miners are.'

'Scum!' The sneer in the voice hit Crispin like a blow. 'Mr Warburton will be interested when he gets back to hear about this. Working in the mines and on the railways! Turncoat to the Boers and offering a bribe.' He looked across the yard at the manager and the station-master and the other officials hurrying towards the assembled horses and the trap and he said, delivering his words in an undertone and their sibilance dancing with droplets in the air, 'Those natives won't get far. Sixty-odd deserters without rail-passes! My name's Lemmer, not Marwick or Drake! I don't pander to their "noble savage" as they pretend to do and I've just dispatched a message to the army to come in with support. These boys will all be back at work before noon. And your two will be in jail! I'd have you in jail too if you were worth the trouble, but there will be a report on Mr Warburton's desk the day he returns from Cape Town. What Mr Warburton can do for the prospects of a man is hardly worth contemplating. I'd pack up and disappear if I were you.'

A turncoat to the Boers and offering a bribe! Crispin stood as Lemmer walked away as if his skin had been stripped from his back. He stood until they had driven off and the yard of the station was empty but for a sweeper hovering here and there with a desultory broom, nudging the flying mounds of dust from place to place.

Viljoen's Drift was just across the Vaal, the first siding on the far side of the border. Five miles, no more. Crispin took his bicycle and mounted it and rode out, fighting the wind that swept in across the veld.

He rode fast, mile after mile. Then he heard the horses' hooves. A rumour far back from his flying wheels. Closer. Closer. He did not turn to watch for them. The road started up a hill and he had to dismount, breathless, thrusting his bicycle before him. They passed him then – a small contingent, armed and businesslike – covering him with dust, oblivious of him at the edge of the road.

Then they were gone, over the rise and the words shouting in his throat to stop them and fire in the muscles of his thighs as he raced after them.

He was on the bridge when he heard them. He stopped, held the rails with one hand, incredulous.

Shots.

Deliberate shots.

Over and over. Shots and no voices, just the whinny of a horse, raised in fright.

And then the stillness and the slow sound of the water unwinding beneath the bridge, reasserting itself against the fading echoes.

Crispin flung himself onto his bicycle and rode it down towards the siding, abandoning it in a culvert and cutting across the veld, taking a shorter route, running the last half mile through stands of khaki weed and ploughed lands.

The dust and the desolation. Soldiers milling and the train drawn off a way, the windmill in the station-master's garden sending the jagged shadow of its vane spinning across it. The carnage. The dry earth of the siding-yard greedy for blood.

There were men huddled against the horror, guarded by a sergeant. There were men lying on the ground. Nine. Ten. A dozen of them. Still. Still as if they were deep in sleep, their blankets abandoned around them.

Here a hat, there a shoe. And there a man, lying on his face in the dirt with arms flung out in supplication. Crispin ran towards the train, going from truck to truck, shouting Tom and Reuben's names.

None replied and he stared from the white light of morning into the gloom of those trucks, into the eyes of men, dead to his voice, crouched on floors, herded together in their fear.

He said, shaking a man, 'What happened?' And he spoke in Xhosa then, 'Tell me, what happened?'

'They stopped the train. They looked at the rail-passes. Those that did not have were made to get out. It was the Sotho workers. The soldiers told them to return to the mine. They refused. They stood together and they took up stones that they found lying there on the ground. Once more the soldiers said that they must go with them. They refused again. The soldiers surrounded them. They were standing close, those men, right in the eye of the gun. Then the soldiers fired.'

Crispin went on, all down the line, calling for Tom and Reuben. Where are Tom and Reuben? Tom and Reuben, where are they? He turned then and walked towards the soldiers guarding the wounded, lifting the injured into the shade of a corrugated shed. He went among them, unheeding of the train dragging slowly away, and then he stood among the dead, searching their faces, 'Tom and Reuben.'

'What's it you want, boy?' A soldier and not unkindly.

Crispin did not answer, gazed past him as if he had not seen him. 'Tom and Reuben.'

He went among the bodies, heedless of a lieutenant pluck-ing at his sleeve. From face to face and a sobbing in his breath. From face to face. The leader with his pale skin – a Bushman mother, delicate and light – very still in the glare of the sun and already the drone of flies coming to the feast. Tom and Reuben. Tom and Reuben. From face to face. From face to face.

They had died together. Side by side.

He found them at the edges of the little battlefield.

And he stooped to them and felt the warmth of their skin and saw the dark stain of blood seeping from Reuben's neck. The branchlet of the *mphafa* tree was still clasped in Tom's protective fingers. Crispin prised it out gently and touched each heedless shoulder with it. Then he divided it in three and put the pieces in his shirt against his skin. He retreated then, not turning back, careless of the soldiers watching him. He found his bicycle and wheeled it down the road and waited in the culvert until he saw them ride away, marching the re-maining men before them, bringing others on makeshift stretchers to a waiting cart. By evening they were gone.

He returned to the siding. It was deserted. He stood a short while by the mound of the communal grave among the gum trees at its edge. Tom and Reuben Pumani, bartered for cattle, buried among strangers, dispossessed of the right to lie beneath the earth where those they loved might tend them. Vagabond shades for ever.

That night he packed his bag, left money for the Boer woman for the room and found a transport wagon and asked to go with it. He waited in a small town which had no name he could remember until he found a place on a train. Another cattle truck, and people going south, the three twiglets in his bag and a silence so unassailable that none had spoken to him.

Again the journeys and the veld grey with deserted crops and deserted grazing, and the cattle trucks crammed with men. Day and night and night and day and at last the Orange River, brown between its banks and recumbent sand-bars.

Day and night, night and day and hills rising up, lifting off the plain, aloe-covered and the flowers still blooming red among the ironstone. Here a shepherd's tree, there the seams of bush willows along some long-dried stream and, as the train moved south, the candelabra branches of euphorbia in the folds of hills and the blue-green plumes of *msenges* pushing up above the brush.

Each should have been a friend welcoming Crispin home. To see them again, to know so well the smell of each of them – even from the confines of the train – to know the feel of the dust on leaves and which birds hid in their shade, should have lifted his heart, reprieved him with the promise of a glimpse of the distant, far, far hills all of a hundred miles away: St Matthias slumbering in its valley. Such things would heal and absolve.

Until then, he knew there could be no reprieve. These once-loved, familiar scenes crept by as if they'd turned their backs on him. Strangers to him. Aloof with their own brooding. He carried with him a burden that he could not lay down. And God was silent.

If he slept it was there beneath his lids – the silence and the carnage of that dusty siding. If he woke and looked out at the empty stretches where an abandoned farmhouse or the skeleton of a drought-ravaged tree slid past in silhouette against the sky, it was still there. No escape. He carried it inside his head. Then he would turn his eyes away and take up his bag and open it enough to probe for the three stems of the *mphafa* tree that lay on his clothes and he would feel them and in withdrawing his hand, snag his skin on their small, hooked thorns. Small drops of blood beading up on the surface of his palm: if he could leach it all, let it flow away inexorably, he might exorcise remembrance from his heart.

He dreaded the night. In the day the talk of the other passengers banished the voices in his head. But at night their whisperings went back and forth, back and forth through his mind. And the sound of the wheels on the track were the sound of the hooves of the soldiers' horses: step by step and step by step – until he could have beat his head against the cold iron sides of the carriage to escape it. Wakeful, he would watch the stars, hanging low in the great arc of the sky. So far. So dauntless. To have been cleansed, to have felt the coolth of their benediction. To have slept among them, light and free!

And he repeated to himself, saying over and over, like a litany to keep the thoughts away, 'Queenstown tomorrow. Dohne. Stutterheim. Queenstown tomorrow. Dohne. Stutterheim.' From there he would walk down the Donsa, right along the southern slopes of the Amatolas, fasting like a pilgrim, and find, at last, St Matthias safe among its trees.

And in returning he'd expunge his burden. Set it down and walk away. The voices that announced his guilt – tormenting him – would soon be still.

If he could just get home.

But nothing could expunge it. Even within the safe-embracing walls of the house, the sanctuary of his own room with his boyhood things around him, the gestures of concern from those who loved him, he could not lay that burden down.

The most familiar things – the taste of bread baked in a pot, the smell of the kraal, the sound of the bulbuls at evening, the caress of the sun as he lay on the grass in his mother's garden, back pressed to the ground – by their very familiarity, amplified the dark, bewildering silence in his heart.

He went to the church. And the silence there was greater than in the quiet of the night when he lay awake, waiting for the dawn.

He could not escape it, nor the eyes that followed. Not those of Tom or Reuben or Sonwabo. But his own.

Father Charles could see it in his face. It was as if Crispin watched for something just beyond his reach. But he would not speak of it. He did not seem to have the words or know the way to say them. Father Charles waited but Crispin only told the facts of what had happened and went to the Pumanis' kraal with Benedict and when he had returned – exhausted – he said no more. It might have seemed as if he were himself: boyish Crispin with the mission lads flocking round him and his smile ready for them all, content to play cricket or kick a ball until the evening bell.

399

He asked if he could help in the workshop and he stayed there in the day with Groenewald and his helpers, never leaving until the old man chased him out. He would come to the house then or follow his father to his office, bringing his carving with him or sit and whittle at it in the sewing-room with Miss Smythe or his mother near. It occurred to Father Charles that Crispin – despite the familiar gestures of affection, his smile, his usual quiet – dared not be alone.

He did not go fishing any more.

He did not hunt.

He kept to the mission grounds in the company of Benedict. It was something he had never done before.

After church on the second Sunday of his return, Father Charles was in the workshop pottering among his tools, buffing them with a cloth as he often did when he was composing a sermon, sitting sometimes deep in thought. Crispin came in through the door – in haste – and Father Charles looked up startled and said, 'What is it, lad? Is something wrong?'

'Nothing,' said Crispin, leaning back against the door jamb as if to get his breath. 'I wondered where you were.' He rubbed his hand across his hair in that small familiar gesture, making it stand up. And yet, there was something strangely injured in that movement, the handing off of pain. Father Charles looked at him, alert.

Crispin sat on the work-bench beside him and took up a cloth and some spanners and cleaned them methodically.

'Good to have you home at last and another pair of hands to help,' his father said. 'Will you stay a bit?'

'I won't be going back,' said Crispin.

'I am glad,' said his father, inspecting him a moment. 'You are needed here.'

Crispin glanced at him. A brief boyish eagerness, suddenly extinguished, as if he'd been recalled from it. He bent and picked up another tool, saying nothing, but Father Charles could hear him swallowing and swallowing again. To ease the way for words he said, 'The first important task I ever gave you was the care of these, do you remember?' He turned a chisel over in his hands. 'And they are just the same ones too. Good and strong and made to last for years. It will give me

400

pleasure to see you use them now. Then, you were such a little lad you couldn't even lift the box.'

'The last time I used these tools was to repair Reverend Brompton's musical-box,' Crispin said.

'Ah, poor man.' Father Charles folded his cloth and smoothed it on his knee.

'I believe he died.'

Father Charles nodded. 'Yes, lad. He died. A greater rest, I think, than he could ever find among us here.'

Crispin put the tools down carefully, ordering them on the ground before him. Then he arranged them – with ritual care – in their old wooden chest and he lifted it and put it on the high shelf against the wall.

Father Charles saw him stand a moment with his hands resting on the lid. He said then, 'Will you come with me to the church?'

But Crispin shook his head. He said awkwardly, glancing back, 'I told Miss Smythe I'd give her my carving for the retreat house chapel. I'll take it down to her now.' He seemed to hesitate at the door as if negotiating with himself the distance to the house. And then he was gone.

Disturbed, Father Charles sat on the bench in the half-gloom of the workshop. Seldom had he seen that fleeting look in any eyes. That absolute retreat.

Crispin went to the house and opened his suitcase and he took the figure he'd carved from among his things. He looked at it from every side. Persistently Frances, despite his intentions to carve a madonna. The figure emerged from the wood, rough in places where he had not finished working it, lovingly smoothed in others, a long hand in repose against the babe.

He took it to the retreat house, to the little chapel there. He found Helmina cleaning the candlesticks. He stood in the doorway and she turned and said, 'Oh, how lovely, Crispin. Did you make that?'

'I thought of this place,' he said and his voice was gruff to hide its breaking. 'I was on my own so I didn't have much else to do.'

He waited for her to speak but she said nothing, only took

401

the figure and set it carefully on the flower-stand and stood back to admire it.

'She has the wrong face for a madonna. A bit wild.' His voice echoed up and down the little room. 'That's why she reminds me of Frances. Only, Frances is more beautiful.' He paused. 'And more sad.'

His resolve wavered and he turned back to Helmina, but she stood so hesitantly that he did not know what he could say.

Helmina said, 'Shall we play bagatelle after tea?'

Her words seemed to come from a great distance, a far-off time. He nodded then and looked a moment at the figure on the stand and he half smiled and said, 'Yes.' And he went away.

The late light of afternoon. A Sunday quiet in the house and the old roof easing joints before the sun went down. Crispin found his mother in the kitchen stirring a sauce. She glanced round at him and said, 'Crispin dear, fetch some parsley from the garden. This gravy wants a bit of flavour.'

He went to his mother's vegetable garden. Another unobtrusive ritual. One that he'd performed so many times: the choosing of the parsley or the radishes or mint. He picked a bunch and took it in to her and she smiled at him and bent to sniff it. He sat at the kitchen table, watching as she chopped it. He said, 'I wish that Frances was here.'

'She will be soon,' his mother said, sprinkling the herb into the sauce. 'Like you, I think she's coming home.' Her voice held a small unsteady note in it. 'I have missed her so.' She did not look at him. 'I wish I'd told her.'

Suddenly brisk, she took the gravy to the stove, stirred it, coaxing it to thicken. She did not speak as she poured it into the porcelain sauce dish but she set the empty pot on the table before him with a tentative smile. 'Do you remember?' she said, bringing a slice of bread from the pantry. He nodded. He took the bread from her and held it in his hand: when he was small he had always asked to lick the spoon and clean the sides of the pot with a crust.

He did not move. She lit the lamp and fetched the plates

and set them on a tray and still he did not move. The pot grew cold, the lip of gravy congealing on the rim. He could hear her in the pantry, gathering cutlery together. He put the slice of bread down on the table.

Quietly Crispin rose and set the chair straight and went from the room. He walked down the passage to the hall. He took his gun from the rack. He loaded it – another precise ritual – checked the breech – methodical, well-trained by Victor – and walked from the house.

He went down the path between the banksia roses, through the gate to where the thorns crept up against the orchard hedge. Looking up he saw the spur of the Kaboosie dark and far against the evening sky. And the Pirie Bush was dreaming in the shadows of its deep ravines.

Chapter Twenty-Seven

The last Sunday evensong at Mbokothwe. The last meeting of the choir. Walter's boxes were packed and his trunk had been sent ahead to Stutterheim to the station. The train was due on Saturday. His ticket had been booked. The roomy carpet-bag, awaiting daily essentials, remained open on the floor of his room. The little house stood forlorn with its crooked furniture and only the fire-irons for company. The teapot and mugs and the milk jug and the caddy would be left to welcome the next incumbent.

And yet the room remained persistently familiar, as if it would not relinquish him, as if it were only waiting for him to return for the grate to glow and the small windows to shine and wink out across the valley and to invite the wind down the chimney again.

And to crown it, Pusey said as he stood in the doorway, with Walter's surplice over his arm and waiting to accompany him to the church, 'I do not see you gone, *Mfundisi*. Your shadow is sitting fast in its chair.'

'That is only old Plotz preparing for the spring,' Walter said and the words, though incomprehensible, brought no surprise.

'And the beans are growing nicely. They are growing in happiness. Why would a man leave his bean-patch and his chickens when they are brooding. Tell me that?'

'You must understand that I can't stay any more.'

'Bring a wife. *Lobola* one. There are many you can have if you look. Then you will be glad to be among us always.'

And Walter laughed. Bring a wife indeed. 'I am not the sort to marry,' he said.

'No,' Pusey glanced at him shrewdly. '*Mfundisi* Brompton was not a man to marry. He was not a man to know the heart of any other person. This he could not do because his own heart was too full of fear. But you, *Mfundisi* – I never saw a man who was wishing more for marriage,' and Pusey took his snuff container from his belt and pinched a little in his fingers. 'I can see here,' and he placed his hand at different heights, 'so many sons. And here,' indicating with the other hand, 'so many girls.' One. Two. Three. He sneezed delicately. '*Kanti* — and even yet, it is so.' And he went off towards the church with such an air of certainty it seemed as if nothing could disrupt the daily routine despite the empty cupboards and the bulging carpet-bag in the house. Following him, Walter wished it could be so.

The church was full to the doors and the voices embraced the highest rafters and the light in the sanctuary was soft and red. Walter looked long at the faces raised to his when he turned to the congregation to speak. He did not give a sermon, he used no Bible text. He said, in Xhosa, his words confident at last, 'I leave you with my respect and with my love. I wish you prosperity. I wish you strength. May God protect you and may the shades of those that have gone before stand with you in wisdom at your sides.'

And when he had spoken Pusey mounted the step and came and stood beside him and swept his eye across the congregation and he raised his arms, a true praiser and *imbongi*, and he cried:

> It was he who came in the cart with the horse
> with the eye of a crow and the face of a mule,
> It is he who is known as *mfundisi*
> Never-Rest for he is a man that watches
> the papers in his books even when the
> sun has set and even when the moon is high.
> It is he, the writer of words, and the
> singer of songs, that leaves us now.
> It is he who brought good things to
> this place, Mbokothwe, with a heart
> that has ears and a spirit with
> a quiet tongue and wisdom that rejoices
> first in the happiness of other men.

The people came from their benches and put their hands upon Walter, crowding round in a communal embrace. With a song, a lament of farewell, they went with him from the church. Long after they had gone, he could hear that song as they walked home along the ridges of the hills, phrases strung like stars linked out across the sky, the drift and fade and rise of harmonies reaching up to him. He listened and then he turned back into the church and looked about at the dim, whitewashed walls and the slim brass cross and the panes of the windows barred to the deep evening green of the twilight sky.

Walter prayed alone, kneeling in the front pew with a candle still burning on the altar in the plain enamel stick sending up the glow of its light and the shadowed blue of smoke wisps.

Once this building had held a foreboding, once its sacraments had been desecrated, and once the voice of the musical-box had wept its notes into the night air. It had been a place of omens. Mbokothwe, the grinding-stone. Now, it was a sanctuary.

And in kneeling there, he knew at last a healing benediction. No debates or prayers of supplication, no excuses for what he did intruded in the moment of acceptance. Then he went to the vestry and he took off his surplice and cassock slowly and hung them on the nail behind the door and looked at them a long moment before he turned away.

Pusey was waiting when he got back to the house. He had made a pot of tea and Walter invited him to share it at the table with him. They drank in companionable silence and lit their pipes and smoked awhile and then Pusey went out with a small salute and left him.

Walter went to the bookshelf and examined the collection of little gifts that the children had brought him that day. There was food and there were texts drawn laboriously by hand and there was a beaded tobacco pouch and a holy picture surrounded by crochet-work. So many small mementoes to take with him, gestures of regard and love. He lifted them into his bag.

He reached for his worn Bible and paged it slowly. He went to the door and opened it, sitting on the step to watch the moon rise full above the hills. He read as he sat there and he listened to the sounds of the dark. Such a quietness, such a peace indeed. He put the Bible down and gazed along the dim lip of the slope, suddenly intent. He listened, a small unease in his throat. Nothing stirred. Nothing but the softness of the bergwind blowing and the limpid light of the moon lying on the contours of the hills.

But that echo hovered at the edges of his thoughts intermittently that night and all the next day and the next, nudging at him in the busyness of his final preparations.

On Wednesday afternoon the telegram came.

Pusey brought it. It had been delivered by a runner from the post office in Stutterheim, carried to a trader, sent on to another and then across the hills with a boy. It was from St Matthias, dated Monday. It said:

> Pumani sons all dead. Crispin Farborough
> has disappeared. Father Charles requests
> you come.
> Benedict Matiwane.

Walter held the telegram in his hand, silent. Mechanically he put the last of his clothes in his bag and closed it.

He was leaving the next day. At first light. Permission to travel since martial law had been imposed in the Colony was difficult to obtain. He had his permit in his bag and he would have ridden on Boggis to Stutterheim, sold him – Judas's thirty pieces of silver – and taken the train, heading north and then west, circling St Matthias and no intention of returning.

And now this.

As if it were predetermined.

And so, in the morning, as the sun was coming up and a cold wind swept across the valley and the bare-headed hills, Walter saddled Boggis and stood a moment among the people who had gathered in his yard, rising well before dawn to bid him goodbye, wrapped against the cold in blankets and hands icy when their fingers reached for his. He rode out, turning sometimes to raise his hat to the dark assembly beside the church – Plotz and Pusey side by side, somewhere there among them – and Mandlankosi Jingiso framed by the drunken bell, his great declamatory voice thrown up and out in a last farewell.

407

Walter cantered down the slope, putting a distance between himself and the little settlement on top of the hill. And instead of taking the road to Stutterheim, he travelled west and south, he and Boggis. West and south.

A telegram was sent to Victor too. Father Charles sent it, directing it to Cape Town where Victor had been summonsed by Mr Warburton, a temporary leave from the ILH requested: there were great things in store for Victor. The Government Native Labour Bureau was being formed and only the best men were being recruited to its ranks. Victor's reputation had gone before him. He had been there no more than a few days when the telegram arrived. He cursed it silently. Again, Crispin's vagaries had interfered. Reluctantly Mr Warburton had given him permission to leave.

He said, 'Go on then, Drake. Telegraph me when you have an idea of when you're likely to be back in Johannesburg. I'll be on my way on Tuesday next and in the office by Friday. You'll have to hand in your commission. Enough war-mongering now. You have more valiant things to do.' He looked Victor over. 'They're impressed with you. I'll be sad to second you to the Labour Bureau, but there it is. They need good men to get it going and to my credit, I offered them the best,' and he shook hands with Victor with the air of a schoolmaster sending off – in magnanimity – a favourite scholar. 'I trust the news from home will give us no further cause for alarm. I hope you find young Farborough and can bring him with you.'

Victor did not pass through Grahamstown. He avoided it. He who had faced the barrage of fire at Elandslaagte, had lain in a dangerous delirium in Ladysmith, had dared with the devil at Maritsane, could not face Frances. He was too afraid. The wedding plans proceeded, he knew from his mother, he knew even from the short, detached letters that Frances sent, but she was lost from him as if she had disappeared with Crispin into the Amatola foothills. He would marry her – she had indicated nothing to the contrary – and he would spend the rest of his life fighting to regain her.

And so, taking another route, passing almost within sight of her, he arrived at King William's Town and found a place on the post-cart going to The Hoek. No journey had ever been more tedious than those last thirty miles, no horses shambled on so slowly. He had raged in silence, wishing he could whip them up. He arrived in the village at noon and saw the familiar trap drawn up outside Nettleton's store. He took his bag and hurried across to it through the milling tribesmen, scattering chickens in his haste. His Uncle Charles came to meet him, Aunt Emily sat in the trap, unbent but fragile with anxiety and fear.

Father Charles was gaunt from days of searching the mission lands, tracking through bush where he had not been in years. He was an old man and the serenity Victor had always known had gone from his face.

Both of them reached for him, in a new and discomforting dependence, as if, by his presence, they might be redeemed from the fear of loss, just two old people, assailed with uncertainty. 'Thank God you are here.' Father Charles's voice broke as he embraced Victor.

Victor climbed up beside his Aunt Emily and put his arms about her. 'Oh, Victor,' she said. 'You know every place he's ever hunted. Find him, Victor, please bring him back. I can't bear to think that he might have fallen into a game-trap or hurt himself or been harmed in any way. The uncertainty is terrible! We've had every native on the mission searching, every neighbour, the police. There's no trace of him at all.'

And so it was that the mission seemed deserted on that limpid morning when Walter Brownley arrived, riding Boggis down the Donsa road into the empty yard, abandoned by the ubiquitous Kobus with his broom and his following of old men. Every man, every boy was out scouring the hills and only the cattle of Kobus Pumani grazed on, unconcerned, among the water-furrows.

It was as if Walter were returning home to find that no one lived there any more but heard voices, echoing with the notes of laughter lost. He seemed to see the shadow of a fleeting figure when he raised his eyes to the Nolovini ridge: Frances moving through the grass, sitting with her skirts about her and her cape pulled up against her cheeks and he so silent and so clod-footed, dragging Boggis up the slope. He looked again and there it lay, far and still and only the wind bending the grass.

He went on, walking down through the orchard and the garden to the house. He found it empty, though the doors stood open and the window sashes had been raised. The first fellow-creatures he encountered – as though they had materialised from another world – were two small girls hovering in the shadow of the retreat house walls. Then the spell was broken and they ran inside and he heard them call, high voices fluting like grass birds, '*Ngumfundisi*. It is a priest. *Ukhona ngaphandle*. He is outside.'

He followed them to the back door of the retreat house and stood on the threshold of the kitchen, waiting. A large kettle steamed on the wood stove. A small cream-painted dresser, its door worn away at the corner where dozens of fingers – over years – had hooked it to open it, was arranged with a tray of cups and a starched cloth. A large refectory table stood in the middle of the room. He let his gaze rest on each of these familiar things as if greeting old acquaintances. He heard quick footsteps, recognised them at once. He smiled.

'Father Charles?' The voice was the same. There she was at the doorway opposite. He held his hat, looked up as she descended the two narrow steps towards him. She paused a moment, poised, as if she'd caught her breath, seeing him in silhouette against the light.

'Miss Smythe?' he said. 'Helmina?'

She ran to him wordlessly and he took her hand and covered it with his own and then he bent and kissed her cheek and said, 'Was I expected? I came as soon as I heard.'

'We didn't think you'd be here so soon,' she said. 'Thank God you've come. Oh, thank God!' And her words faltered and he retained her hand and said, 'I've been wandering around unchallenged for half an hour and you're the only living soul I've seen except for the small girls you had posted outside. The place is quite deserted.'

'They're all searching for Crispin,' she said. 'Everyone has gone to help. There are men out looking all the time. Father Charles and Mrs Farborough have driven to The Hoek to

410

fetch Victor. He's coming from Cape Town. He left as soon as he got the telegram. Once he's here and the police from The Hoek arrive, they'll be going further, up into the Pirie Bush. It's so vast, they have only been able to search the edges and Father Charles has not wanted to risk another accident by pushing in too far until Victor is here.' She averted her face then and struggled a moment, gesturing with her hand that she could not speak.

Coming to her rescue, Walter put his hat on the table and said, eyeing the kettle on the stove, 'I hope that's boiling away for me and you'll give me a cup of tea and have one yourself and sit with me a minute.'

Grateful for the diversion that he'd offered, Helmina turned to the stove and the little dresser and fussed about the tray, filling the pot with a spoonful of tea-leaves and replenishing the sugar basin. She glanced back at him as if he were a phantom.

It was good to see her standing at the stove, making the tea as he had so often watched her do in the past: a moment of familiarity in the uncertainty of his return. She was unchanged, deferential in her smallness and timidity. She smiled at him unsteadily, composed herself and took the tray into the parlour and set it on the table.

He sat opposite her, accepted a cup and stirred his tea slowly before he said, scanning her face to see if she were able to speak, 'Tell me.'

'I'm sorry you had to come on such an occasion,' she began, drawing a deep breath and turning her spoon in her saucer.

She began tentatively, speaking of Tom and Reuben and Sonwabo Pumani and Walter heard her words like echoes from some distant, fearful place, given to him here in the quiet of the small retreat house where nothing had changed: it was not possible when surely, if he stood and looked out of the window he would see Tom or Reuben walking with the goats or Sonwabo sauntering behind, whistling for them to wait for him, and laughter in the air long after they were gone.

When she had finished she sat examining her hands, regaining her composure. Then she refilled his cup and he heard the note of her voice waver as she said, 'Crispin came home. He arrived one day. He looked dishevelled and wild and I feared he was ill. But in other ways he seemed himself and after he had told us and Kobus the whole terrible business,' she paused again, mastering her voice, 'he worked with Mr Groenewald in the carpentry shop for a few days and was useful about the house and spent time carving as he always liked to do.' She looked up at Walter. 'But I knew,' she said. 'I knew he wasn't right. I couldn't reach him. Nor could Father Charles.' It was some time before she could continue. 'It was as if he was no longer with us.' She put her hand to her eyes and then withdrew it, folding it in her lap. 'On Sunday afternoon' – and drawing a breath – 'he came to the little chapel here. He brought a carving of a madonna that he'd made and he put it on the flower-stand by the altar. I told him how beautiful it was and I sensed that he wanted to tell me something.'

Walter leaned forward. 'Go on,' he said.

'And I didn't know how to let him.'

'What did he say?'

'Nothing. He just stood there and watched me. It seemed as if he didn't know how to begin.' She cast about with her hand as if trying to gather words. 'If only I had spoken!' Walter could hear the sob in her voice. 'Instead, I said he should come back to the house and play bagatelle with me. He used to like that long ago when he was a child. We played often – just he and I – especially if someone had been cross with him or he felt lonely.' Walter waited for her. She struggled on. 'It wasn't enough! It wasn't nearly enough! I went back to the house and he didn't come. I waited and waited. I was too . . .' she took a breath, 'diffident to go and find him and make him tell me what he needed to say.' She opened her hands, let them fall into her lap. 'My diffidence was cruel. Oh God, it was cruel!' She looked up at Walter and the tears were crowding in. 'And now he's gone.' She bowed her head, struggling for control. She said, 'He took his gun – that was all – not even a jacket.' She was silent. Then she said, 'And now he'll never come back.'

Walter was hesitant. 'You speak as though he were dead.'

'He is. I have known it since Sunday evening. I have said nothing to anyone because I have no proof. Just a stillness suddenly. Just knowing.' She rose and said, searching her pockets for her handkerchief, 'Come and see what he made for the chapel.'

She led him through to the small retreat house chapel, built between the guest rooms, and opened the door. She beckoned him in. On a stand by the altar stood the slim wood-carving of the Madonna and Child and she said, 'He made it in that lonely time in Johannesburg while he was searching for the three.' She paused. 'He said to me when he put it there that he thought it looked like Frances, except that Frances is more beautiful and sad.'

Walter turned to the carving poised on the stand and he heard Helmina withdraw behind him, her step deferential, easing the way for him in her timid selflessness, leaving him a moment with his thoughts. He looked at the figure then, slim and straight, the head inclined towards the babe. He did not see it though. He gazed beyond it at its shadow cast against the corner of the wall: a presence at its side.

When he returned to her, closing the chapel door behind him, she said, the tears still thronging in her throat, but her voice steady and low, 'Won't you ever come back to St Matthias?'

'I'm on the way to Grahamstown to say goodbye to the Bishop. I sent in my resignation some weeks ago.'

'Are you leaving?' And the sudden movement of her eyes belied her calm.

'I'm taking the steamer from Port Elizabeth next Friday.'

'To England?'

'Yes, I'm going home to England.'

There was a small silence and he could hear the leaves of the trees outside lapping at the wind. She was having difficulty again and her face was turned from him.

As if he had divined her thoughts, Walter rose and took his hat and said, his hand briefly on her shoulder, 'It has always worried me that our goodbye was so inadequate. I'd like to think you didn't judge me harshly for it.'

She shook her head, unable to speak.

413

He said then what he had meant to say and never had, 'I'm sorry. At the time it seemed that there was nothing else that I could do. It was unforgivable of me.'

She looked up at him and her eyes found his a moment. 'You are missed,' she said, then she rose and took up the tea-tray and turned to the kitchen door and set her small shoulders and he heard her busy about the sink. He watched her from the step: if he could have put his dreams aside as quietly and as acceptingly as she and offered himself to his work the way she had done! There was heart and valour in Helmina Smythe indeed!

Helmina wrung out the dishcloth and hung it across the basin and she turned to him briskly and said, 'They should be back any minute. Leave your bags here and let me take you to the house. Father Charles has been fretting about whether you had received the telegram Benedict sent. He'll be so relieved to see you.'

She led him up to the Farboroughs' house and into the living-room to wait for Father Charles and Emily. She touched his arm briefly and withdrew, saying, 'I will go and prepare tea for them all and something to eat. I know Victor will be impatient to go out and search as soon as he arrives, but I doubt that he has had either a decent meal or any sleep since he left Cape Town.'

She was gone and Walter stood and looked about the room, waiting at its threshold as if he was intruding by going further. There, the old familiar sofa, and there the Bible that Father Charles used nightly at the family prayers, and there the vase that had its discarded mate in Mzantsi's little house, and there the wax fruit that stood on the sideboard and the fireplace with the logs laid in readiness and the cabinet in which Emily Farborough kept her family china and her posset cups. There the photographs in the silver frames: Frances, young and grave, with her hands in her lap and her solemn eyes; Victor; Crispin. And there the piano. He had not seen a piano since he had left this house and he had not played on one since he had played the Corelli: if he turned she might be sitting by the chair on the low stool with her hair caught at her nape in its velvet ribbon and her fingers linked about her knees.

He was still standing there when he heard the trap arrive. He went to the window and watched it draw up at the porch. He saw the frailty in Father Charles as he climbed down and the smallness of Emily, her hair much greyer than he remembered and no familiar briskness in her movements, no alertness in the way she looked up at the steps but as if it had become an effort to negotiate them.

And Victor.

In his uniform and his boots, he was leaner, broader-shouldered than before, his face honed by months on campaign. No more a boy. Seeing him, Walter wanted to retreat, feeling his own slightness and shabbiness. Then he took his hat from the mantel, impatient with himself, and he went to the door to greet them. The reception from Father Charles and Emily Farborough swept aside any notions of inadequacy.

Father Charles reached for Walter's hand as if stretching out across a gulf and Emily put her arm in his, drawing him to her. 'Thank you,' she said. 'I never doubted that if you had received our message, you'd come.'

And then it was his turn to acknowledge Victor and he looked up at him and Victor shook his hand and said, 'Mr Brownley.' That the eyes should meet and before they have looked, retreat in haste from the thing that they might see.

'I am at your disposal,' Walter said. 'For whatever needs to be done.'

'Thank you.' Victor turned to Father Charles. 'I would like to get the mission boys together at once so we can plan the search properly.'

'Most of them are out at the edge of the Pirie Bush, waiting for you with Kobus,' Father Charles said. 'I sent them ahead this morning. I told Benedict to ride out with them and then return so we would know exactly where to find them. He should be back by now and ready to direct you. I gave him the mare and told him to saddle Hector. The police will be arriving as soon as the sergeant and some of the men can be spared, but you may start without them. I shall take the cart with Mzantsi and drive it as far as I can along the track, in case you should need it.' He hesitated then, fighting to hold his words steady. 'Have you a horse, Brownley?'

'Yes.'

'Would you ride with Victor and Benedict then?'

And so it was arranged and Walter left Victor to a hasty tea and went in search of Benedict.

He found him in the printing-room. He had seen the mare tethered outside and he walked up and stood a moment in the doorway. Benedict was seated at the table, scanning proofs. Suddenly, as if he had sensed a presence, he turned.

'Benedict.'

Benedict pushed back his chair and returned the greeting with warmth but with a weariness as if, in facing each other here in the printing-room, they were acknowledging some moment of defeat. Or predestination.

Walter scanned his face. 'It is so good to see you again and our dear old printing-room. How are you, Benedict?'

'Black in my heart,' Benedict said and his eyes shifting to the yard beyond the door where he could see Victor walking up from the house. He turned back to the table, moved the papers around.

'Crispin?' Walter said.

'All of them. And much more.'

'Miss Smythe told me a little about Tom and Reuben and Sonwabo.' They stood in silence a moment, remembering, unheeding of Victor's approach. 'And now, what of Crispin? Did he speak to you?' Walter said.

Benedict nodded. 'He spoke.'

'Miss Smythe fears he has gone deliberately . . . She is sure he is dead.'

'Miss Smythe sometimes reads a heart better than any,' Benedict said. 'Especially Crispin's.'

'Do you think she is right?'

'Yes. I think she is right.'

'The devil take her.' Both Benedict and Walter turned, startled. Victor stood in the doorway. 'I hope you have said nothing like this to Mrs Farborough. It's preposterous nonsense, an old spinster's superstition.'

'You did not see him,' Benedict said. 'You did not see the sickness in his heart when he came from Johannesburg, but I did. And I know that there are places where a man may go

416

before he dies where other men have never been. I saw it in his eyes. That is why I think that she is right.'

'Why on earth would he kill himself? What for?' Victor in retreat: such ideas were inadmissible.

'Tom and Reuben died.'

'For God's sake, I know all that,' Victor said. 'I've heard nothing else on the way back from The Hoek.' He searched for words to still his own confusion. 'It was rotten luck and an iniquitous business but I shall make sure that there's a full enquiry into the circumstances when I get back to Johannesburg.' He cast about. 'Despite that, it doesn't follow that Crispin should run off just because they're dead or because of how they died, tragic though I know it was.'

'They were killed at a station trying to get home. Unarmed men, harming no one,' Benedict said, overriding Victor's voice, continuing inexorably, emphasising every word as if he had rehearsed them for this moment. 'And were you told that they were shot by British soldiers, acting on information from a man from the Native Affairs Department and a mine manager?' He paused. 'Father Charles and Mrs Farborough do not know it all. Crispin did not tell them. But he told me.'

Victor stared at Benedict.

'They were brave men, those Basotho,' Benedict said. 'They were brave to do that thing and to defy British soldiers. And when Crispin saw Tom and Reuben among the dead, with nothing but their old bag from St Matthias and a branch from an *mphafa* tree that they were bringing home for their brother Sonwabo, he brought the pieces here and he went with me to Pumani's homestead and he laid those branches down at his door and he said, "Here are your sons Tom and Reuben and I have brought a third, because I have not found Sonwabo. When I went to the jail where he had been, they said none should come in search of a sodomite for such filth deserves to die and needs no burial and no friends." That too is what the missionary said to Crispin. And after that Crispin could not look in that man's face for anger at his words and could not be his friend nor go with him to preach in compounds.'

'Why didn't he tell his father this?' Victor said.

'How can you tell these things that have taken your own belief and killed it like a python strangling a goat, and show it to a man whose life depends on Faith? He might as well have taken an axe and chopped down the cross on the altar in the church or struck it into the heart of Father Charles. So,' Benedict paused, 'Crispin came to me and he said, "Benedict, I have killed three men. I have killed Tom and Reuben and I have failed Sonwabo Pumani. What price must I pay for that?" I told him that his father would tell him to pray, for then – if there is indeed guilt – God would take it on Himself and release him. But that is not the way with Crispin. He does not give his burdens to others. He said to me, "All our lives we have played games with each other. We have been soldiers and we have been priests and we have dug gold out of the earth. But that's over. Now we are men, we know it is no longer a game and we will have to decide how to end it." And he went away and I did not see him again.'

'Surely you don't blame him for this?' Victor looked at him and a frown had closed in to mask the disquiet.

'Blame him?' Benedict gazed back steadily. 'No, I do not blame Crispin. Some men would say it is fate, some accident, some bad luck. Some would even say it was *umthakathi*. Only God has the power to lay blame. Perhaps He might blame you.'

Victor stared at him. 'Blame me?'

'So many events,' Benedict said. 'To start with, the cattle advances.'

Walter saw the blood rising in Victor's face. 'Who told you that?'

'Mr Klaus Otto. It was clear to me that you had sent him to recruit me as a runner, even though he did not give your name. It was easy to guess who was behind the cattle advances. Nor did he deny it when I asked him.' He glanced at Victor and away. 'You take me for a fool because I am black and dependent and think I cannot see the truth behind these things? Perhaps you do not even know the truth yourself. You have the power to act without much thought and still achieve the things that you desire. That is your strength, but it will trap you and you will pay for it one day.'

'I do not take you for a fool or I would never have sent Klaus Otto to you. I believed you would be glad of the opportunity to earn yourself some independence. I shan't be so misguided again. I should have remembered your confounded insolence.' Victor's voice was cold and quiet: he was mustering an armoury against the rising tide of doubt. 'What have the cattle advances to do with Tom and Reuben's death, tell me that? Every man who recruits successfully, recruits with cattle or cash advances. I did not shoot the miners at the station and I would have had the official arrested who sent for the army. How dare you suggest that I had any hand in it.'

'It is not what you do, it is what you fail to do, that has always made you different from Crispin. That is why he has been somewhere out there on his own, looking God in the eye, and you are here.'

Benedict went to the window of the printing-room and gestured at the pasture beyond the church. 'Look, there are Kobus's cattle. How Kobus loved those cattle until they took his sons! Now he is running like a man with a swarm of bees in his head, in confusion and shame, crying out for help from his shades. If he cannot hear them speak then he will sit in the church and he will say prayers that he does not understand and he will weep for his sons and never know if he failed them or not. He knows that he has been duped but he cannot say exactly why.'

Benedict turned to Victor and he said, 'We are all expendable to each other, no matter what we say. You will go from here and I will go as well and perhaps we will return some time and we will remember the games we used to play and give some thoughts to each other and to the ones who are dead, resurrecting them just for a moment, and then we will go away and think of other things.' Benedict took a step towards the printing-table and leaned across and picked up a newspaper lying there. He held it out. 'I am not just talking of us here at St Matthias. There are men like Soga and Rubusana who see, who know, that when you have finished this war of yours and have raised your flag all over this country and brought it to the glory of your Empire – the one that we, as black men, are supposed to revere for having bestowed on

419

us an education, faith, prosperity and all the other high-sounding gifts – that you will sell us out – perhaps against the advance of metaphorical cattle – and say it is expedient. Political, economic, moral expedience – call it what you like. You will sacrifice our rights in order to secure your peace with the Boers and shrug us off and find some expedience to pin it on.' He paused. 'It is for this expedience that men like Tom and Reuben and Sonwabo Pumani are dead. There will be thousands like them in the time to come.'

Victor looked at him and then he looked away and the sweat was creeping all along the edges of his hair. He said to fill the silence, his voice flat and quiet, 'I am riding up to the Pirie Bush. I believe you and Mr Brownley have been asked to accompany me, but I am going now and if you wish to follow you may suit yourselves.' And Victor pulled open the door and went outside alone. Following, Walter saw him untether Hector from the hitching-post, mount and spur the horse away, goading Hector past the place in the road where he usually balked, riding him as if pursued.

Chapter Twenty-Eight

The Pirie Bush. Ravines and slopes and forests, deep with shadow and caves set in among the broken rock-faces and high above, far, far beyond the crowns of the trees, a distant sky and a pale sun. Victor had seen the mission workers sitting around a small fire, waiting, but he had taken another route and gone alone, forcing Hector up along small paths that criss-crossed the edges of the forest where wood-gatherers and hunters came. At last the footpaths dwindled in the undergrowth and he tethered Hector, marking where he was and took his gun, slinging it on his shoulder. Despite the cool dampness of the shade, he was drenched with sweat and flies hovered at his face. He brushed them away, cursing them, his voice breaking in his throat. He thrust saplings and low-growing plants aside, crushing them underfoot.

He worked his way up the slope until he came to a clearing and he stopped and wiped his forehead on his sleeve and looked around, unable to decide on a direction, realising that when they'd come here as boys, even little more than a year ago, it had always been he who had led, he who had decided what ravine to take, what outcrop to explore, never Crispin. If Crispin had led, perhaps now he would have had some notion of where to go. He stood like a man whose memory has deserted him in familiar surroundings, leaving him with no idea of how to proceed.

Aimlessly he went from swelling shoulder to swelling shoulder, blundering through the undergrowth and the fallen boulders. Alone. And afraid. Benedict's words hovered in his thoughts: 'It is what you fail to do that has always made you different from Crispin. That is why he is out there somewhere on his own, looking God in the eye, and you are here . . .'

Benedict was wrong. He *was* looking God in the eye and he could not bear the fire of that scrutiny.

He went on down a kloof, hardly aware of the bush about him for it was he – not Crispin – who was the hunted in this place. It was as if he could hear footsteps at his heel. He stopped, fighting for breath. Water trickled down the rocks, broadening into a stream, flanked by flat river stones. He stretched out on one of these to drink. He turned on his back then and lay a moment in the great, breathless silence with his face to the sky, his arms flung out, exposed to the Gaze-of-God. And Victor knew, that moment, what Crispin must have felt: the abyss glimpsed, the darkness closing in, and he struggled up, drawing his limbs in as if they were an armour and he stood, shaken. 'Crispin!' He shouted. 'Crispin!' And the echoes ringing and the trees aloof and heedless. He retrieved his gun. Almost running, he went back the way he had come. He would rather have faced the fire at Elandslaagte again, the exploding shells, the bodies of his comrades flung among the rocks, the screaming horses, than stand alone in the silence of that kloof under the Eye-of-God.

He climbed an outcrop, his concentration fixed to every step and foothold in the stone. Sweat stung his eyes, his breath was ragged, his shirt ripped at the sleeve. He reached the summit and he scanned the bush around. Way, way below him he could see the string of men winding up towards the edges of the forest, Benedict and Walter Brownley leading them. A group of policemen were tethering their horses to a stump beside the track where the mission cart stood. He could see, even at that distance, the small, white gleam of Father Charles's helmet and Mzantsi unharnessing the mules. He whistled but there was no response. They were too far away. He loaded his gun and raised it, sending a single shot off into the still air. The men making for the edge of the forest stopped. Victor laid down his gun and waved both his arms. Benedict responded and Victor clambered down the rock, working his way back towards them.

It had been six days since Crispin had gone and the wind and small wild feet had sent away the signs of his passing. Benedict kept his eyes to the path as he walked, searching for footprints, crushed leaves, broken stems. If Tom and Reuben and Sonwabo had been there, they would have found him. They could read a spoor as if it were a book, directions clearly printed. They would have known the hidden glades where the shades of warriors were gathered and the places where a man might go to inspect the thoughts of his heart. Benedict stopped, abruptly.

Inspect the thoughts of his heart . . .

He had not remembered. He had not recalled it until now, standing there in the gloom of that forest as he had once stood in the forest at Mbokothwe, the day he and Crispin and Walter Brownley had searched for the Reverend Brompton. They had gone together and they had stood in silence after the sound of shots had died away and they had sung a hymn, beckoning Brompton forth from his lair: 'Abide with me, fast falls the eventide; the darkness deepens, Lord with me abide . . .'

No – no song would bring Crispin out. He had gone in silence, not wishing to be found, not driven from them – as Brompton was – but withdrawing from them, withdrawing his thoughts from the closeness of them, closing himself away from them, lest he falter. He had gone, taking only his gun and this burden of the heart, unable to separate himself from the shades that he had brought with him all those days and nights from that distant station where Tom and Reuben Pumani had died.

What would he have done in Crispin's place? Where would he have gone? And he remembered how he had stood at the depression in the ground in the forest at Mbokothwe, where the *isivivane* cairn was made at its edge, and tried to expunge the little burdens of his own heart and offer them up to whatever Presence waited in the shadows to receive them. How small they seemed now. But he remembered it and he remembered too how he and Crispin had each taken a stone and laid it on the *isivivane* cairn and said, '*Qamata, ndiphe amandla*' – God give strength to me – and then how Crispin had remained behind, hanging back as he'd walked on, to stand a moment at the edge of the hollow in some reverie of his own.

Benedict could see Victor waiting at the curve in the path ahead. Behind, he could hear Walter Brownley's steady steps and the voices of the beaters and the police sergeant, directing his men. He reached Victor and he said, 'Somewhere here there will be a place where men go to confess the sorrows of their hearts. Perhaps you know of these places yourself? They are ancient things, holes dug in the earth. Crispin saw one with me at Mbokothwe and we stood there a long time together and he placed a stone on an *isivivane* cairn with me. It is where one makes peace with the shades and with God. It is such a place that we must find.'

'Crispin is a Christian,' said Victor brusquely, as if he did not dare explore the words that Benedict had said. He scanned the bush, searching for a new strategy. 'Why would he hope for reconciliation with the shades? What shades, anyway? He will not find his grandfathers here.' He whistled, summoning the stragglers. 'You boys form groups of three.' He spoke in Xhosa. 'We will work up each ravine, going from right to left and then spread out across each ridge which links them.' And in English, 'Mr Brownley, this will be a strenuous climb, perhaps you should go along the lower path, at the edge of the trees, and join up with Mr Farborough's trap, making a loop back towards the drift.' Walter inclined his head, acquiescent. It was not the time to argue. 'Sergeant, will you and your men come with me?' Victor had taken command but he'd aligned himself, moving closer to the policemen, needing strangers then – those who would not see his fear – secure with order and precision.

'You are wasting your time because I am sure I am right,' said Benedict quietly. 'I was at Mbokothwe with him.'

Victor looked at him and the hesitation – and retreat – were there in his eyes. He said, 'I will follow my plan. You may follow yours. You will know where to find me' – he pointed – 'I will be moving consistently in that direction.' He gestured to the gathering to follow, adding – an afterthought – 'You can take one of the boys with you, if you wish.'

'Mr Brownley will come with me. He knows these places. He has seen them too.'

Victor gazed a moment at the ground and then glanced from Benedict to Walter. He said, 'Take my gun. If you have more success than us, fire a shot so we can find you. The sergeant will do the same if we discover Crispin.'

Benedict took the gun, checked the breech. One bullet. He nodded. Victor stepped back and Benedict turned down into the lower path.

424

Victor did not raise his eyes to Walter as he passed. Walter almost paused beside him, put out his hand to touch his arm – a gesture in recognition of what he saw in his face. But Victor had turned abruptly from him, with an order to the men to follow. And he was gone.

It was Benedict who found him. A glade – as he had guessed – not far in, the trees more spare and the undergrowth more open, a place where cattle might have strayed to rest in shadow from the midday sun, yet hidden by a sudden slope from travellers on the path above. A sanctuary it was, facing out towards the gentle ridge of the Kaboosie, a company of old grey rocks surrounding it, like ancient watchers lost in vigil. There they found the cairn. There they found the leafy hollow in the ground, and all around the denser bush rising out and up towards the higher land.

It was Benedict who heard the flies long before they reached the clearing. Walter saw him stop ahead, stand alert, his head inclined. Walter stood with him, searching for a sound and then he heard them too, sensing them minutely: the low murmur of incessant feasting, a hum that fell and rose and sank again to silence, secret from the careless ear.

They went together, slowly then, afraid to blunder in.

The cairn. The hollow. The rock. A small plant, a flower, star-pale and fragile, anchored by a root-hair high up on its face. And the flies – dancing, dancing – in its shade.

Crispin lay in the leaf-mould, his rifle at his side, half of his chest blown away. Walter and Benedict stood in silence, a little wind tugging at the tree-tops high above.

Walter went to him. He stooped to him and the aura of flies lifted and swayed and settled in again.

Walter did not flinch from touching him. He laid his hand on Crispin's forehead and he blessed him quietly and turned to Benedict.

Without speaking, Benedict picked up a small stone from the ground and walked to the traveller's cairn and stood beside it. There, on the top, another stone had been newly placed. He touched it, saying, 'This is Crispin's.' And then he raised his eyes to the trees and the old rocks and the mountain far beyond and brought them back to rest on Crispin and he said in Xhosa as if he were addressing God on his behalf, 'May God and the shades of our fathers walk with us in our hour of need,' and he spat on the stone in his hand and placed it beside the other on the cairn. '*Qamata, siphe amandla*' – God give strength to us. Then he slipped back the safety-catch on Victor's gun and raised it to his shoulder, setting the sights at the even blue of the sky. And fired.

In the morning, just before the early dawn had faded in the rising light, Benedict had gone. Unobtrusively he went, without farewell. He had said what he had had to say beside the *isivivane* cairn and no further words were needed. Walter Brownley had been there with him and he would be his witness. There would be no lamentations, no recriminations: Walter Brownley would speak for him and Father Charles would hear the words in wisdom and in love. He knew that too.

He let himself quietly out of Mzantsi's house, carrying his bag, and he went to the printing-room. It had been his refuge, the place where he had learned his skill and found his talent: a gift derived from the hand of unknown shades. He took a piece of paper and he wrote:

> I have gone and wherever I have gone,
> I will hold this place in my thoughts
> and my remembrance.
> It was the womb in which I was conceived,
> in which my spirit has been moulded and to which
> my heart will return, no matter what the exile.
> But now I must be born. I must go forth alone.
> And if I should return, I will return in freedom.
> For without that freedom, I can never call myself
> a man.

And he drew the hat from his head: the little hat that he had always worn, with the feather of a crane sewn in its brim, and he laid it on the table with the words that he had written and he closed the door behind him. Then he walked away. He reached the gate of St Matthias Mission, securing it with a careful hand. And the miles were light before his feet: somewhere far beyond the furthest hill, the sister of Sonwabo Pumani would be waiting for his coming. As she had promised.

It was Walter who discovered that he had gone. Directed by Emily Farborough to prepare the church for the funeral service with Helmina and Benedict's help, he went in search of him, asking anyone he passed if they had seen him. None had.

Thinking he might find him in the carpentry shop where Mzantsi and Mr Groenewald were preparing a stand for the coffin, he hurried across the yard. Near the church the gravediggers worked where the ground was hard and flinty beneath the oak. They dug with a spare song between them, heaving the dark brown soil, striking roots and rocks. They looked up as Walter passed, shook their heads at his enquiry, resting on their shovels, sharing an enamel beaker of sour porridge between them. No, they had not seen Benedict Matiwane since he had carried Crispin Farborough into the house from the cart the night before.

Walter took the path to the printing-room. He glanced through the window but the room was empty. He knocked at Mzantsi's door but there was no response. He hurried down towards the workshops and found Mzantsi speaking to a group of catechists, newly arrived from the outstations, preparing them to assist with the service. Walter beckoned him outside. 'Do you know where Benedict is?' he said.

'No. I have not seen him. Is he not in the printing-room perhaps? He often leaves the house before sunrise to work with the press and to write. I am so used to his hours I do not notice any more when he comes and goes.'

'No one has seen him,' Walter said. 'He has not been to the house.'

Mzantsi looked at him and his tongue edged along his lip. 'Last night,' he said, and he made a clucking noise deep in his throat, 'when we had brought Mr Crispin from the Pirie Bush, I asked Benedict if he would join with me in prayers but he went to his room and he closed the door. He would not eat and he would not keep me company although I wished to

427

speak of Mr Crispin and to think of him – remembering – and knowing that his mother was sitting with him in the house.' His face puckered. 'It seemed wrong to sleep when Father Charles was watching through the hours.'

Mzantsi stared out across the yard. 'Come,' he said. 'Come with me,' and Walter followed him to his cottage, walking fast, too fast to speak, Mzantsi going ahead as if seized by some conviction. He opened the front door and went inside. 'Benedict?' There was no reply.

Walter followed him to Benedict's room. Beyond the door, Walter could see the bedstead against the wall. The long, bevelled mirror on the wardrobe reflected a dozen bedsteads in its face, diminishing in size. Mzantsi opened this cupboard and peered inside. It was empty. There were neither clothes nor books.

'Gone!' Mzantsi turned to Walter, threads of spittle strung between his lips. 'Gone!'

'He has nowhere to go,' said Walter.

Mzantsi shook his head. 'Gone,' he said. 'This time, yes.' He seemed to stand in some bewilderment, mouthing words. 'Gone. And yet, he never said.'

Mzantsi looked about him, as if gathering in with his eyes all that was familiar and sure. 'He never said,' he repeated, his face crumpling. '*Jesu, Jesu.*'

Walter left Mzantsi standing in the doorway of his house and hurried back towards the printing-room. Surely Benedict would not have abandoned their beloved press so easily, or gone without a word, without a gesture of farewell? He closed the door behind him, standing still to catch his breath.

A chair stood squarely at the editing table beside the press. Walter approached – and yes – there it was. A piece of paper was lying on it. Weighting it was Benedict's hat. Just so, laid beside it with ritual precision. Walter took up the paper and held it to the light at the window and he read the words that Benedict had written, announcing his own exile.

'. . . now I must be born, I must go forth alone. And if I should return, I will return in freedom, for without that freedom I can never call myself a man'.

He stood a long time at the window of that small room, the

428

one-time sanctuary of their work, holding Benedict's message in his hand. Beyond, he could see the sweep of the hillside, red with ironstone. Thunderheads were pushing up above its edge, citadels of silent cloud, heralding the first rains of early spring. Far away and low, he heard the first faint thunder.

He turned from the window and looked at the old Albion standing in the middle of the floor, lovingly polished by Benedict. What would become of it, brought from Mbokothwe, dragged from the wilderness to wheeze and clank and grind? It had given Benedict a voice he did not know he had. From it had come articles and poems, stories and reviews that had been published and acclaimed. It had given him the first glimpse of the freedom that he sought.

Dear old press. Walter touched its sides, almost a caress. How he had loved it too. Who would work it now? Who would feed it oil and rub its head with a soft, unabrasive cloth and coax the print together on the page? Would it be discarded, left to rust, abandoned as it had been once at Mbokothwe?

Wearily Walter pulled out the chair. He felt for his pipe but he left it unlit on the table.

Frances.

She had come here sometimes, bringing him tea and a plate of buttered bread, standing in the doorway, saying teasingly, 'You and your old machine, Mr Plotz! Are you writing a book that you spend so long in here in secret?'

And there had been the time when she had waited, tremulous, and said, 'Your tea will be cold if you do not drink it,' and he had turned his back on her, too afraid to ask her what was wrong, and knowing she was waiting for a word to beckon her to him.

Oh, Helmina had been right when she had said that diffidence and silence could be cruel! Never to have said the things he should have said! Never to have turned to her and told her what he felt! In all that time he'd kept his silences – in diffidence and fear.

He sat a long time in the printing-room, heedless of hunger or discomfort, heedless of the traps and carts arriving at the gate, heedless of the sounds of hooves or voices as the yard filled with people from the distant outstations and The Hoek. Heedless of the rising wind.

He was roused by the sound of hurrying feet, someone striding up the path towards the door. It was thrust open hastily by Victor. He was dressed in full uniform. 'Mr Brownley?' Walter turned. 'We've been scouring the place for you.'

'I'm sorry.' Walter rose. 'I was preoccupied with my own goodbyes.'

'Mzantsi says Benedict has gone.'

Walter picked up the paper from the table and held it out to Victor. Victor read it and his face seemed to move. He did not look at Walter. He stood, his head bent to the letter in his hand, marshalling composure, tutored to reveal nothing. He looked up at last and said, 'Shall we go?'

All the mission people were gathered in the church. All, but Benedict Matiwane. The old men who had dug the grave and the cleaners and the washerwomen, the men from the small foundry and the clerk from the post office. The teachers and the nuns from the girls' boarding-house. The young and the old. The orphans and apprentices.

Emily Farborough and Victor Drake sat apart, Helmina just beyond. Near them, with a deferential space, were Harold Stanbridge, Mr Erskine the magistrate, the Nettletons, the Blacklocks and the Butlers, Dr Fraser and his wife, their daughters, and the minister from the Lutheran church. Further back, the constable and the ladies from the Benevolent Society and the postmaster. Behind, the faithful and the tribesmen of the mission, throng on throng.

The coffin, borne in with the procession, was placed before the chancel steps. Helmina had made a bower of irises and daisies and ferns at the base of its stand. On top lay a small bunch of wild flowers that she had gathered alone. At its head, the flames burning true, three candles stood side by side. For Tom. For Reuben. For Sonwabo.

Valiantly Father Charles led the service, asking that Walter attend him closely. He seemed to draw strength from him and, vigilant, Walter kept watch at his side.

'Neither death, nor life, nor angels, nor principalities, nor powers, nor things present, nor things to come, nor height, nor depth, nor any other creature, shall be able to separate us from the love of God, which is in Christ Jesus our Lord . . .'

As Father Charles spoke and Mzantsi repeated what he said in Xhosa, Walter let his eyes rest on the mourners in the first pew. Emily Farborough remained quite still and straight, tranced, her head turned slightly towards the coffin, her fingers curled across the edge of the prayer-book which remained unopened in her lap. What titanic will had made such calm, he could not guess. It was humbling to see.

Beside her was Victor. He loomed above her, the great squareness of his shoulders in his military regalia, the patrician fineness of his face. Manhood's triumph. How often, when he'd contemplated Victor, the phrase had come to Walter's mind: see the conquering hero comes! Sound the trumpets, beat the drums! Perhaps such a presence was Victor's burden: the expectations of him, much too great to carry. As he watched, Walter saw Victor put out his hand. He saw him place it tentatively in Emily's, not giving comfort, but seeking it himself. Such a gesture Walter had not seen before, could never have imagined. He turned from him in sudden compassion. Strange, that the first prayer that he wished to say – and which he uttered now – should be for Victor. And when he raised his head, Victor had been looking at him and their eyes had met in quietness.

Mzantsi sang a note, a note taken up here and there, swelling, until all the congregation held their chord. Then the dear, the familiar words of 'All Creatures of our God and King', Crispin's favourite hymn, filled the church. Walter did not sing. He listened. He had heard this hymn so often sung by parish choirs at home: good, hearty voices, true sopranos, vigorous baritones. Here, under Mzantsi's hands, beckoning forth the falling notes of the hallelujahs, it became a lullaby, a lament. Somewhere in the hymn, somewhere in its trailing cadences, was the shadow of the great, brooding forest, the emptiness of windswept hillsides. Somewhere within the predictable Protestant harmonies, was the breath of something else that hovered like a shadow beneath the words.

As the last notes fell away and Charles Farborough turned

431

to the congregation to continue with the burial service for his son, a summer storm broke with its own wild orchestrations beyond the dim sanctuary of the church's walls. There was a great stillness among the mourners as they waited for Father Charles to speak but before he began, he paused to listen to the beating rain, the sounding of the thunder way across the Amatolas. These were the things that Crispin Farborough had understood. Wind and storm and the smell of rain-washed ironstone and skies wide and wild with heat or cloud.

Ah, Crispin. To lie closed in the earth so soon, away from the sight of the sun.

Chapter Twenty-Nine

And so the time had come to go. Walter shared a last meal with the Farboroughs and spent the evening with them in their living-room. At nine o'clock Helmina had drawn the tea-table nearer the hearth and closed the shutters against the night as she had done so many times before.

Emily sat beside the fire, looking at the flames, her hands resting on the arms of her chair. Father Charles was opposite, his eyes closed wearily. He had had no sleep in days. The old head drooped every now and then, startling him awake, and he would gaze about and then subside once more.

Walter watched Helmina pour the tea, a ritual shared since that distant afternoon when he had first arrived at St Matthias. But this time there were empty places at the table: no Crispin with his hair awry, eating bread and butter and licking his fingers secretly; no Frances peeping at him brazenly, deciding that he resembled Kobus's bush goats; no Benedict standing at the porch with a catch of eels and a smile of pride.

Victor came in from the stables and Father Charles roused himself and without looking up said, 'Is that you, Victor?'

'Uncle Charles?'

'There you are. Sit now and have tea. We haven't spoken of your plans yet but I believe you have been asked to help reconstitute the Government Native Labour Bureau? A feather in your cap,' and he looked up at Victor and smiled wearily. 'Mr Stanbridge knows all your doings. He detained me in The Hoek once for hours describing your success with mine disturbances. It is strange how a man will find his calling. I remember when we sat in this room and spoke of mining and recruiting. I never thought what it might mean.'

Victor did not reply. He drank his tea, his eyes on the rug, and Father Charles did not lead the conversation further. That had all been said and laid aside. Tom and Reuben and Sonwabo would be left in peace that night. He said, 'Are you going straight to Johannesburg from here?'

'To Grahamstown,' said Victor and he had cleared his throat, as if his words had stuck.

'A telegram was so harsh a way to tell her about Crispin,' Father Charles said tiredly. 'So cold. So incomplete. But what else could we do? Will you explain it gently, Victor? And, one day, will you bring her home? Even for an hour if she will not stay longer. I'm an old man and desolate without her.' He put his hand to his eyes and rubbed them, drawing them together and watching the fire intently and, taking up the poker, leaning forward to adjust a log, his breathing heavy.

In the silence Helmina lifted the milk jug and put it down and turned the teapot handle and set the teaspoons straight on the saucers and Victor said to Walter, 'How are you getting to Town?'

'I'll ride in, sell my horse and take the first train to Grahamstown and the coast. I don't wish to be too late to catch the steamer in Port Elizabeth. I can't afford to delay a moment.'

'Boggis has been a fine old horse,' said Father Charles from the depths of his chair. 'I remember the day you brought him home. He looked such a mule but it didn't take him long to acquire a dignified air. I used to laugh sometimes seeing you go out and he trotting as if he were imitating Hector.'

'I'm a Judas to sell him,' said Walter. 'I shan't know how to look the old man in the eye when I say goodbye to him. I fear it will break my heart.'

'Oh, Mr Brownley, you can't sell Boggis!' Helmina exclaimed in dismay. 'All those times he took me up to teach at the little school and such a faithful companion to you.'

Walter said, as though he stood accused, 'I can't take him with me. I would far rather leave him here with you than have to sell him to a stranger. But I have no way of getting to King William's Town without him and I dare not miss the train.'

'Klaus Otto was at the funeral,' said Victor.

'I saw him,' said Walter, 'but we had no opportunity to talk.'

'I spoke to him.' Victor looked down at his hands and then smoothed back his hair from his brow with a quick, impulsive gesture. 'He's outspanned at The Hoek tonight and going to King William's Town tomorrow.' He glanced at Walter. 'I'm sure he'd be glad to take you. If you ride to The Hoek in the morning, you can leave the horse at Nettleton's. I have a telegram to send and I'll fetch him on the way. I'll be glad to buy him from you and keep him stabled here. Miss Smythe can ride him, she seems to have such a fancy for him.' And he glanced at Helmina and smiled fleetingly.

'I need no payment for Boggis if he's to stay here,' said Walter and he looked at Helmina's flushed face. 'It would offend his so-called dignity entirely if he were bartered! Miss Smythe would certainly ensure he doesn't back-slide into muledom again and she could use him in the cart to take the boys and girls on outings!'

'You are both teasing me!' said Helmina.

'Not at all,' said Victor. 'It's a relief to have a happy idea for once.'

'And I would leave with an easy mind knowing my old friend was with you,' said Walter and he put his hand out to Helmina and took hers a moment and squeezed her fingers and saw the colour fly about her cheeks.

'More tea?' she said, all but bolting from her chair and taking the pot to fill it in the kitchen.

Suddenly Emily Farborough said, still looking at the fire, and not turning her head, 'Hearing you talk, it is very strange to me to believe you'd choose to leave, Mr Brownley. Why are you really going?'

Walter put his cup on the table with care, feeling Victor's eyes. 'I believe,' he said, choosing his words, 'that I do not have a vocation.' There was a silence. Emily was waiting. 'And I'm homesick, Mrs Farborough,' and as he said it, it was not Daisy's drawing-room in Alton that rose in his mind's eye, but the small deserted house at Mbokothwe with its crooked pair of chairs at either side of the fireplace and its dung floor. He was appalled.

'We heard from the Bishop what you had achieved,' Emily said and, despite the exhaustion, there was something of the old asperity in her voice. 'We know what you did here. It seems a wicked waste.'

'I'm sorry.' It was all he could say. And still he could feel Victor's eyes on him.

'My dear,' Father Charles put out his hand to his wife, reaching across and inclining his grey head to hers. 'What he has achieved is a foundation of rock for his successor. It is not for us to question a man's vocation.' And he patted her hand and he said, as if to himself, 'But I never thought I'd wish a man proved wrong as much as he.' He turned and regarded Walter. 'Nor have I ever wished a curate to the devil like I have the unfortunate young man they are sending me next month!' He sighed again. 'To have had my friends around me . . .' and he retained Emily's hand, chafing the fingers in his. 'That would have been a blessing indeed.'

The logs were shifting in the grate, easing themselves and settling, the embers falling. Walter rested his eyes on the piano and let his gaze move up slowly to the picture of Frances standing on its top.

Absorbed, Walter looked at it and then he glanced across at Victor and he knew that Victor had been watching him and had followed his gaze. Victor's eyes flickered away from his and Walter saw a small movement in his temple as though he had unlocked his jaw and locked it once again, to keep the words inside.

Oh, Victor knew why he had gone from Mbokothwe. Victor knew!

Then Father Charles rose and he said, 'Let us say our prayers and go and rest.'

Helmina went for the Bible but he put it aside and said, 'We will say the Lord's Prayer and the twenty-third Psalm tonight. We will say them for our mission lads that we have lost and we will say them for Crispin and for ourselves,' and he had bowed his head and they had gathered round him. Dear old man, with Emily beside him and the firelight soft about the room and the words to sustain them all. When he had finished he blessed them, 'In the Name of the Father and of the Son and of the Holy Spirit', and embraced them, each in turn.

As Walter took his leave to go to his bed in the curate's lodge, Emily said, 'Mr Brownley, even if it should make me

436

weep again, will you play that piece you played one night just before you left us? I remember Frances asked for it . . . and Crispin was here, carving his wood.' She glanced at Father Charles, summoning strength from him. 'Just a phrase or two.'

So Walter sat at the piano and he opened the lid and he looked again at the pictures on the piano top as if he were addressing them: at Victor in his colours cap and blazer; at Crispin with his gun, with life and joy and gladness in his face; at Frances with her solemn eyes.

And so to the Corelli. Once again.

Last partings. All the mission workers came to see him off. Kobus stood in the yard without his broom, a gaunt man in his greatcoat, and the old men gathered near, heads turning as one to follow Walter's progress down towards the stable and a murmur between them. Groenewald, the carpenter, raised his hat and Nowasha brought a package of cold meat and bread for the journey.

The herders and the washerwomen and the stablehands and the sweepers were all there and, as if they too were waiting in farewell, the familiar places seemed to salute him: Mzantsi's little cottage and the school pegged out in newness on the hill and the workshops and the forge. He turned towards the printing-room. The door was closed and bolted. He paused, then slowly he put his hat on his head and walked towards the church. It stood with the light on its windows and the nests of swallows still sheltered under its eaves. Wanderers they were, migrants, travellers of the great tides of the air, returning undaunted every year to breed.

He let himself into the church through the great double doors and walked up the aisle to the vestry. He went in and stood in the stillness, feeling the pale green light about his feet, a benediction on his face. A silence. A presence in its shadowed space.

He went, not turning back, his footsteps even on the flagging of the floor.

Boggis had been saddled and brought to the front porch. There was Mzantsi, holding the bridle, his watch chain looped across his chest and wiping his eyes sporadically with his handkerchief. Beside him Helmina stood with her hand at Boggis's neck as if she were forging a bond in remembrance of him. To see her there with Boggis and the children waiting for her at the gate in eagerness! He went to her smilingly and kissed her cheek and said, 'I shall think of you and all your little children and dear old Boggis more often than you can imagine.'

On the step, Emily and Father Charles and Victor waited. To each he said goodbye – a small, fierce embrace from Emily, a word of prayer – and he had almost wept to feel the grip of Father Charles's hand, the strong old fingers clasped in his.

Recovering himself, he turned to Victor, his gaze steady, 'Goodbye, Victor,' and he paused but he did not look away. He said, 'Care for her. Love her. Godspeed to both of you.'

And then he went, hearing the voices of the children and the workers raised in song, a hymn to send him out and through the gate and up onto the road beyond.

He rode, and only at the bend, when he was too far for anyone to see, he dismounted and looked back at the old grey church among the trees and the valley and the thread of the Mtwaku and the little homesteads gathered on the hills and the line of the Kaboosie rising up towards the sky. And then he put his face in Boggis's neck and wept. And Boggis stood in patience and looked at him from the corner of his eye with his lip drooping in its own doleful way.

And so Walter had left him too, tethered to the Nettletons' hitching-post, with his nose in a fodder bag, awaiting Victor, and Boggis had watched him with what had seemed to be complacence, chewing slowly as if he – in his old-mule wisdom – divined some Other-Whim-of-God.

Frances rose and drew the curtain aside and looked out at the night and the town beyond. She sat on the window ledge, leaning her head against the cool panes of glass, the musical-box open before her. The telegram from her father lay inside with Walter Brownley's letter. She took it up and held it to the light of the single candle-flame. She knew the words by heart:

Crispin has taken his life in the Pirie Bush.
Devastated by the death of the Pumani boys
in Transvaal. Letter follows.
Our loving prayers and thoughts . . .

Crispin had gone. By his own choice and by his own hand, risking the possibility that there might be no gathering of shades to welcome him but only the void, the inescapable pain of sin and the sentence of an unforgiving God. His Creator – half-heathen and half-mission – fluctuated in a way he never could explain. Now would be the reckoning for his dyadic soul.

Crispin had gone and with him all the games that he and Frances had played – the little rituals that made a sense of life since they were small: fishing with red flannel in the furrows for eels, bird-games by the river, calling in imitation of the neddickies and bulbuls and shrikes. Secret words, affirming their belonging, and Benedict presiding over them as if the union of their childhood could never end.

This day, Crispin would have been offered up in their father's church and buried by the oak, planted by their mother, growing near its walls. The prayers their father would have said would have been a supplication – made in trust – that he would rest in peace. And yet, Frances knew – fiercely she believed it – that Crispin would be laughing somewhere in the hills, in that slow, self-deprecating way that he had always had – he and the hunters of the bushbuck and the hare, roaming free with Tom and Reuben and Sonwabo, the bergwind blowing, off with their hunting sticks: they who, as children, had once been locked in the church by Victor, they who had been soldiers in the mock battles by the river, they who had hunted and sparred in the great *umngeni* joust. Yes, he would be with them now, out beyond the homesteads where the forest climbed the steep ravines, too young, as yet, to be revered as shades, too old still to be shadowless, as little children are who die.

Frances walked about the room, fighting to suppress the unremitting pain that held her. If she could only turn away from this and from herself – standing clenched with all the icons of this house surrounding her – as Crispin had! If she could walk out in the bush, as he had done, and leave behind the things tormenting her! If she could weep, she knew it would relieve the great, burning hurt of its distance. But she could not weep – not in the cold restraint of her room in Victor's mother's house, not so far removed from all that was familiar and loved. She dared not weep for fear that she might loose tumultuous, angry, bitter grief. She knew that it could turn on her – implacably dark – and swamp her.

On Wednesday morning another telegram came. Frances heard the gate swing and click closed but she did not go to see who called, nor answer the knock on the door. Victor's mother opened it herself and she came to the living-room with the envelope in her hand and tore the seal and unfolded the paper, looking up, her eyes moist, 'Victor will be here at twelve.'

Frances took the telegram and she read it:

> The train at twelve. Wednesday.
> Sent with my love. Victor.

Frances folded it and put it on the table. She looked at it a moment, lying there, and then she took it up again and she went upstairs with it and she put it in the musical-box. It belonged there, that strangely worded message . . . sent to you with my love . . . The train at twelve. Wednesday.

It was a quarter to eleven. Frances went to her cupboard and she opened it. She searched among the skirts and blouses, the slight, elegant dresses that Aunt Alice had had made for her. She found her old travelling dress that she had worn on the day that she had come from St Matthias. She took it out and she laid it on the bed. She took her walking boots from her trunk and she took her cape.

She unpinned her hair from its arrangement on the top of her head and she brushed it and tied it back at the nape of her neck. Then she went downstairs.

Aunt Alice said, 'Frances, dearest, you are not meeting Victor like that, are you?' Gently admonishing. 'I have just told the groom to get the trap ready so he can drive us both to the station. The wind is chilly but I'd hoped you'd try the costume Miss White delivered yesterday. I had it in mind especially for his home-coming. You look so pale in that dark cape . . .'

'I won't go in the trap, Aunt Alice. I wish to walk and I want to speak to Victor alone.'

Alice Farborough looked at her and her chin quivered as she spoke. 'You are not yourself, Frances,' she said. 'I know you have had a terrible shock, but you are entirely not yourself. Perhaps I should go to the station alone and leave you here to rest. Victor will be back in no time and everything will be all right.'

'I am myself, Aunt Alice,' Frances said quietly. 'And I will walk all the same.'

She went to the door but she hesitated at it and then she returned swiftly to Alice Farborough standing in the passageway and she reached up and kissed her cheek and laid her fingers on her arm. 'Thank you,' she said. She paused, looking for words and then she went, closing the door behind her and hurrying down the steps.

Frances did not think of what she would say when she saw him. These were things that one could not anticipate: just a word or two, just the trite structure of a sentence to destroy. She doubted she could do it.

And yet she knew she must.

She could not tuck her hand within the crook of his arm and walk along the platform and go home with him and sit in the garden and weep for Crispin and then, when she had dried her tears, she could not take him in and show him how many trunks had been packed for Johannesburg. She could not play the child to exasperate him or to glean his comfort. She could not let him kiss her and surrender to the need to hold and touch and feel. For if she did, she would be a liar and a thief. Taking what he had to give and hiding it away in an empty heart.

Going down the streets into town with the stone pines standing sentinel up on the eastern hill and the church in High Street brooding over wagons in the square, it seemed impossible – walking on a Wednesday morning in early spring, as if on an errand to the post office or the bank – that she was on her way to redirect her life. Her father had said – and she had kept the words in her remembrance: seek the truth and live by it even if it means that you must be alone.

The awesome fear of that.

She'd fought to overcome that fear and she was walking to the station now to conquer it at last. With truth. With love.

And as she went, she noticed each and every thing she passed, as if it were imperative that she remember while she may. She watched a ginger cat on a wall, slit-eyed in the sun, furtively appraising a sparrow. She noticed how the little bell of the Cathedral School in Huntley Street hung at an angle, dangling its rope against the wall. She heard the voices of the children singing in their classroom, hearing their words right to the corner of Bathurst Street. She would remember always what they sung – a small, fugitive refrain, echoing in her mind.

The trudge up the street towards the station made her hot. She took off her cloak and dangled it across her arm, trailing the hem in the dust, and the wind was cool against the damp-ness of her cheeks, flushed from the run. She stood by the waiting-room door and she watched the guard gathering himself to welcome a train and she heard its signal far, far off and her heart beat fast.

There were other people on the platform: a man who looked like a clerk from the Revenue Office and a woman with small children and a group of black men, sitting on bales and waiting with luggage gathered around their feet, and a sweeper on the tracks, looking every now and then along the rails, head cocked and listening.

What would she say?

What would she say when Victor stepped from the train and saw her there? He might be commanding or distant, off-hand or hesitant. He might be humorous or ardent. How lives may turn on such small, prosaic moments.

She could hear the train more clearly and she looked away, letting her eyes follow the opposite slope and rest on the wall of the town's cemetery and the spires of cypress trees beyond.

442

The engine, hauling the carriages, entered the station, heaving with the work of the final gradient, steam pushing fiercely from its sides and wisping up into the air. The doors opened, people got down and luggage was passed from the windows. Frances's throat was dry.

There were soldiers, alighting with the camaraderie of men parting for a time. Frances scanned their faces. No, he was not among them. They looked shabby and older and shorter and less valiant than Victor. Perhaps he had changed his mind and stayed at St Matthias. Perhaps – as he had done before – he would remain away to fuel her anxiety and then arrive unexpectedly to claim her.

The soldiers dispersed. The woman with the children met a man with a large portmanteau and the Revenue clerk was shaking hands with a kindred soul, equally black-suited and drab. There was a group of children, accompanied by a teacher, an old man and woman, looking for baggage, and a porter pushing mail-sacks. No – no Victor. He must have missed the train.

The platform emptied. The sweeper climbed aboard, knocking his broom against the door. Frances turned towards the station steps, the wind tugging and lifting her cape as she stopped to pull it round her shoulders.

There was a man walking down the platform. He carried an old carpet-bag. He stopped to fumble in his pockets. He brought out a pipe and matches and he turned his back to the wind to protect the flame.

Frances stared.

That preoccupation. That stance, and there – the pipe satisfactorily lit. He stood and he looked off up the hill, with the bag at his side and his hat pulled down and the little wreaths of smoke from the pipe bowl, rising round him.

She remained poised, and the wind busy about her. He turned then, as if he had sensed her and he looked in her direction and he took the pipe from his mouth.

He stood. And she stood. Oh, an eternity they stood on that little empty platform with the old train settling in to rest on its tracks.

She ran to him. She ran to him and he pushed his pipe into

his pocket. She ran to him and his hat fell on the platform and his bag was overturned and the sweeper in the train forgot his broom and his dusters and the empty compartments as he peered from a window.

'You came for me,' she said.

'It was you who came for me,' and a smile, mustering his old wryness and looking into her face as if to drown.

'I thought that you had gone,' she said – with tears – but laughing to see his face and his hair standing up where she had knocked his hat off. 'And yet, today, I think I might have waited here for ever till you came.'

And the sweeper, gazing still, watching through the window of the train, made a clicking in his throat, half of disapproval and oblivious of how he stared.

'Will you take me home?' she said, reaching to find his lips again.

'To St Matthias?'

'To Mbokothwe. I want to set your crooked old furniture straight and see to your supper. And besides, you're a danger to yourself.' She pulled away from him and flapped her cloak at him. 'If I weren't here now, you'd have set yourself on fire!'

And Walter glanced down at his jacket pocket where his pipe was smouldering unheeded. He extracted it, laughing, and he retrieved his hat and bag and then he took her by the hand and drew her arm through his and turned her down the platform. In the station yard he stopped suddenly and he said, 'How did you know I was coming on this train?'

She said, looking just beyond him, the salute soft in her words, 'The train at twelve. Wednesday. Sent with my love.'

'From Victor?'

'Yes,' she said. 'From Victor.'

444

READ MORE IN PENGUIN

In every corner of the world, on every subject under the sun, Penguin represents quality and variety – the very best in publishing today.

For complete information about books available from Penguin – including Puffins, Penguin Classics and Arkana – and how to order them, write to us at the appropriate address below. Please note that for copyright reasons the selection of books varies from country to country.

In the United Kingdom: Please write to *Dept. EP, Penguin Books Ltd, Bath Road, Harmondsworth, West Drayton, Middlesex UB7 ODA*

In the United States: Please write to *Consumer Sales, Penguin USA, P.O. Box 999, Dept. 17109, Bergenfield, New Jersey 07621-0120.* VISA and MasterCard holders call 1-800-253-6476 to order Penguin titles

In Canada: Please write to *Penguin Books Canada Ltd, 10 Alcorn Avenue, Suite 300, Toronto, Ontario M4V 3B2*

In Australia: Please write to *Penguin Books Australia Ltd, P.O. Box 257, Ringwood, Victoria 3134*

In New Zealand: Please write to *Penguin Books (NZ) Ltd, Private Bag 102902, North Shore Mail Centre, Auckland 10*

In India: Please write to *Penguin Books India Pvt Ltd, 706 Eros Apartments, 56 Nehru Place, New Delhi 110 019*

In the Netherlands: Please write to *Penguin Books Netherlands bv, Postbus 3507, NL-1001 AH Amsterdam*

In Germany: Please write to *Penguin Books Deutschland GmbH, Metzlerstrasse 26, 60594 Frankfurt am Main*

In Spain: Please write to *Penguin Books S. A., Bravo Murillo 19, 1° B, 28015 Madrid*

In Italy: Please write to *Penguin Italia s.r.l., Via Felice Casati 20, I–20124 Milano*

In France: Please write to *Penguin France S. A., 17 rue Lejeune, F–31000 Toulouse*

In Japan: Please write to *Penguin Books Japan, Ishikiribashi Building, 2–5–4, Suido, Bunkyo-ku, Tokyo 112*

In South Africa: Please write to *Longman Penguin Southern Africa (Pty) Ltd, Private Bag X08, Bertsham 2013*

A choice of fiction in Penguin

THE PENGUIN BOOK OF CONTEMPORARY SOUTH AFRICAN SHORT STORIES
Stephen Gray (editor)

Twenty-seven stories from the best of the new generation of South African writers in English. Most of them break with the conventional realist work of past tradition and search for new ways of story-telling. This work is an introduction to recent South African fiction at its most robust, uninhibited and accomplished, and to writers who are significantly contributing to South African literature in the making.

THE SECRET LETTERS OF JAN VAN RIEBEECK
Robert Kirby

An acerbic collection from South Africa's leading satirist.

CIRCLES IN A FOREST
Dalene Matthee

The story of a boy growing up in the shadows of the Knyana forest and his enthralment with 'Old Foot', the leader of the last remaining elephant herd within the forest.

JIMMY'S PLACE
Vincent Pienaar

In any bar the guys spend a lot of time sorting out the problems of the world. After all, taking care of the ozone-friendly leak in the greenhouse is a lot easier than taking care of a wife and a dog-box full of screaming children.

ANCESTRAL VOICES
Etienne van Heerden

Winner of the CNA Literary Award and the Hertzog Prize for Prose

Truth and fantasy, the past and the future, life and death are indiscriminately mingled on Toorberg, home of the Moolman family.

CASSPIRS AND CAMPARIS
Etienne van Heerden

'A brilliant exposé of our present day society'
– Cape Times

Originally published in Afrikaans *Casspirs and Camparis* won the Rapport Prize for Prose in 1992, and received Honourable Mention in the Noma Award for Publishing in Africa – a first for an Afrikaans work.